Praise for the
No... of Allison Chase

Her ...

"Charming.... Enterta... ...ments tested at the beginning of ... ...t the unflinching examination of the ... ...orian culture, making this a real treat for fans of both history and romance."
—*Publishers Weekly*

"Chase showcases her talent for creating unique mystery/romances in this Her Majesty's Secret Servants installment. The mystery is exciting, the romance strong, and Chase's writing engrossing. Here's a novel for those who crave an out-of-the-ordinary read."
—*Romantic Times*

"Extremely entertaining.... I found myself not wanting to put down this book ... a fresh, unique feel to the romantic historical."
—Night Owl Reviews (Reviewer's Top Pick)

"A little history, a little mystery, a little science, and a lot of passion ... a great read you will not want to miss." —Fresh Fiction

"Nineteenth-century fans will appreciate this engrossing read as the amateur sleuths seek motives and opportunities while chasing after clues and falling in love." —Genre Go Round Reviews

Most Eagerly Yours

"This romance has an intelligent heroine and a sexy hero, plots against the queen, intriguing twists and surprises.... All of this makes Chase's first Her Majesty's Secret Servants novel a page-turner."
—*Romantic Times*

"A perfect balance of history, mystery, and romance that promises further adventures in this series." —Fresh Fiction

"A wonderful beginning, leaving me eager to know how the other sisters may act as the Queen's 'secret servants.'"
—Romance Reader at Heart (A Top-Pick Rose)

"Fast-paced.... Fans will enjoy the opening act of Her Majesty's Secret Servants as dueling investigations lead to a traitor and love."
—Genre Go Round Reviews

continued ...

The Blackheath Moor Novels

Dark Temptation
Winner of the *Romantic Times* Award for Best Historical Romantic Gothic

Recklessly Yours

HER MAJESTY'S SECRET SERVANTS

ALLISON CHASE

A SIGNET ECLIPSE BOOK

SIGNET ECLIPSE
Published by New American Library, a division of
Penguin Group (USA) Inc., 375 Hudson Street,
New York, New York 10014, USA
Penguin Group (Canada), 90 Eglinton Avenue East, Suite 700, Toronto,
Ontario M4P 2Y3, Canada (a division of Pearson Penguin Canada Inc.)
Penguin Books Ltd., 80 Strand, London WC2R 0RL, England
Penguin Ireland, 25 St. Stephen's Green, Dublin 2,
Ireland (a division of Penguin Books Ltd.)
Penguin Group (Australia), 250 Camberwell Road, Camberwell, Victoria 3124,
Australia (a division of Pearson Australia Group Pty. Ltd.)
Penguin Books India Pvt. Ltd., 11 Community Centre, Panchsheel Park,
New Delhi - 110 017, India
Penguin Group (NZ), 67 Apollo Drive, Rosedale, Auckland 0632,
New Zealand (a division of Pearson New Zealand Ltd.)
Penguin Books (South Africa) (Pty.) Ltd., 24 Sturdee Avenue,
Rosebank, Johannesburg 2196, South Africa

Penguin Books Ltd., Registered Offices:
80 Strand, London WC2R 0RL, England

First published by Signet Eclipse, an imprint of New American Library,
a division of Penguin Group (USA) Inc.

First Printing, December 2011
10 9 8 7 6 5 4 3 2 1

Copyright © Lisa Manuel, 2011
All rights reserved

SIGNET ECLIPSE and logo are trademarks of Penguin Group (USA) Inc.

Printed in the United States of America

PUBLISHER'S NOTE
This is a work of fiction. Names, characters, places, and incidents either are the
product of the author's imagination or are used fictitiously, and any resemblance
to actual persons, living or dead, business establishments, events, or locales is
entirely coincidental.

The publisher does not have any control over and does not assume any responsibility for author or third-party Web sites or their content.

*To my sister-in-law, Holly, whose love of horses
helped inspire the heroine of this book.
And to the young women who inspire me: our daughters,
Sara and Erin; our nieces, Heather, Liz, and Theresa;
and our grandnieces, Savannah and little Maggie.
Always believe in yourselves, ladies, and always
stick to your guns—no matter what!*

ACKNOWLEDGMENTS

Thank you to the Carriage Association of America for helping me sort out the Windsor Mews, specifically what existed, and, more important, what didn't yet exist, in the spring of 1839.

Thank you to my parents for all those riding lessons I took as a kid—see, they finally paid off.

And a huge thank-you to my editor, Ellen Edwards, for her continued support, guidance, and patience (she knows what I mean).

Chapter 1

Windsor, England
Spring 1839

A violent jolt clacked Holly Sutherland's teeth together and shocked her out of a fitful doze. Her eyes flew open, and she spied high stone walls and an open gate just before the brougham she'd traveled in throughout the night rolled to a halt on a cobbled drive.

The carriage listed as the footman stepped down from his perch on the rear footboard, but Holly swung the door open before he'd come round to assist her.

"Are we here?" She leaned out, eager to be free of the dim and confining carriage, and just as eager to see what the next minutes held in store.

"We are, miss. Please wait while I set down the step." Roger, a towering youth with a head of dark, wavy hair and the handsome features typical of many young footmen, unfolded the step and offered an arm to assist her down.

The sight that greeted her took her aback. The morning mist shrouded a grim, two-story edifice sporting several pairs of closed double doors; above them, a row of dingy windows struggled to reflect the first glimmers of dawn. A stale air of neglect hung over the place, lending it as much cheer as a prison.

Is that what it was? Had the queen sent for her because

an inmate had escaped, and it would be Holly's task to track him down? The villain might be some deranged brute who had threatened England's twenty-year-old monarch. There had been several attempts against Her Majesty's life in the two years since she had ascended to the throne. . . .

The notion should have frightened Holly, but, on the contrary, exhilaration raced up her spine. A weight in the reticule dangling from her wrist provided a heady boost in confidence that sent her chin inching upward. Could she pull the trigger of the repeating revolver she had brought along for added protection?

Most certainly, if it came down to protecting the queen's life, her own, or that of an innocent bystander. And if she held the weapon in two hands and braced her feet firmly, she could even aim it fairly straight.

Behind her, the gates whined and then clanged as a pair of guards pushed them shut. The stark sound sent her forward with a spring in her step, while over her shoulder she asked the footman, "Where is here, exactly? And how do we get in?" The doors all appeared to be locked up tight.

"We're at the Windsor Mews, miss. Her Majesty's stables. And not that way, miss. That is merely the carriage house."

She stopped a few feet shy of the first set of doors, a ripple of disappointment dousing her excitement. Stables were rather less spine-tingling than a prison, though perhaps Victoria wished to supply her with a speedy mount on which to pursue her quarry.

Glancing up, she caught a glimpse through the mist of Windsor Castle's Round Tower poised high above the landscape like a monarch on her dais. She regarded the seedy brick structure before her. "These mews are rather less grand than one would expect for England's queen."

"There are plans for new ones to be built later in the year," he replied in a bored tone. "Now, if you'd follow me please."

"Is the queen to meet me here?"

Of course he didn't answer. He had tolerated her questions long enough. His job was not to supply information, but simply to deliver her to her destination. "If you please, miss, follow me."

They threaded their way through a maze of courtyards, stables, and outbuildings, Roger's steady pace prompting Holly to grit her teeth to keep from asking him to please hurry. Voices reached her ears, along with the clanging, clunking, and sweeping of the stable hands beginning their morning tasks. She rounded a corner into another enclosure, where a team of workers scurried back and forth carrying buckets, brushes, rakes, and armfuls of snaking tack. They seemed to have reached the very heart of the mews. The footman stopped before a heavy-looking door, reached into his pocket, and brought out a jangling set of keys.

She was surprised to step into a cozy room furnished with a faded but comfortable-looking settee and a small oak table and chairs; a cheery fire flickered in a small brick fireplace. The effect was of a slightly shabby retreat, the furniture too worn to remain in a drawing room but adequate enough to accommodate the queen's hunting parties.

"Her majesty's private salon, miss," Roger explained, confirming Holly's guess. "Do make yourself comfortable, if you please." With that, he turned on his heel and left her alone. She had no choice but to contain her impatience and wait.

It was all very puzzling. But even more puzzling had been the note Roger himself had delivered, only hours ago, to the Knightsbridge Readers' Emporium, the London bookshop owned jointly by Holly and her sisters.

> *Dearest Holly,*
> *I need you—and only you. You must come to me at Windsor at once! Tell no one. Except your sisters, of course. But please make no delay!*
>
> *Yours,*
> *V*

She'd barely had time to comprehend the note's meaning—that, like her sisters Laurel and Ivy before her, she was being called to the service of her country—before she had found herself scurrying to pack a bag, bid her sisters good-bye, and board the waiting brougham. Without further explanation, she had been whisked out of the city and across a moonlit countryside.

A clatter of footsteps echoed in the hall. Just before the door swung wide, Holly jumped up from the settee. A petite figure swathed in a cape of sumptuous forest-green velvet swept through the doorway, and England's queen flipped back her hood and stretched out her hands. "My dearest Holly, thank goodness you are here!"

They rushed to each other, and Holly found herself enfolded in an embrace that for several lovely seconds renewed every sweet facet of the friendship that had marked her childhood years.

Here before her stood the only real friend she and her sisters had known during their sheltered upbringing at Uncle Edward's country estate—and vice versa. As heir presumptive, little Princess Victoria had been allowed precious few influences beyond those of her mother and John Conroy, a man who early on had designs on controlling the throne Victoria would eventually occupy. At her mother's insistence, the common-born Sutherland sisters had been tolerated against John Conroy's advice only due to their father's military ties to Victoria's father, the deceased Duke of Kent.

The past, with all of its childish secrets, promises, hopes, and dreams, flooded Holly's heart as she pressed her cheek to Victoria's. They had been orphans together, the Sutherland sisters and this dear, lonely little girl. But as Victoria's importance to England grew, Holly and her sisters were deemed less and less suitable to be her companions.

Now she was their queen and could acknowledge their friendship openly if she chose to, which she did not because of one imperative matter.

We will always be your friends . . . your secret servants if need be. Holly and her sisters had spoken those words to the child Victoria nearly a decade ago, on a sunny summer's day in Uncle Edward's rose garden. At the time, none of them could have guessed what that pledge would lead to. In the past year, Laurel, the eldest, and Ivy, Holly's twin, had each risked death in the service of their queen, though neither had quite explained to Victoria the dangers they had faced.

Risk, danger, fear . . . The vow had incurred all that and more for Laurel and Ivy. And now—oh, now it was Holly's turn to finally stray from the safety of everyday life and embark on her own adventure.

Did that frighten her, even just a little? Good heavens, yes. It was a sensation that made her feel alive, vibrant, *important*. . . .

Victoria's arms came away, and Holly stepped back to gaze into her friend's face with a smile she could hardly restrain. "What is it you need me to do?"

Victoria rattled off her needs like items on a shopping list. "Prevent an international incident. Save the monarchy. Save *me*."

Chapter 2

Victoria tapped her foot nervously on ground left slightly muddy from recent rains. The morning breeze stirred the dark curls framed by her bonnet brim, and she absently blew away a tendril that strayed across her cheek. "Now that you've had a good look, tell me what you think of him."

Holly hesitated, no less puzzled now than she had been at the outset of her journey. The "him" to which Victoria referred snorted and stamped his foot, then swung his head in an arc that showed his impatience to be free of the lead rope presently coiled around the head groom's hand.

William, a man who barely reached above Holly's shoulder yet whose stocky physique possessed the strength to control a half-trained Thoroughbred, had spent some ten minutes putting the two-year-old colt through its paces in the paddock behind the royal salon. Even after another several minutes of being walked sedately around the ring, the animal's flanks rippled in agitation, a sign of its unseasoned youth. Standing some fifteen hands high, the colt was sure to gain another several inches before it reached maturity.

For a second time, Holly made a slow circuit of the animal, careful to stay well out of reach of the back hooves. The ebony mane and tail made a dramatic contrast to the bay coat; a white marking gleamed beneath the forelock.

She peered over the horse's muscular neck to Victoria. "He's an Ashworth colt, isn't he?"

The queen smiled astutely. "You recognize the star."

"The distinctive Ashworth star," Holly mused with a nod. At the very mention of the name, a faint stirring quickened her pulse, a sensation she could no sooner ignore than she could stop breathing. What had this matter to do with the Ashworths? She reached out to finger the horse's midnight mane. "There is no mistaking that marking, or the quality of the animal."

"He was a gift," Victoria explained, "from the Duke of Masterfield himself before he departed the country last week. Have you met the man?"

"I know *of* him, that he is the patriarch of one of England's premier families. I am acquainted with the younger Ashworths, though only just."

"Colin Ashworth is well acquainted with your brother-in-law, is he not?"

Holly merely nodded, afraid her voice might reveal her sudden discomfiture. Ordinarily the Sutherland sisters would never have set eyes on such noble personages as the Ashworths, but all that had changed when Ivy married Simon de Burgh, Marquess of Harrow.

Holly had first met Colin Ashworth, Earl of Drayton, at the wedding, and on several occasions over the past months. Each instance had been marked with strained silences and awkward pleasantries that left her perplexed and certain the man held her in small regard. Then there had been that last encounter, only a few weeks ago. Her insides fluttered at the memory of how they had found themselves alone in Ivy's morning room one day. The earl had drawn her to the window overlooking the gardens, had stood closer to her than he ever had before, and spoken softly in her ear. For a moment Holly's limbs had turned to molten jelly, for something in his stance, his manner, his very hesitation, had led her to think perhaps he was going to . . .

She dismissed the memory with a quirk of her lips. He had merely asked if she knew the variety of a certain box hedge edging the gazebo, which she had not.

Victoria cocked her hip in a decidedly unqueenly gesture and set a hand at her waist. "Well? What do you think of him?"

"The earl is a . . . a courteous gentleman. Well informed on numerous topics of conversation . . ."

"No, no, not Colin Ashworth. We'll get back to him. I mean the colt."

"Oh. Yes, of course. Er . . . he appears very well proportioned. Glossy coat . . . bright eyes . . . perspiring moderately from his exercise . . . good muscle tone. His fetlocks are sturdy, his gait steady. He carries his head high and . . ." With thumb and forefinger she raised the colt's top lip. He tried to snap at her and she pulled her hand out of his reach. "His teeth are even and a good color. I'd say he is top rate. A fine animal and exactly what one would expect of the Ashworth stock."

Frowning, William bent his grizzled head and dropped his gaze to his feet. Before Holly could fathom the reason for that odd reaction, Victoria huffed and waved a gloved hand in the air. "Yes, yes, he promises to make a champion racehorse someday. But is he the most extraordinary of horses? Does he surpass all others of his ilk? Does he . . ." She moved beside Holly, reached out to stroke the colt's nose, and said in a hush, "Does he fill you with a sense of awe?"

"I'm afraid I don't understand."

Victoria's arm swung down to her side. "I thought not. And that is because this is not the same colt the Duke of Masterfield presented to me. *This* horse"—she jerked her chin at the animal—"is an imposter. Switched, possibly while William and the other grooms were exercising my horses in the Great Park."

Holly flicked a gaze to the high stone walls enclosing the paddock, and remembered the iron gates guarding the entrance of the mews. "Is that possible?" she asked the groom.

Color darkened William's leathery complexion. "If it happened in the park, then I'm afraid so, miss. A host of us went out the day before yesterday. Grooms, trainers, some of the younger lads as well. We brought a dozen horses, several of which hail from the Ashworth stud and look a great deal alike—dark bay with black points, the Ashworth star." He brushed his thumb across the bold white mark between the animal's eyes.

"It was a scene of some confusion, then?"

"Not confusion, miss, but a good bustle of activity. Not all the horses were exercised at the same time. And I suppose it is possible—not easy, mind you, but possible—that someone might have stolen in through the trees and made the switch while her majesty's colt was awaiting his turn with the trainers."

Holly was about to comment when Victoria said, "Thank you, William. That will be all for now."

The groom bowed and led the colt away, and Victoria and Holly tramped back across the paddock and reentered the parlor. Victoria swept to the window that overlooked the enclosure and set her hands on her hips. "Oh, if that man weren't a duke's son, wouldn't I simply come right out and accuse him of horse thievery!"

Holly's mouth dropped open. "Surely you can't mean . . ."

"Indeed I do." Turning back into the room, Victoria yanked off her gloves and slapped them against her palm. "Who better to understand the colt's potential than the man who bred him, the duke's own son? I realize Colin Ashworth has connections to your family, so I hope you will not be offended by the theory I've formed."

As in the paddock, mere mention of the name raised a commotion inside Holly. She schooled her features carefully. "Dearest, you know you can speak freely with me."

"I believe it is possible Colin Ashworth resented his father giving me the colt because he wanted the animal for himself. Who could blame him, really?" The queen tossed her gloves onto a nearby tabletop. "But I cannot accuse a peer's son of theft. Not without irrefutable evidence."

Oh dear. Dismay settled like a leaden shawl around Holly's shoulders, tempting her to drop into the nearest chair. However little regard Colin Ashworth had shown her during the months of their acquaintance, he was Simon's good friend and stood high in Ivy's esteem as well. And now Holly was to ascertain if the man had sunk as low as the lowest of vagabonds—a horse thief.

As if she of all people possessed the power to insinuate herself into his life, to become close enough to examine the state of his character. Other than his brief and unsuccessful inquiry into box hedges, he had hardly exchanged a handful of sentences with her during the entirety of their acquaintance.

She nearly laughed at the irony. Instead she tugged off her own gloves and used them to fan her suddenly overheated face. "Are you utterly convinced a crime has been committed? Did you call in the authorities?"

"The authorities—bah! They took notes and nodded and ever so cautiously insinuated that my head was full of stuff and nonsense. But I tell you, *my* colt, the one given to me by the Duke of Masterfield, can be compared to no other. I cannot explain the particulars; there is no outlining the differences between the two. It is a superiority one senses, but cannot accurately define. With your uncanny way with horses, I am certain that when you find my colt, you will know it beyond a doubt."

Alarm shoved Holly a half step backward. When Her Majesty had called upon Laurel, it was to investigate a royal cousin whom Victoria had suspected of treason. When Ivy's turn came, she was charged with recovering an electromagnetic stone that had been stolen from the royal apartments at Buckingham Palace. In both cases, the cousin and the stone had been known to exist. They had been *seen*, not only by Victoria, but by others of her household and acquaintance as well.

But this colt! How could Holly be sure the head groom wasn't at this moment settling the animal back in its stall? Especially when William himself could not with any authority prove the colts were not one and the same?

She tried to choose her words carefully. "What if . . . just supposing . . . I am unable to find your colt?"

Victoria strode to her and seized her shoulders. "Oh, but

you must. You see, I don't intend keeping him for myself. He is to be a gift to His Royal Highness, Prince Frederick of Prussia. The prince has already seen the colt and expects to take possession of him directly following the Royal Ascot a fortnight from now. Delivering any but the promised colt could be seen as an insult, a mockery, and could spark an international incident."

Victoria spoke in a desperate rush that left her breathless and flushing bright crimson. Holly pressed a hand to her cheek. "Do calm yourself. Of course I shall help you. Let us make ourselves comfortable on the settee, and you can explain everything."

Only slightly more composed, Victoria plucked at her skirts as she settled on the cushions, then found Holly's hand and clung to it. "Prussia's king is infirm and aging, and it is only a matter of time before the younger Frederick assumes the crown. Lord Melbourne feels the prince provides us with the perfect opportunity to strengthen our ties with Prussia, for if the wars with Napoleon taught us anything, it is the benefit of strong allies."

"Yes, of course." Holly's brows drew inward. "And you wish to give Prince Frederick the colt as a gesture of goodwill."

"Exactly. The prince greatly admired the colt when he was here last week. He's traveling now, but he fully expects to claim the colt at the closing of the Royal Ascot. I even named the animal Prince's Pride, and though he is too young to race in this year's meeting, my intention was to show him off and create a bit of a stir in the racing world, thus adding value to Frederick's gift. He's quite a horseman himself and a racing enthusiast."

"I see. But . . ." Holly patted the back of Victoria's hand as she quickly debated the wisdom of repeating her doubts. She concluded that with such a tenuous mission, she owed it to her monarch to be honest. "In the event the original colt cannot be found—"

"You *must* find him." Victoria released Holly's hand and sprang to her feet, beginning an erratic circuit of the room.

"My reign so far has been . . . less than smooth. There are those who say I have made mistakes. . . ."

Victoria's voice trailed off and Holly thought of the recent headlines. Earlier this spring, Victoria had publicly but wrongly accused one of her ladies-in-waiting, Flora Hastings, of being with child. Lady Flora had proved chaste but gravely ill, and the queen's behavior over the incident had caused a dreadful scandal. The wave of disapproval had barely died down when Lord Melbourne had temporarily fallen from power, and Victoria had refused to honor the request of her new prime minister, Sir Robert Peele, that she replace her Whig ladies-in-waiting with those from Tory families. Her stubborn denial had resulted in another political turnover, with Peele stepping down and Lord Melbourne returning to office.

There had been whispers that the queen and Lord Melbourne had plotted together to circumvent the will of the people. Others had accused Her Majesty of being a spoiled child, unfit to wear the crown.

Holly believed neither of these allegations, but she understood that Victoria could ill afford another embarrassing incident. She came to her feet. "The majority of the people adore you. They understand you are young and these things—"

Victoria silenced her with a vigorous shake of her head. "The opposition to the monarchy, and to my reign especially, grows daily. Not mere whispers, mind you, but rumbles capable of toppling a thousand years of English tradition."

The possibility rendered Holly's throat dry. They had spoken of such rumblings before, when Victoria had first reestablished ties with the Sutherlands and asked Laurel to investigate her cousin. The crumbling of the monarchy seemed far-fetched—impossible—yet in recent times, more and more people rejected the notion of the divine right of kings. The French, for a time. The Americans . . .

"Holly, these negotiations with Prussia provide me with a chance to regain the people's confidence and admiration.

If I can be seen as instrumental in forging a strengthened alliance . . ."

"I understand. And do not worry." She reached for her friend's hands and gave them a squeeze. For at that moment, with her eyes opened wide and her brow furrowed tight, England's queen appeared young and vulnerable and very much in need of a friend's reassurance—however much that friend lacked certainty in her own ability to fulfill the promise she was about to make. "I will find your colt."

The tension drained from Victoria's youthful features. "Thank you, my dear friend. I knew I could count on you."

Victoria threw her arms around Holly, and as they hugged, a realization prompted Holly to pull back from Victoria's embrace. "There is one matter we haven't considered. My disguise. Laurel used an alias during her mission, and Ivy disguised herself by wearing trousers and posing as a young man. But the Ashworths *know* me. How shall I—"

The queen waved a dismissive hand. "That has become a moot point. Since your sisters' marriages, you have been out in society. *Everyone* knows who you are. You'll simply investigate Colin Ashworth as yourself."

"But . . ." Holly could raise no valid argument, but if she had been doubtful about this mission so far, she was doubly so now. Laurel and Ivy had both attested to using their masquerades as shields; being someone else had armed them with confidence and a sense of invulnerability they would not have otherwise possessed.

Holly would have no such advantage. Her name, her reputation, her very future, would be at risk.

But she had long ago taken a vow, and she had no choice. When she nodded her acquiescence, Victoria pressed her hands together. "Now, you'll need a cover story, and a chaperone, of course. . . ."

Victoria's enthusiasm burgeoned in direct proportion to Holly's growing qualms. Once their plan had been laid out, she expressed one final misgiving, this time having nothing to do with herself, but with the man she was being sent, possibly, to apprehend, whose life she might very well destroy. "Do we in this country . . . still hang horse thieves?"

Victoria raised a haughty eyebrow. "We do not. Unfortunately. For, although I am no great proponent of the death penalty, I should very much like to make an exception in this case, were I able."

Holly's relief proved short-lived as Victoria added, "The culprit is perhaps even now sniggering behind his hand, believing he has got away with his perfidy. That, I tell you, is something the Queen of England shall not abide. Mark my words: he will pay, and pay dearly."

Chapter 3

"I tell you, Grey Momus will take the Gold Cup again this year. There is no other can touch him in the two mile flat."

"You are altogether too confident, Bentley. A champion one year might lug in at the next. It doesn't do to toss all of one's hopes on a single prospect."

The two gentlemen, both influential members of England's Jockey Club and personally responsible for many of the new rules governing the sport of horse racing, stood side by side, hands clasped behind their backs, chins tilted at forty-five-degree angles as they gazed up at the team of workmen three stories above them. Racing across the Ascot heath, a vigorous breeze shoved bright clouds across a wide blue sky. A swirling haze of dust rose from the track, prompting both men to grasp the brims of their beaver hats. The younger of the pair, Mr. Stuart Bentley, coughed and shielded his mouth and nose with his free hand.

Then he turned to bestow an indignant sneer upon his older companion. "Lug in? *Lug in*, did you say?"

Colin Ashworth stood a few yards away on the grassy verge between the racetrack and the newly erected grandstand. He had been paying scant attention to Bentley and the podgy Lord Kinnard, the queen's Master of the Buckhounds. Instead, he watched the construction crew use a system of ropes and pulleys to raise a ten-foot section of the iron and wooden balustrade to the stand's third-story balcony.

Construction of the new building had begun nearly a year ago, though delays and setbacks had led Colin and his fellow Jockey Club members to despair of its completion in time for this year's Royal Meeting. That only the balustrades still needed to be positioned came as a welcome relief. Since old King William had preferred to sit at home with his wife and his hounds rather than attend the races, Ascot had become sadly neglected during his reign. The attendance last year of his niece—young and fresh and promising to usher in a modern age—had brought a resurgence of racing enthusiasm not seen at this course in nearly two decades.

Colin stole a moment to scan the colonnaded building front. The tiered balconies alone would hold hundreds of spectators, never mind the drawing rooms, betting halls, and refreshment parlors inside. A new era for Ascot demanded new accommodations for the masses, both wealthy and poor, and the new stand promised to oblige those needs with modern efficiency and a fashionable flare.

A sudden screeching set his teeth on edge and jerked his attention back to the workmen. A corner of the railing had slipped from the ropes, and the section swayed precariously high above the ground. Colin's limbs went rigid. The piece, consisting of heavy oak and adorned with intricate curls of wrought iron, weighed a good ten stone. It would surely break apart if it hit the ground.

As the section swung outward from the building, Colin lurched forward. "They're going to drop it." He cupped his hands around his mouth. "Slow down, men. Steady those ropes."

Bentley and Kinnard continued their debate of this year's Gold Cup favorite, seemingly oblivious to the danger. Colin squinted against the sun's glare and gritted his teeth. The remaining ropes seemed to be holding, but the railing swooped back and forth at its awkward angle, scraping the building's fresh paint as the workers on the ground heaved to feed the ropes through the pulleys. The section nearly cleared the second story. Four carpenters peered down from the rooftop balcony, attempting to steady the apparatus from above.

"Damned fools," Colin murmured, "in too much of a hurry."

"For my part, I'll set my money on Drayton's mare, Satin Flower," Kinnard said as if the outcome of the races, still a fortnight hence, were the only concern of the moment.

"Your money shall be wasted," Bentley declared and pressed his lips together.

Colin had a particular interest in seeing the Royal Meeting begin—and, more important, end—on time, and it had little to do with the investments he and his fellow Jockey Club members had riding on the event.

He was about to walk closer to the building to instruct the workers to proceed with caution when high-pitched shouts prompted him and the other two men to pivot. Whether the cries were male or female, and signaled enjoyment or distress, Colin couldn't be sure, but a warning shivered across his nape. He shaded his eyes with his hand and searched the flat heath stretching beyond the racecourse. In the distance, several trainers and jockeys were exercising their mounts; Colin saw nothing amiss among them.

To the west, however, a rising cloud heralded an open phaeton barreling along in a dervish of dust. As more cries echoed across the landscape, the driver steered his pair of bays straight toward the course.

The very same course that had recently seen considerable sums in renovations and resurfacing in preparation for the coming meeting.

Colin strode across the track and onto the sprawling lawn at its center. With growing consternation he watched the phaeton speeding toward him like a steam engine hugging its rails. Frenetic laughter bounced along with the shouts. He perceived two figures huddled on the box—one wearing dark, masculine clothing, the other in a bright, fluttering gown that billowed and surged like a sail at full wind.

Anger rose up as he recognized the bays, the phaeton, and the pair of lunatics apparently intent on destroying the newly resurfaced track, not to mention putting two perfectly good carriage horses at risk with such a madcap pace.

He stared across the distance and clung to the hope that the approaching phaeton would turn and swerve away, that the driver would poke fun at him with a mocking wave before *she* guided the team back across the heath.

The passing seconds only brought the carriage closer, and Colin's hopes sank.

"Damn you, Sabrina," he muttered. "And you, too, Geoffrey. You both know better."

"Isn't that your brother and sister?" Lord Kinnard stood now at Colin's right shoulder, gaping.

Bentley came up at his other side. "Have they lost their wits?"

"No," Colin replied with a frustrated sigh, "they cannot have lost what they never possessed." And yet even as he spoke, he knew the words were not quite true. Sabrina in particular could be rash and rebellious, but she never put horses at risk.

Never.

"Oh dear . . . Good heavens . . ." Kinnard stumbled backward as the phaeton bucked and skittered ever closer, as it became clear that Colin's sister had no intention of stopping before she reached the track. "The new surface— they'll gouge it dreadfully," Kinnard mumbled.

"Never mind the track," Colin said with false outer calm as inside, frustration swiftly congealed to a solid lump of fear. He raised his arms, waving them in a desperate attempt to warn Sabrina to change direction.

Could she maneuver the track's sharp western curve? Or would the horses trample pell-mell across the turf and up onto the inner verge, which might very well send the team careening and the carriage tumbling?

Bentley's and Lord Kinnard's arms went up as well; the three of them must have looked like broken windmills.

Their efforts did nothing, however, to attract his sister's attention and halt the stormy momentum of the bays.

Colin's breath froze in his lungs as the carriage left the uncultivated heath with a jolt that sent the vehicle airborne. As the horses scrambled for their footing, the carriage arced awkwardly across the swale and bounced with what must have been a teeth-jarring crash onto the turf. His heart seized as the skidding wheels spit plumes of dirt into the air. His blood iced as he perceived the faces of his brother and sister, both still laughing, blissfully and infuriatingly unaware of the danger should the carriage roll.

The phaeton neared the western curve, and Sabrina allowed the team their heads. *Foolish girl!* Why didn't she slowly rein them in, check their momentum?

Make the turn, make the turn . . .

A roar from the grandstand broke Colin's concentration. Were the workers cheering Sabrina and Geoffrey on? But no, those were not cheers but shouts of dismay. Colin didn't dare turn around to view the fate of the balustrade. He could not have turned his head if he wished to. His neck muscles had locked in place.

The phaeton entered the curve—damn the Jockey Club for not insisting upon widening that dastardly bend. But it had been designed for skilled jockeys on horseback, not out-of-control carriages. The bays stretched out their necks and pressed their ears flat. Even from the distance, Colin could see the panic glazing their eyes and flaring their nostrils. Turf flew in chunks behind them. The carriage rumbled and creaked; the wheels howled against the ground. Suddenly Sabrina's wide silk bonnet took flight like an exotic bird winging skyward before it lost the wind currents and bounced on the track behind the carriage.

Bentley clutched his lapels and whistled between his teeth.

Kinnard held up the flats of his meaty hands. "By God, they're going to tip."

The prediction sent ripples of dread up Colin's spine and a cold sweat dripping down his sides. The carriage had reached the apex of the curve, and in horror he saw the right-hand wheels lift from the track and spin uselessly in the air. The horses apparently felt the shift in the vehicle's center of balance. Their stride broke, became choppy, treacherously haphazard. Sabrina slid on the seat and fell against Geoffrey's shoulder, and for an instant the two of them formed a knot of reins and limbs and flurrying hems. Their squeals—of laughter, or had they finally recognized their peril?—blended with the terrified shrieks of the bays. The phaeton tipped farther, then farther still, until every muscle in Colin's body braced for the impact. His legs were coiled to run—run and disengage his brother and sister from the twisted, shattered wreckage. . . .

And then, by some improbable miracle, the carriage made it around the bend and righted itself. The previously lolling wheels slapped the course and engaged the traction of the turf. The horses regained their footing and their stride smoothed. Sabrina shoved herself back into position and slowly, with heart-pounding precision, brought the carriage to a halt directly in front of the royal enclosure, some two dozen yards from where Colin, Bentley, and Lord Kinnard stood.

For several seconds Colin couldn't move, could barely draw air in and out of his quivering lungs. His anger frothed, but deep beneath it churned the terror of having nearly lost two members of his family.

A fresh burst of laughter from the phaeton snapped him out of his stupor. Geoffrey's and Sabrina's voices rang out in strident harmony, making Colin's temples throb and setting his feet in motion.

"Get down from there," he shouted before he'd covered half the distance to them. "Both of you. Get down this instant."

Though the order immediately stifled their laughter, neither moved to comply. When Colin reached them, whatever his features conveyed sent Geoffrey scrambling down from his side of the carriage. In his haste he missed the step, half slid, half tumbled from the seat and barely landed on his feet. His flailing hands managed to latch on to the side of the footboard, thus preventing him from falling to the turf on his rear.

Sabrina suppressed a giggle, her bravado slipping as she wrapped shaky fingers around Colin's stiffly offered arm. Once on the ground, she caught her bottom lip between her teeth and regarded him from beneath her lashes. Yet she rallied quickly enough and lifted her chin. "Really, Colin, would it pain you *very* much to develop a sense of humor? Must you always be so frightfully grim?"

On the other side of the phaeton, Geoffrey let go a squeak, though whether of laughter or fear, Colin couldn't say.

He flicked a glance at his brother, at the horses' shivering flanks, at the newly gouged furrows scarring the track for some fifty yards in the carriage's wake. His gaze narrowing on Sabrina's haughty expression, he drew breath to deliver a dressing down sure to scrub the arrogance clean off her face.

Chapter 4

"Willow? What are *you* doing here?"

The look those words produced on her younger sister's face made Holly immediately regret them. According to the plan she and Victoria had formed, she had expected Ivy, *only* Ivy, to join her here at the Robson Hotel in the tiny village of Ascot. As a married sister, Ivy was to serve as her chaperone to prevent tongues from wagging. Willow's presence, on the other hand, was sure to complicate an already difficult task.

A burly porter begged their pardon and lumbered through the doorway to deposit two armfuls of bags in the suite's sitting room. At the same time, Willow exchanged a disconcerted glance with Ivy, then lifted her chin with wounded dignity. "Is that any way to greet your sisters? No welcome? No how do you do? We arose at the first glimmer of dawn, you realize, to make the journey here."

Willow needn't have elaborated. Having made the journey herself, Holly was well aware of the unconventional traveling arrangements one endured at the queen's request. But it was the fatigue blanching Ivy's complexion that raised her concern and reminded her of her manners.

"I'm so sorry. Please come inside. Ivy, are you feeling unwell?"

Ivy pressed a hand to her belly, then quickly let it drop when the porter straightened from his task and turned toward them. "I shall be fine after a little rest," she whispered. "And perhaps a cup of tea."

"*Now* do you see why I had to come along?" Willow threaded an arm around Ivy's waist and flashed Holly a significant look. Once the porter had closed the door behind him, she added, "I couldn't very well let Ivy travel alone, not in her delicate condition."

Holly sighed. "No, I don't suppose you could."

That afternoon Ivy napped while Holly and Willow unpacked and settled into their lodgings. The Robson Hotel on High Street was a brick and stucco edifice that stood four stories tall; the suite Holly and her sisters shared looked out over the north side of the village and across a stretch of heath to the racecourse. Holly presently stood in front of the open armoire with a dress draped over each arm. "Do you suppose, Willow, that you might have left me a tiny bit of space?"

The rooms had proved small and inadequate, but little wonder, for Victoria had planned for only two of them. Holly's first impulse had been to take one of the two bedrooms for herself—this was *her* mission after all. But it had soon become apparent that the slightest exertion weighed heavily on poor Ivy, and she would need a room of her own if she was to get her proper rest.

Without a word, Willow went to the armoire and shoved her gowns to one side. A few minutes later as she attempted to squeeze between Holly and the clothespress, she bumped Holly's elbow and sent the stack of chemises she had been about to place in a drawer tumbling to the floor.

"Oh, sorry," they said in unison, both bending to pick up the bundle. Their heads clunked together.

"Ow!" Willow was the first to straighten, rubbing her temple. "Did I hurt you? I'm sorry again."

Holly massaged her forehead and felt the beginnings of a small lump just below her hairline. "Never mind. It's all right."

"No, Holly, it isn't. It isn't at all." Tears sprang to Willow's eyes.

"Whatever is the matter?"

"Oh . . . everything!" Willow went to the bed and sank onto the edge. "Nothing is as it should be, and I—I miss the way things were. I miss having my sisters always around me. I miss Thorn Grove and our little Readers' Emporium. I miss the life we used to lead, and . . ."

Holly sat beside her and slid an arm around her waist. "What is it? You can tell me."

For a moment Willow said nothing, but leaned her cheek on Holly's shoulder and returned her embrace. Then she straightened and scrubbed away the single tear that had spilled over. "Everything is changing, and I fear I'm being left behind. When Victoria first came to the emporium seeking Laurel's help, I thought how exciting it all was. How important the four of us had become. Finally, oh, *finally*, we were no longer children but women of independent means who *mattered*, who meant something, albeit secretly, to their queen and their country."

"Yes, and all that is still true."

"Perhaps, but for how much longer? Laurel and Ivy are both married and soon to be mothers. With each mission I have lost a sister."

"You haven't lost them, Willow. They are still our sisters, and we are almost as often together as we ever were. Why, here you are with me and Ivy both. How can that signify losing anyone?"

"But a married sister isn't the same. Don't you see? Laurel and Ivy are no longer Sutherlands. Their hearts, their loyalties, the greater share of their very lives now belong to their husbands, and soon to their children. Here we are embarking on a third mission, and beyond a doubt there will soon be a third husband. And I . . ." Her eyes misted again and she hiccupped a quiet sob. "I shall be the only Sutherland left. Oh, still a sister, but alone, an outsider in each of your homes."

Holly stroked Willow's coppery gold hair and smoothed the bittersweet smile dawning on her own lips. "First of all, you seem in a dreadful hurry to marry me off, when in fact I have no prospects I care to acknowledge."

How true. Laurel's and Ivy's marriages had left Holly the next eligible sister, and she had seen no dearth of suitors eager to attach themselves to her wealthy brothers-in-law, an earl and a marquess respectively. With a moue of distaste she considered the middle-aged and miserly Sir Robert Hodges, and the handsome and thoroughly conceited Lord Padstone. And then there was the awkward and sweaty-palmed Emerson Stoke-Brandish, who never let her forget that he would someday inherit ten thousand a year.

That was to name only a few of the hopefuls who had recently vied for Holly's hand, none of whom could have named her favorite book or pastime or even venture an opinion as to the color of her eyes.

"You are wrong, Holly, utterly mistaken. With each mission comes a husband. That is how it works."

"Don't be silly." But Holly's conviction drained from her voice by the last syllable. How could she dissuade Willow of such a notion when she herself had come to believe that that was indeed how *it* worked, it being the magic that seemed intertwined with these secret missions for the queen?

For it was true that after their missions, Laurel and Ivy had married—gloriously—each finding love with a man who in turn adored his new wife, not for her wealth or position, of which the Sutherland sisters had none, but for themselves.

But how many other such men could be waiting to sweep a Sutherland off her feet? In Holly's estimate, none. Besides, she was just now experiencing her first delicious taste of freedom. And of true purpose. To her, marriage seemed a bitter medicine to swallow.

She continued stroking Willow's hair, so beautifully silky, and so unlike her own unruly red locks. "Don't you fret, dearest. I hear no wedding bells in my foreseeable future. I don't wish to hear them. I am not like the rest of you; I never have been."

Willow's head came up, her eyes shining. "You mustn't listen to what other people say. You are neither brassy nor gauche and you *never* embarrass the rest of us. So what if you like to gallop your horse across Hyde Park? And who cares if you prefer sturdy riding boots to dancing slippers? Or if you sometimes express your opinion in mixed company when other ladies wouldn't dare? You'll make some fine man an excellent wife someday, and he'll value those traits in you."

Holly chuckled. "We shall see about that, I suppose. Just remember that you are next in line after me, and one of these days Victoria will call on you. If there *is* some strange enchantment about the vow we made her, I've no doubt that you, darling Willow, will reap the most thrilling reward of all."

She expected that to bring a smile to her sister's face, but Willow regarded her gravely. "I doubt that very much. Soon enough, Victoria too will marry. She will have Albert to champion her and will no longer need us. My turn may never come. And then I'll be alone. Very much alone."

Holly studied her younger sister's features: her dark blue eyes, her creamy skin, and the high, round cheeks that always hinted at the velvety petals of Uncle Edward's prized Bourbon roses. Of the Sutherland sisters, Willow was the striking beauty, and the one usually so sweet of temperament that, of them all, she should least have feared growing old alone.

"I'm very glad that you and Ivy are here," Holly lied. Truly, she would have preferred her mission to more closely resemble Laurel's and Ivy's, to allow her to work alone and at her own discretion. Willow was right—this was not how *it* was supposed to work. Rewards aside, Holly feared this new complication could very well hinder her from recovering Victoria's horse and exposing the thief.

She sighed. She would have to make the best of it. At the very least, do her best to make Ivy comfortable and Willow less sad.

"I'm sorry I snapped at you about the wardrobe," she said.

Willow gave a delicate sniffle. "I'm sorry I made you drop your linens."

Holly glanced about the tiny room, which seemed to close in around her. "These walls are too confining for two people to move about at once. You finish unpacking while I go out for a walk. Take all the space you need in the dressers and armoire. When I return, we'll all three go downstairs and see what the chef has prepared for supper."

Willow rallied at the suggestion. After a quick check on Ivy, who had awakened from her nap and was now relaxing with a book, Holly decided she had done everything presently in her power to ensure the contentment of both sisters. The slanting sunshine and bracing breezes of the clear afternoon called to her. She soon left the precincts of the tiny village and headed off across the heath in the direction of the Ascot racecourse.

"Have you lost all capacity for rational thought? Do you not comprehend the damage you might have inflicted upon yourself, your brother, the horses . . ."

Himself. Could his sister not comprehend what havoc her antics had wreaked on *him* as he waited to know whether he would suddenly find himself without his two youngest siblings? Colin wished to shake her till her teeth rattled, or grasp her neck and thoroughly wring it, or thrash some small amount of sense into Geoffrey—sense the whelp sorely lacked—because damn it, *damn it* . . .

He clenched his fists and dragged air into his lungs. As he calmed, an image flashed in his mind, that of the laboratory he happily shared with his colleague, Errol Quincy. Confound it, he should be in Cambridge now; he and Errol were close, *so* close to the breakthrough they'd been seeking these several years. Just before he'd been called home, Colin had sensed success, felt it right down to his bones. A few experiments more promised to finally lead to the development of a blight-resistant grain that could essentially end the periodic famines that threatened England's population each year, not to mention the country's fragile economic stability.

But no, before he could save the country he must first

find a way to save his family's future, without ever letting them know their future was at stake . . . or that he, the eldest and heir to the Masterfield fortune, had resorted to horse theft to stave off brewing disaster.

They would never understand. Neither would the queen. There were moments when he scarcely understood what sardonic devil had prompted him to press his advantage as the queen's chief horse breeder, steal onto the royal property and reclaim what his father should never have given away.

He wondered if dear old Papa had acted in blind ignorance or bald-faced spite before he had sailed away from England last week. Was the old bastard even now standing on the deck of the America-bound *Sea Goddess*, laughing into the wind?

A string of curses streamed through his brain, but he fought them back and summoned a shred of cool and, in his opinion, fair reason.

Before he could speak, Bentley touched his elbow and pointed to the grandstand. "Looks like your carriage survived, old boy, but the railing fell and shattered."

Colin pinched the bridge of his nose and regarded his siblings. "A torn-up track, a broken balustrade—you two have much to answer for."

"Bother the track," Sabrina shot back. "A few men with rakes will set it to rights in no time. And you can hardly blame us for some old balustrade shattering." She looked to Geoffrey for concurrence. The boy shrugged a shoulder and looked away.

Colin turned to Bentley and Lord Kinnard. "Would you excuse us, please." He waited for the two men to walk out of hearing range, then rounded on his sister. "If not for your ridiculous stunt, my attention would have been on the workmen. Who knows but that I might have issued a warning that could have saved the railing? Have you any notion of the cost of either the workmanship or the materials?"

"A pittance, most likely." She tossed her golden curls. "I hardly see what all this fuss is about."

"Then I shall educate you. Until the damages are repaired and paid for, neither of you will see so much as a ha'penny of your allowances."

"Our allowances?" Ruddy color suffused her face. "You can't do that. You haven't the authority."

"Don't I? Until Father returns from the West Indies I am head of this family. One short note to our bankers in London is all it will take. Unless . . ." He leaned in closer, drawn by a flicker of vulnerability in his sister's eyes. He raised a hand to gesture at the sweating horses. "This exceeds even your wildest penchant for mischief. I've never seen you mistreat a horse, not in your entire life."

He paused as her cheeks reddened yet more, became mottled. The slightest of quivers shook her chin. Or was it only a passing shadow?

"Why today, Sabrina? What is different about today?"

She ignored the question and asked one of her own. "So then, I managed to capture your interest, did I?" Her mouth quirked with disdain. "Too little, too late, brother."

"What are you talking about?" When she only glared at him as though he were some disgusting insect to be trampled, he shifted his gaze to Geoffrey. "What is she talking about?"

"Don't ask him," his sister snapped. "Ask yourself. Where were you when I appealed to you for help? Where was your precious attention then? I'll tell you. In that repulsive laboratory of yours. And because of you—"

Sudden tears filled her eyes, reflecting the bright sunlight. She clamped her lips into a tight line. Her characteristic bravado falling into place like the painted backdrop of a play, she held her skirts and set off toward the grandstand. "I believe I shall ride home with Mr. Bentley," she murmured over her shoulder.

Colin pushed out the breath he'd been holding. Meanwhile Geoffrey had moved beside the carriage, half hiding behind the nearest horse's flank. He pressed tighter to the horse's side as Colin approached him.

"What did she mean?"

Geoffrey shoved his hands in his coat pockets; the sun flashed on his blond hair as he stared at the ground.

"Geoff!"

The boy's chin came up in an abrupt gesture reminiscent of Sabrina's defiance. His blue eyes sharpened as they met Colin's. "Frederick Cates became engaged last week. Sabrina got word of it this morning."

Colin's mouth dropped open and a single syllable came out. "Oh."

"Oh." Geoffrey shoved away from the carriage. "If I go with Sabrina and Mr. Bentley, will you drive this rig home?"

Colin nodded and watched his brother saunter down the track to the little group still milling near the grandstand. He wanted to join them, wanted to take his sister aside and apologize and . . .

It was too late. Sabrina had put her hopes in Frederick Cates, fourth Earl of Redmond, and to all appearances, her expectations had not been in vain. Redmond had even spoken to Colin's father, but for some reason no one could fathom, Thaddeus Ashworth had refused to give his permission. Colin suspected he had been holding out for an even better—more lucrative—offer, for titles alone didn't interest the duke, nor even wealth. It was power the Duke of Masterfield respected, and how that power might be of use to him.

Sabrina had written to Colin begging him to intervene, but by the time he had been able to leave Cambridge, their father had already embarked for America, where he would remain these next several weeks as he surveyed his plantations and purchased more land.

"I'm sorry, little sister," he muttered to himself, then stepped up into the phaeton and hoisted the reins. "Once again, Father, you've managed to leave devastation in your wake."

Sabrina . . . Briarview . . . it seemed neither would emerge unscathed from Thaddeus Ashworth's disregard. Colin could do nothing now about his sister's dashed hopes, for

Frederick's engagement could not be undone. But Briarview Manor, the family's estate in Devonshire, was perhaps another matter.

Good God, he was a scientist, not a shaman. But when Thaddeus separated the colt from the Devonshire herds, he had, in the minds of the local folk, unleashed an ancient curse meant to protect a native breed of ponies—a breed whose blood ran in the colt's veins. The Briarview tenants believed themselves and their land to have fallen prey to this curse, which supposedly explained the recent falling in of the Brocktons' barn roof, the stillbirth of a pair of the Wileys' lambs, and the flooding of the river, which washed away a goodly portion of pastureland.

It didn't help matters that his grandmother, the dowager Duchess of Masterfield, who lived at Briarview Manor, believed in the curse just as strongly. "We are doomed unless the colt is returned immediately," she had insisted in her urgent letter to Colin.

Doomed. Yes, because they assumed it was so. He had tried reminding them all that the roof had needed replacing, the lambs had been a rare pair of twins born too small to survive, and the river, which flooded every four to five years, had been due again to overflow its banks. And it wasn't that the Ashworth coffers lacked the funds needed to make restorations. But in Devonshire his logic wasn't worth a tin farthing, and neither was his coin. The villagers and tenant farmers *believed*, and work had come to a wary, stubborn standstill.

All he wanted—*all*—was to resolve his family's troubles and return to Cambridge, to his work, his friends, and the life he had built for himself there. At the university, he felt free to be the man he truly was, not the man he was born to be. Some would argue the two were the same, but the rigid reality of being Thaddeus Ashworth's son and heir bore no resemblance to the worthwhile niche he had carved out for himself as a scientist, scholar, and educator.

He picked up the pace, intent on studying the horses'

strides to determine if Sabrina's reckless driving had done them any damage. So absorbed was he in watching the rise and fall of the animals' shoulders and hindquarters, he didn't see the woman crossing his path until it was nearly too late.

Chapter 5

The openness of the landscape drew the full heat of the afternoon sun, but Holly nonetheless shoved her bonnet back from her brow and lifted her face. The Ascot heath was a wide, flat expanse that seemed endless and endlessly bright, accustomed as she had become to the close streets, looming buildings, and deep shadows of London, or the forested acreage surrounding Thorn Grove. The heath dwarfed the village she had left behind, so that from here it appeared no more than a huddle of bricks and stone in the middle of a vast emptiness.

No, not quite empty. Before her, sudden and stark, stood the rear walls of the neoclassical stands that edged Ascot Racecourse. To her left rose the royal stand with its sweeping drive and grand portico. To her right sat the betting box, where great sums of money exchanged hands during each Royal Meeting.

Between those structures now stood a brand-new grandstand that replaced, she had been told by the hotel desk clerk with no small amount of pride, a smaller and outmoded structure. Almost overnight, Ascot had gone from nearly forgotten to England's premier racecourse, all because the new queen had attended last year's meeting. The presence of workmen in and around the building attested to the unfinished state of the new facility, and the rush to have it completed before the opening of the races two weeks hence.

A sudden rumble snapped Holly out of her musings just in time for her to spot a sporty, open phaeton swinging out from between the stands. The vehicle barreled down the lane straight toward her.

Scrambling to move out of the way, she darted across the road but realized the driver swerved in the same direction in his effort to avoid her. With the phaeton almost upon her, she could chance about-facing and hurrying back across the road . . . or dive into the roadside foliage.

Holly dove.

She landed facedown in a bed of peonies and primroses and something that prickled. Tiny pebbles pelted her back, and she heard hooves crunching on gravel and wheels skidding to a stop somewhere behind her.

An instant later, as she attempted to untwist her skirts from her legs, a pair of boots landed with a great thump beside her. A pair of strong hands closed around her upper arms and began lifting her from the ground.

"Madam? Good heavens, madam, are you hurt? Did the carriage strike you? Can you speak?"

All this rushed out in a deeply rumbling baritone, and a familiar one at that, before she was even upright. Her bonnet had tipped askew, covering one eye, and with the other she peeked out from under the brim. Could the man who had nearly run her down be who she thought he was?

Could she be so lucky?

She reached up and shoved her errant bonnet back off her brow so hard it slipped off and bounced from its ribbons against her back.

"Madam, I am dreadfully sorry. I never expected anyone to be walking to the course today and was not paying proper attention—"

As his mouth dropped open she drew a steadying breath. "Lord Drayton, good afternoon."

He gaped at her for more seconds than any self-respecting earl should ever gape at anyone or anything. "Miss *Sutherland*?"

She nodded, unnecessarily of course, for disheveled though she may be, there could be no question as to her identity. Colin Ashworth knew her well enough.

"But . . ." His apparent astonishment could have been no greater than if she had fallen out of the sky. "What are you doing here?"

"I . . . er . . . that is . . ." With the back of her fingers she brushed tattered flower petals from her lap.

"Good grief, forgive me." He slid an arm around her back and, rising, gently pulled her up alongside him. For a few tantalizing seconds she savored the strength of his arm around her. Then it slipped away. His hand, however, hovered just beneath her elbow, as though he feared she might suddenly topple. He bent his face close to hers, his sharp blue eyes roving over her until her skin heated. "Are you quite all right? Shall I bring you to a physician?"

"No, no, I'm fine. Truly." She paused a moment to assess the accuracy of that statement. She felt no blood trickling from anywhere, nor anything more serious than a dull ache in her hands and knees from when she'd struck the ground. She smiled an assurance. "No lasting damage. Oh, but I cannot say as much for the flowers."

A Holly-sized depression marred the perfect symmetry of the flowerbed that lined the drive from the road to the portico of the royal stand. Lord Drayton gazed down at the crushed chaos of pink, yellow, and violet, released a long-suffering breath and shook his head.

"Flowers can be replanted," he said, yet the shadow that momentarily darkened his countenance suggested he regretted the demise of the flora more than he cared to admit. True, as a top breeder of Thoroughbreds, Colin Ashworth was a member of the Jockey Club, which meant that everything to do with the Ascot Royal Meeting would be of vital interest to him.

Even, she supposed, the gardening.

Then it struck her: his claim of not expecting anyone to be walking to the course today smacked of an admonishment, as if he blamed her for being there. He would never say as much, of course, but that flicker in his eyes betrayed a hidden emotion. . . .

She shrugged away the thought as he held her hand and helped her step back onto the gravel lane.

"How coincidental that of all the people I might nearly have run down today, it should be you, Miss Sutherland," he said. "What will your sisters think of me?"

"Actually, I believe the word is *providential*, my lord, for I'd hoped to run into you while in Ascot. Not literally, of course, but all the same." She untied her bonnet strings, swung the beribboned silk and straw chapeau back on her head, and tied the bow off to the side, close to her ear. All this she did without taking her eyes off him, except for a brief down sweep of her lashes. She made the dimple in her right cheek dance. "And you may ask my sisters for yourself what they think of our near collision," she said. "Willow and Ivy are here in Ascot with me. Laurel couldn't come, of course. As you must know, my eldest sister is nearing her confinement. She and Aidan are delighted." She didn't add that Ivy, too, was expecting.

He politely inquired after Laurel's health. After an awkward pause, he added, "You've come to attend the Royal Meeting, then."

"Most assuredly, but . . . what are you doing here?" She lifted her chin and widened her eyes. "Last I heard, you and Mr. Quincy were shut up in your laboratory at Cambridge, mixing potions and peering at mold."

He flashed a ghost of a smile. "I am here for the Meeting as well. A good number of the Ashworth Thoroughbreds are entered."

"Oh, yes, I'd nearly forgotten your family's involvement in horseracing." Oh dear, had she gone too far with such a bald-faced lie? Probably, but he would never contradict her, not openly. "In fact, you are a member of the Jockey Club, are you not? Were you inspecting the track?"

"I was." That earlier shadow returned to veil his expression. "Unfortunately there have been a couple of small setbacks in the preparations." A muscle in his cheek bounced. "I can only hope the Meeting will not be delayed."

"Oh, no, and here I have added to those setbacks by ruining the lovely landscaping along the approach." She sighed with regret.

"Hardly your fault, Miss Sutherland." And yet his eyes narrowed as if he were taking her measure. She decided it wouldn't do to linger here any longer, with him scrutinizing her beneath the glaring sun.

But neither would it do to lose a heaven-sent opportunity. She glanced over his shoulder at the stands. "As long as I am this close, may I venture a peek?"

That seemed to rouse him from his wariness. "Where are my manners? Of course you may." He offered his hand and helped her up onto the carriage seat.

As he turned the team in a wide arc, Holly laughed as if she hadn't a care in the world. "How splendid, a private tour."

"You do realize," he said over the grind of the carriage wheels, "that the races don't begin for another two weeks?" Did she hear another slight note of accusation? Before she could reply, his eyebrows gathered tightly. "Why providential?"

She blinked, well aware that for a redhead, her eyelashes were thick and dark and, when lowered, cast coy shadows over her cheeks. "Your nearly trouncing me to death? My sisters and I aren't here only for the races. We wish to acquire a racehorse of our own. I thought perhaps you could assist us."

He drew back a little against the seat, his frown deepening. "*You* wish to purchase a racehorse?"

"Certainly. Is there a reason why not?"

"Women don't typically own racehorses, Miss Sutherland. The Jockey Club—"

"Yes, I know." She held her bonnet against the breeze. "The Jockey Club has rules against women entering horses in the races. Then Simon will enter our horse. Surely that is allowed?"

"Speaking of Simon, does he know you are here?"

"Of course Simon knows." She released a chuckle to hide how much the question annoyed her. Was she a child that she needed a man's permission before leaving home? "Why, Lord Drayton, you sound as if my sisters and I were acting on the sly."

She paused to gauge his reaction to that, but he gave no hint to his thoughts. He faced straight ahead, his profile squarely set as he maneuvered the horses through the narrow gap between the stands. "I only meant that the purchase of a Thoroughbred entails a good deal of practical experience and knowledge. There is much to consider."

"Indeed, Lord Drayton. But I happen to know a fair amount about horses in general, and surely you'll be good enough to lend us the benefit of your expertise when it comes to Thoroughbreds in particular."

"I should be honored, Miss Sutherland."

He didn't sound honored. He sounded . . . wary again.

"For instance," she went on brightly, "which would you recommend: a seasoned racer or a colt?"

She put light emphasis on that last word just to see if he would react, but if she had expected him to flinch or gasp or incriminate himself in any way, he disappointed her with his calm reply. "There are benefits to both. Generally, the sooner you wish to enter your horse in the races, the more experienced you'll want him to be when you make your purchase."

The phaeton lurched where gravel gave way to lawn. The wheels hissed through the grass, and the shadows between the buildings fell away as they emerged into the almost blinding dazzle of the Ascot Racecourse. The brightness wasn't due simply to a lack of trees that might otherwise impede the sun, but to the fresh white paint coating the towering stands, the flash of daylight on expansive windows, and the track itself, bleached pale and reflecting the cloudless afternoon. Holly blinked rapidly, not in flirtation this time but to help her eyes adjust to the assault.

The track was longer and wider than she had expected, and the distance between the front and back straights much more extensive. She was used to paddocks and woodland trails where a horse might canter, but achieve a gallop for only short distances before the terrain forced a slower pace.

Here on this flat, smooth track that stretched beneath the expansive sky, she easily envisioned horses at a flat-out gallop, their ears laid back, nostrils flared, legs extending to their full reach while the ground streaked beneath them.

The mere thought set her heart pounding, and in her excitement she stood up on the footboard while the phaeton was still moving, her mind's eye conjuring roaring spectators, thunderous hooves, tumultuous clouds of dust. . . .

"Miss Sutherland!"

Like an iron cuff, Lord Drayton's hand wrapped around her forearm. With the other hand he drew back on the reins, and the phaeton rolled to a stop that could not have been any smoother considering the grass had just given way to the track. Holly nonetheless swayed precariously, only to be caught in Lord Drayton's arms as he rose from the seat beside her.

The fragrance of his shaving soap inundated her senses; she leaned against his solid front and breathed him deep into her lungs. It wasn't until the clamor of voices, hammering, and sawing penetrated the haze of her pleasure that she pulled away.

"I'm quite steady now. Thank you."

Oh, such a lie. No more than a few seconds could have passed, but in those seconds Holly discovered how easily and quickly her mission could veer out of her control.

Lord Drayton's arms still hovered halfway around her, continuing to impart his heat though he no longer touched her. "Miss Sutherland, you shouldn't go standing in moving carriages."

"No. How foolish. I was just so taken aback . . ."

His annoyance gave way to a grin, his mouth widening to expose even teeth and score his cheeks with intriguing lines, like dimples but longer, deeper. It was the first truly uninhibited smile she had ever seen on him—except for one other occasion, months ago.

"Ascot has that effect on people," he said in a low, confiding tone that tripped the beat of her pulse. "Especially since the renovations. Ah, but wait till opening day."

A quiver passed through her. "I long for it."

Something high above them, on the roof of the new grandstand, clanked and then banged, and Lord Drayton's arms fell to his sides. But he continued to lean slightly over her, his grin in place, his eyes alight with an interest he'd never shown her before. "I knew you enjoyed riding, Miss Sutherland. Do you remember that morning we rode with Simon and Ivy?"

"Indeed I do, sir." But it startled her that *he* did. He had never once referred to it, not in all the months following, and that he did now raised a joyful little chorus inside her. "I remember we left Simon and Ivy far behind."

"You left *me* behind for a time as well, and I had to spur my mount to catch up. I should have guessed you'd be a race enthusiast."

Careful. She mustn't make him wonder why the subject had never come up before; he must believe her interest in the turf to be a recent development, as indeed it was.

"In truth, I am not *such* a race enthusiast—not yet. But I wish to be. It seems such an exciting diversion, especially now that our book emporium is being run by an employee—"

"Colin, what are you doing back? We thought you'd abandoned us ages ago."

A young woman whose golden curls spilled from her bonnet came strolling out the wide double doors of the grandstand. Two gentlemen in top hats followed, trailed by a gangly, towheaded youth who scuffed his feet sullenly. All four crossed the terrace and came down the steps to gather beside the track.

Holly immediately recognized both the blonde and the youth as Lord Drayton's sister, Lady Sabrina, and his brother, Lord Geoffrey, who presently scrutinized her from beneath an untidy forelock. Lord Drayton and his younger siblings, including another brother, Lord Bryce, had attended Simon and Ivy's wedding last autumn. She had never met the two men in top hats, the older one plump and round-faced and the young one leaner though rather pear-shaped.

Before Lord Drayton could reply to his sister, her gaze lighted on Holly. "Miss Sutherland?" She shaded her eyes with her hand. "Miss Holly Sutherland, can that be you? Why, how splendid to see you!"

Her striped skirts billowed as she hurried to the phaeton. Lord Drayton assisted Holly down, and though she prepared to dip a curtsy, the next thing she knew, she'd been captured in Sabrina Ashworth's enthusiastic embrace.

The young woman's zeal took Holly aback. While the Ashworths had seemed to accept Ivy, now a marchioness, into their aristocratic set, upon their first meeting Sabrina Ashworth had spared precious few words for either Holly or Willow.

Lady Sabrina stepped back and held Holly at arm's length. Her delighted expression fell. "Good gracious! What happened to you?"

Holly had forgotten about the state of her walking dress, smudged with dirt here, stained from the flower petals there. Looking down, she spied a small tear near her knee.

"An accident," she said with a nod. "Neither I nor his lordship was paying attention—"

"Colin, did you run Miss Sutherland over?" A scowl rumpled Lady Sabrina's smooth brow.

"Indeed not, Sabrina."

"Then how do you account for this?" Her hand shot out, encompassing Holly's tousled state. "Poor Miss Sutherland, narrowly escaping death. And I am to be condemned as a reckless driver? The pot and the kettle, Colin, the pot and the kettle." She slipped an arm around Holly's shoulders. "What a fright you must have suffered."

"Only for a moment. Lord Drayton startled me with his approach, and I tripped getting out of the way—"

But Lady Sabrina suddenly tired of the subject, or so it seemed, since she changed quickly to another. "Have you come to see the improvements to the racecourse?"

"I cannot know what those improvements may be, having never been here before."

"Never? Then I shall enlighten you." Lady Sabrina linked her arm through Holly's and walked with her back to the steps she and the others had just descended. "We'll begin with the new grandstand. We may only proceed to the second story, mind you, since the work is not completed above, but . . ."

Colin watched his sister sweep Miss Sutherland away, unsure if he should be annoyed or relieved. Surely now, with distance between them, his pulse would ease back down to its normal pace.

Not that he believed for a moment that his sister played the accommodating hostess out of purely unselfish reasons, or that she had developed a sudden admiration for Miss Sutherland. Sabrina was toying with him, no doubt devising ways she might use Miss Sutherland to strike back at him for his failure to intervene when their father withheld his permission for her to marry Frederick Cates.

His gut tightened at the thought of her dashed hopes. He supposed he should have come home sooner, instead of lingering in Cambridge, hoping for a breakthrough in his experiments. Then again, if Cates had had any true feelings for Sabrina, he would have shown some patience rather than proposing so readily to another woman. Colin found the man's behavior all too telling . . . but Sabrina wouldn't see it that way. Not yet, while she was still hurting.

Instead, she seemed intent on pressing her advantage with information Colin had months ago predicted he would have cause to regret. At Ivy and Simon's wedding, his astute sister had quietly studied him, noting his every movement and expression, until, satisfied she had guessed the truth, she had confronted him with a shrewd smirk.

Why, brother, it appears you are quite taken with the new Lady Harrow's sister. A former shopkeeper, no less.

Don't be ridiculous.

Oh, but your scowl tells all. You like her, but you don't wish to like her....

It had been the red hair that had first caught his notice. He had always loved thick, fiery curls, and Miss Sutherland possessed those in abundance. He'd never forget that morning soon after the wedding when he, Simon, Ivy, and Miss Sutherland had gone out riding together at Simon's Cambridge estate. Miss Sutherland's cap had gone flying off and her hair had tumbled down her back....

Whether she'd noticed or not, she'd kept riding, urging her mount faster until she had opened a substantial distance between herself and the others. Worried for her safety and leaving Simon and Ivy behind, Colin had spurred his mount to catch up, only to discover her completely in control and barely winded from her gallop. When they'd finally stopped beside the river to rest the horses, she'd turned to him with laughter spilling from her generous lips, joy glittering in her verdant eyes, and her wind-tossed curls dancing like flames about her rosy cheeks.

To this day he didn't know if it had been the red hair, the laughter, or the realization that here was a woman unafraid to express her delight. What a refreshing departure from the icy debutants the society matrons forever tossed in his path, prudish young women who wanted him for his future title and fortune and little else.

That day, he had discovered countless tiny details about Miss Sutherland that he liked—liked exceedingly well. But that hadn't stopped a single, formidable obstacle from standing between them.

He was the Duke of Masterfield's son, and from an early age he'd known it was his duty to marry an heiress, a woman who would bring land and further wealth to augment the Ashworth holdings.

More important to Colin, he was Thaddeus Ashworth's son. He bore a scar or two to prove it, and there was no way in hell he'd ever bring an innocent, ingenuous woman like Holly Sutherland within arm's length of a man like his father.

Chapter 6

"Willow, Ivy, are you ready to leave? The carriage is waiting out front."

"I'm coming," Willow called from the bedroom she shared with Holly.

Holly stood at the front window of their suite, holding the curtain aside and peering down. Yesterday, her visit to the Ascot Racecourse had yielded a prize: an invitation, for her and her sisters, to Masterfield Park, the Ashworths' nearby estate and stud farm. The invitation had come from Lady Sabrina, and while her brother had readily echoed his sister's sentiments that the Sutherlands must come on the morrow, a reservation had darkened his bright eyes.

"One more moment," came Ivy's delayed and distracted reply from the other room. With a sudden concern, Holly hurried into her bedchamber, where Ivy sat hunched at the dressing table.

"Are you feeling ill again?"

Ivy shook her head. The quill she held made scratching noises on the paper in front of her. "I'm just finishing a letter to Simon so I can get it in this morning's post."

"You haven't been gone two full days yet. What can you possibly have to tell him?"

Willow's giggle carried from the sitting room. "That she *loves* him! But do hurry, Ivy. The invitation is for ten o'clock, and it would be rude to keep the Ashworths waiting. We must maintain the best of relations with them if we are to benefit from their Ascot connections."

Holly couldn't deny the advantage of being on good terms with the Ashworths. Through them, she and her sisters would have access to virtually all of racing society gathering daily in Ascot for the upcoming races. Neither she nor her sisters quite believed that Colin Ashworth had stolen the queen's colt, but unless Victoria was mistaken that Prince's Pride had not yet been taken from the area, the Ashworths would provide the best opportunities to discover the animal's whereabouts.

Ivy dipped her pen, her sigh sending Holly to kneel at her side. "Surely nothing is wrong at home?"

"Oh, no, it's not that. Not that exactly." She tapped the end of the quill against her chin. "I just hope he heeds me."

Holly didn't mean to read her sister's private thoughts from around her shoulder, but words such as *have a care*, *do nothing rash*, and *wait for my return* leaped off the page at her. She laid her hand on Ivy's shoulder. "You're frightening me a little, Ivy-divey."

"I don't mean to, honestly, Holly-berry. But you remember Victoria's stone, the one she had me recover from Simon's sister last autumn."

"As if I could ever forget anything remotely related to the stone or to the events of last autumn. Why, it's a wonder you are sitting here talking to me at all."

Ivy's skin flushed at the memory that still had the power to make them both tremble. "Simon has the stone back again," she whispered.

Holly's eyebrow shot up in astonishment. "How . . . ?"

"Victoria sent it to him—with Albert's blessing—as a reward for all he suffered in helping recover the stone. She is allowing him to continue his experimentation with its electromagnetic properties and . . ." She trailed off. Setting down her quill, she turned in her chair and gripped Holly's hands. "I'm so afraid he'll blow himself up. He's so impetuous. So damnably enthusiastic when it comes to scientific advancement. And without me to temper that enthusiasm . . ."

"Ivy, dearest, Simon may be a bit rash at times, but he's also brilliant. And if you ask me, he learned some valuable lessons last fall that he won't soon forget. Besides"—Holly smiled at her—"he has more reason now than ever to be careful."

"Yes, he does, doesn't he?" They both glanced at her belly, as yet revealing no indication of the precious secret within. Ivy blinked rapidly and gave a suspicious little sniffle.

"Besides, I realized something yesterday," Holly said.

"What is that?"

"I need you for this mission. Victoria and I both need you here, and as more than a chaperone. Colin Ashworth . . . Oh, how do I put this? He is far more forthcoming with you, and with Willow, too, than he'll ever be with me."

"I can't think why you say that. Surely you don't believe Victoria's suspicions concerning Colin could be true. Do you? I know him to be the most sincere and honorable of men."

Holly didn't know how to reply, but Willow saved her from having to by appearing in the doorway. "Ivy and Holly Sutherland, how are we to ever find Victoria's elusive colt if you two idle away the entire day?"

Some fifteen minutes later, Holly gazed out the carriage window at the gently rolling vista of Masterfield Park. The property was all she might have expected of a duke's estate, and perhaps more. The house was sprawling but graceful in its proportions, with an ingenious seaming of older architecture with modern additions, so that if Ivy, who had visited here before, hadn't pointed them out, Holly would never have noticed.

But it was the Ashworth stud—the stables, pastures, paddocks—that left her awestruck. She had believed the stables owned by her brothers-in-law to be extensive and well appointed. But even from this distant view, she realized these would dwarf those other stables, as well as outshine them in their design.

As the carriage approached the wide front steps of the house, Lady Sabrina, elegant in a riding habit of deep blue serge trimmed in dark plaid, came down to greet them. "Everyone is already down at the stud. The races are to begin shortly."

"The races?" Holly exchanged puzzled glances with her sisters. They had known only that they would be viewing horses this morning.

"Didn't you know?" Lady Sabrina leaned around Holly and Willow to regard Ivy at the opposite end of the seat. "It was winter when you visited, Lady Harrow, so I don't suppose there was any reason for my brother to show you the racecourse he installed last year."

Holly surveyed the riding attire that emphasized Lady Sabrina's trim figure and brought out the vividness of the blue eyes and blond hair that were so like her brother's. "Do you intend to race this morning?"

She emitted a burst of ironic laughter. "If I thought my brother would tolerate it, certainly. But no, my role is relegated to putting a couple of the fillies and colts through their paces, to show off their potential as hunters. Not all of our Thoroughbreds are destined for the racetrack."

Holly was surprised Colin Ashworth tolerated his sister even in this role, for it did, after all, amount to putting her on display before their guests. Not all men were as open-minded as her sisters' husbands, willing to admit that women were capable of achieving skills equal to those of men. Judging from the sardonic look on Lady Sabrina's face, her brother had probably deemed this a necessary compromise to prevent her from attempting something even rasher.

Holly couldn't help secretly cheering for the young woman. "How you must enjoy your life here," she said.

Lady Sabrina gave a shrug.

Circling the house, the driver followed a gravel lane that skirted formal gardens and continued for about half a mile. The Ashworth holdings were considerable and impressive. Willow apparently thought so, too, for she continually craned her neck as Lady Sabrina pointed out sites of particular interest.

The lane ended in a circular forecourt enclosed by three

expansive buildings of whitewashed stone with slate roofs.
Corinthian columns, carved embellishments, and beveled,
diamond-paned windows put each structure on a par with
the manor house itself. A host of carriages lined the pave-
ment, attended by teams of drivers and footmen, some bus-
ily attending the vehicles, others lounging and chatting.

"And these are our stables," Lady Sabrina said unnecessarily. She pointed far to the right. "Over there is the carriage house. Before us are the stables proper, with our
personal horses to one side, and racehorses to the other. To
the left is the veterinary annex."

The carriage stopped and she hopped out without waiting to be assisted. "I hope you aren't opposed to walking.
The racecourse is through there, past the paddocks and just
down a little ways."

The main stables comprised two wings that straddled a
wide archway. They passed through the arch, the air redolent
of hay and horses. On either side, double doors stood open,
revealing wide aisles that disappeared into shadowed interi-
ors. Holly glimpsed stable hands walking up and down, their
arms filled with equipment. She longed to detour down one
of those aisles and see what equine treasures they contained—a longing born from both her own desires and her
duty to Victoria.

They emerged back into brilliant sunlight amid a patchwork of neatly fenced paddocks where grooms were walking a dozen or so horses. Far beyond, on the pastureland
surrounding Masterfield Park, mares and tiny foals grazed
and played in the morning sun. Closer, at the base of the
enclosures, an assembly of some one hundred people
milled about, a moving mosaic of top hats, parasols, and
bright, beribboned bonnets. Some sat in chairs placed
along a split-rail fence; others strolled through the grass or
helped themselves to refreshments beneath the shade of a
wide elm tree.

"Oh, what a breathtaking scene," Ivy exclaimed.

"And good gracious, it appears as if the whole of racing
society is assembled here."

Lady Sabrina regarded Willow with a moue of surprise. "Of course. What had you expected?"

Holly and her sisters exchanged significant looks.

"Lord and Lady Wiltshire, may I present the Sutherland sisters: Lady Harrow, Miss Holly Sutherland, and Miss Willow Sutherland. Ah, Lord Beecham, this is . . ." Lady Sabrina made the introductions as they proceeded through the crowd.

In every instance they were met with outward civility, but Holly perceived an underlying curiosity that made her and her sisters objects of scrutiny. Who were these newcomers to the racing scene? many of those inquiring looks asked. Did these green chits know what they were about? Would they be properly guided by their menfolk? And would they pose any true challenge to the status quo and thus upset the well-established equilibrium of the turf?

"They are viewing us as potential threats to their purses," Holly murmured after Lady Sabrina excused herself and disappeared into the throng.

Ivy snapped open her parasol. "Fortunes are made and lost in these arenas, and we bring an unknown quotient to the mix."

"Pay sharp attention to everyone you converse with and jot down notes as soon as you can," Holly reminded them. "You did both remember to bring notepaper and pencils?"

They nodded, and Willow gave her reticule a pat. "Espionage is so very exciting, isn't it?"

Ivy shushed her. "We want to blend in, Willow, not cause a stir."

"Too late for that," Holly pointed out. She passed a gaze over the crowd, raising a hand to wave at familiar faces. "We must use our present notoriety to our advantage."

"Notoriety? Whom do you mean? Do I have a guest on whom I must keep a close watch?"

Holly whirled about. Colin Ashworth stood just behind her, his expression both quizzical and amused. How long had he been there? How much had he heard? She quickly recounted all she and her sisters had said. "I—I was speaking in general terms ... about—about racing," she stammered, hoping her pounding heart wasn't just then sending a revealing blush to her cheeks.

It didn't help that he wore a riding coat of rich brown velvet that made his hair flash brighter gold and his eyes darken to cobalt, or that those eyes crinkled as he flashed a devastating smile. "Were you, indeed?"

"Of course. We are here to learn all we can."

Something in those wide eyes of hers raised a suspicion that Colin had interrupted a conversation not meant to be overheard. While her sisters smiled at him, Holly Sutherland blinked up at him as she seemed to gather her composure and prepare to ...

To what? Unless he was greatly mistaken, she had flirted with him yesterday at the track, employing those thick lashes and that single dimple in her right cheek as persuasively as a highwayman employs his blunderbuss. Except instead of valuables, the item in danger of being stolen was Colin's heart.

The darker-haired Ivy stepped forward and grasped his wrists. With the privilege of a best friend's wife, she kissed his cheeks and then stepped back without releasing him. "Colin, you scoundrel! Do stop teasing my sister, won't you?"

From over her shoulder he watched Holly blow out a little breath; the stain faded from her cheeks. Surely her flirting had been nothing more than an effort to procure an invitation here today. She had spoken rightly a moment ago; if she and her sisters wished to learn about racing and Thoroughbreds, they would certainly achieve that goal at Masterfield Park. But that notion left a pertinent question bandying about his brain.

He took Ivy's hand in his and raised it to his lips. "Why didn't you write to me and let me know you were coming to Ascot? Surely you knew I'd have replied immediately with an invitation to stay here at the Park."

"Oh, we didn't wish to inconvenience you and—" She paused, her bottom lip easing between her teeth. "And our decision to come was rather sudden. I had been feeling under the weather previously and—"

"You're better now, I hope?" He leaned in closer. "Simon told me the happy news. You look wonderful. You positively glow."

"That husband of mine." Ivy smiled fondly. "It's hard to believe a man who once kept so many secrets now cannot cling to a single one."

"Not when the secret is as happy as this," he said. "But never fear. He did swear me to silence for the time being."

He turned to Willow then, waiting silently beside Holly, and reached for her hand. "I hope you, too, are well, Miss Willow. Are you still dabbling in watercolors?"

"I am, indeed, though not to the extent I was."

"Good. Then perhaps you shall not ask me to sit again. I am afraid I made the most capricious of subjects last time. My portrait could not have turned out well."

"On the contrary, your likeness was one of my best."

With a hand to his chest he professed disbelief, and together they laughed.

Why was it so easy with her? Though as unmarried as her older sister, he could hold her small, warm hand in his own and feel nothing but an acceptable brotherly affection.

Oh, he knew the answer: he had no desire to be Holly Sutherland's brother.

Ivy moved beside Willow and nudged her shoulder. "Aren't those the Fenhursts over by the refreshment table? Come, we must greet them."

They moved off, and Colin wondered if it had been his imagination that Ivy had tugged her younger sister away, purposely leaving him standing alone with Holly. He caught her staring at him with a perplexed expression, as if she couldn't quite make up her mind about something. An instant too late she lowered her lashes and flicked her glance away.

"Sabrina told us there are to be races today," she said overbrightly, turning her face toward the racecourse, where the grooms were tending the waiting horses.

He studied her for a moment, until her gaze skittered back to his. "Maybe you'll tell me why, since Ivy would not."

She arranged her features into an ingenuous smile. "Tell you what?"

"Why she didn't write to let me know you were coming."

"Oh . . . that." She gave a little shrug. "As she said, we decided at the last minute."

"Ah." He offered her his arm, and she slipped her fingers lightly into the crook of his elbow. Strolling with her toward the track, he said casually, "And yet you were able to procure lodgings in the village."

"Yes, at the Robson."

"Mm. Quite a feat, that."

Her fingertips tightened against his coat sleeve. "What do you mean?"

"I mean, Miss Sutherland, that reservations for the Royal Meeting are made months in advance. I am astonished that the Robson could accommodate you on such short notice."

"Perhaps . . . they'd had a cancellation."

"Perhaps." Why did he have the distinct impression—a slight prickle at his nape, really—that there was more to the sudden appearance of the Sutherland sisters than they were willing to say?

They reached the fence bordering the racetrack and stood side by side, watching the grooms on the other side make a last check of the bridles and girths. Her subtle perfume drifted to his nose, making him forget what they'd been discussing. She didn't smell flowery as most women did, but spicy, almost peppery. Did he detect a hint of cinnamon? He breathed the scent in, turning his head a little toward her, and was very nearly tempted to bury his nose in her hair.

He shook his head to clear it and turned back toward the track. "Miss Sutherland, are you quite certain Simon knows you are all here?"

She jerked her chin in his direction, her eyes sparking green fire. "That again?"

"Please humor me, Miss Sutherland. I've only you and your sisters' best interests at heart."

Her lips thinned, then relaxed. "I suppose it was Simon who must have worked whatever magic got us our rooms."

"With his wife in her condition?"

"Lord Drayton—" Her hand closed over the rail in front of her, and even through her glove he could see her fingers straining. "As Ivy herself said, she is quite well. A woman doesn't suddenly become breakable simply because she is . . ." She darted a furtive gaze around her, then whispered, "And if you would only stop mentioning it, no one need be the wiser."

"Forgive me."

She narrowed her eyes at him, then relented with a quirk of a smile. "There is no need. I thank you for your concern for my sister. And after all, you were kind enough to invite us here today. What kind of guest would I be to reprimand my host?" She unclenched a hand from around the railing to gesture to the horses, now being led to the starting line. "Which among them is favored to win?"

"My own." He raised his arm to point, and as she leaned closer to follow the line of his outstretched finger, he was again pleasantly assaulted by a waft of her fragrance. "The tall one in the middle. His name is Cordelier. In fact, I should be taking my place right about now."

"Will you be racing him yourself?"

"Most assuredly."

Her mouth dropped open; her eyes flared with excitement. "Isn't it dangerous?"

"Not very." Her head tilted in disbelief, and apprehension flitted across her face. Was she worried for him? Or were her concerns directed toward the horses? "This track is too small to allow the sort of speed achieved at courses like the Ascot. It's merely a demonstration track, designed to show off the potential of the Thoroughbreds for sale."

"Having never seen a race before, Lord Drayton, I'm sure I'll find it thrilling all the same."

"You'll watch, then? Not all the ladies do."

"I certainly will. I'm in the market for a horse, aren't I?"

"And should you see anything you like," he murmured, leaning close enough to see the faint freckles sprinkling her cheeks and the bridge of her nose, "you'll be sure to let me know. Won't you?"

Her eyes widened and he stared down into them, drawn by the tiny specks of gold like a pirate to secret treasure. Oh, wouldn't he like to plunder lovely Miss Sutherland. To take her in his arms and claim first her sumptuous lips and then the rest of her glorious body hidden beneath the folds of her clothing. He imagined that, as proficient a rider as she was, she must have the sculpted thighs and hips of a goddess. . . .

She was speaking to him, wishing him luck, bidding him to have a care. He straightened, managed a word of thanks, and strode off, giving himself another shake that did little to clear away the haze that had settled over his senses.

Holly stood gripping the rail, looking about for Willow and Ivy. Colin Ashworth suspected . . . something. Or at least he did before she managed to distract him away from the fact that their story didn't quite add up. She needed to warn her sisters.

She spotted them through the crowd, speaking to Mr. Charles and Lady Elizabeth Dalton. For a moment she considered going to them and drawing them away, but she remembered that last year Mr. Dalton, a renowned London barrister, had achieved sweeping victories at the Ascot, Newmarket, and Epsom races. The man knew everything and everyone connected with the turf. Better she let Ivy and Willow continue their conversation.

Besides inquiring into the attributes of racehorses in general, they planned to prompt horse owners to expound on their latest acquisitions and their prospects of raising a future champion. Would the thief, through pride and believing he'd gotten away with his crime, say something to give himself away? Holly hoped so. She hoped someone—anyone—here would slip up, as long as it wasn't—

She turned her attention back to the racetrack. Footsteps crunched as a man and woman picked their way down the track to where a finishing post had been erected on the swale beside the outermost edge of the course. Holly nearly raised a hand to wave at the woman. Tall and trim, she moved with a familiar stride that held both a dancer's grace and a nimble, almost impatient quickness. That, and the curls flashing golden in the sun from beneath a feathered hunt cap, had tricked Holly into believing for an instant that it was Lady Sabrina proceeding down the track. Further scrutiny revealed a gray tarnish to those curls, and a waistline that, though still slender, showed the thickening that comes to women of later years.

"That's the duchess," said a woman in a tall, flowered bonnet who had drifted beside Holly. Holly nodded. The Duke and Duchess of Masterfield had not attended Ivy's wedding, but she would have known the woman anywhere because of her striking resemblance to her daughter. "The gentleman with her is Her Grace's brother, Lord Shelby," her neighbor added.

The duchess carried a bright red flag that fluttered gaily at her side. Two chairs sat directly beside the post, and after stomping bits of turf from their boots, the pair, talking and laughing, took their seats.

Willow came up on Holly's other side, panting as though she'd been running. "Don't look now," she murmured, "but there *he* is."

"Who?" As Holly waited for Willow's answer, she continued studying the track. The curves were wide and generous, the straights smooth and level. As Lord Drayton had indicated, this was a demonstration course, not one to set rider or animal at risk.

"It's *Lord Bryce.*"

Willow's urgent whisper sent Holly's glance sidewise through the crowd. The second-oldest Ashworth sibling stood at the edge of the elm tree's shadow, managing to appear solitary despite being surrounded by people. Even among his family, Bryce Ashworth stood out as different, his hair a darker shade of blond, his features too blunt to be called handsome, and his gaze too piercing to be considered affable.

When Holly had met him at the wedding, something about his somber manner had captured her interest, even her sympathy—although why she couldn't quite say. She pondered Willow's reaction to the man. "Do you have a reason to dislike the fellow? Has he offended you?"

"Of whom are you speaking?" Ivy said as she appeared at Willow's shoulder. "Who offended you, Willow?"

"No one."

"She's worried about Lord Bryce," Holly told her in a whisper.

"Where is he?" Ivy craned her neck. "Oh, I see him." She raised a hand to wave, but Willow swatted her arm down.

"Don't attract his attention."

"Why ever not?"

A slight shudder shook Willow's shoulders. "He frightens me."

Ivy huffed with impatience. "Bryce is a lovely gentleman."

"He is forever scowling, and he is altogether too quiet, as if he knows secrets about people. And his hands . . ."

"Willow, you are being unkind." Ivy clucked her tongue in admonishment. "The scars on his hands are the result of a boyhood accident. And while I'll admit his is a severe countenance, I'm certain he means no harm to anyone. Least of all to you."

"Well, he is so . . . so not at all like Colin."

The comment filled Holly with perplexity. Just the fact that Willow thought of him as *Colin*, not *Lord Drayton*, spoke of how differently he behaved with her than with Holly. Except for those rare moments when he let down his guard, as he had seemed to very briefly, moments ago.

Or had she only imagined him leaning closer and softening his voice, as on that day in Ivy's drawing room?

As if a man like Colin Ashworth would ever kiss a

woman like her. If he had any interest in her at all, it was merely to sell her a horse.

A note on a horn stifled conversations and sent the spectators vying for places along the fence. A gate opened and six men entered the course, all in knee-high boots, lambskin breeches, and smartly tailored riding coats.

He was among them, standing nearly a head above the rest. He went to the side of the horse he had pointed out to her—Cordelier—a magnificent bay with dramatic ebony points, not like those that had pulled his phaeton yesterday, but taller, sleeker, and with the distinctive Ashworth star above his eyes. Like the colt Holly had seen in Victoria's mews, except that this horse was clearly more mature and more powerful about the flanks and shoulders.

Nimbly Lord Drayton set his foot in the stirrup, his thigh muscles rippling beneath his form-fitting breeches, and with no visible effort he swung up into the saddle. Holly had been used to Colin Ashworth the scholar and scientist, an observant man attuned to the minutest of details. As she watched him now from a distance, he became, not the scientist, or the acquaintance who perplexed her, but a figure that commanded attention, that exuded power and confidence. For the first time she found herself glimpsing the essence of the man and all his finer qualities—his breeding, his nobility, his authority. It was none of it blatant, but implied in the relaxed set of his shoulders, each deft flick of his hand, each calm word he spoke to his horse.

Gripping the rail, she leaned out, absorbed in the potency of his nobleman's profile—the intelligent brow, the determined nose, the square and obdurate chin.

"Holly, if you aren't careful you're going to tumble over the fence."

Ivy's warning brought her back to her senses. She blinked, and was taken aback to recognize another of the riders, just now approaching the mount that stood beside the earl's.

"Is that Geoffrey Ashworth?"

Willow shaded her eyes with her hand. "I believe it is.

Why, I wouldn't have thought it. He was so retiring when we met him last autumn. I'd think him too timid for racing."

"He'll surprise you, then," Ivy said with a secretive smile.

Lady Sabrina strode through the gate and stood on the swale a few feet beyond the horses. How splendid she looked, as confident and commanding as her eldest brother, with her bright curls tamed at her nape and her feathered cap tipped to a rakish angle. The breeze gently flapped the neat little tails of her riding jacket and filled her skirts, affording fleeting glimpses of red-trimmed boots.

She raised a blue flag over her head. Taut energy rippled through the air. The crowd stilled. The horses stood frozen but for the eager quivering of their flanks. Holly held her breath, excitement building inside her. On either side of her, Ivy and Willow stood at rigid attention. A whistle blew, and Lady Sabrina snapped the flag down to her side.

The horses thundered past, the noise and the momentum stealing Holly's breath. She forgot all else as the race absorbed the whole of her attention. The line of Thoroughbreds spanned the track until they reached the far corner. Then they stretched out into a single-file line, all vying for the innermost position.

They came around, passing Holly and her sisters again in a blur. She leaned forward and tried to make out Lord Drayton among the knot of riders, then saw his hair flash gold in a shaft of sunlight. Around her, people waved hands in the air and cheered their favorites on; caught up in the enthusiasm, she found herself calling out Lord Drayton's name, and that of his stallion.

They rounded the far curve again, and as they neared the straight Lord Drayton edged his horse to the outside and began putting several horse lengths between him and the other riders. But then another came on close behind him, then alongside. The horses' flanks brushed, and even from here she saw Lord Drayton's triumphant grin fade beneath a sudden apprehension.

Gasps flew among the spectators.

"They're too close!"

"They'll tangle!"

"They'll fall!"

"Why, isn't that young Geoffrey?"

Holly's knuckles whitened against the rail, her nails digging into the wood. Willow pressed against her side. Ivy's lips moved stiffly in urgent, silent prayer.

As they pounded into the eastern curve, Colin tightened his knees, pulled back slightly on the reins, and pressed one heel snug against Cordelier's flank. The stallion slowed almost imperceptibly, but enough. At the same time, Cordelier eased to the right, giving Geoff and his mount enough room to make it around the bend without both horses' legs tangling. Colin held his breath and kept firm, trusting Cordelier to keep his pace even.

Rock steady. The stallion didn't let him down.

From the corner of his eyes he saw Geoffrey blow out a breath of relief, the fear in his eyes fading. It had been close. But it hadn't been all Geoff's fault, not entirely.

As they'd come down the front straight for the second time, Colin had spotted Holly Sutherland, a blur of red curls framing her face, her impossibly green eyes pinned on him as if to guide his every move, as if she alone could deliver him unharmed to the finishing post. He'd even heard her shouting his name.

Damn it, he knew better than to allow a distraction from the crowd to break his concentration. He held his gaze directly in front of him now as he gave Cordelier his head and let the stallion glide past the finishing post. His mother and uncle dropped their flags, proclaiming him the winner. Only then did he glance over his shoulder to see Geoffrey coming several paces behind him to take second. The rest of the pack swiftly followed.

Slowing to a walk, Colin rode Cordelier around the track once more, then dismounted and handed him off to a groom. His guests spilled through the gates, their shouted congratulations humming in his ears. He waited for Geoffrey to climb down from his mare and strode to his brother's side.

"You all right?"

Geoff darted a look at him from under a shock of disheveled hair. "Fine."

"And the mare?"

"Fine, too."

"Good race, though. You did well. I'm proud of the work you've done with that horse. She's bound to have a distinguished career on the turf."

Geoff said nothing; he started to walk away.

"Wait a moment. What's wrong?"

His sixteen-year-old brother stopped, turned, and with a grim expression, held out his arms. "I lost. And I nearly killed us both."

"You came in second, and we're both still very much alive."

The boy scowled. "You don't need to dip it in honey. God, I hate it when you do that." He pivoted and strode off, and soon disappeared among the laughing, delighted spectators.

Colin sighed.

"He doesn't like it when you make excuses for him," a voice said at his shoulder. He turned to see Sabrina smiling shrewdly up at him, the feather in her velvet cap shivering in the breeze.

"I wasn't making excuses for him. I was merely—"

"You see," she interrupted, "he doesn't realize that if your horses *had* collided, the fault would have been yours as much as his. Perhaps more so."

Before Colin could react, she placed a hand on his upper arm and leaned closer to whisper, "I watched you as you came out of the east curve. Something in the crowd caught your attention, or you would have anticipated Geoff's move as the most logical response to your sprint for the lead." She leaned away, a teasing smile bringing beauty to an angular face that often appeared too sharp. "I wonder what that something was. Or whom?"

The smile in place, she sauntered off, gathering a circle of guests around her as she led the way to the refreshment tables. Stuart Bentley was among them, and offered Sabrina his arm.

Colin felt as though a fist were pressing on his breastbone. His sister was right, on both counts. Geoff couldn't stomach excuses, or compliments for that matter, because in his short life he'd been afforded so few of either. Their father didn't believe in indulging his children or encouraging them with praise . . . or forgiving their faults.

"Geoffrey, surely you aren't going to take that *from your sister, a mere girl? Never mind that she can outride you, outrun you, and outsmart you."*

"Geoffrey, don't you wish to prove to your brothers that you are no less capable for being so much younger? Unless, of course, you are *less capable."*

"Geoffrey, everyone knows you're powerless to stand up to your siblings, but must you always make such a mewling, cowardly display of your disappointments?"

Thaddeus had Geoffrey convinced he'd never measure up to what a duke's son should be—whatever the blazes that was. How to undo the damage? How to persuade a young man of his worth, when his own father professed to find nothing of value in him?

The track had all but cleared. Colin's mother and Sabrina, with Bentley close at their heels, were urging their guests to fill their plates and enjoy countless cups of punch. He noticed Bentley try to offer Sabrina a cup he had filled for her, but either she didn't notice or she ignored the gesture as she gathered acquaintances around her. Bentley poured the contents into the grass, handed the cup to a passing servant, and dragged his heels as he strolled away. Colin couldn't help feeling a little sorry for him, but if Bentley had only asked, Colin would have told him that Sabrina was far from ready to settle her affections on a new suitor, especially on one more than a dozen years her senior.

When Colin exited through the gate, he was surprised to

find all three Sutherlands waiting for him on the lawn. Ivy gave him a quick hug and proclaimed her relief that both he and Geoffrey had emerged unscathed. Miss Willow congratulated him on his win, but she seemed preoccupied, her gaze darting to the elm tree. She nudged Ivy.

"Come. You should eat something and have some punch. It won't do for you to become overheated."

The pair walked off, leaving Colin alone with Holly for a second time. Her eyes flickered—with unease? Shyness? A warning prickled his nape. His preoccupation with this woman had nearly resulted in a racecourse calamity.

He cleared his throat. "Can't we tempt you with some of our treats, Miss Sutherland?"

"I'll go along in a moment. Thank you. It's just that . . . for having won the race, you don't look at all happy, Lord Drayton. And I wondered . . ."

"Yes?"

"That is, I believe this to be one of the subtleties of racing I have yet to understand. How is it your horses failed to maintain a proper distance between them?"

The same way he couldn't seem to keep a proper distance from her. Aloud he said, "They take their cues from their riders. As soon as I realized the danger, I signaled for Cordelier to ease away."

"Your command was invisible. I saw no signal, yet you averted disaster."

"Cordelier and I know each other well." He turned, holding out the crook of his arm.

She laid her hand on his triceps and together they walked toward the company milling beneath the elm. "Your rapport is remarkable. I assume you must have begun training him at a very early age, to establish such a strong bond."

"He's been with me since just after his birth."

She stopped suddenly and swung about to face him with a beaming smile. "You've quite convinced me, then. My sisters and I must have a colt. Oh, not one fresh from its mother's side, but young and malleable enough to be hand-raised as a champion."

"You'll find that potential in any of the Ashworth colts, Miss Sutherland."

"Oh, but I want something extraordinary. An animal that . . . surpasses all the rest. Do you have such a colt, Lord Drayton?"

At those words, he gave an inner flinch. What could Miss Sutherland know about extraordinary colts? Without stopping to consider the consequences, he reached out and grasped her chin, tilting her face to his.

Chapter 7

Holly held her breath and injected as much innocence into her gaze as she could muster.

But, of course, she hadn't asked that last question innocently—not at all. She had decided to press her luck and risk all because of Lord Drayton's near accident during the race. The incident had left him more shaken than he might care to admit, more than his outward confidence revealed. A brief but taut altercation with his brother had immediately followed the near accident. Holly didn't think any of the other guests had noticed. *She* might not have noticed if not for Ivy.

Ivy had recognized the tension between Lord Drayton and his youngest brother, and had pointed out the earl's continued discomfiture. But it had been Holly who decided now would be a good time to question him, to dispense with caution and shake Lord Drayton yet more while his guard was down. She watched him closely as her question seemed to strike home; she caught the widening of his pupils just before he blinked, shuttering his expression.

"What do you mean by that?" he asked in a quiet tone.

She had her answer ready. "I mean to win, Lord Drayton. Owning a Thoroughbred might be an entertaining hobby to my sisters, but I intend for our horse to become a legend of the turf. I want to upset the racing world and tip the established scales. I want a champion."

He held her chin a moment longer, his gaze locked on hers until she dizzily felt herself spiraling into the endless blue of his eyes, so like the color of the sky. Then with a nod he released her, and she filled her lungs in relief.

"I understand you, Miss Sutherland."

"And?"

With a hand at her elbow, he coaxed her to continue their trek across the lawn. "Our stables are open to you and your sisters. But ultimately, only you can decide which animal meets your standards."

"Oh, but surely—"

"You will know it when you find him . . . or her, for a mare can make as great a champion as a stallion. You must trust your instincts." His voice softened and dipped to a low, resonating note. "Can you do that, Miss Sutherland?"

Hadn't Victoria used nearly those exact same words? But presently, Holly's instincts could not be trusted a whit, because Lord Drayton's proximity, the rumble of his voice, and the masculine scent of his starched cravat draped like muffling velvet over her common sense and lulled her into a muddle of confusion.

She would have stumbled over a root in the ground if he hadn't kept his steadying hand at her elbow.

"I'll be back."

Before Ivy could respond, Willow slipped away, intent on following her quarry.

During the race, while the guests and even Holly and Ivy had turned all their attention to the track, Willow had kept a wary eye on Bryce Ashworth. Swathed by the deep blue shadows of the elm tree, he hadn't shown so much as a flicker of emotion, not even when his brothers rode neck and neck and almost went down. He had made no move closer to the railing; no sounds of warning came out of his mouth. He had simply stood watching, his jaw clenched, his expression as grave as always.

Now, as everyone gathered for refreshments, he seemed to shake himself out of a trance. He scowled at the intrusion into his shady haven and moved off, despite his mother's suggestion that he join the others in enjoying the small feast. He passed Lord Geoffrey without a word, but the youngest Ashworth halted and watched his brother stalk off with a puzzled frown.

Willow couldn't help wondering what had so occupied Lord Bryce's mind that he had failed to be moved by a threat to his brothers' lives. If anything, his sullen behavior could be seen as—good heavens—disappointment. The realization that with Colin out of the way, Lord Bryce was next in line to inherit set Willow's feet in motion.

He strode back past the paddocks, toward the stables. A few guests also strolled the area, and Willow managed to stay hidden within them and the steady stream of servants carrying covered platters to and from the racetrack. Not that her concealment mattered, for Lord Bryce never once looked back.

At the main stables, he veered suddenly to the right, toward the building Lady Sabrina had dubbed the veterinary annex. Might he be checking on an animal he didn't dare display openly among the rest? Could Victoria's colt be tucked away in a secret stall, where even Colin wouldn't stumble upon it? Raising her hems off the ground, Willow peered over her shoulder to make certain no one was following, and sped her steps.

When she reached the veterinary hospital, Lord Bryce was nowhere in sight. A closed red door confronted her like a warning against her brazen actions. *For Victoria*. Thus assured, she set her hand on the latch.

"Where are you going?"

Willow gasped and spun around. Her heart reached up into her throat.

His mouth a forbidding slash, Bryce Ashworth stared at her from beneath the disapproving jut of his brows. "Guests aren't typically admitted to this area."

"I . . . er . . . the crowd became so confining and I . . . well . . ."

"Thought the confines of the veterinarian wing would be a relief?"

She opened her mouth to reply, then closed it. Was he accusing—or joking? She searched his serious features for some hint. One eyebrow hovered slightly above the other. Irony, or censure?

"I'd thought I might . . ." Goodness, what?

"Are you interested in horses, Miss Sutherland? I mean, as other than a source of exercise."

"Horses are lovely animals." Though in truth she far preferred cats and dogs and other smaller, furrier creatures to horses. She enjoyed pets she could cuddle and carry about. But he didn't need to know that. "Did not your brother mention to you that my sisters and I are considering purchasing a racehorse?"

Had he just stepped closer? Or, with the door at her back, did she simply feel hemmed in by his greater height and solid physique? He studied her as if imagining what she might look like without her clothing. The notion sent flames to her cheeks, a quiver of uncertainty to her knees. "In that case," he finally said, "do accompany me inside, and learn about the potential hazards racing poses to a horse."

His voice held an admonishing note that burrowed under her skin even as his baritone caressed her insides. Did he disapprove of racing? She flinched as he leaned to reach an arm around her. Her gaze dropped to his hand, and she glimpsed the raised scars across the backs of the knuckles and over the fingers. Afraid to be caught staring, she flicked her gaze upward just in time to see determination claim his expression. Did he mean to grab her and pull her inside? Willow sucked in the breath she'd need to cry out for help.

But he only gripped the latch and opened the door. "After you, Miss Sutherland."

Her better sense clamored a warning. Then again, she wouldn't be alone with him, for there must be an extensive staff inside, caring for the sick and injured horses. She might learn something to aid in their mission. Her bottom lip clamped between her teeth, she stepped across the threshold.

"Where has Willow disappeared to?" Ivy peeked from beneath her parasol's scalloped edges. Her skin was flushed, her brow glistening.

Holly pressed her palm to her sister's cheek. "Do you need to rest? The day has grown quite warm. I'm sure no one would mind your seeking shelter in the house."

"I'm fine. Did Willow tell you where she was going?" Ivy scanned the crowd spreading out around the uppermost paddock. Within the wide fenced circle, a carefully raked course snaked in and out of posts that had been set up to create obstacles. There were also four steeplechase jumps, each about waist high.

"Don't worry. Our baby sister is hardly a child anymore, though the rest of us are apt to think of her so. I wouldn't doubt that she has found a barn cat with a nest of kittens and is at this moment naming them all."

Ivy laughed and nodded. A rapping on the fence post drew their attention, and that of the guests around them, to a platform that had been set up beside the paddock's gate. Lord Shelby, the duchess's brother, stepped up and raised his arms to quiet the crowd. "Ladies and gentlemen, the first demonstration will be by Lord Henry Braxton on Necromancer."

A moment later a rider trotted an ebony-coated mount into the paddock. One by one he maneuvered the obstacles, horse and rider moving as one. Holly's watched his progress with admiration, noting how instantly, with no visible signal, the rider changed the horse's direction from right to left, forward to backward, or proceeded from a walk to a trot to a canter.

"He's mine," a voice behind her murmured uncomfortably close to her ear, so close a breath grazed her nape beneath her bonnet.

She glanced over her shoulder, her heart lifting at the

sight of Lord Drayton. Yet he stood some several yards away observing, and could not have whispered in her ear.

She turned full around to discover one of the gentlemen she had met at the Ascot Racecourse yesterday. With a smirk she felt sure was meant to be a confident grin, Stuart Bentley bowed over her hand and raised it to his lips. "Should you not find what you are looking for in Ascot, Miss Sutherland, you must come to me at Newmarket."

He continued to hold her hand beyond what was proper. Taken aback, tugging unsuccessfully to free her fingers, Holly took in his too-weak chin, sloping shoulders, and wide hips that even skilled tailoring couldn't quite conceal. A certain smugness in his tone—and in that lingering smirk—suggested he might be discussing something other than horses. The directness of his gaze, unwavering from her own, bordered on insulting.

Necromancer exited the paddock to a round of appreciative applause, giving Holly the excuse she needed to yank her hand from Mr. Bentley's grasp. Horse and rider entered another fenced enclosure across the wide, grassy aisle. Necromancer was unsaddled, walked, and then left to his leisure.

Lord Shelby announced the next horse and rider. He stepped down and strolled to his nephew's side. The earl seemed to pay scant attention to his uncle's comments, which were clearly about the horse now cantering around the course.

Holly angled her gaze away. If Lord Drayton was ignoring his uncle, it was because he was watching her . . . and Mr. Bentley. She glanced back at him around the edge of her bonnet brim and tried to read his expression. Puzzled? Annoyed?

"That is Dark Rider, another of my colts." With his chin, Mr. Bentley gestured at another ebony-coated horse that stood waiting in the nearby paddock. Reluctantly Holly returned her attention to the man—a Jockey Club member, and therefore someone not above suspicion when it came to Victoria's colt.

She stretched her lips in a smile. "A fine-looking animal, sir."

"I've many more like him." He eased closer still, his gaze boring into her. Holly retreated a step, then glared back and held her ground. "I am certain I could find you something suitable to your needs," he said.

Oh? And what, exactly, did he believe those needs were? "I should very much like your opinion on what makes a racehorse a champion," she lied evenly. She angled another look at Lord Drayton, then instantly dipped her chin when she discovered his gaze still squarely on her. To Mr. Bentley she said, "What traits should I seek?"

The man looked inordinately pleased with himself as he launched into an explanation that Holly heard little of. She concentrated instead on his tone, expressions, and body language. Detecting arrogance but no trace of deceit in his manner, she decided Stuart Bentley simply wasn't clever enough to have stolen Prince's Pride. He possessed no subtlety, no cunning; given his present conduct, he seemed the sort of fellow to play his hand with an open fist.

Odd, but he hadn't behaved this way toward her earlier. If anything, he'd seemed unduly interested in Lady Sabrina. . . . *Ah.*

Understanding washed over her. Stuart Bentley wasn't any more interested in her than he was in the white-socked chestnut that presently entered the paddock and shied from the first obstacle. She'd wager it was Lady Sabrina's notice he hoped to attract, even if he must do so at Holly's expense.

That certainly changed matters . . . although perhaps not from the earl's perspective. She peeked over her shoulder, then pretended merely to be brushing a curl off her cheek when she discovered him still watching, almost—goodness— seething from beneath the fringe of golden hair the breeze had shoved across his brow. A sudden and unquenchable urge rose up inside her to comb that forelock back through her fingers, to press her lips to that intelligent brow, to assure him—

Of what? That she could never return the attentions of any man who did not have the distinction of being him? That she would rather die alone than spend a moment of her life with a fop like Stuart Bentley?

Good heavens, where had that come from? She didn't love Colin Ashworth. She couldn't; she didn't even like him. Well, she supposed she did, but *he* didn't like *her*. Not that he was ever unkind or treated her as Mr. Bentley did, without the proper respect. But . . .

He never treated her as he treated her sisters. He showed her none of the easy, brotherly affection he always showed them. He never ran to fetch things for her, or joked with her, or invited her to stroll among the shrubbery, as he had with Willow the last time they had all been at Ivy's home of Harrowood, in Cambridge.

When Holly had remarked upon his oversight, Ivy had told her she might have gone with them if she'd spoken up sooner. But she hadn't wanted to speak up, hadn't wanted to impose her company on a man who clearly didn't seek it. She had wanted . . . *still* wanted . . .

An ache pushed its way from her heart to her throat, and she swallowed, blinking sudden moisture from her eyes. Mr. Bentley had kept up a steady stream of conversation that had required little more from her than the occasional nod, until now.

"My home is always open to you, Miss Sutherland," he said in a less-than-decent whisper.

She drew back and raised an eyebrow in her best imitation of Victoria. "Why, thank you, Mr. Bentley. Should my sisters and I fail to find the right horse here, *we*"—she emphasized the word—"shall certainly accept your gracious invitation to visit your stud. However, I confess I do have trouble believing Newmarket can offer anything superior to what may be found here in Ascot."

Bentley's jaw stiffened. "That remains to be seen."

"Indeed." Still smiling, she turned her back on him as a dark bay with black points entered the paddock. From the platform, Lord Shelby tugged his coat into place and announced, "Ladies and gentlemen, Lady Sabrina Ashworth riding Sport o' Kings."

Holly pressed forward, Mr. Bentley all but forgotten behind her. She was curious to see how well the noblewoman rode, not to mention a little envious of any woman fortunate enough to have such opportunities at her disposal.

Apparently, not everyone agreed. "Blast Drayton for allowing his sister to take such risks," Mr. Bentley murmured.

Perched sidesaddle, Lady Sabrina cantered once around the paddock, catching Holly's eye as she rode past her and flashing a grin Holly couldn't help returning.

She flinched when Mr. Bentley, moving up beside her, called out, "Do have a care, Lady Sabrina!"

If the young woman heard the warning, she gave no indication. Mr. Bentley waited until she came round again, then raised a hand in a salute as she did. Again, she made no response, but steered her mount toward the first of the obstacles.

The horse glided in and out of the posts, its stride smooth and steady. "Oh, Lady Sabrina is quite good," Holly exclaimed, her pulse accelerating even as the young woman quickened the pace.

Beside her, Mr. Bentley grumbled, "If their father were at home, he'd never allow it."

"Allow what?" Holly tilted her head at him, though she kept her eyes on Lady Sabrina. She had neared the end of the first row of obstacles without mishap, and was about to come around again and take the first jump. "Why do you fret, sir?"

Eyes narrowing, he mumbled his excuses and pushed away. He soon disappeared behind the guests crowded along the fence.

Holly returned her attention to Sabrina Ashworth. She took the first jump smoothly, but as she approached the next, the animal balked, threw his head up, and swerved hard to the right. Unprepared, Lady Sabrina wobbled in the saddle. Gasps shot through the spectators. She quickly recovered her balance, but the horse's footing remained erratic. It shied away from the next obstacle and again, the sudden motion threatened Lady Sabrina's balance. She hung on and tried to steady the animal, but to no avail.

"She's in trouble," Holly announced to no one in particular.

"Good God, not again," replied a voice she hadn't expected.

Lord Drayton stood at her shoulder, his brow knotted in a scowl of concentration.

Sabrina came around the paddock toward them, her horse kicking up enough dust to attract first Colin's attention, then his concern. He studied the animal's stride, heard the faltering beat of its hooves striking the ground. Around the fence, spectators pulled back and covered their mouths to ward off swirling clouds of earth.

The filly, Sport o' Kings, was the half sister of the colt that had replaced the one his father had given the queen. Marked with the same Ashworth star across her brow, she represented the finest of the Ashworth stock, destined to become a star of the turf.

Then why was she struggling to maintain a smooth canter as Sabrina tried to maneuver her back toward the obstacles?

"It's become a battle of wills," Miss Sutherland said softly. The breeze shifted, bringing her spicy scent to tantalize his senses. For a moment he forgot his sister and thought only of the beauty beside him. What had she and Bentley been talking about?

Bentley—if ever a man had been in danger of having his neck snapped, *he* had in those minutes he'd claimed Miss Sutherland's hand. And yet what business was it of Colin's whose hand she held? She wasn't his. She could never be. Period.

"My lord, your sister is typically a proficient rider, is she not?"

The urgency in her voice snapped him back to his senses. "This isn't at all like Sabrina," he said. Not until yesterday, at least, when his sister had lost control of the carriage team. Now she seemed to be doing all the wrong things and making matters worse. He cupped his hands around his mouth. "Sabrina, ease up and go with her, not against her."

The filly stopped, lurched, and attempted abrupt changes in direction while Sabrina fought to hold her on course. Miss Sutherland leaned forward over the rail. "Something must be done. If she doesn't loosen the reins, she risks rendering the animal head shy."

The term set off an alarm inside him. "I'm not about to let that happen."

He strode to the gate, swung it open, and entered the paddock. Sabrina came round again, still clearly struggling, the filly increasingly agitated. Colin moved into their path, his arms extended to attract the horse's attention. The animal knew him; he'd conducted the greater portion of her training and had long since won her trust. He could have approached her in any field, held out his hand, and within moments had her nibbling oats from his palm.

Not today. When she saw him, her eyes rounded and her nostrils flared. Colin sensed her apprehension just before she whinnied and swung wide. The filly reared and Sabrina's little plaid riding cap flew off. Colin's gut clenched as he expected his sister to tumble to the ground after it, but her well-honed sense of balance kept her in her seat. Even so, confusion and fear flickered in her eyes.

Colin started toward them again. He was still some yards away when hoofbeats surged from behind him and a lengthy shadow swept past him.

Chapter 8

Holly didn't wait to see if Lord Drayton would meet with success. As he hurried to his sister's aid, she hefted her skirts and ran to the opposite enclosure, where other horses awaited their turn in the paddock.

The closest horse to the gate was a bay, already saddled and tied to the rail. The animal didn't bear the star, but everything else about him suggested he hailed from the Ashworth stud.

"Miss? Excuse me, but what on earth do you think you're about?"

Holly ignored the groom as she hastily unwrapped the reins from the fence and pulled herself into the saddle. With no time for niceties such as adjusting her skirts so she could approximate a sidesaddle position, she slipped her feet into the stirrups. The youth's face was a streak of ruddy color as she urged the colt past him.

"Miss! Come back here! You can't—"

She cantered the colt through the open gates and into the larger paddock. A shocked twitter rippled through the crowd, but she ignored the gasps and set her sights on Lady Sabrina and the filly.

The colt's energy pulsed beneath her like surging ocean waves. She must be careful or she could just as easily lose control and find herself in the same predicament as Lady Sabrina. She glimpsed Lord Drayton's face as she rode past him, saw his surprise give way to consternation and then anger. She took no heed as he shouted her name.

Sport o' Kings danced about, shaking her head and pulling at the reins, giving Lady Sabrina a jolting ride. It appeared the young woman could barely manage to hang on. Praying she could keep the colt calm, Holly urged him to the filly's side.

"Give her her head and allow her to follow my lead," Holly called softly to Lady Sabrina. The girl nodded and carefully loosened the reins.

Holly wagered on a horse's instinct to run in a pack, and on the filly and the colt having a rapport. The filly acknowledged the colt's presence with a twitch of her ears and a momentary easing of her erratic movements. Holding her breath, Holly stole the opportunity to squeeze with her knees and set the colt to an even, comfortable lope.

With a burst of triumph she watched the filly take her cue from the other horse. Matching his pace, she fell in beside him, her stride smoothing and elongating. After a lap around the paddock, Holly ever so gradually slowed the colt to a trot, then a walk, and then finally brought both animals to a halt.

Sport o' Kings's fatigue showed in her snorting breaths and her quivering, sweating flanks. Holly leaned over to run the flat of her hand along the filly's damp neck. Lady Sabrina's hands shook where they lay in her lap, still clutching the reins.

Lord Drayton ran up to the filly's side. "Are you all right?"

Her brow furrowed, her gaze pinned on the black mane in front of her, Lady Sabrina nodded faintly. Her brother raised his arms to grasp his sister about the waist. She leaned in to him and allowed him to lower her to the ground.

Around the paddock, the onlookers called out their relief for Lady Sabrina and the filly. Both Lord Drayton and his sister ignored them. Having witnessed Lady Sabrina's haughtiness in the past, Holly waited for her to heft her chin, glare into her brother's face, and make excuses. She did none of those things, but continued to stare downward, a ridge of perplexity scoring her brow.

"You were fighting her, Sabrina," her brother said quietly. "You know better than that."

"She has never behaved that way before. . . . I don't understand it. . . ." Lady Sabrina regarded the filly, standing calmly now and rubbing her head against the colt's neck.

As Lord Drayton and his sister continued their murmured conversation, Holly became aware of the twittering onlookers.

My goodness, did she really ride in astride?

Did you see how her skirts flew up to expose her ankles?

She did save the day, albeit in a rather scandalous manner.

Her family? They're nobody, really. . . .

She glanced around at the shocked and curious faces, her cheeks heating. The urgency of the situation had sent her scurrying for a remedy, the only one she could think of. Only now did she realize how she looked to the others, sitting astride in the saddle with her skirts tucked round her legs and her ankles on display.

And where was Ivy? Or Willow, who should have been back by now? Had she so embarrassed them that they'd slipped away somewhere? She remembered the earl's angry look as she had ridden by him. Her heart sank and her cheeks flamed hotter.

"Miss Sutherland?" He had moved beside her horse, and stood with his arms extended to her.

"Lord Drayton, I am sorry. I only thought to—"

"Yes, but not now, Miss Sutherland. Please, just let me help you down."

His hands braced her sides at her waist, and what should have been a simple gesture of assistance set off a firestorm of confusion inside her. She forgot to lean and set her hands on his shoulders so he could lift her from the saddle. She knew only that he touched her as he had never touched her before, and that she wished him to go on touching her, touching more of her, touching her endlessly. His hands were strong and warm and sure, as she had always known they would be, all those times she had peeked at them and tried to imagine them on her.

She'd gotten her wish, but to what purpose?

"Miss Sutherland, is something wrong?" Oblivious to her untoward musings, he lowered his arms. "You seemed in control, but perhaps you were injured?"

She shook her head, more to clear it than in reply, so aloud she said, "I was not hurt, my lord."

Why do you suppose she just sits there?

Can you hear what she is saying to him?

The continued speculation sent fresh waves of heat climbing from her chin to her hairline.

The earl raised his hands to her again. "If you please, then."

"Oh, yes. How silly of me."

This time she set her hands on his wide, sturdy shoulders. He seemed to bear her weight with no effort at all. As he lowered her to the ground, she leaned more fully in to him—she couldn't help herself—and her thighs brushed his, and then her breasts briefly grazed his hard chest, sending a shock of awareness through her.

"There you are," he whispered. Her feet touched the ground, but he didn't release her. They stood toe-to-toe, bodies no longer touching but close enough for his heat to penetrate her clothing, for his breath to graze her cheek, for her lips to feel drawn to his as if by a magnetic pull.

His chin lowered a notch. "Will you do something for me, Miss Sutherland?"

She inhaled his starchy, masculine scent and nodded. "Anything."

"Sabrina? Oh, my darling girl!"

The shouted endearment sent Lord Drayton stepping away. The sudden loss of his bulk in front of her left Holly feeling as though she might fall on her face. She braced her feet and struggled to regain her composure as the Duchess of Masterfield swept into the paddock. Lord Shelby was already at his niece's side, and now Lady Sabrina was enfolded in her mother's arms.

"I was still down by the track with some of our guests when someone came running to tell me your horse had gone stark mad."

"Not mad, Mama. Just a bit nervous. Please don't make a fuss."

"Why, my only daughter is nearly thrown and trampled by a mad horse, and I am not to make a fuss? Come. We are going to get a nice cup of strong, hot tea in you." Her arm securely anchored around her daughter's shoulders, the duchess walked her out of the paddock. Lord Shelby followed them, but he went no farther than the grassy aisle between the paddocks. Holly could hear him reassuring the guests that all was well.

Lord Drayton gathered the colt's reins. Just as he reached for the filly's, a groom ran to relieve him of both animals. The earl turned back to Holly. "That favor, Miss Sutherland." A flick of his chin indicated his sister and mother, the pair looking very much alike from behind, though the younger woman's hips were more slender and her hair gleamed a brighter gold. "Will you go with them?"

Did he long for her to be gone? The notion sent her heart sinking to her knees. She glanced again at the Ashworth women, proceeding slowly toward the house, Sabrina's head on her mother's shoulder. "I'm not sure my company would be needed just now, my lord."

"It would, Miss Sutherland. I assure you it would. Please go."

Please go. The words jabbed at her heart, especially the *please*, as if he could scarcely wait to be relieved of the embarrassment she must have caused him. To keep her chin from trembling, she clamped her lips together. Then she lifted her chin and swept out of the paddock. Ignoring the raised eyebrows and whispers of the guests was easy. She simply let their disparagement shoot like dull-tipped arrows over her head. But Lord Drayton's censure weighed heavily, unbearably, even after she'd put considerable distance between them.

Chapter 9

W ith a cautious step Willow entered the veterinary wing of the Ashworth stables. She had expected dark, cavernous rooms where it might be dangerous to be caught alone with a man, but she instead encountered whitewashed walls, scrubbed stone floors, and high-set windows that let in generous sunlight.

Two stable hands cast her curious glances, and one seemed about to question her when Lord Bryce followed her through the doorway. The redheaded youth tipped his cap and resumed his chores. Immaculate stalls lined the long room. Though many stood empty, some half dozen were occupied by animals boasting the Ashworth traits of dark chocolate coats and black points, and white markings on their brows.

She crossed to the nearest animal and reached out to stroke its nose. "Are these horses ill?"

"Several were colicky but are better now," Lord Bryce said behind her, the echo of his voice booming in the tiled room. Willow only just managed not to wince. "That one before you has a strained tendon."

"Is that serious?" The horse jerked its head up and out of her reach, but instead of pulling away, she remembered what Holly had told her about remaining still and calm, and gaining the animal's trust.

"Nothing that time and care won't heal. My brother has

instituted a new form of therapy that uses electrical stimulation." He gestured into a room that opened onto the one they occupied, and, craning her neck to see inside, Willow saw a jumble of machinery and wires.

"Oh, yes. I'm quite familiar with the technique. My brother-in-law Simon has a laboratory at Harrowood that houses nearly identical apparatus. He says electro-stimulation of muscles has yet to be fully accepted by the scientific community. Many of his peers consider it hardly more valid than alchemy. What do you think, my lord?" She peeked over her shoulder at him, and discovered him standing much closer than a moment ago. His strong features and piercing eyes filled her view, prompting her to swing her chin forward again.

"The results speak for themselves," he said in a murmur that prickled her nape and tingled down her spine.

"Oh, I—I agree. My sisters and I have seen those results for ourselves, for Simon served as his own first subject, regenerating his shoulder muscles that were all but destroyed last autumn." The horse, having kept his eyes on her all this time, finally lowered his head, so low, in fact, he began nuzzling the silk bow at the front of her dress. "Please don't eat that," she said with a chuckle.

"That sounds like Simon de Burgh," Lord Bryce said, "to experiment on himself."

"Oh, that is the least of it, much to my sister's dismay." But instead of elaborating on matters she'd been sworn to keep secret, she reached up and scratched around the horse's ears. She couldn't hide her pride as she added, "Did you know my sister helped him develop the process?"

He nodded. "My brother is grateful they shared their research with him."

Something in Lord Bryce's tone made Willow stop petting the horse, her hand hovering in midair. Did he have some reason to disapprove of his brother's efforts when it came to the care of the Ashworth herds? "Are you a horseman, my lord? I noticed you neither raced nor showed any of the hunters."

His loud footsteps startled her as he strode away from the stall. His failure to reply any other way to her question reinforced her opinion that Lord Bryce was indeed a strange man, not open and steady like other gentlemen, but shuttered and dark, changeable and unpredictable. Giving the horse one last stroke, she forced herself to follow in his wake and keep him talking. "I'm sorry, my lord. Did I say something wrong?"

"Perhaps we should be getting back to the others, Miss Sutherland. Your sisters might be wondering where you are."

Did he wish to have her out of the stable? Was there something beyond this room he didn't wish her to see? Maybe his sudden reticence had nothing to do with her question and everything to do with the process of electro-muscular stimulation. Perhaps a certain colt was even now undergoing that very process, right here in this building. Now that she thought of it, the results of electrical stimulation could have been why the colt had appeared so extraordinary to Victoria—and could very well be the secret to the Ashworths' remarkable successes on the racing circuit.

Good heavens, perhaps this mystery had less to do with one missing colt, and everything to do with Colin Ashworth having devised a means of cheating, of giving his Thoroughbreds an unfair advantage in the races. Or was Lord Bryce the culprit, a man who appeared to have little or no interest in horses. Who would ever suspect him? Maybe not even his own brother.

Lord Bryce stood waiting, scrutinizing her with his own inscrutable gaze. She tried to smile, to shrug as if she hadn't a care; as if the mood between them hadn't inexplicably changed. "Oh, well, bother my sisters. And we've been gone only a few minutes. I long to see the rest of your facility here, Lord Bryce. I find it all so . . . fascinating."

Would he balk? Make excuses? Surely that would be as good as an admission of guilt. She held her breath, trying not to let her eagerness—or suspicions—realign so much as a muscle in her face.

"As you wish, Miss Sutherland. This way, then."

He led her into the surgery, a room lined in shiny white tiles and filled with steel instruments that flashed sunlight into Willow's eyes. He explained how some of those instruments were utilized, making Willow scrunch her eyes closed and shudder. From there they entered a square room, smaller and darker than the previous ones, the floor strewn with straw and the windows curtained in rough brown cloth that emitted scant light.

"This is nothing like the other rooms," she remarked with a twinge of unease.

"This is the breeding room, Miss Sutherland." His deep voice hung heavy in the quiet, and Willow realized she could no longer hear the lads working in the main room. She was now very much alone with Bryce Ashworth.

"The breeding room," she repeated, for no other reason than to fill the silence that felt more than awkward, but . . . wrong. And then it hit her. *Breeding room.* Where stallions and mares were brought to . . .

"Oh, my."

"Is something wrong?" He eased closer than she deemed proper or comfortable. Had bringing her here, to this breeding room, been a prelude to improprieties he imagined he might take with her? Her heart jolted at the thought, and fear climbed into her throat.

His eyes, that peculiar dark shade—a deep, stormy ocean blue—that none of the other Ashworths shared, held her immobile but for the sudden trembling of her fingertips. The stern slash of his mouth promised nothing good, nothing favorable. He stole her oxygen, then rendered it back to her laden with the scents of starch and wool and something mysteriously, disturbingly male.

"I—I think perhaps you were right," she stammered. "My sisters must be searching for me . . ."

"We'll go in another moment, Miss Sutherland. I just remembered something I believe might be of great interest to you. Come." He held out his hand, and even in the dimness, she once again saw the scars that crossed the knuckles and stretched nearly to the wrist, the skin mottled and twisted as if it had been held to an open flame. What had happened to him? Ivy had told her only that an accident had occurred when he was a boy.

Willow shivered, her mind a maze of uncertainty. "What—what is it you wish to . . . er . . . show me, sir?"

"A surprise." His height and the width of his shoulders crowded her, making her feel vulnerable. The touch of his thumb and forefinger sent a sparklike charge to her chin. "I think you'll like this very much, Miss Sutherland."

He released her, and she clutched her hands before her. Gracious, would he show her Victoria's missing colt? No, that could hardly be his intention. Her instincts urged her to flee. She stepped backward, nearly tripping over her hems.

Yet there she stopped, or rather her feet stopped and wouldn't budge another inch. Deep, deep inside her, a longing rose up to stay, to learn what, if anything, he wanted from her.

He beckoned with a forefinger as he turned and opened a door, leading her into an even darker room. Against her better judgment, Willow stepped into the twilight of a space also strewn with hay, the windows also shielded from the sun. Lord Bryce stopped in the center of the room, waiting for her to advance beyond the doorway. Clutching the doorframe, she was about to turn around and flee when a faint mewling sound reached her ears.

"Is that . . . ?"

Lord Bryce nodded and did something that stole Willow's breath, clutched her heart, turned her knees to jelly, and contradicted every disagreeable quality she'd ever accused him of possessing. He smiled—a full smile that smoothed away the severity of his features and brought a youthful handsomeness to his face. His hand came up toward her again, and this time she crossed to him and grasped it, hardly noticing the bumpiness of the scars beneath her fingertips.

He brought her to a shadowy corner, where the straw

strewn about the floor had been piled into a little nest. A fat yellow barn cat lay stretched on her side, while half a dozen kittens, their eyes still closed, squirmed and prodded one another as they each vied for a teat.

"Oh ... oh ..." One hand still warm in Lord Bryce's hold, Willow pressed the other to her lips. "How precious! How old are they?"

"I can't say exactly. I noticed them yesterday."

"Oh, my goodness ... they're darling, just darling!"

"You like kittens, Miss Sutherland?"

"Oh, more than anything. More than horses or fine frocks or ... or anything. Oh ... they're so tiny and new. I don't suppose we should touch them just yet?"

"Perhaps just a light stroke or two would be all right. Their mama doesn't appear overly disconcerted by our arrival."

He was right. The mother cat peered up at them from beneath sleepy, half-closed lids. While her hungry brood pulled and pushed at her tummy, she appeared to take it all in stride, even, perhaps, slightly bored by her progeny's antics. Willow knelt down and ran a fingertip down the back of a yellow-and-white-striped kitten. It took no notice, but went on suckling greedily.

Willow released a contented breath and rose to her feet. "Lord Bryce, thank you. Why, I'd thought ..." She'd thought all manner of unseemly things, from the theft of the colt to Lord Bryce attempting to steal her virtue. When all along, all he'd wanted to do was— Oh, imagine her thinking he might be attracted to her, that he found her alluring.

About to laugh at her own folly, she stole a peek at him to discover him peering back at her *most* intently. Oh, but she wouldn't fall prey to fanciful speculation again. She smiled. "Lord Bryce, I—"

Not another word passed her lips, for he abruptly leaned close, pressed his lips to hers, and kissed her—kissed her deeply, wholly, until she ran out of breath and her insides melted away.

Just as abruptly, he pulled back, looking astounded, almost frightened by what he'd done. His mouth opened, and for an eternal moment during which Willow's heart pounded deafeningly in her ears, no sound came out. Then, like a man suffering from shock, he murmured faintly, "Forgive me, Miss Sutherland."

Before she could gather her composure to reply, he turned and strode away, retreating back through the rooms the way they had come.

"I should never have gotten on Sport o' Kings." Lady Sabrina's voice quivered with emotion. She held Holly's gaze for an instant, then turned abruptly away to stare out across the gardens. "I was angry and . . . and she knew it."

Perched beside her on the terrace's wide stone balustrade, Holly untied the ribbons beneath her chin and set her ruched silk bonnet in her lap. The duchess had left them some minutes ago to consult with her housekeeper and butler about the evening's entertainments. The woman had meant well, but Holly had had the impression that her efforts to comfort her daughter had done little to ease Lady Sabrina's agitation. In Holly's estimate, it wasn't assurances the young woman needed, but simply someone who would listen.

"That was why I lost control," the noblewoman continued in a tight voice. "Sport o' Kings and I have practiced those exercises countless times. We could do it blindfolded."

Far below them, the slate rooftops of the stables framed the base of the gardens. On the other side of those structures, the demonstrations were continuing. Holly should be there. She should be asking questions and persuading the guests to boast of their latest equine acquisitions and confide in her about their hopes for future successes on the turf.

But as much as Victoria needed her, she couldn't leave Lady Sabrina.

"I was so angry with *him*," Sabrina said softly, almost mouthing the words. Her head went down, her chin nearly touching her chest.

"Whom do you mean?"

Sabrina's head swung up. "My brother. Colin."

"But what did he do?"

"It's what he didn't do, Miss Sutherland. It is because of him that the man I expected to marry is now— Oh, it is so humiliating." She lowered her head for a moment, then looked up with eyes that sparked with indignation. "He is engaged to another woman."

"But . . . what could your brother have done to change matters?"

"He could have insisted my father give his permission before he left for the Americas." An angry blush stained the girl's cheeks. "He could have come home when I asked him and confronted our father."

"But, Lady Sabrina, your father is a duke. Surely no one can bend his will once his mind is made up."

"Father's mind *wasn't* made up. He was stalling or preoccupied or simply didn't care. . . ."

"Excuse me for saying so, my lady," Holly said as gently as she could, "but if that was the case, your gentleman, if his heart was true, would have waited."

Lady Sabrina ripped a handful of leaves from the plant growing in the pot beside her, crushed them between her fingers, and threw them over the balustrade. Holly braced for a retort, but the girl surprised her. "Perhaps you're right, Miss Sutherland. Perhaps it had nothing to do with my father or Colin, and everything to do with me. I drove him away."

"No, my lady, surely not. I didn't mean that. But your heartache certainly does explain your difficulty in the paddock. A horse can sense the troubled mind of its rider."

Lady Sabrina nodded. "Yes. And something is happening to me, Miss Sutherland. Something strange and inexplicable is rendering me a danger to our horses."

"Don't be silly. All you need do in future is maintain a calmer state of mind."

"You don't understand." The woman startled Holly by suddenly seizing her hand. "Yesterday at the Ascot Racecourse, Colin believed I intentionally drove our carriage onto the track. He believed I urged the team to a dangerous gallop across the heath."

"And didn't you?"

"Of course I didn't." Her grip tightened until Holly's fingers began to throb. "Oh, I pretended it was all in fun. But just as today, I'd lost control. A rabbit had darted across our path and spooked the team. But it was more than that—*much* more. I've dealt with startled horses before without mishap. Yet nothing I did either yesterday or today made the slightest difference. It is as though . . ."

"Yes?" Holly leaned slightly forward, searching Lady Sabrina's features. Panic flickered in the noblewoman's light blue eyes.

"It is as though the animals suddenly loathe me. Fear me."

Holly wiggled her fingers until Lady Sabrina's hold loosened a fraction. "Did you explain to your brother what happened?"

"Good lord, no. I cannot have Colin or even Geoffrey realizing the truth." Her voice sank to a whisper. "I pretended to have done exactly what Colin accused me of. My family mustn't know. No one in the racing community must ever know."

"I still don't understand, my lady. What must people never know?"

"That I have completely lost my abilities as a horsewoman. Don't you see, Miss Sutherland? These horses are all I have. Without them, there is nothing. *I* am nothing. Nothing at all."

"Nonsense." Holly slipped an arm around the girl's shoulders. "These recent mishaps are merely that. An expert horsewoman does not lose her abilities overnight. Why, tomorrow you'll saddle Sport o' Kings and ride to your heart's content. You'll see."

Lady Sabrina blinked down at her lap, an effort to clear away tears, Holly guessed. When she looked back up, a determined expression had wiped her vulnerability away. "I don't know why I've confided in you, Miss Sutherland. Perhaps because you do not hail from our world, because you are not truly part of it and will therefore not judge me as the others would. But you are nonetheless a skilled horsewoman. I recognized that today. I respect you for it. And I thank you for what you did earlier."

Those words produced a pang Holly did her best to hide. If only her brother felt the same.

"I must beg you to afford me the same respect, Miss Sutherland. Please speak of this to no one. Not even to your sisters and most especially not to any members of my family. May I count on you to keep my confidence?"

"I assure you, my lady, no one will hear anything from my lips."

Lady Sabrina came to her feet. "If you'll excuse me, I must change into a proper gown and then see if my mother needs me. You and your sisters are staying for supper?"

"We are. Thank you."

Lady Sabrina swept away, the train of her riding skirts trailing behind her on the flagstones. She gathered the train over one arm and entered the house through a pair of French doors. At the same time, a footfall sounded at the base of the terrace steps. Someone started up.

Holly gasped when his face came into view. "Lord Drayton." Her gaze darted to the garden below. "How long were you . . . ?"

He paused at the top of the stairs. "Listening?"

She compressed her lips in reproach.

"I am sorry, Miss Sutherland. I hadn't intended to eavesdrop." His brusque tone and the determined speed of his stride as he approached took her aback.

She drew herself up, her spine gone rigid. "Your sister was speaking to me in confidence, my lord. No matter what you heard, I cannot discuss anything she said."

"I didn't seek you out to talk about my sister."

He had sought her out? Before she could decipher what he could mean, he was beside her, sitting disconcertingly close and—her heart lurched—grabbing for her hand. "Miss Sutherland, I want you to promise me you'll never again do anything like what you did in the paddock today."

Dismay sank like a stone inside her. "Lord Drayton, I—I apologize. I know you had matters well in hand, and then I came along and embarrassed you before your guests—"

"The devil take my guests."

"What?" She blinked in surprise. "Aren't you angry with me?"

"Angry?" His eyebrows shot up in incredulity. "Miss Sutherland, you may have rescued my sister from grave injury. Perhaps even saved her life."

"But earlier you seemed so . . ." She trailed off, trying to remember what exactly he had said.

Please go . . .

"Miss Sutherland, the truth is I did *not* have matters well in hand. I am eternally grateful for your quick action, and I want you to swear you'll never do anything so foolhardy again."

He still held her hand, almost squeezing it as his sister had done, and now he gave it an urgent shake. His words made scant sense. He was grateful but at the same time he seemed angry, or at least perturbed, and—she hardly knew what else. His proximity and his touch threw her into confusion, elation. She could think of no reply, not even when he repeated his demand that she never endanger herself again.

He fell silent. His blue eyes held her, and she might have been soaring in a clear summer sky. A taut energy arced between them; it pulsed through her, hummed in her ears. There was so much she longed to tell him, so much more she longed to hear him say. The silence stretched, not exactly uncomfortable, but filled with puzzlement and an expectation that sizzled like her brother-in-law's electrical wires . . . until voices from the garden severed the connection between them.

Down below, on the main garden path, top hats, beribboned bonnets, and parasols bobbed above the shrubbery. Laughter drifted through the foliage.

Lord Drayton came to his feet. "Excuse me, Miss Sutherland," he said, and was gone.

Conversation and Mozart faded to a muted hum as Colin melted into the shadows and descended the terrace steps. The torches dotting the gardens threw elongated shadows across his path, their irregular shapes reflecting his troubled thoughts.

He had more than done his duty today as acting head of the family and a leader in the racing world. A full dozen of the Ashworth two-year-olds already had prospective buyers, along with several more race-ready three- and four-year-olds. Of those, several purchasers had expressed wishes for their animals to remain at Masterfield Park for training. His solicitors would begin negotiating terms tomorrow and the bargains would be struck before the Royal Meeting commenced. His father could have nothing to complain about upon his return from the Americas.

Are you still laughing, Father? Ah, but Colin would have the last laugh, assuming he could convey the colt safely back to Devonshire without anyone finding out, and then somehow convince the queen the replacement colt was the one Thaddeus Ashworth had given her.

By God, he needed a miracle.

A seductive murmur followed by a higher-pitched giggle came from somewhere beyond the box hedge to his right. As he proceeded across the gardens, more soft laughter drifted on the breeze. It seemed his guests were thoroughly enjoying his hospitality. As long as all parties were willing, it wasn't his business to interfere. He kept going, not pausing until he reached the stable yard, where he stopped to gauge the brightness of the moon. Nearly full, the orb hung plump and bright in a cloud-free sky, spreading a carpet of silver across the paddocks and the more distant meadows.

Perfect, as long as he kept to a conservative pace.

Nate, the night groom, snapped to attention when Colin walked inside the stable. "Cordelier, milord?"

Colin nodded. While the gangly youth went to collect

saddle and tack, he strolled down the aisle, lit by the lanterns hanging high on their pegs, until he reached the stall of his favorite horse. Something about this place, its sounds and smells, never failed to calm him.

Cordelier stood sleeping with his head in the far corner, but at Colin's soft summons the stallion turned and stuck his nose over the stall gate. "Halloo there, boy." Colin reached into his pocket for the small apple he'd secreted there earlier. As Cordelier munched it from his palm, Colin ran a hand down the animal's powerful neck. "You did exceptionally well today."

Another stallion might have panicked when Geoff's horse bumped him, might have reared, kicked, fallen. Colin shut his eyes to block out the images of what could have happened. He stroked Cordelier's neck again. "You're a good, steady friend, old man."

Cordelier should have been sold off years ago. The most promising of the Ashworth colts at the time, he had known no shortage of eager buyers. In fact, Thaddeus had nearly sealed a deal that would have taken the potential champion far north to Yorkshire.

But Colin had wanted him—no other horse would do—and he had put his foot down. If his father wanted his continued cooperation in the breeding and raising of champions, then he would yield to Colin's wishes.

Cordelier finished chomping the apple and pressed his nose to Colin's coat front in search of another. "Sorry, old boy. Only brought the one this time."

He touched the star half hidden beneath the stallion's ebony forelock. He loved this horse, had raised him from a foal and trained him up to be the champion he might have been, had Colin been willing to let him go.

"Sometimes, old boy, I wonder if I did you any favor in keeping you from the turf. Racing is in the very chemistry of your blood. You might have been a legend. Ah, well, I suppose you've served an even greater purpose, if a rather less celebrated one." The horse seemed to nod in agreement, and nuzzled Colin's shoulder. "How about a ride beneath the stars, shall we? You know where we're going, my friend." Scratching behind Cordelier's ear, Colin lowered his voice to a whisper. "My partner in crime—"

"Milord?"

He jumped at the interruption, and turned to see Nate standing with his arms empty and at his sides. Colin frowned at the delay. "Is something wrong?"

Nate nodded and came closer, speaking in an undertone. "There's someone about, milord. A lady. I thought you should know."

"Well, who is it?" Had Sabrina sneaked away from the bustle of the supper party? When she was younger, she'd often slip out of her room at night, and Colin would find her down here, brushing her pony and confiding in the gentle animal about her future hopes. One of those hopes had been recently dashed, and he didn't doubt she'd seek the same solace that had once eased her hurts.

But Nate was shaking his head. "She's no one I know, my lord. One of your guests, perhaps. She's down the east aisle, moving quietly from stall to stall, a bit strangelike. She's actually slipping into the stalls."

"Did she see you?"

The groom gave another shake of his head.

Colin moved away from the stall. "Thank you, Nate."

"Shall I saddle Cordelier, sir?"

"Hold off for now."

Chapter 10

Good heavens, they were all the same. Horse after horse essentially identical, with bay coats and ebony points, the only differences being that some bore the Ashworth star, some only a streak, while others boasted no white marking at all beneath their forelocks. Those last two, of course, she ruled out immediately. Victoria's colt bore the star. But Holly still had to examine each horse, because the marking wasn't always immediately apparent if covered by the forelock. And the stable's dim lighting didn't help.

"This will never do," she murmured beneath her breath. Finding Prince's Pride would be like finding the proverbial needle in a haystack, except that every bit of this hay exactly resembled the needle.

She sidestepped to the next stall. She had decided to examine the Ashworths' private stables first, for it made more sense to her that Victoria's colt would be hidden among the animals not readily available for public viewing. She hadn't counted on there being so many!

"What can one family possibly do with all these horses?" she whispered in response to the sleepy snort that greeted her at the next stall. She ran her hand up the nose, moving the mane aside and checking for the star. This one had it. As she had done several times already, she unlatched the stall gate and stepped in. First she checked to see if this animal was a colt. Then she hesitated, waiting for . . .

Good gracious, for some magical quality to come over her. She simply didn't know what she was supposed to feel when—if—she finally encountered Prince's Pride. Victoria had said she would *know*, that she would sense the colt's remarkable superiority.

She felt nothing but the heat wafting from the animal's flanks, sensed nothing but that this particular horse had suddenly awakened from his doze and noticed her intrusion into his stall.

His head swung around, one large velvet eye regarding Holly with a gleam of surprise. The flank beside her quivered and shook, a back foot stomped. The tail swished in agitation.

"There, there now," Holly cooed gently. "It's quite all right. I don't believe you're the fellow I'm searching for, so I shall be going now."

But as she attempted to retrace her steps, the horse shifted his formidable bulk and blocked her path.

"It's all right," she whispered again. "If you'll only move over a bit . . ."

She moved alongside the animal, smoothing her palms over his flank as she went. The action seemed to have a calming effect. The tail switched back and forth but the horse stood his ground and tolerated Holly making her way to the stall gate. She reached the colt's front shoulder and stretched her hand toward the latch—

"Who's there?"

The barked demand startled her, and she let out a cry of alarm. With a whinny, the horse lurched and tried to swing about; his massive shoulder struck Holly and shoved her off balance. She landed on her rump in the hay.

Footsteps advanced toward the stall at a run. Holly attempted to gain her feet while the colt stomped and thrashed dangerously about his stall. Head down, Holly thrust her arms up in front of her and shimmied back as tightly against the side wall as she could to avoid the frantic hooves.

The gate was thrown open, and a pair of hands made a grab for the colt's halter. The horse fought and shied, trying to find a means of escape within the close confines of the stall.

"Miss Sutherland," Lord Drayton called out as he struggled to gain control of the animal, "have you been injured?"

"No, my lord." He maneuvered the horse to one side, allowing Holly room to stand. She wasted no time in scrambling to her feet and out of the stall.

Lord Drayton spent the next few minutes soothing the horse. Finally he secured the gate, and turned to regard Holly. "You're quite certain you're all right?" he said very low, in a queer tone that spread goose bumps across her back.

She nodded, then crossed the aisle and stood beside him, in front of the stall. As if the past moments hadn't happened, the horse stuck his head over the gate and calmly nudged her with his nose. "Is the colt all right?"

"He's done no harm to himself that I can detect."

"I'm sorry. I . . ." She heaved a sigh. "I keep saying that to you today, don't I?"

A powerful hand closed over her shoulder. "Come with me."

Just as earlier, his touch cast her into a state of bewilderment. Barely aware of her surroundings, she let him convey her down the aisle, around a corner, and out into the night air. She thought he'd turn toward the house, but he chose the opposite direction, walking with a purposeful stride, one that made her hasten her steps to keep up. Then he came to an abrupt halt.

Empty and silent, the paddocks, racetrack, and pastures beyond spread like a moonlit patchwork before them. The hush unnerved her, as did the silence of the man beside her, charged as it was with an emotion that pulsed off him in waves. He'd taken her hand and tucked it into the crook of his arm, and as they stood side by side, she stole a glance at him. His nose pinched and his jaw sharply square, he stared hard into the distance. She could only guess he was searching for words adequate enough to rebuke her for her foolishness.

When she could stand it no longer she swallowed and said, "I'm sorry. I only wished to see the colt up close."

"The fault was mine, Miss Sutherland. I shouldn't have sneaked up on you as I did." He broke off, turned her to face him, and seized her hands with the same intensity as earlier that day on the terrace. "But you could have been seriously injured."

She found herself toe-to-toe with him, dwarfed by his greater size, the breadth and strength of his shoulders, his broad chest. As he stood poised above her, his face was a fierce shadow framed by the night sky, his eyes gleaming with the sharp clarity of the stars.

The emotion blazing in those eyes made her look away, gasp for breath. And then she realized what he'd said and looked back at him. "You purposely sneaked up on me."

With a sheepish lift of his brows, a quirk of his mouth, he nodded and released her hands.

"You thought I was . . . ?" She didn't finish the question, for the obvious truth was that he'd suspected her of doing exactly what she *had* been doing: spying. Her pulse rattled a warning that she was glad he couldn't feel.

"I am extremely protective of the horses," he confessed. "The racing world is not an entirely ingenuous one. Rivalries and greed often drive people to extremes."

Her heart thudded against her stays. Had *he* been driven to an extreme act? She wondered how close she had come tonight to discovering Victoria's colt. Perhaps no more than a stall or two away.

His expectant look broke into her thoughts. It was her turn to say something, and she realized that despite his apology, he waited to gauge her reaction to that last statement. He was testing her as much as she was testing him.

If ever she needed to deceive, it was now. For Victoria. For her country.

"And you thought perhaps I was . . . up to no good?" she said with a touch of dramatic flair. Feigning astonishment, she pressed a hand to her bosom. "You thought I might be ferreting out the secrets of the Ashworth racing success?"

His lips pursed, and one corner lifted in a lopsided grin. "It does sound rather ridiculous when spoken aloud. But you were *inside* the stall, Miss Sutherland. Surely you realize how unusual that appears."

"But how can one properly judge good horseflesh without getting as close a view as possible?"

Eyebrows drawn, he seemed to weigh this statement. "You do realize you were on the private side of the stables, where we keep our own horses."

Indeed, she'd been very much aware of that fact. She widened her eyes. "Was I? Then I must have misunderstood your sister earlier. I could have sworn. . . . Well, there has been so much to absorb today, I don't wonder I got it wrong."

The crickets and night rustlings filled her ears, became all but deafening as he studied her and she willed every muscle in her body not to quiver, not to give her away. Suddenly exhausted by her game of deceit, she wanted to demand what he was looking for, and what he was hiding. Perhaps it was a delayed reaction to being nearly trampled beneath the horse's hooves, but she wished for the safety of her hotel room, where she might bury her face in her pillow and—goodness—cry. Let flow tears that she couldn't explain. She knew only that her heart suddenly ached, and she longed for relief.

"Return tomorrow for a private tour of the stables," he suddenly said. "And a ride, if you wish."

What? "Really?"

He nodded. "If you like."

"I would like that very much—"

She was interrupted by a voice calling out from the stable yard. "Colin, are you here?"

They both turned in the direction of the hail. Silhouetted by lamplight, Lady Sabrina approached from the archway between the stable wings.

The earl quickly opened a wide space between him and Holly. "Yes, Sabrina. What is it?"

"I've been looking for—" Lady Sabrina broke off and

craned forward, peering through the shadows. "Is that Miss Sutherland with you?"

He swore under his breath, and Holly wondered what his sister would think to discover them standing here together in the dark. But there was nowhere to hide, nothing to be done but square her shoulders.

Lady Sabrina met them partway as they walked back to the stable yard. Holly wanted to shrink from the curiosity arching the young woman's brows. "It is actually you I've been searching for, Miss Sutherland."

"Me? Is something wrong? Is it—"

"Do not be alarmed, Miss Sutherland," Lady Sabrina hastened to say. "She is all right, just a bit of a faint. Mama called for the smelling salts and some tea, which quite did the trick but—"

Colin stopped her with a hand on her wrist. "*Who*, Sabrina?"

"Ivy," Holly murmured, confirming her own worst fears. "Oh, no!"

Panic gripped her. Hefting her skirts, she stood poised to set off at a run. The earl pressed forward on the balls of his feet, too, and Holly remembered that Ivy was the wife of his closest friend.

Lady Sabrina stepped in front of them, blocking their path. "I didn't mean to frighten you, Miss Sutherland. Lady Harrow is at this moment sitting with her feet propped up in Mama's blue parlor, sipping tea. And"—she leaned closer and lowered her voice—"no one but Mama and me is any the wiser."

"Oh. I—" The open acknowledgment of her sister's condition brought Holly up short. Was Lady Sabrina also acknowledging Holly's compromised position of having slipped away with her brother? Not that she *had* slipped away with him, but surely that was how it must appear. "Thank you."

The girl gave a conspiratorial wink that made Holly unsure whether or not she had found an unlikely ally in the young woman. As if to suggest she had, Lady Sabrina linked her arm through Holly's. "Come, I'll take you to your sister."

"Yes, and we'll need our carriage brought round immediately."

"Oh, indeed not, Miss Sutherland," Lady Sabrina replied in a tone that brooked no debate. "Mama will not hear of your returning to your hotel. You and your sisters shall remain here, where Lady Harrow may be properly looked after. You may make a list of everything you'd like fetched from your rooms. I shall send a footman and my maid."

Holly looked uncertainly at Lord Drayton, who had yet to add his approval to this turn of events. She glimpsed myriad emotions flickering across his handsome features: startlement, hesitation . . . fear? All this passed in the span of blink, and then he recovered his poise and gave a nod. "A prudent plan."

That was all. Lady Sabrina chatted all the way back to the house, seeming oblivious to the heavy silence that cloaked both her brother and Holly. Holly should have been elated at this further opportunity to observe the Ashworths, and Lord Drayton in particular. But those emotions she'd witnessed nagged like a sore tooth. Were they an admission of guilt?

"For the third time, I did not faint," Ivy insisted. "I stood up too quickly and became the tiniest bit light-headed."

Perched at the foot of the bed, Willow shifted her legs beneath her and leaned against a bedpost. "You fell," she insisted. "I saw you."

"I lost my balance."

Holly poured another cup of tea and passed it into Ivy's hands. She searched her sister's face for the slightest sign of illness. The color had returned to her cheeks, and the cup and saucer remained steady between Ivy's hands. "Lady Sabrina insisted you passed out," Holly reminded her.

"Lady Sabrina exaggerates. I became a trifle disoriented, but only for a moment."

A knock at the chamber door cut their debate short. The

door opened, and the Duchess of Masterfield stepped inside. "I do hope I am not disturbing you."

"Of course not, Your Grace." Holly and Willow slipped off the bed and dipped curtsies. Ivy started to follow suit, but the duchess held up an imperious hand as she crossed the room.

"Lady Harrow, do not dare rise from that bed." She came to stand at the bedside. "You do look much improved. It must be the tea. Greerson, my abigail, is a veritable catalog of old remedies. I daresay there is no illness the woman has not the recipe to cure. Why, when I was expecting my eldest . . ."

Perching on the edge of the mattress, the duchess relayed her own experiences with the malaise of increasing. Her hand settled with motherly affection on Ivy's, giving it the occasional pat of reassurance.

Seated on the other side of the bed, Holly used the opportunity to study the woman who had raised such a diverse and contrary brood.

Like her daughter, she was not exactly beautiful, though her features were well formed and spoke of intelligence. The directness of her gaze declared her a woman who missed little, yet she lacked the spark that was immediately detectable in her daughter's bright manner. The duchess's eyes were not the gemlike blue of Lady Sabrina's and her eldest son's, but a faded hazel, and something in her bearing suggested a vivacity that had also faded with time.

"I hope you are all contented with your accommodations?" the woman asked.

Holly and her sisters assured her they were.

The duchess smiled kindly at Ivy. "I should leave you to your rest." She turned to Holly and Willow. "Breakfast is laid out at half past nine. Country hours, you know. You'll find the morning room down the corridor beyond the library." She patted Ivy's hand once more. "I'll have a tray sent up for you, Lady Harrow."

"I assure you, Your Grace, that will be quite unnecessary."

"Indulge me, dear." Leaning closer, the duchess stretched out a hand to touch Ivy's cheek. Her lace-edged sleeve rode up to expose her wrist.

Holly's eyes widened at the sight of a weal a couple of inches above her hand, the faded ghost of an injury that had left a blotchy discoloring around her wrist. The woman lowered her arm and stood, her sleeve once more concealing the mottled skin. Holly darted a glance at each of her sisters to see if they, too, had noticed, but their expressions revealed no hint that they had.

She glanced down at her own wrist, and encircled it with her other hand. A faint unease gathered in the pit of her stomach, the sensation lingering long after the duchess had left them. And for some reason she couldn't quite name, she hugged her sisters tighter than usual as she bade them good night.

"Good morning, Lord Drayton. I hope I'm not too early."

Dawn had barely broken over the horizon, and the stable yard lay in chilly shadow. The other guests would be hours yet in their beds, but Miss Sutherland was freshness itself as she stood before Colin, the crisp folds of her emerald riding habit elongating her figure and deepening the fiery hue of her hair.

His reaction to her made him forget the fatigue that clawed at his frame. He'd spent a restless night—thinking about her, and the fact that she lay sleeping under his roof. From countless angles he had imagined her generous curves covered only in some diaphanous chemise and a light coverlet, her rounded cheek plumped from the pillow beneath it . . . her lips softly parted . . . and he, merely down the corridor and around a corner, so close. And very much awake.

"We can postpone, my lord, if this proves inconvenient for you."

Good God, he'd been mutely staring. He gave himself a shake. "Not inconvenient at all, Miss Sutherland. I am merely surprised to see you up and ready so early."

"There is nothing like an early-morning ride," she said, slightly breathless, her green eyes glinting.

"I agree. Most people don't realize what they are missing, sleeping half the morning away."

"Just so. We were all early risers, growing up at Thorn Grove." She grinned, and while they stood another moment without speaking, somehow the silence had become companionable, comfortable.

No, not comfortable. *Hardly* comfortable. He felt exhilarated, bedazzled, aroused. Dizzy. She made him dizzy with wanting her. Her spicy scent, her riot of curls, her lovely, lightly freckled skin . . . Just once he'd like to pull her into his arms and take in all of her, absorb her, drink in his fill.

Ah, God, did he truly think *just once* would satisfy such a craving?

"Where are my manners?" he asked, turning his thoughts to a safer subject. "How is your sister? I trust she is recovered?"

"She insists she suffered from nothing more serious than light-headedness. But we are grateful for the duchess's hospitality. And yours, my lord."

"No thanks are necessary, Miss Sutherland. Especially as it worked out so conveniently, since I did promise you a tour this morning." Once again he let his gaze drift over her riding habit, from the green feather in her cap to the train looped over one arm. "And a ride, of course."

"I apologize again for last night. I realize I shouldn't have—"

"My guests are welcome to explore any part of this estate, at any time."

"Are we?" She seemed inordinately pleased about that.

He nodded. "But I thought perhaps we would begin with the horses that are actually for sale."

She blushed, but with a grin that sparked his pulse. A little flame grew inside him, a much more pleasant sensation than he cared to admit.

Side by side they strolled up and down the aisles. He told

her the names of the horses, their ages, their prospects. She listened carefully. Her comments impressed him and convinced him she had spent many hours not only riding but also being among horses and grooms. Her knowledge seemed a combination of natural instinct and firsthand experience, and his admiration for her increased by the moment, a circumstance that unsettled him.

He sought refuge in the one subject he could share with Miss Sutherland without fear of treading too close. "Have you seen an animal yet that strikes your fancy?"

"I've seen many such. The horse you raced yesterday—" She looked about her. "I don't see him here. What was his name?"

"Cordelier, and no, you won't find him among our investment horses."

"Oh? And why is that?"

"Because he is mine, Miss Sutherland. I raced him only to demonstrate what an Ashworth Thoroughbred is capable of. He is not for sale and never shall be. "

Her brow furrowed. "Not even for the right price?"

"No price could induce me to part with Cordelier. To me, he is vastly more than just a horse."

Damn, but he'd said too much. There were too many memories and too many emotions coiled around his rare triumph over his father.

Her eyes narrowed and a smile hovered on her lips. "What is he, then?"

He allowed his own mouth to curve. "Perhaps nothing more than a young man's folly, Miss Sutherland. But I've always thought of him as my challenge to myself." Yes, this he could share without exposing too much of himself, without ripping open the old wounds. "You are aware of my scientific interests?"

"Oh, yes. My brother-in-law has spoken of the experimentations you and your colleagues engage in at Cambridge."

They resumed walking. She moved close at his side, her swaying skirts brushing his thigh. The rhythm of each *swish, swish, swish* invaded his mind and made it difficult to focus on what he was telling her. He trusted his mouth to form the correct words while the rest of him swam in a heated haze that blurred their surroundings yet sharpened every luscious detail about her.

They crossed the arched entryway and entered the private side of the stables. "Cordelier is the first horse I ever bred entirely on my own. I combed our breeding stock for just the right qualities. His father is Harvest Moon, his mother Pilgrim's Delight. Both champions."

"Oh, my, even I have heard of them. With such a bloodline, one would think you'd be eager to race him."

"Only privately. I couldn't bear to part with him, not even long enough for him to be properly trained for the turf. But he sired several of the horses you just saw."

"A stud without a track record?"

"His breeding speaks for itself. Cordelier's progeny are extremely sought after in the racing world. Ah, here we are." They stopped at Cordelier's gate, and the horse circled the stall to offer his ears to be scratched. "Halloo, old boy."

Seeming eager to please, Miss Sutherland pulled off one kid glove and worked her fingers at just the place Cordelier most preferred. Colin couldn't help grinning at the happy glaze that entered the animal's eyes. "I believe you've won him over, Miss Sutherland."

She ran her hand beneath the horse's forelock. "Do all Cordelier's offspring bear the star?"

"No, not all, though most do. Actually, I find myself fascinated by how and when the star makes its appearance. It began several generations ago, in a horse called Shooting Star."

"Yes, I believe I've heard of him . . . or read about him. Isn't he listed in the Ascot racing annals? Wasn't he owned by the king himself?"

"Two kings, Miss Sutherland. Mad King George owned him first, and then his son, George IV."

"Then Cordelier is a descendant of Shooting Star?" When Colin nodded, she pushed a low whistle through her lips. "I am standing before a legacy of racing history."

Her enthusiasm was infectious, and his heartbeat accelerated. "Cordelier is more than that, Miss Sutherland. He has played a significant role in my theories of heredity, of how some traits prevail and are passed visibly from generation to generation, while others rest dormant in a bloodline until they surprise one with their sudden appearance."

Her hand strayed to the braid coiled at her nape. "Like my red hair. None of my sisters are so burdened. A bequest from my maternal great-grandmother, or so my uncle Edward told me."

"The man who raised you," Colin mused more than commented. Ivy had confided some of her family history to him, how their parents perished in a house fire, and the four sisters were raised at their uncle's modest Surrey estate. A sad look came over Miss Sutherland, and he found himself searching for words to banish it.

She rallied with a brisk laugh. "My extraordinary luck, this hair of mine."

"It may be. You see, Miss Sutherland, it is sometimes those dormant traits that endow one with unexpected strength. That is what I have been working to achieve among our stock. To determine the most beneficial characteristics, not only of stamina and speed, but also of resilience and the ability to withstand disease and injury."

"It sounds as if you have set yourself against nature." Cordelier nudged her arm, and she resumed petting him.

"Not against nature so much as an attempt to use nature to its best advantage. Traits are not good or bad. Each has its purpose, and in learning what those purposes are, we can breed the ones that will best serve a particular species. Racehorses, unfortunately, are susceptible to a wide range of maladies that too often make it necessary to destroy the animal. If I could only find—"

He stopped, realizing how impassioned he'd become. He stood with hands fisted, shoulders bunched, legs braced as if he'd just entered the boxing ring, as he sometimes thought of his laboratory.

Her hand stilled on Cordelier's mane. "Such an applica-

tion might benefit more than mere horses, Lord Drayton."
One reddish gold eyebrow arched astutely. "Might one suppose your ambitions extend to human beings?"

That she had made the jump and questioned him so
calmly, so entirely without any look of judgment, sent a
thrill through him. "Inasmuch as hereditary illnesses might
someday be better understood, and even eradicated, yes."
Some impish impulse sent his forefinger reaching out to
trace a burnished tendril curling about her ear. "But as for
the traits that make each of us who we are, Miss Sutherland,
I would not desire to interfere with those."

Her bosom rose and her lips parted on a delicate little
sigh that melted directly over his loins. Aching to draw her
into his arms, he instead clamped his teeth against his desires and turned back toward Cordelier.

Holly Sutherland would wither among a family like his.
He might not believe in curses, not in the mystical sense, but
his was a family defined by bitterness and greed. These
weeks of his father's absence had been like a gift, a heady
relief. But Thaddeus Ashworth would return home soon
enough, bringing scorn and animosity with him.

Colin, Bryce, Sabrina, Geoffrey . . . all of them bore the
scars of their childhood, some physically, others buried
deep inside. Their mother, too. The Duke of Masterfield
loved no one and nothing as much as his brandy, and his
brandy made him mean, unremorsefully so.

"We tarry overlong, Miss Sutherland. You did not come
here to talk, or to hear my ridiculous theories."

"Didn't I?" Her voice emerged as a wisp of its usual timbre.

He couldn't take much more of standing beside her, of
inhaling her scent and imagining the warmth of her skin
beneath all those layers of linen and wool. He forced his
gaze from the double row of buttons that marched up her
jacket, emphasizing the swell of her breasts. "Certainly not,
Miss Sutherland. Or do you not long for a brisk ride across
the pastures?"

"Oh, I do. I most certainly do."

Chapter 11

Something in Lord Drayton's tone, in his gaze, convinced Holly he understood, even better than her sisters, what horses and riding meant to her. That to her, riding was freedom itself, akin to sailing over the hillsides like a low-flying bird, powerful and tireless and unhindered. The closest comparison she could think of might be Ivy and her science, how she and Simon harnessed the earth's mightiest powers.

While she was growing up, Uncle Edward had always frowned upon her antics, as he had termed them; he had called her reckless and unladylike, until she had grown ashamed of the abandon that filled her during her madcap rides. She had stopped riding astride, and rarely galloped except when she felt safe from disapproving eyes.

Lord Drayton was busy adjusting something on Cordelier's halter that didn't seem to need adjusting. "What you did in the paddock yesterday was not the act of a casual rider, Miss Sutherland, and most especially not typical of a female rider."

Oh. Mortification crept hotly up her neck. He shot her a glance. "Don't misunderstand. I admire your skills. I merely meant that such abilities are not acquired haphazardly. So what shall it be, Miss Sutherland? We have several dependable geldings available, or perhaps one of the older mares will do?" The slant of his lips issued a challenge she could not resist.

"No old mares or geldings for me, Lord Drayton. A stallion, if you please."

"We shan't be riding in a paddock," he warned. "Are you certain you are equal to a gallop across the open pastures?"

She grinned, then grinned harder when his features lit with the same eager enthusiasm. Yet it was with the utmost gravity that he asked his next question. "Sidesaddle or astride?"

Hoping for just this opportunity, she had worn the doeskin leggings she'd had made specially some years ago. Her reply must have shown on her face, for without waiting for her answer, Lord Drayton called for his grooms. If the lads found the unorthodox instructions shocking, they gave no indication.

"His name is Thunderbolt," he told her some ten minutes later, just before he leaned over and laced his fingers to boost her up onto the animal's back.

"Oh, dear. That sounds rather formidable."

He unlaced his fingers and straightened. "Second thoughts?"

Ah, another challenge. She lifted both a foot and an eyebrow, and waited for him to lace his fingers again. When he did, she set her knee into his palms and gathered the reins. Supported by the strength of his arms, she fairly floated into the saddle. The horse shifted beneath her weight and stomped his back foot. Then he settled down as she leaned forward to stroke his neck and murmur reassurances.

The earl swung up onto Cordelier, and they clip-clopped out of the stable yard. Once they had passed the paddocks, he clucked the horses to a trot, and then to an easy canter that took them beyond the racetrack. The sun was just climbing above a bank of clouds on the horizon. It was a fine, cool morning, and Holly filled her lungs with the scents of lush spring grass and the pungent tang of horse and leather.

At a smooth, steady pace they traversed a rolling field and circled some low hills. Holly found her patience growing short. Despite all his intimations to the contrary, the earl seemed intent on keeping to a safe speed—safe for a lady. The notion threatened the prospect of a vigorous morning ride.

He surprised her by bringing them to a halt. Twisting in his saddle, he gestured back toward the way they had come. "As you can see, we are no longer visible from the house."

"Aren't we?" She twisted around, too, and saw only the gentle swell of the fields in all directions.

He replied with a question of his own. "Are you ready, Miss Sutherland?"

Her heart leaped. She smiled, and he gave Cordelier some invisible signal. The horses broke into a gallop that devoured the ground beneath them.

True to his name, Thunderbolt stormed across the open terrain. His body elongated and his head and neck stretched straight out. As the countryside streaked by, Holly felt her very soul expand, even as her lungs filled with sweet, crisp air. Yesterday's concerns flitted away. It had been so long—too long—since she'd felt such power beneath her, conveying her into the wind in defiance of earthly gravity. A whoop escaped her, and then another.

Lord Drayton rode Cordelier beside and a little ahead of her. He turned his face toward her and smiled, and a sudden realization stole a portion of her elation. Theirs was no wild pace determined by the impulse of the horses, but rather one carefully controlled by the earl himself.

He wasn't acknowledging her abilities as a horsewoman; he was merely indulging the lady's fancies with a symbolic pat on the head while keeping her safe from any real risk.

It would not do. Not now, with the thrill of true freedom so close at hand. Holly squeezed with her knees and leaned lower over Thunderbolt's neck.

The horse shot forward in a burst of vigor that confirmed her suspicions that he'd been held in check. As she passed Lord Drayton's surprised countenance, she laughed. "Don't be afraid, sir. I'm certainly not."

Then she leaned lower still, her fingers splayed over her horse's mane, the reins looped loosely through her thumbs.

In many ways she relinquished control to the stallion, but it was a control based on mutual trust, one she felt confident of resuming whenever she liked.

Would the earl be furious with her? Her last glimpse of him had revealed his consternation. She braved a peek now over her shoulder. He had fallen several horse lengths behind. Then he, too, urged his mount faster. As he gained ground and pulled up alongside her, their gazes met, his glinting with admiration. He made no effort to curb their speed, and with a nod she thanked him.

Then she squeezed Thunderbolt's sides again and once more resumed the lead, even if only by a nose. She directed their course over the wide swell of a hill, around a copse of birch trees, across a narrow stream. To the west, several rolling hills converged to form a soft, shady vale that invited exploration. Holly headed Thunderbolt in that direction.

"Miss Sutherland!"

Suddenly he was no longer several feet away but so close she might easily have touched him. Her name boomed again from his lips, and she drew back in the saddle. Thunderbolt's pace immediately slowed. In the next instant Lord Drayton leaned over and snatched the reins from her hands.

Gradually Colin slowed the horses to a canter, then a walk, and finally a halt. As the animals stood stamping and snorting, Miss Sutherland's obvious anger shot like green arrows across the space between them.

"Why on earth did you do that? There was no danger and I certainly was not pushing Thunderbolt beyond his limits." A kid-gloved hand went to her slender hip. "Or do you still doubt my horsemanship?"

"I never doubted your horsemanship, Miss Sutherland. Though I do not doubt that if left to your own devices you would run pell-mell into the eye of a raging storm."

Her mouth dropped open, and though sounds of indignation poured forth, no actual words formed. He tossed back her reins and turned Cordelier toward home. Thunderbolt would follow. The stallion's impetus had been snipped short, and now he would long only for a good brushing down, water, and the treats he would receive upon being handed back to the grooms.

They rode in silence until the racetrack came into view. By then Miss Sutherland's brooding scowl had eased to puzzled curiosity.

"Was it the vale? Did you not wish me to ride down into it? Does some danger exist there?"

Indeed it did, to him and everything he held dear. But she had supplied him with a convenient excuse. "The terrain there is treacherous, Miss Sutherland. I could not have you rushing headlong into marshy bottomland."

"You might have simply said as much, my lord. I'd have gladly changed direction."

Would she have? At the time he hadn't believed so. The look on her face, that whoop she'd let out—both were evidence of a bold, unstoppable spirit. She had reminded him of himself, but not the self he was here in Ascot . . . and not as any other living soul ever saw him. Except perhaps for his grandmother, of course, who sometimes watched from her bedroom window at Briarview while he galloped with the ancient ponies across the Devonshire hills. Infused with the spirit of the Exmoors, he became as fearless and undaunted as they were; even thoughts of his father couldn't shake his buoyancy.

He had seen the same fortitude in Miss Sutherland's eyes as she'd headed for the vale. And he had believed there was no other way of stopping her. She would have laughed and kept going, ridden between the hills and into the trees, and discovered the secret that could destroy everything he was striving to preserve. Even now, despite her insistence to the contrary, he didn't believe matters would have gone any other way.

When they reached the stables, she didn't wait for him to help her down but swung from the saddle on her own, landing with a light footfall on the ground. "Thank you for the ride, Lord Drayton, and for the tour. I enjoyed both immensely."

Irony bit through each word. He wished he could apologize. But he'd become careless this morning. Instead of using his brain he'd allowed a lower region of his anatomy to take charge. He must be more careful, even if that meant playing the boor whenever he confronted Miss Sutherland's charms.

He returned her thanks with a correct and impersonal bow, then raised an eyebrow as if taking her measure and judging that she fell rather short—another lie, the worst of all. "If there is any other way I can assist you and your sisters in your purchase of a racehorse, you have only to ask, Miss Sutherland."

"Thank you again, sir." Arching a coppery eyebrow of her own, she met his mockery and raised the stakes with the stiffest of curtsies, one that conveyed far more indignation than respect. Every sleek line of her body radiated pride and indifference that would have cut him to the quick if it hadn't been exactly the reaction he'd hoped for. Even so, the haughty sweep of her skirts as she stalked away left his insides stinging.

"And where were you two?" Stuart Bentley's voice echoed from within the archway between the stables. A moment later he emerged into sunlight. "Up rather early with our pretty Miss Sutherland, weren't you?"

Colin didn't like the man's tone, or the insinuating look in his eye. "She is a guest, Bentley. I often ride with our guests in the morning. Especially ones with Miss Sutherland's equestrian skills."

Bentley smirked and tapped his riding crop against the flawless sheen of his right boot. "Is that all she is skilled in?"

A burst of fury sent Colin across the paving stones. His pulse surging, he seized Bentley's riding crop. His first impulse was to use it on the other man; only a steadying breath and an effort of will prevented him from doing so. Instead he bent the crop between his hands, stressing the leather-encased wood until it snapped.

The crack penetrated his anger, leaving him calmer, if still breathing heavily and feeling no less adamant. "Miss

Sutherland is the relative of a close family friend," he said evenly. Bentley had backed against the stable wall. He stared at Colin and swallowed. "I will not tolerate that kind of talk about her, nor about any guest in my home." He handed Bentley the two halves of his riding crop. Then he backed a couple of steps away from the other man. "Clear?"

"Quite." Bentley rubbed the back of his neck. "Didn't mean anything by it, old man. A jest, nothing more."

Just as he hadn't meant anything by sidling up to Miss Sutherland yesterday during the demonstrations? Colin still burned to know what he'd said to her, but he wouldn't give Stuart Bentley the satisfaction of asking. On the turf, and when administering Jockey Club business, they were colleagues, even allies. But never quite friends. "A jest in rather bad taste."

The man gave a quick roll of his eyes. "Apparently."

Colin gestured at Bentley's black riding coat. "I'll order a horse saddled. Your own, or one of mine?"

In preparation for the races, Bentley had stabled several of his Thoroughbreds there, as well as his personal mount.

"I, er, think I've changed my mind about riding." The man shoved away from the wall and moved to make his retreat. "Later, perhaps."

"Let me know when and I'll join you."

Bentley assured Colin he would, but Colin would have wagered a hefty sum that the odds of that happening were low, at least for the duration of that day. He'd overreacted, to be sure. His response to Bentley's comment had come on lightning quick and with equal intensity, a fact from which he derived little pleasure. It meant that he'd conquered very few of those emotions that had barraged him months ago, on the first occasion of finding himself alone with Holly Sutherland.

Now, as then, there seemed very little logic attached to the urgent need to have her in his arms, a desire that reduced his Cambridge-educated mind to that of a caveman. Her. Here. Now.

But if he'd had reasons *then* not to become involved with

her, those reasons had now increased tenfold. He was a horse thief who had chosen the queen as his victim.

And that constituted treason.

No, Holly Sutherland was not for him. But, heaven help him, if *he* couldn't have her, he'd be damned if a dandy like Stuart Bentley would have her, or would have his way *with* her, which was no doubt more what the other man had in mind.

"But surely you questioned him."

"You certainly spent plenty of time with him this morning. If you didn't question him, what *did* you speak about?"

Holly lifted the pearl brooch from the dressing table and held it in her palm. So smooth and round in its simple gold setting, so perfect. So pure. During the past two days, there had been moments when Holly wished her life could be as unsullied as that pearl, free of deceptions and suspicions, with no crimes to be investigated and no criminals to apprehend.

She had envisioned excitement and intrigue, not a tangle of emotions that left her confused and reluctant to continue her mission. Ah, but the brooch, she remembered, had been a gift from Victoria, one of many. She closed her fist around it. If a girl younger than she could rule a country, then certainly Holly should not begrudge the small part she had been asked to play in helping secure the crown on the head of that very young girl.

But this morning Holly had nearly forgotten her mission. Last night, she had stolen down to the stables alone to search for the missing colt. Oh, she supposed an animal whisked from the Royal Stables would have been secreted in a far more clever place than the Duke of Masterfield's private stables, but it had been worth a look. This morning, however, missing colts couldn't have been farther from her mind, especially with the ground blurring beneath her and her heart thundering from the presence of the dashing man galloping beside her.

Even now, she was doing it again—forgetting he was

under suspicion, thinking only of how her insides heated at the sight of him, and the fact that he alone seemed to recognize the spark she tried so hard to conceal, but never quite could, because it sometimes burned too bright, too intensely, inside her.

She opened her fist. Looking at herself in the mirror, she gave a nod of approval. Her curls had been dressed to their best advantage, upswept and held with combs at her crown while spiraling tendrils danced above her shoulders. Her dress, with its plunging neckline and cinched bodice, was all the rage in London and Paris. Her jewelry was costly, but sparse and simple: earrings and the matching brooch. She affixed the piece to the aqua-blue silk, close to her shoulder. Then she turned to her sisters.

"I didn't question him this morning," she said in reply to Ivy's question. "I thought it best to allow the conversation to take its natural course."

"And?" Willow tugged her evening gloves on and smoothed the satin that reached above her elbows. Holly might look the proper lady tonight, but her youngest sister was positively angelic in soft rose trimmed in velvet and georgette. The three older Sutherlands always considered Willow the most beautiful of them all, and tonight she promised to steal the heart of every man attending the Ashworths' ball. "What did you speak about?"

Ivy turned from the swivel mirror, where she had been scrutinizing her reflection to reassure herself that her condition had not yet become evident. She tilted her head expectantly.

"We spoke of"—*everything but missing colts*—"horses and the sorts of traits that sometimes hide within a bloodline. And science. He, Lord Drayton, has the most extraordinary ideas about breeding. He doesn't leave it all to hired breeders. Nor are his efforts only for racing, but for the good of the species as a whole. Diseases, injuries . . . he hopes to ease those burdens and someday—this is most extraordinary of all—he aspires to apply his findings to humans, and—"

She paused for a quick breath and stopped. Ivy and Willow were regarding her as if she had taken leave of her senses. She quickly realized it wasn't what she was saying that puzzled them, for scientific principles were no oddities to them, especially not since Ivy had married Simon. But it was *how* she had been running on, her voice rising a full octave in her excitement.

"Interesting," Ivy said with a smile that suggested she wasn't referring to the earl's work. Plucking her fan from the top of the bureau, she snapped it open and fluttered it before her face. "It would certainly seem that you two connected on an academic level."

Holly didn't miss the teasing sarcasm. "It wasn't like that at all, Ivy. Just because you and Simon fell in love over the gears and gadgets in his laboratory is no reason to believe two people can't have an intelligent conversation without becoming moon-faced over each other."

Ivy stilled her fan, her eyes peeking innocently over the lacy edge. She glanced at Willow and winked. "Did I imply any such thing?"

Willow stifled a giggle and returned her attention to Holly. "You were gone for a good two hours. Surely you didn't talk about breeding the entire time."

"The rest of the time we rode."

"Ahhh," her sisters said in unison, and traded looks of comprehension.

"Oh, never mind. What about the two of you? Did you have a chance to question more of the guests?"

"I had tea with Colin's uncle, Lord Shelby, along with the Fenhursts, Lord and Lady Arnold, and the duchess." Ivy smoothed her hands over her amber silk bodice and glanced in the mirror again. "Holly, are you certain no one can tell?"

"Yes, as long as you don't repeat your fainting spell. Now, what happened during tea?"

Ivy shrugged. "I detected nothing unusual. I even tried provoking Lord Arnold into a bit of a tizzy by challenging him to name a colt who could ever take Grey Momus's place. Mr. Bentley happened to be close by. He immediately championed my claim. A heated debate ensued, but there were no shifty eyes or hesitations or prevarications of any kind. Nothing to signify anyone having something to hide."

"Not all criminals have shifty eyes," Willow pointed out.

Holly considered the guests. No one was above suspicion; even the most elderly race enthusiast could have hired someone to steal the colt. She supposed it might be time to expand her investigation and wrangle invitations to the other area stud farms. But so far, no one had mentioned the Ashworths' extraordinary colt, not even in passing. That suggested that the existence of the animal was not common knowledge, that no one outside of the Ashworth family had ever seen it.

Which pointed the guilt toward the Ashworths themselves. Not that any of them had mentioned the colt, either.

"What about Lord Bryce?" she said. "Have either of you had the opportunity to speak with him?"

Willow turned away, but not before Holly witnessed the blush flooding her face.

"Willow? Have you and Lord Bryce conversed?"

"Ah, no . . . not about anything significant." On her way to the wardrobe, she changed course and opened one of their trunks that had been placed beneath the window. She rummaged through the contents.

"What constitutes 'not really'?" Ivy prodded. "And when did you speak to him?"

Kneeling, her head all but hidden inside the trunk, Willow replied, "Yesterday . . . during the demonstrations. He showed me the veterinary annex." A chemise and a pair of stockings flew over her shoulder to land on the floor behind her.

"Why didn't you tell us?" Holly folded her arms across her chest. "We thought you'd gone up to the gardens with some of the other guests."

When Willow didn't answer, Holly went to her, grasped her shoulders, raised her to her feet, and turned her about. Though she'd have thought it impossible, her sister's blush had deepened. "Good heavens, Willow, what happened in the veterinary wing?"

"Nothing. Lord Bryce . . . showed me kittens. That is all."

"That is all?" Over her shoulder, Holly exchanged a glance with Ivy. She looked back at Willow. "Those must have been extraordinary kittens."

"It is nearly nine," Willow said in a swift change of subject. "We are expected downstairs presently."

With a sigh, Holly released her and stepped away. "I have a plan and I'll need your help. Once supper is over, I shall slip away and search the duke's private office. Lady Sabrina mentioned earlier that that is where the record books on all the horses are kept."

"And you think you'll open one of those books and see, 'Remarkable colt given to and then stolen back from Her Majesty the Queen'?"

"No, Ivy, I do not expect to find that written in the ledgers. But surely the duke made a notation of his gift, perhaps with some specific identifying qualities I might use to differentiate the animal from among countless others that look virtually the same." Holly went to the dressing table and picked up her fan, then stood tapping it against her chin. "Will you both help me or not?"

"Of course we'll help you." Looking infinitely calmer now, Willow came up beside her and slipped an arm around her waist. "I am guessing you want us to distract the others so no one notices you've gone."

"You do that, Willow," she said. "If anyone asks, make my excuses. Just don't say I developed a headache or any other ailment, or the duchess will insist on following so she can nurse me back to health. I plan to exit the ballroom onto the terrace and reenter through the corridor near the library. Ivy, should someone decide to search for me, you come through the house and warn me."

Ivy nodded her understanding. Holly did a quick survey of her sisters: their coifs, evening gowns, and glowing faces. "Causing a distraction shouldn't be difficult. You both look ravishing."

Ivy beamed at her. "As do you, dearest. You are certain to dazzle."

The image of striking features and strong arms flashed in her mind, and the notion of whether *he* would find her dazzling heated her through. She shook the thought away. Now was the time to concentrate, not fall prey to girlish fancies. With a toss of her curls, she pulled up straighter and opened her fan. "For Victoria, then. Are we ready?"

Chapter 12

In awe Holly considered the evidence of wealth that shimmered in every crystal-dripping chandelier, every flaw-
lessly polished mirror, every gleaming gilt frame and
carving and clock that graced the Ashworths' ballroom. It
was said the Duke of Masterfield's peers often shook their
heads at his propensity to dirty his hands in trade. If the
extravagance of marble and silver and sumptuous silk could
speak, it would tell the story of a man who believed himself
to have the last laugh. As Victoria had told her, the duke
was even now on his way to the West Indies to survey his
plantations and purchase more land.

A string quartet and a pianoforte tucked into an alcove
provided the music. As the duchess began pairing off her
guests for the next quadrille, Holly avoided her by ducking
behind a flock of plump matrons who declared their disin-
clination to dance by closing ranks and embarking on a
rousing commentary about what the other ladies were
wearing.

Holly had already danced a quadrille, a minuet, and a
waltz, but this one she meant to sit out, or rather move
through the room long enough to establish her presence.
Should anyone inquire after her, people would say, "Oh,
yes, I was just speaking to her. She went off that way. . . ."

Near the center of the room, Willow stood paired with a
tall young man whose thatch of dark hair insisted on falling

in his eyes despite copious amounts of pomade. Ivy had
taken a seat on one of the satin-covered settees along the
far wall. The very young Countess of Huntley sat beside
her, nervously fluttering her fan and darting her gaze all
about her. As Holly watched, Ivy placed a hand on her companion's wrist and appeared to set about distracting her
from her cares.

The music began, and the dancers commenced the opening steps. Holly deemed it safe to disengage herself from
the camouflaging matrons, but before she left them she
joined briefly in their debate over the merits of feathers
versus jewels versus ribbons in the latest headdresses.

"Does not a ribbon or two, and perhaps a small, carefully
placed jewel, suffice?" she asked, then awaited their re-
sponses as if their opinions were of the utmost importance
to her.

Lady Bidsworth raised her lorgnette to study her, her
sharp eyes nearly swallowed by the plump folds of her aged
face. "Only when the wearer is as young as you, my dear.
Enjoy simplicity while yet you may."

Smiling, Holly moved on, greeting people as she went,
stopping to exchange pleasantries and trade opinions about
the day's demonstrations and activities. She didn't remain
with any group longer than a minute or two, but worked her
way steadily across the room.

As she neared the open terrace doors, she stopped and
turned for a final surveillance of the ballroom. The dancers
had formed two elegant lines and were presently tracing a
graceful pattern down the center of the room. The rest mingled along the room's perimeter, watching, talking, laughing,
all beneath the solicitous eye of the duchess. A middle-aged
couple, husband and wife, drifted past Holly and out onto
the terrace, tipping their heads to her in greeting. She was
just about to turn and follow them out when her gaze lighted
on Lord Drayton, standing in front of one of the room's
several fireplaces. He looked magnificent in ebony tails and
a white silk waistcoat, his equally pristine neckcloth tied
simply.

He didn't need artifice; didn't need embellishments to outshine his peers. He need only stand with his shoulders broad and relaxed. Powerful without effort, he was a man equally at home in a ballroom as in the saddle.

Her stomach dropped. Beside him, smiling up at him, was the golden-haired beauty who had arrived that afternoon with her parents: Lady Penelope Wingate, whose father owned profitable shares in the Ashworths' West Indies plantations.

"My father is pushing the match," Lady Sabrina had whispered in Holly's ear earlier that day. "She's exquisite, isn't she?"

Holly had to agree, whereupon Lady Sabrina had leaned closer to confide, "She's also a distant relation to the queen, which is why Father is so keen on Colin marrying her. Personally, I don't like her. Despite her lineage there is a commonness about her that borders on vulgarity, as well as a look in her eye that prompts one to suspect her of clandestine thoughts."

"Vulgar royalty?" Holly had asked with a chuckle, while her insides turned queasy.

"She is only *just* royal."

Holly shouldn't have asked her next question, but she hadn't been able to refrain. "What does your brother think of her?"

She had held her breath as she waited for the answer, dread pitching and churning in her stomach.

Lady Sabrina had laughed without humor. "One never can know precisely what Colin is thinking."

Based on the significant looks passing between Lord Drayton and Lady Penelope, Holly would say he liked her exceedingly well, despite her exaggerated curls and overabundance of jewelry.

A misery as cold as hoarfrost settled over Holly's heart. Her thoughts tumbled back to her tour of the stables that morning, to the many insights Colin had shared with her. Did he share his aspirations with Lady Penelope? Was he even now explaining his theories of prevailing and dormant traits to the eager young *royal* chit batting her eyelashes at him?

"Miss Sutherland. A pleasant evening, no?"

She started, then disguised her flinch with a flick of her fan. Stuart Bentley stood at her shoulder, gazing out over the ballroom as if to join in her contemplation of the proceedings.

"Superlative," she said, barely suppressing a huff of exasperation. She had just been about to make her escape, *would* have made it, if only she hadn't lingered over Colin Ashworth's conquest of the simpering Penelope Wingate.

Pivoting on his heel to face her, Mr. Bentley tipped a bow. "And how is it that such a lovely lady is not dancing?"

"I mean not to dance this set, sir. The day has left me weary and—"

"Ah, but a new set is just beginning. Will you not do me the honor of standing up with me?"

Oh dear. Oh *no.* The duchess chose that moment to hasten across the ballroom, honing in on them like an arrow to its mark. "Yes, delightful! Mr. Bentley, Miss Sutherland, do lead the others into the next waltz."

Holly could hardly refuse without appearing insufferably rude. When the quadrille ended and the next number began, she had little choice but to place her hand in Stuart Bentley's and walk with him to the center of the gleaming parquet floor.

"Is it not most fortunate, my lord, that our fathers' interests coincide so agreeably?"

"Indeed, Lady Penelope," Colin murmured in reply, though to what he had just agreed he wasn't quite certain. As she nattered on, his gaze drifted over the ballroom, then abruptly stopped. What was *this?* Bentley and Miss Sutherland were dancing a *waltz.*

What was Bentley up to? Colin thought he had made himself perfectly clear at the stables that morning. Had Bentley forgotten, or had he grown a substantial pair of bollocks in the interim?

Beside him, Penelope went silent. Colin shifted his gaze back to her, at the same time wondering why he put up even the slightest pretense of interest. Despite his father's well-vocalized wishes, he had no intention of marrying her. Not now, now ever; not even if she were next in line to the throne.

Especially not then.

She blinked, her lips curving in a smile that struggled to be sophisticated. "But perhaps such matters are best left unsaid."

"Matters?" He tried to remember what she'd been talking about, but Miss Sutherland's bright blue skirts swept the corner of his vision and drove all other thoughts clear from his mind.

"Business, my lord. Commerce." She half mouthed the words as if they were blasphemies.

"Nothing untoward about business, Lady Penelope."

"Then you agree with my father's opinion on the subject?"

He wished Penelope would stop talking so he could concentrate on the elegance of Miss Sutherland's arms, the curve of her nape, the tightness of her cinched waist as she circled round and round the ballroom. Colin shouldn't have been surprised at her agility. Riding would have sculpted her figure to perfection—he'd wager a small fortune on the potential magnificence of her thighs—while the subtle nuances of maneuvering a mount would have taught her a dexterity that easily translated to other physical endeavors . . . such as dancing.

He yanked his attention back to the young lady beside him. "I'm sorry. What?"

"Do you agree that England should empty its debtors' prisons, not to mention repeal the Abolition of Slavery Act, in order to provide a viable workforce to our protectorates around the world?"

"What?"

Just then, the music ended. After a bob of curtsy, Miss Sutherland scurried away from Bentley's side. Colin followed her progress down the long room. She paused near her sister Ivy, then continued on until she reached the terrace doors. As she crossed the threshold, the torchlight outside set brilliant highlights dancing in her hair, gilded the folds of her gown, and tinged her skin with a warm, inviting glow.

It was a summons he couldn't resist, even if it hadn't been directed at him.

"If you'll excuse me a moment, Lady Penelope." Without hearing her reply, he bowed and wasted no time in striding away.

"Colin, there you are. Has it been your intention to ignore me all night?"

At Ivy's approach, he halted in his tracks.

"Of course not. Are you enjoying yourself?" He tried his utmost not to let his impatience show. "I see you are not dancing."

"I confess I'm a trifle fatigued tonight...." She linked her arm through his, leaving him no choice but to let her lead him on a stroll along the edge of the room—away from the terrace.

His mother unwittingly came to his rescue by inquiring whether he and Ivy meant to dance together. "I believe Lady Harrow could do with some punch first, Mother," he replied before Ivy could speak. "And I'd not be tempting her out onto the dance floor until the occasion of another sedate quadrille."

"Oh, you are quite right." His mother's eyes widened with alarm. She slipped her arm through Ivy's and drew her to her side. "Come, my dear, let us endeavor to make you comfortable."

"Oh, but—"

Confident he'd left Ivy in capable hands, he cut a determined path toward the terrace.

"Lord Drayton."

He bit back an oath as he ground to another halt. "Miss Willow."

She stepped into his path and earnestly thanked him for

the splendid ball. And suddenly something didn't sit right with him. He'd watch one sister disappear out the terrace doors, and when he tried to see where she was going, the other two sisters conveniently headed him off.

Before the youngest Sutherland could engage him any further in conversation, he smiled, gave her gloved hand an affectionate squeeze, then excused himself and walked briskly off. If anyone else called his name, he didn't hear it.

The terrace was sparsely populated, with Miss Sutherland nowhere in sight. His first thought was that she'd stolen down to the stables again. But to what purpose? He had shown her everything that morning. The horses, the facilities, everything. An uncomfortable sensation crept over him.

Did her interests lie merely in the purchase of a racehorse? He had believed that her enthusiasm for all things equestrian had been what had sent her down to the stables the night before. But if not, what was the tantalizing Miss Sutherland searching for?

The ballroom lay at the easternmost end of the house, and she could have gone in either of two directions: down the steps and into the gardens—and perhaps the stables beyond—or westward, toward the other rooms that opened onto the terrace.

The former notion brought a bitter taste to his mouth. Had she stolen into the shrubbery for a tryst? Who would it be? Bentley? No, Colin had just left him behind in the ballroom, dancing with another young miss.

Besides, his instincts denied the possibility that Miss Sutherland had scampered outside to compromise herself in the shadows. As sensual and alive as she was, she was no fool of a chit bent on ruination. Like her sisters, she had good sense about her.

Then . . . ?

He began strolling casually until he got beyond the torches and the candlelight spilling out the ballroom windows. The music faded into the chirping of crickets and the swish of the trees. He considered the row of darkened windows and French doors stretching out beside him. Where had she gone, that she couldn't have accessed more easily from within the house?

Unless she hadn't wished to be seen.

Willow watched Lord Drayton—or Colin, as she sometimes dared to call him—stride out to the terrace. She had done her best to delay him, but she hadn't been clever enough. Had Holly gotten enough of a head start?

Whirling, Willow craned her neck until she located Ivy walking arm in arm with the duchess. Ivy, too, cast worried glances toward the gold-tinged shadows of the terrace.

With a flutter of her fan, Willow caught Ivy's attention. Then she flipped her fan closed again and pointed its tip in the direction the earl had gone. Ivy's brows knitted in comprehension. Willow pressed a hand to her bodice to suggest that she go, but Ivy shook her head. She said something in the duchess's ear, then began threading her way out of the ballroom.

Willow's instinct was to follow Colin. Perhaps his leaving had nothing to do with Holly. Wishing to set her mind at ease on that count, she headed for the terrace, hoping to find him leaning on the balustrade, enjoying the night air and speaking with guests.

"Miss Willow." Lady Sabrina's satin-clad hand settled lightly on Willow's shoulder, effectively holding her in place. "There is someone who wishes to dance with you, but he is afraid to ask you himself."

"Oh, I . . ."

"Please, it would mean the world to him, I'm certain."

"Good gracious, why would anyone be afraid to ask me?" Yet the answer seemed obvious. It must be Geoffrey, the youngest and most retiring of the Ashworth siblings.

"Why, here he is now." Lady Sabrina reached out her hand, but the wrist she caught and the figure she drew closer were far too solid and imposing to belong to the youthful Geoffrey Ashworth.

Lord Bryce's stormy gaze—so much darker and more

mysterious than those of his siblings—shifted to encompass Willow. It descended on her with near physical force, rendering her slightly weak in the knees. "Good evening, Miss Sutherland."

"G-good evening." Her voice fluttered like the diaphanous wings of a moth.

"Bryce, Miss Sutherland appears not to be engaged for this set." His sister raised her eyebrows; her narrow chin thrust forward as if to impale her brother should he show the slightest prevarication.

He hesitated for an instant, an eternity that made Willow squirm inside with mortification. Then the word *delighted*, uttered in his deep, brooding voice, caressed her ears, and she discovered her hand tucked into the crook of his arm, her fingertips tantalized by the hardness of the muscle beneath his sleeve. The music began. In Lord Bryce's guiding arms Willow found herself swept round and round in determined circles, flying, soaring, until the room blurred and she lost track of where they were, lost track of everything but Lord Bryce's severe countenance, his steady hold, and the inscrutable gaze that never left hers.

Chapter 13

Perhaps Ivy had been correct in predicting that the duke's private office held no evidence of the colt's disappearance, but Holly believed she had discovered something equally noteworthy. She had flipped through one ledger containing pages and pages of names—horses and buyers, races and winners—with corresponding numbers that indicated prices, sizes, weights, and speeds. Nothing unusual there. But the second ledger she chose held a fascinating clue: references to the Ashworths' Devonshire estate.

She had not previously considered that a significant number of the Ashworth Thoroughbreds were not bred at Masterfield Park, but rather some two hundred miles away at the family's remote country home. Could Prince's Pride have hailed from faraway Briarview? That would explain why none of the racing enthusiasts here seemed to have heard of the extraordinary animal. And despite Victoria's conviction to the contrary, Prince's Price could have been secreted out of Ascot days ago.

Or perhaps not. That morning, Lord Drayton had curtly turned their horses back toward home after Holly attempted to ride into the vale. The small valley contained dangers, he'd said.

But could the vale contain more than marshy bottomlands?

The clicking of a brisk tread along the terrace brought

her up sharp. With a gasp she sprang up from the desk chair and blew out the single candle she'd lit. She headed for the door, then remembered the ledger book still in her hands. She doubled back to the desk, fumbled with the drawer, and shoved the ledger inside. The footsteps continued their approach, echoing briskly against the side of the house.

Lord Drayton? A footman who might report back to his employer about finding her here?

Indecision held her frozen. The office itself didn't open onto the terrace. She had reentered the house through the library next door, passed through the corridor, and come into the office.

She cracked the door open and listened. Did she have time to slip back into the corridor and get far enough away before whoever it was emerged from the library? Or should she remain where she was and hide? With a glance over her shoulder she quickly dismissed that idea. The room offered no concealment but the small space beneath the desk. If she were going to be apprehended, she was not going to suffer the added ignominy of being caught crouching on all fours beneath a desk.

Her resolve sent her across the threshold. Having no idea where the corridor led, she shut the door behind her and set off as fast as her feet could take her.

Colin walked through the library, and when he reached the corridor, he paused, listening to the retreating footsteps. Light footsteps, like those of a lady in dancing slippers. Louder, silk and taffeta rustled like a chorus of crickets. Colin smiled, though not altogether pleasantly.

He wondered if she had merely been in the library and had slipped out right before he stepped in from the terrace. But why the harried escape? Perhaps she had been elsewhere—say, in his father's office. But what could possibly hold her interest in all those volumes of horse statistics and estate records?

It occurred to him that this wasn't the first time he'd caught her skulking about, assuming, of course, that it *was*

Miss Sutherland and not another guest sailing along the corridor ahead of him. Each soft footfall drew him on like a tender call to battle—a fragrant, beguiling but equally perplexing battle.

He started after her, but then another sound, a heavier footfall, stopped him cold. He pricked his ears as, up ahead, a hush blanketed even Miss Sutherland's taffeta crickets.

Her flight had been interrupted. Or perhaps it had never been a flight. Perhaps she hadn't detected Colin and had not been running away at all, but rather hurrying *to* something. Someone.

His insides ran cold—the murderous sort of cold that throughout history had prompted men to wrap their hands around other men's throats and squeeze and squeeze. He pivoted and without hesitation retreated the way he had come, back across the library and out to the terrace.

Who was it? he wondered bitterly. Bentley? Loathing congealed in his gut. Colin had left the other man in the ballroom, but that didn't mean the insufferable blighter hadn't made his way through the interior of the house to the appointed place. Bentley had been a guest here many, many times over the years, and he knew the layout nearly as well as Colin did. Yes, probably Bentley. He couldn't think of who else it might be.

Damn it. *Damn it.*

Holly hurried around the corner, praying she might find the main corridor and cross back to the east wing before Lord Drayton—or whoever—found her. Footfalls in the darkness behind her brought her to a halt. When she stopped, the other tread stopped as well, nearly propelling her heart out of her chest.

She could just make out the closed doors on either side of her. Another corner loomed ahead of her. Behind her, the corridor lay empty. Where had the sound come from? She saw no one, detected no movement. But then it came again: *step, step* . . . followed by the light squeak of a floorboard beneath the runner.

Her heart now reaching into her throat, she gripped the closest doorknob and gave a twist, but just before she could push the door inward and dive inside, an arm slipped around her waist from behind.

A cry rose up inside her. She was roughly spun about, her breasts and belly crushed against a solid form. Arms closed around her, cutting off escape. A face, shadowed and indefinable, loomed above hers.

"Lord Drayton, please . . . I—I can explain. . . ."

A whisper fell against her cheek. "Not Lord Drayton, my dear."

Colin lingered in the rectangle of light spilling from the ballroom doors. Damn, and damn again. He couldn't do it—couldn't stroll back inside, take up where he had left off with Lady Penelope, and lead the next waltz as if nothing were amiss.

He turned about, beginning to feel like a child's top, going round and round. She wouldn't thank him for interfering. She'd be mortified. But if nothing else, he owed it to Ivy to make sure her sister was safe, that she hadn't encouraged a situation that exceeded her expectations, not to mention her experience.

Feeling obligated to make sure Stuart Bentley or some other fop didn't at that very moment have her pinned against a wall, his hands tunneling beneath her skirts, Colin broke into a sprint.

Not Lord Drayton? The shock of the revelation slammed the breath from Holly's lungs. She struggled against the arms that held her, trying to claw her way free.

"Release me this instant!"

"No, my dear." The sour taste of wine wafted beneath her nose. His face drew nearer and she tried to make out his features, but in the paltry light she could only see that he was older than the earl, heavy featured, his graying hair slicked back off a high forehead. He looked . . .

Like any number of men from the ball. Had this man seen

her slip away from the crush unaccompanied, and believed she'd hurried to these quiet halls for a seductive adventure? Did he perceive her struggles as a game, a challenge?

He bent his head closer. Did he mean to kiss her? Revulsion rose in her throat. She wedged her arms between them and tried to shove away. The hands gripped her relentlessly while his slash of a mouth peeled open and hot laughter scalded her skin.

"Whatever you want, I have no interest. I demand you let me go this instant."

His only response was his obscene laughter.

"Sir, you are in your cups." She tugged for all she was worth. "Come morning you will regret your actions."

"Shall I, *mon amie*?"

"Indeed, yes!" She lashed out with her hand, her palm striking the side of his head and not the cheek she had aimed for. But she was not Laurel Sutherland's sister for nothing, nor Aidan Phillips's sister-in-law, for that matter. They had taught her how to fight, to defend herself. If this man refused to behave like a gentleman, then it was time for her to stop behaving like a lady. She lifted her foot—

Her knee hit squarely in the man's groin. He let out a yelp, his arms loosening and opening a fraction of space between them. As he bent over, she seized the opportunity and swung her fists, jabbing at his throat, and something fleshier—his cheek this time? When he howled and lurched backward, she ran, blindly, having no notion in which direction she went. She only hoped she would end up at the library where she could escape to the terrace and the safety of the ballroom.

"Miss Sutherland, is that you?"

She collided with a torso—solid like the stranger's yet familiar, protective. Arms closed around her, wrapping her in safety. "Lord Drayton? Please let it be you this time."

The bravado that had saved her from that drunkard's lascivious intentions now abandoned her in a torrent. Sobs choked her voice, strangling the syllables of his name. Until this moment, she had not realized how frightened she was.

Who had accosted her? Could it have been Mr. Fenhurst, who had always been kind to her and her sisters? Or Lord Arnold, whose youthful wife proved he had a penchant for younger women? The man in the corridor had seemed larger and stronger than either of those two, but could her fear have magnified his size and strength?

She buried her face against Lord Drayton's shoulder.

"What is it? What happened?" The questions came sharply, penetrating her fear, demanding an answer. "And what did you mean, by 'this time'?"

She pressed her cheek to his coat front. "There was a man. At first I thought he was you following me, but . . ." She raised her face, taking in the firm lines of his chin, his jaw, the stony contour of his cheek. "It wasn't you."

"I did follow you, Miss Sutherland, but when I heard you stop in the corridor, I assumed—" He broke off. His hand cradled the back of her head, his fingers gently stroking her hair. The library door stood open beside them. Lord Drayton held her tightly, his lips tickling her ear as he made soothing sounds to calm her. She relished the reassurance of masculine superfine, and the muscle beneath, against her cheek.

"It was my own fault," she said. "He must have seen me leave the ballroom and followed me. He must have assumed I went looking for . . . for . . ."

He framed her face in his hands and raised it from his chest until their gazes met. His voice, when he spoke, was as steely as a knife-edge. "What did he do?"

"He . . ." Now that she was safe, it all seemed a blur. He had seemed to materialize out of nowhere, from the shadows themselves.

An ill sensation rose, wrapped in layers of shame that forced her head down. There were reasons decent young women didn't wander alone through dark corridors. She drew a steadying breath. "He seized me and refused to let go."

The earl's hands tightened until she could feel the calluses, acquired from years of riding, against her cheeks.

"Did he take privileges with you?" When she didn't answer, he spoke more loudly, more fiercely. "Did he hurt you?"

"He didn't hurt me exactly. In fact, I may have injured him. I struck him and kicked him as hard as I could. Then I ran."

She couldn't be quite certain, but she thought the corners of his mouth lifted in what might have been a smile.

"Come." His strong arm looped about her waist. As he walked her into the library, she didn't know if it was lingering fear and shock that made her knees wobble, or the intimacy of his hold. But if not for his steadying arm and the solidness of his side against her, she would have toppled. He brought her to the settee before the fireplace and gently handed her down onto the cushions. "Wait here."

"Where are you—?"

But he had already gone, leaving her alone with nothing but the unsettling images of the last several minutes flashing through her mind. She couldn't stop herself from pondering what might have happened if she hadn't gotten away.

A nearby object gleamed in the moonlight coming from the window, and she jumped up from the sofa. Taking the iron fire poker from beside the hearth, she gripped it in both hands and sat back down. Her fright hardened to anger, and she scowled at the empty room, the open doorway.

"If you think I caused you pain earlier . . ." She tightened her grip on the poker. Let him try again, and see what she would do.

A sudden memory bristled the hair on her nape. Laurel had been attacked in Bath last year. Could this incident be related?

But this had been different from Laurel's attack. Her sister's assailant had pressed a knife to her throat. Laurel would surely have been killed if Aidan hadn't come along when he had.

She stiffened at the sound of approaching footsteps.

"I couldn't find a trace of anyone."

She sprang to her feet and crossed the room to Lord Drayton. "I'm not making this up. He must have found his way back to the ballroom; he—"

The earl held up his hand. "I wasn't insinuating that he didn't exist. I was merely stating that he is no longer anywhere to be found. You may be right that he has returned to the ballroom. Or he might have left. The house is wide open tonight. Invitations to this ball went out to all the fine families in the area, so he could have been anyone. By God, I loathe the thought of either a guest or a neighbor behaving in such a despicable manner. If I ever get my hands on him . . ."

"He might not have realized what he was doing," she said reasonably. "He was certainly drunk. He reeked of wine." A shudder ran through her, and Lord Drayton came closer.

"You're shaking." He took the poker and stood it against a table. Then he closed his hands around her upper arms and rubbed them up and down the bare skin above her evening gloves.

His touch spread fire through her, but he released her all too soon and returned her to the settee. He took a moment to light a lamp before going to the cabinet in the corner and pulling a stopper from a decanter. When he returned he crouched at her feet and pressed a cut crystal cordial glass into her hand. "It's sherry," he said. "Drink."

She tried to obey, but swallowing proved difficult with him kneeling in front of her, his chest grazing her knees. Her free hand disappeared beneath his very large, very warm palm. His fingers closed around hers, disconcerting and heavenly.

"Did you recognize anything about him?"

She tried to focus on his question, rather than on those calluses across the base of his fingers, or on how she might lean over and press her lips to the silky hair at the crown of his head. "It was too dark. I could make out only that he was older than . . . than you. Not quite elderly, I shouldn't think. Middle-aged."

"Did he say anything?"

"Very little. He said . . . that he wasn't you."

The earl responded with a curious lift of his eyebrow, making her regret the disclosure. *Don't ask. Please, don't ask.*

He drew back a little. "Of all things, why would he declare that?"

"Because . . ." She sipped her sherry, wishing she could crawl into the glass and drown.

He grasped her wrist, and gently lowered her arm. "Why, Holly?"

The echo of her Christian name reverberated through her, then settled with a heated thrum deep in her belly. She had often heard him speak her sisters' names, Ivy and Willow, even Laurel. But never Holly. Never once had he looked at her and allowed his lips to form her name.

How sweetly it rolled off his tongue, making her pulse leap, her heart swell. His presence suddenly filled the room, her world, and each breath she drew came laden with his musky scent, fueling a sudden longing to toss her sherry aside and throw her arms around his neck.

"Holly?"

She shut her eyes, blocking out the tempting sight of him. "I told you, I thought he *was* you. I thought you had been following me, and when he caught me, I . . . cried out your name." Good heavens, she kept digging herself in deeper. What questions would he ask now? What answers would he demand?

"I *was* following you," he said quietly but harshly. His subdued fierceness quickened her pulse. He rose higher on his knees, his hands sliding along her thighs to settle at her waist. His palms cupped her hipbones, raising an ache between them that nearly made her cry out his name all over again. She shut her eyes.

He swore under his breath. "I heard you running down the hall, and I followed until I realized you weren't alone."

Her eyes snapped open. "You heard him?"

"Yes, damn it. I could have spared you the entire unsavory experience had I not deemed my interference less than welcome."

"You thought I'd gone to tryst?" Her stomach tightened into a ball of dismay.

It was his turn to lower his face in silent rumination. Holly slipped a hand beneath his chin, his evening bristle rough against her fingertips, disquieting and oddly reassuring at the same time.

Reassuring? By his own implied admission, he had believed the worst of her. The fact of it stung, but she couldn't help repeating her question, though this time it came out as a statement. "You thought I'd sought an assignation."

His nostrils flared. His eyes flashed defiance, but beneath it, uncertainty. Apology. "Yes. I am sorry. But yes."

"You think that because I enjoy riding fast, I *am* fast."

He seized her wrist. "Damn it, *no*."

Chapter 14

"I came back," he said, the words both an avowal and a plea. Her wrist was small and warm, so delicate in his hand. He gazed down at it, then upward to the satiny whiteness of her arm, the skin so much paler, purer, than his own. "If I had believed you to be fast, I would not have come back to stop you. I would not have wished to save you from a grievous error."

The error of giving herself to an undeserving boor like Bentley, or for that matter any other man on the face of the earth.

Any man that wasn't *him*.

Never mind that he was the one man who couldn't have her, not now, not at any time in his foreseeable future.

"You came back for me. . . ." Her voice melted to a soft little whimper that undid his remaining composure—and his resolve.

"Yes. God yes, Holly."

He released her wrist and rose onto the settee beside her. Then she was in his arms, sinking into him, her fragrant warmth spreading across his shirtfront. Months and months of standing firm fell away like a house of cards in a sudden draft, leaving him exposed, vulnerable, wanting.

He tried telling himself he'd allow nothing more than a brief touch of their lips, a small taste of what he could not have. But her lips were full and moist and at the slight prod of his tongue, they parted for him, invited him in, and sent him spiraling headlong into pleasure. She tasted of sherry and sweetness with a dash of spice, and every irresistible thing he could think of.

Until he could no longer think at all.

His hands began moving, exploring her through her clothing, and once or twice beneath as he raised her hems to reveal a silk-covered ankle, a shapely calf. His fingertips trembled over long, elegant lines and tight, exquisite curves. He had been correct about the riding. Where other women were soft and malleable, she was firm and sculpted, an artist's masterpiece, but warm, alive, unknowingly seductive.

His lips trailed his fingertips down the curve of her chin, the underside of her jaw, and down, slowly down to the silky skin of her throat. He set his open mouth on the pulse in her neck, savoring the tease of her pulse point against the tip of his tongue. With her lips curved and her head tossed back, she gave a purr and arched in his arms, bringing her body more tightly against him. The slight wiggling of her bottom against his thighs made his throbbing erection unbearable, but he tamped down every urge to proceed any further. If it killed him—which he feared it might—he would take no more from her than could be winked at in the morning.

For he knew—beyond a doubt—that Holly Sutherland would wink at none of this. She was no experienced paramour, no sophisticated, spoiled society lady, and this was no conquest for her, no game of *seduce the earl* with which she would regale her friends afterward.

He would have bet a piece of his soul that each kiss, each touch, held meaning for her, or she would not be here, would not be kissing him back. All the more reason to let her go before another of their heartstrings tangled. He would not be like his father, a man who dallied with innocence, taking what didn't belong to him without a qualm.

But he didn't let her go. He held on and inhaled the fragrance of her skin and hair so deep as to never, ever forget it. He kissed every part of her that he dared—her throat, her shoulders, her lips—so he would always remember the feel of her, the taste of her on his tongue.

Then a thought, a prayer, sprang to his mind: perhaps someday . . .

But when? How long? With horse thief added to his list of attributes, maybe never. No, he couldn't ask her to wait.

Just another moment; then, one more. His silent plea hadn't concluded before she lowered her head with a shy smile that held more seductive power than the most practiced flirtation. Her skin was flushed, her eyes darkened with desire—a desire he felt as a sharp and poignant stab that began at his heart and pierced through to his loins.

"And to think I'd believed you didn't care for me," she whispered, pushing back a curl that had fallen from its pins to dangle against her cheek.

Her voice held a chuckle, but a tear glimmered in the moonlight. That tear might as well have been a bullet aimed straight for his chest.

Ah, God. He sealed the gaps between them. "I am sorry I gave you reason to think that."

And even sorrier that she would come to think it again. Would there be tears then? He didn't want to hurt her. He wanted only to protect her and preserve his own sanity.

But when she looked at him as she was doing now, her eyes alight, her cheeks flushed, her lips moist from his kisses, he thought *to hell with sanity*. And honor and duty and every other ideal he had been born to. He pressed his lips to hers, taking her mouth deeply, thoroughly, in a kiss meant to see him through the rest of his life.

This was the last time, he swore.

But when the time came to lift his mouth from hers, it was not the steel of his resolve that spawned the action. With her pressed sweetly up against him, her lips ingenuously open to his, he had no resolve. *None.* It wasn't honor insisting he do the right thing, but the echo of footsteps coming down the hall.

Holly stiffened against him. "Do you hear that? Could he have come back?"

He struggled to remember the *he* to whom she referred. His arms still around her, he raised his head and listened. "It isn't a man. The steps are too light."

"Ivy!" she hissed, and pulled away from him.

"Holly?" The urgent whisper shot along the corridor. "Where are you?"

Holly pressed her lips together and quickly smoothed her hands over her skirts.

"How would she have known . . . ?" Colin narrowed his eyes in puzzlement, but there wasn't time for answers. Holly came to her feet.

"Your neckcloth," she whispered.

He raised a hand to straighten the knot. A glow filled the hallway outside the doorway.

"My hair . . . is it . . . ?"

He took her hands in his own. "Your hair is fine. Just follow my lead."

The approaching footsteps fell silent. He turned to see Ivy poised in the doorway. She raised the candlestick she held.

"Holly?" she whispered. The light spread through the room and she saw them both. "Oh!" Then she clamped her lips shut.

Before questions could form in Ivy's mind, Colin walked a few steps toward her. "Ivy, I'm glad you're here. Your sister needs you."

"Oh?" she said again. She shot an anxious glance past him. "Holly, what is it? Has something happened?"

The subdued alarm in Ivy's eyes, alarm that had been there *before* he spoke, most garnered his interest. It was no accident, her showing up this way. She obviously had known where her sister would be, and Colin suspected she knew exactly why Holly had come to this part of the house.

Behind him, Holly said, "The ball had grown wearisome, and I thought I'd find a quiet corner all to myself for a few minutes. I went searching for the duchess's reading room."

Ivy's puzzled gaze shifted back and forth between them. "Yes, and . . . ?"

"There was a man," Holly said.

Ivy's eyebrows surged.

"In the corridor." Holly gestured unnecessarily to the doorway. "He must have thought—that is, he reached for me...."

"Good heavens!" Ivy rushed to Holly and threw her arms around her. "Did he hurt you? Who was it? Colin, did you apprehend him? Where is he now?"

"Please, one question at time," came Holly's muted plea, spoken against Ivy's ruffled neckline.

Before many questions were answered, Colin bade Ivy to take Holly to their rooms. "She can finish telling you the details, but see to her comfort first."

"Yes, yes, of course," Ivy agreed. "You poor dear. What a fright. And such an insult." Her eyes snapped. "What I wouldn't give to have that villain here before us ..."

"I'll walk you to the main corridor," Colin said, "and see that you arrive safely. I'll send Miss Willow up as well. Then I must find my mother and apprise her of what has happened."

"I wish you wouldn't do that." Holly clasped her hands at her waist. "Your mother has been so kind, and I wouldn't want this incident to color her opinion of me."

"My mother would not think less of you for something that was not your fault," he said.

"Many people would think less of me because of it," she replied quietly, "no matter who was at fault."

He couldn't deny it. Many a young woman had been ruined for less. If others had seen Holly leave the ball, they would already be wondering why, speculating about whom she might have gone to meet. If the slightest hint of what had happened to her became common knowledge, there would be no stopping the gossip.

He wanted to go to her, take her in his arms again, and assure her she had nothing to regret, not about the man in the corridor, and not about what happened here between them. He wished to do so much more than that—wished he could make everything right by openly declaring for her.

That wish was nothing new. Neither was the fist that closed around his heart each time he thought of her.

"How can you be certain that man has no connection to the one who attacked Laurel last year?" Ivy asked.

"Yes, that horrible Henri de Vere," Willow said breathlessly. "Did you get a good look at him? Did he speak French?"

The question triggered a memory that drew a gasp from Holly's lips. "He called me *mon amie*," she said. Then she frowned. "Oh, but many an Englishman uses that term. And the way he whispered . . . I cannot say for certain if he spoke with an accent or not."

Ivy sat on the bed beside her. "Holly, tell us again exactly what he said to you."

She tried to focus, to see past the glorious images crowding her brain, to think past the earl's masculine scent still lingering on her skin. He had called her Holly, and the sweet timbre of it vibrated against her ear even now, a rumbling caress not unlike the touch of his callused palm, or the bristle of his chin across her cheeks . . . her bosom.

Steeling herself with a breath, she repeated the few guttural words spoken by her assailant, while the things Colin had said—yes, *Colin* now, and never again Lord Drayton—floated through her soul on gossamer wings.

But as her sisters compared the details of tonight's incident with Laurel's attack in Bath last year, Holly acknowledged that those moments in the library had been anything but joyous and carefree. Like those calluses marring his palms, those moments had been marred by . . . sadness. And when he had bid her and her sisters good night and his gaze had fallen upon her, it had seemed as if a curtain had been drawn across his eyes, sealing in their light, their life. She had heard *good night* fall from his lips, but the echo inside her had been of *good-bye*.

Pain pressed upon her heart as she admitted he wasn't coming back to her, not in the way he had revealed himself tonight, with his defenses down and his heart open. No matter how naturally passion had sprung up between them, no matter how utterly right it had felt, it would not be repeated. Her throat tightened until she could barely breathe. She might see Lord Drayton tomorrow, but *Colin* would not be back.

Beneath her sorrow, questions hovered. Why had he pushed her away previously, and why again now? What did he fear? What might he be hiding?

"Assuming this man *was* one of the guests," Ivy was saying, "and assuming it was drink and not malice that prompted his deplorable behavior—"

Holly blew a strand of hair away from her face. "I doubt very much he'll remember what he did come morning."

Ivy nodded. "It would still behoove us to proceed with care. We mustn't go anywhere alone, any of us."

"Agreed." Willow removed her necklace and placed it on the dressing table.

Holly said nothing. She could make no promises other than that she would not be caught unawares again. She had an investigation to complete, a colt to find. And two sisters to protect, not to mention a tiny niece or nephew who must not, under any circumstances, come to harm.

She waited until she heard both sisters breathing evenly from their beds before wrapping her dressing gown around her and slipping from the room. She had a plan for tomorrow and she would need help, but not from her sisters. Quietly she made her way down the corridor and around a corner. The light shining from beneath a closed door filled her with relief. Her hunch had been correct that the person inside would still be up. She knocked softly.

The door opened, and a surprised face blinked out at her. "Miss Sutherland."

"Lady Sabrina, may I come in?" Although the other woman had changed from her gown into her night chemise and her maid had taken down her curls, she looked wide awake. Still, Holly asked, "Or are you ready to retire?"

The young woman swung the door wider. "I can never sleep directly after a ball."

Lady Sabrina invited her to sit in the easy chair beneath the window. Hoping she wasn't making a mistake, Holly wasted no time in getting to the point. "I need your help. In the morning at first light, I'll need a horse. Can you arrange it?"

At first Lady Sabrina simply stared back at her with a puzzled expression. Then she leaned back in her elegant damask-covered chair, a shrewd smile playing about her lips. "Does this have anything to do with my brother?"

Lady Sabrina was no fool, and Holly didn't attempt to lie. "I cannot tell you why I need a horse. I can only say that it is of the utmost importance. And that I will be indebted to you. Greatly so."

"Hmm." Beneath her satin dressing gown, Lady Sabrina crossed one leg over the other. "I couldn't help noticing that you disappeared from the ball earlier."

"You are mistaken." Holly shrugged a shoulder. "I didn't disappear. I simply grew tired of all the noise and heat."

"Where did you go?"

"The library. It was an accident, really, my ending up there. I am unused to houses on so grand a scale."

The other woman tapped manicured fingernails on her chair's carved arm. "Did you know my brother disappeared from the ballroom as well?"

Holly bit back a groan of impatience. Whatever rapport she believed she had established with this woman during their talk yesterday had been an illusion. She was beginning to believe the members of this family, all of them, took pleasure in toying with other people's feelings, while they themselves were incapable of sustaining a sincere emotion for more than a moment.

"One would assume if your brother left the ballroom," she said evenly, "it was to join the guests playing whist in the card room."

"One might, except I peeked into the card room. My brother wasn't anywhere to be seen."

Holly rose to her feet. "I am very sorry I disturbed you, Lady Sabrina. I'll bid you good night now."

"Oh, do sit down. And call me Sabrina. There is no need for such formality between us. Not when you come sneaking to my room in the middle of the night asking for favors."

"I didn't sneak. I—"

"Please sit," the woman said more gently, the mockery suddenly gone from her voice. "You shall have your horse in the morning."

Holly sank back into the chair. "Thank you."

"You're welcome." She drummed her fingers again; the smile returned to her lips. "He likes you, you know."

Heat climbed into Holly's cheeks. "Pardon?"

"Don't be coy. Colin admires you. I can tell." Her hands closing over the arms of the chair, she leaned forward. "Were you together tonight?"

When Holly hesitated, her cheeks scorching, Sabrina waved a hand in the air and sat back. "Never mind. It is none of my business and I suppose it is most disagreeable of me to tease you. My advice, however, is not to . . ." She heaved a sigh. "Not to put too much stock into it. Into *him*. He does like you, from what I can perceive. But that doesn't mean . . ." Something approaching a scowl sharpened Lady Sabrina's features. "We're none of us prone to tender feelings. We weren't raised on them. They aren't in our natures."

"Your mother certainly seems agreeable."

Sabrina pushed out a mirthless chuckle. "Mother is stretching her wings at present, playing at being the matriarch. But mark me, it shan't last. As soon as my father—"

The other woman said no more, but her reference to the duke sent a chill down Holly's spine. She thought of the bruise around the duchess's wrist. Sitting forward, she placed a hand on the other woman's knee. "My lady . . ."

"I told you, it's Sabrina. And never mind. You need a horse. I shall supply you with one. But there is a price to be paid."

Holly braced herself. "Name it."

"A truthful answer to one question, in so far as you may tell it."

Holly gestured her acquiescence with an open hand, and

triumph flashed Sabrina's blue eyes. "Does this clandestine ride at dawn have something to do with my brother?"

Holly sighed. "Yes."

The lady surprised her by showing no hint of mockery or amusement. "Thank you for admitting it. Now then, you were very kind to me yesterday after the debacle in the paddock, and I shall be happy to return the favor."

Something in her tone prompted Holly to ask, "Why do you dislike your brother?"

That produced a laugh. "Do I? I couldn't say. As far as I know, this is how brothers and sisters behave."

"No, Sabrina. It is not."

"No?" She gave her loose curls a toss that sent them tumbling down her back. "Well, it is how we Ashworths have always behaved."

A sense of sadness swept over Holly. A family so at odds, they didn't even realize how contrary they were. She couldn't fathom it. When she thought of her own family, of the little spats she and her sisters sometimes engaged in, and how quickly they forgave and how staunchly they supported one another . . .

"I'm sorry for you," she whispered, but Sabrina seemed not to have heard her.

"What time tomorrow?" she asked.

"Sunup," Holly told her, then returned to her room.

Chapter 15

Colin tossed a few essentials into the valise gaping at the foot of his bed. His trip to Briarview would commence sooner than he had anticipated. He had planned to wait until after the Royal Meeting, and slip away while dozens of grooms and trainers led their racehorses away from Ascot.

His instincts, however, urged him to set out without further delay. True, by leaving tomorrow he would hazard bringing attention to himself, and thereby risk not only his family's interests in Devonshire, but, more important, those of every villager and tenant farmer.

By waiting he would incur even greater risk. Miss Sutherland and her questions . . . her furtive escapades through the stables and the house. Could she have somehow learned his secret?

For the life of him he couldn't see how. Still. . . .

A tap at his door scattered his thoughts. "Come in."

An oblong wooden cask balanced on one palm, his valet shouldered his way into the room. "I've brought the requested items, sir."

"I appreciate it, Kirkston," he said as he took the box from the older man. "Did anyone see you entering my father's rooms?"

"Not a soul, sir. I made doubly certain no one was about before I slipped inside."

"Good. Not a word of my plans to my family. I don't intend to give them much notice before I leave."

"Very good, sir. Will there be anything else?"

"Not tonight. Good evening, Kirkston."

"Good evening, sir." With silent footfalls, the man retreated and closed the door softly.

The soul of discretion, Colin thought with satisfaction. It hadn't been for Kirkston's skill at pressing shirts or knotting cravats that Colin had taken him on after the valet's previous employer, Colin's uncle Reginald, had suddenly keeled over of an apoplexy. No, it had been for Kirkston's prudence and unerring loyalty, not to mention other, more singular talents.

He flicked the clasp on the casket and opened the lid. The double-barreled percussion pistol inside gleamed in its cushioned bed of deep blue velvet. Etched into the silver handle, his father's initials, a curling T and a bolder A, stared up at him as if to issue a challenge, as if to mock him. Did he have the fortitude to use this weapon if necessary?

He reached in, lifting the pistol and the velvet-covered tray on which it lay. In the deeper recess of the casket, his fingers closed around a pouch tied with a drawstring. He didn't need to open it. He could feel by the weight, and by the light clunking inside, that the bag held a generous supply of bullets.

Had he required a hunting rifle, he might have gone to the gamekeeper's lodge and requested one from several of the gun racks there. This weapon wasn't intended for stopping a fox in its tracks. This pistol was meant for taking down a man, and it allowed two opportunities of doing so. His father kept weapons such as these under strict control, in a locked trunk in his private suite. Didn't Thaddeus Ashworth trust his sons? Did he deem pistols too much of a temptation for them to be kept readily available? Colin smirked. Probably.

The security measures hadn't, apparently, posed a problem for Kirkston.

Tomorrow, in the late afternoon, Kirkston would deliver

an urgent, albeit falsified, message from Colin's friend, Benjamin Rivers, Dean of Natural Philosophies at Cambridge University. It would speak of a sudden dispute between Ben and the board of trustees . . . Ben in danger of being sacked . . . Colin's immediate intervention required . . .

He felt a little guilty involving Ben, however indirectly, in his deception, but it was the best he could come up with on short notice. By suppertime tomorrow, he and the colt would be many miles from Masterfield Park.

It's you who made all this necessary, Father. You who have turned me into a liar and a criminal, damn you.

Another knock at his door prompted him to tuck the pistol back into its box and close the lid. He shoved the box into his valise, shut that too, and pushed it far beneath the bed. "Come in."

Sabrina, looking at least a decade younger in her dressing gown and beribboned nightcap, came into the room. The look on her face, however, was anything but childlike as she tilted her chin and regarded him with a haughty frown. "It's dreadfully late, Colin. What did you wish to speak with me about?"

"It's not so very late, at least not for you, my night owl."

For an instant, a wistful, almost sad emotion darkened her eyes. He used to call her that when she was a child, but many years had passed since then. In fact, until that moment he had all but forgotten the pet name, bestowed upon a little sister who used to defy her governess by staying awake and sneaking out of bed to greet her older brother as he returned home from his late-night jaunts.

How little she had been then, no more than seven or eight, while he had been approaching twenty and enjoying his first taste of freedom during his holidays from university. However adult he had believed himself, he couldn't deny having savored the squeeze of those eager little arms welcoming him home.

Then one night his father had discovered Sabrina out of bed. . . .

Did his features betray the dismal memory? Perhaps, for

she blinked and angled her gaze away. Her lips moved, and he could have sworn she released an oath beneath her breath.

His gut clenching, he crossed the room to her. "I merely wished to ask you to take special care of Lady Harrow and the misses Sutherland during their stay. I don't want them left on their own."

She swung her face back to his and smiled, a gesture possessing far less humor than shrewdness. "No?"

"I want you to see that they are properly entertained. Do you have plans for them tomorrow?"

"As a matter of fact, Holly and I are taking an early-morning ride."

He hadn't missed the significance of the disclosure. "Holly, is it?"

"Yes. She and I have reached an accord." She shrugged a shoulder carelessly. "As one horsewoman to another."

"I see. And later in the day?"

Her eyes narrowed. "Is there a reason you wish me to keep them occupied?"

His senses sprang to the alert. The look on his sister's face, along with her questions, probed too near the truth. Which was that he wasn't leaving solely to protect the colt, or even the folk of Briarview. For he had no proof that Holly Sutherland or anyone else knew about the animal, no evidence of imminent danger other than a nagging sensation that he must leave.

But when he stopped to analyze that sensation, he could only admit it had less to do with the colt and everything to do with Miss Sutherland herself. If anyone was in danger, it was him. That had been amply proven tonight in the library.

He maintained an outward show of calm. "Don't be a goose. The Sutherlands are not merely visitors. Lady Harrow is Simon de Burgh's wife."

"I know precisely who she is, and who her sisters are."

He had the distinct impression they were holding two separate conversations, and that whatever notion Sabrina had seized upon had nothing to do with amusing their guests.

"Can I count on you, then?"

"I shall do my part," she obliged grudgingly.

"Oh, and Sabrina," he said when she started toward the door. "Miss Sutherland can be an impulsive rider. Make sure she doesn't head anywhere dangerous, such as the creek bottom between the hills. You know where I mean."

She turned and answered with the full brilliance of her most charming smile. Which only heightened his worries.

Holly came to a halt in the stable yard, brought up short by the sight of Lady Sabrina waiting for her with two saddled horses.

"My lady, I'm afraid you didn't understand—"

"Sabrina. And I understood you perfectly well."

"But this is something I must do alone."

"And how did you suppose you would ride off all alone without raising suspicions? Do you not realize our grooms report to my brother everything that goes on here? He already knows we are going out—"

"You told him?"

"Of course I told him. If I hadn't, he would have wondered."

Minutes later, Holly and Sabrina trotted their horses past the racetrack and onto the open terrain beyond. Here, away from the shelter of the house, gardens, and stables, chilling dawn breezes rolled off the heath without impediment. Holly shivered and tucked her chin lower into the collar of her riding habit. Deep clouds lumbered across an inky blue sky still dotted with a few stars, while the rising sun, little more than a crescent on the horizon, stretched the first reedy shadows across the landscape.

Instead of Thunderbolt, Holly rode a sedate mare named Maribelle's Fancy, a mount that seemed sure of foot and quick to obey. And like Lady Sabrina, she sat properly sidesaddle rather than astride. No one would have thought anything out of the ordinary, except perhaps that Lady Sabrina and her friend enjoyed riding at an ungodly hour. As Lady Sabrina had promised, the grooms had asked no questions. Which left Holly with one remaining problem.

Lady Sabrina herself.

She showed no sign of leaving Holly's side. Holly had carefully retraced the course she and Colin had taken yesterday, but the nearer to the vale she and Sabrina rode, the more confounded she became. She couldn't risk taking the young woman into her confidence. No matter the contention between Sabrina and her siblings, she was still an Ashworth, and Holly had no intention of testing her loyalties.

Holly slowed Maribelle's pace and waited for the other woman to do the same. "Lady Sabrina . . ."

"Just Sabrina. Cohorts in crime needn't stand on ceremony."

"I assure you, there are no crimes about to be committed. I never inferred any such thing."

"Then why the secrecy?"

"I have my reasons, just as you have yours for agreeing to help me."

"Oh, my reasons are no great secret. My life is a bore and you have provided a refreshing distraction." Sabrina braced her hands on the saddle in front of her and leaned sideways into the space between them. "Whatever you are doing, do let me accompany you. I swear I'll never tell a soul what I see."

"I cannot. And if you insist on trailing me, I shall be forced to turn around and head back. This is not my decree. It is simply necessary."

"Oh . . ." Sabrina released a dramatic breath. "You know you only pique my curiosity with claims such as that. But very well, at least for now. I shall ride off that way." She pointed due north.

Suddenly, despite Sabrina's nonchalance, Holly deduced a possible reason why the young woman might be reluctant to ride off alone. "Are you afraid your horse won't obey your commands? Like in the paddock?"

"That shan't be repeated."

"But you said it wasn't the first time."

"Never mind what I said. I was upset. The filly had no doubt been spooked by the noisy chattering and the milling of our guests. It won't happen again," she concluded with a determined scowl, making Holly wonder who she was trying to convince, Holly or herself.

"I won't be long," Holly said, though she wondered about the accuracy of the reassurance.

"I'm not supposed to let you go that way." With a jerk of her chin, Sabrina gestured toward the vale. "My brother's orders."

A jolt went through Holly until she realized he had probably only meant those orders as a precaution, based on the previous morning. Surely he would have no reason to think she would return there today with his sister. "Wherever I go, I shall proceed at my own risk and my own responsibility."

"Ride on, then, and do whatever it is that might or might not involve my brother. I will give you half an hour to meet me over by those trees." Sabrina lifted a hand to point westward, indicating a stand of pine trees. "If you aren't back by then, I shall assume something dreadful has happened and will have no choice but to come searching for you."

Holly hoped a half hour would be adequate, but she knew better than to plead for more. She was not only indebted to Sabrina, but dependent on her to keep her lips sealed . . . at least for now, as she had said.

After several minutes she glanced over her shoulder to see if the young woman had decided to follow her after all. Bringing Maribelle to a complete halt, Holly twisted round in the saddle and inspected the landscape in several directions for signs of movement. As far as she could discern, a pair of swooping skylarks singing to each other and a rabbit just now hopping across her path were her only company. She continued on.

Within a few minutes, the wide openness of the rolling heath narrowed between two hills where a stream meandered, split, disappeared into crevices, and reappeared to bubble gaily over rocks. Holly followed the sandy bank, the ground sucking at Maribelle's hooves. Colin had not lied about the bottomlands here. At best, a rider who hadn't been warned might very likely render his mount lame. At worst, a horse could lose his footing and go down hard, his rider thrown.

A growing elation made her wish she *could* urge the horse faster. *He hadn't lied. . . .*

She sobered as she realized that the hazards of the place also made it perfect for hiding something. Too steep and muddy for riding or cultivating, the land was of no apparent use to anyone, and presented no reason for anyone to venture in.

At her back, the sun climbed into the morning sky, but the vale, narrowing until it became little more than a gorge, shut out the direct reach of its rays. Sparse pines and the occasional sapling clung to the rocky hillsides, the swishing of the breeze through their leaves like the hushed whispers of a crowd before a race. Up ahead, the stream disappeared around an eroded outcropping of exposed rocks while the rippling current swallowed nearly all the level ground. Sand and pebbles slid out from under Maribelle's hooves.

Holly stopped the mare and dismounted. She had already gone about a half mile into the vale with no sign of anyone or anything having disturbed the area. She would continue only a little farther before admitting there was nothing here to see. With no reason to risk bringing her mount around the bend, she tied the reins to an obliging branch and proceeded on foot.

Water lapping at her hems and seeping into her boots, she pressed close to the outcropping and picked her way around to the other side. There she came to a dead halt and a jarring truth, one that shed doubt on her loyalty to her queen and her friendship with Victoria.

She would rather find nothing, would rather never find any trace of Prince's Pride, or any evidence that implicated Colin Ashworth in theft or any other crime—even if it meant disappointing Victoria and leaving her reign in jeopardy.

Though she hadn't been aware of it, the rhythm of that prayer had been dictating the pattern of her breathing and the pace of her steps: Don't ... let ... it ... be.... Please ... Don't ... let ... it ... be....

Please.

She moved past the outcropping, and the corner of a split-rail fence came into view. Her hopes plummeting, she gripped a wispy yew sapling growing beside her. Gripped it until her knuckles whitened and the stalk bent against her palm. She stood riveted to the spot and stared at the fence while her heart pounded in her throat, her blood roared in her ears, and images flooded her mind.

A darkened library, a pair of strong arms, a flash of golden hair, and the dear, dear perfection of his features as he leaned his face close and kissed her.

A sickening regret pushed a bitter, burning taste into her throat, her mouth. He had caught her virtually red-handed sneaking about his house, and instead of taking her to task he had kissed her, held her in his strong arms, kissed her again. Heaven help her, a ruse. He had surmised that she suspected ... something ... and had hoped to distract her from the truth.

Her regret hardening to cold, solid anger, she released the sapling; it whipped out of her fingers as she ducked beneath the pine branches in her way until she stood right before the fence. Her fists closed on the top rail. She leaned forward.

And saw nothing—nothing but an empty enclosure. Where one end of the fence abutted the hillside, a small lean-to, rough-hewn and half rotting, stood open to the morning air.

It was vacant.

Colin made his way from one end of the terrace to the other, stopping at each linen-covered table to bid his guests good morning. Laughter and conversation filled the air around him. Along the balustrade, a lengthy buffet offered eggs, hot and cold meats, blood pudding, porridge, baked goods, and an array of fruit transported here from the London wharves.

While some of his guests would stay on during the races, others would be leaving later that day, returning to their own estates or taking up residence in rented homes in the area. The solicitors would now go to work, completing the contracts on the horses bought and sold and seeing to details too mundane to warrant the attention of these aristocrats. No, their sights would now be set on the races themselves. Some would profit. Some would wager more than their purses held and end up teetering on the brink of bankruptcy. There would be triumphs and disappointments, unexpected victories and crushing heartbreak.

Colin would be here for none of it.

Feminine voices drew his attention to the base of the garden steps. Holding the trains of their riding habits, Sabrina and Holly started up. He met them at the top of the steps. "Ladies. Did you enjoy your ride?"

"We most certainly did." Holly appeared flushed and slightly out of breath as she raised her chin to look up at him. The moment he beheld her fresh face, rosy cheeks, and her plump, moist lips, the memory of last night bombarded him. The taste of her, the feel of her soft curves pressed up against him, had proved true everything he had imagined and craved for months, only more so—more tempting, more sweet, lush and intoxicating than he could have dreamed.

"Where did you go?" he asked them. He leaned slightly toward Holly. "Nowhere dangerous, I trust."

"Ah, but your sister would hardly allow that, my lord, now, would she?" Laughter bubbled in Holly's voice, and Colin realized he had never seen her quite so buoyant, perhaps not since that very first ride they had taken together in Cambridge. Her mood was infectious, so much so he questioned his suspicions, and whether he truly needed to leave the area that day. "Especially," she added with a wink of the dimple in her right cheek, "after you expressly told Lady Sabrina to keep an eye on me."

"I might have known," he said to his sister in mock admonishment, "that you would not keep that secret. Forgive me, Miss Sutherland, for being overbearing," he said in the same light tone. "But as you can well imagine, I am responsible for the welfare of my guests."

"I do understand, my lord." Her smile dazzled him. "And rest assured you did not curb my enjoyment of our morning ride in the slightest. Isn't that right, Sabrina?"

Could he have been mistaken in thinking she had somehow learned about the colt and decided to search for the animal? Perhaps her ride toward the vale yesterday had been no more than it appeared—a skilled horsewoman seeking a challenge. And last night, she had claimed she had lost her way and thus ended up in the darkened wing of the house, near his father's private office, where the records were kept; but she wouldn't be the first guest to become lost in this maze of a house.

The notion that he might have been wrong in all of his suspicions lifted a weight from his chest, until he remembered that in the end it didn't matter. He was developing feelings for her, ones he dared not entertain because he was a horse thief who hailed from a broken wreck of a family, not to mention a traitor to his queen.

For that reason alone, he must leave Masterfield Park that very day.

Sabrina answered Holly's question with a quick word of agreement, but her eyes remained on Colin, her lips curled in that cunning, feline smile of hers, as if she could see right into his mind. She tapped her riding crop against her skirts. "You two may debate the merits of morning rides as much as you like. I am famished." With that, she stalked away and found a seat at one of the tables.

"So where did you go?" he asked Holly at length, not because he needed to know, but because he didn't want her to slip away. His mind was made up. He would leave within the next hour or so, and it might be a very long time before he saw her again.

Whatever life held for him next, these were minutes he would savor.

Her smile widened; she shrugged. "We went north mostly, past the pastures and onto the heath. It's really rather beautiful, the heath."

"Most people find it tediously flat, of little use except for racing."

"I find the heath intensely peaceful." She turned her face to the sun, lowering her eyelids to shield them from the direct rays. "Though I expect it won't be at all peaceful during the races."

As if by some unspoken agreement, they drifted away from the noisy company, down the steps, and a few strides along the garden path. They stopped beside a box hedge and she turned to him, still with that radiant smile, her cheek dimpling, her eyes clear and green and filled with . . . *elation* sprang to mind. As did the word *beautiful*. Bright and fresh, like the garden around her.

Her lips took on an impish tilt. "I wonder, my lord, if you could name this box hedge?" She pulled off a glove and gestured with her lovely, slender fingers. Laughter danced in her eyes.

For an instant he couldn't guess her meaning—then he remembered. Remembered that morning at Harrowood in Cambridge, when he had decided to dispense with caution. He had gathered his courage and resolved that he would no longer allow his father or anyone else to dictate his life or rob him of happiness. He had found her alone in Simon's morning room, and damn it, he was going to kiss her. Going to speak to her. He had beckoned her to the window. . . .

And lost his nerve. Or rather, he had remembered the simple, sheltered life she had always led, she and the sisters she loved so dearly. He remembered her innocence, her honesty, and the lovely ringing of her sheer, delighted laughter as she had galloped her horse over the woodland paths. And he had realized he hadn't the heart to sully that innocence, that beauty, with the ugliness that lurked in his family.

"I'm afraid I never was much good with box hedges." He had meant to sound flippant, but he couldn't quite summon that sentiment. Instead, the words sounded hollow and sad.

A crease formed above her nose. "Is anything wrong?"

He took her hand and raised it to his lips; he kissed it, then held it there, not caring who might see the gesture or what they thought. After today it would no longer matter.

But what Holly thought did matter, very much, and he mustn't lead her to the wrong conclusion. "I was thinking of last night," he lied, releasing her hand. "You haven't recognized the scoundrel this morning, have you?"

"No, but I haven't been among your guests yet today. Still, I think what you said last night must be true, that he had come only for the ball, or he would have been familiar to me. I'd even feared that perhaps . . ."

"Yes?"

Her gaze drifted to the purple lilacs growing thick on a trellis. "A year ago my sister Laurel was attacked by a man she had never laid eyes on before, but who seemed to know her." She looked back at him, all the light flirtation of the past few moments erased from her features. "We believe him to be someone from our past, someone who knows a good deal more about us than we do. And who has reasons, unknown to us, for wishing us harm."

He wanted to take her in his arms, but stepping closer to her would have to suffice. "And you think the man last night . . . ?"

She was already shaking her head as if she'd only just reached a conclusion. "In all probability, no. Laurel's attacker railed at her in French. But this man . . . what little he spoke was murmured too low for me to be sure. Once he called me *mon amie* . . . but that doesn't mean much."

"No, I'm afraid it doesn't. I've used the term myself many a time." But the possibility that last night's incident had been more than a drunken rascal taking a liberty with a young woman at a ball chilled him. "Holly, I think you and your sisters should go home. Forget about the races. Go to Harrowood or back to London, wherever you'll be safe."

She drew back as if startled. "Aren't we safe enough here, especially if we exercise a bit of caution from now on?"

No, because soon I shall be gone. He wouldn't be here to protect her, and that meant he wanted her somewhere else.

Mistaking his silence, she said, "Unless, of course, we are no longer welcome."

He was about to assure her that nothing could be further from the truth when one of his head grooms walked quickly up the path to them. He slid his cap from his head before he reached them.

"My lord?"

Colin stepped away from Holly. "Yes, Kenneth, what is it?"

Kenneth held up a hand and opened his fingers. A gray pebble, roundish, sharp-edged, about an inch in diameter, lay nestled in his callused palm. "I came across this in the demonstration paddock, lying in the dirt."

Colin frowned and shrugged a shoulder. "What's so unusual about a stone lying on the ground?"

The groom, about Colin's own age, flashed an indignant look, almost a scowl. "My lord, I supervised the raking of every inch of that paddock myself. Pure, soft dirt, that's what there was. I'd never miss a stone like this—it could have lodged in a hoof, left one of my lord's fine hunters lame."

"Then how do you suppose it got there?" Colin held out his hand and Kenneth passed him the pebble. He held it up to get a good look at it.

The groom shuffled his feet, stuffed his hands in his coat pockets.

Colin shifted his gaze from the stone to the man before him. "Kenneth?"

"I was thinking, sir, about my lady's trouble with Sport o' Kings."

"Are you insinuating someone might have thrown this at the horse?"

"A rock like this would sting a hide much like a bee, my lord. Could make a horse jumpy and irritable afterward." Kenneth shrugged. "I hope I'm wrong, sir."

"Did you check the rest of the paddock?"

"Of course, sir. Twice."

"Thank you, Kenneth." The groom left, and Colin stood staring down at the pebble in his palm, wondering what it meant.

Holly, who had remained silent during the exchange, touched his elbow. "That would explain Sport o' King's behavior. And put your sister's worries to rest."

Colin looked up. "Sabrina's worries?"

Her eyebrows went up and she compressed her lips; then she just as quickly recovered her composure and said, "She blamed herself. She feared she had done something to cause the horse to rebel."

"But who would throw a rock into the paddock?"

Holly reached for the stone. Holding it between her thumb and forefinger, she narrowed her eyes. "Someone, perhaps, who disapproved of Sabrina riding that day."

"Please don't dissemble if you've a name in mind. Who disapproved of my sister?"

She met his gaze. "I could be wrong. I'm *probably* wrong."

"Tell me whom you mean."

She blew out a breath. "Mr. Bentley as much as said that if your father had been here, he would never have permitted Sabrina to take such a risk. And he said 'Blast Drayton for allowing it.'"

"Damn him." Colin raised his chin, searching for Bentley up on the terrace.

"But disapproving is a far stretch from throwing stones," Holly said quickly. "I'm sorry. I should not have mentioned it."

"No, you did right." Still searching, his gaze landed on another face that prompted him to take Holly's hand. Lady Penelope stood near the balustrade, and she also appeared to be searching. Before that lady could turn and spot Colin here in the gardens, he hurried Holly down a side path that took them into the concealment of the tall topiary hedges.

"My lord?" Holly's feet lagged, and he gently tugged her along. "What are you doing?"

He stopped behind an evergreen giraffe and her faltering steps brought her bumping into his side. He felt tempted to swing an arm around her and gather her even closer, but instead he grasped her shoulders and held her at arm's length. "I have an important favor to ask you."

She either sensed his urgency or saw it in his features, for the perplexity smoothed from her brow. "What is it?"

"If you're intent on remaining at Masterfield Park, will you look after Sabrina for me? Stay with her, ride with her, but do not let her out of your sight. Form a constant group with your sisters and mine, and keep one another safe."

"But . . . you sound as though you are going somewhere. Are you leaving?"

He pulled back, realizing how desperate his appeal had sounded. "No, but with the races little more than a week away, I fear my attention will often be engaged elsewhere. I would rest easier knowing the four of you were always together, never off anywhere alone." He released her shoulders and reached for her hands instead, giving them a squeeze. "Will you promise me?"

"Of course. You needn't worry."

An earnest thank-you formed on his lips, but as he leaned closer to speak them and her sweet face filled his view, he kept leaning. Their lips met, and while hers parted on a little exclamation, no doubt of surprise, his opened on an uncontainable burst of emotion. He pressed deeper, imparting against his will everything he felt for her, his desire and devotion, his wish for more between them, his sorrow that he must leave her.

Straightening, he turned away before he could witness her reaction to the impulsive kiss, before this last image of her could burn itself in his brain, before she could ask any questions. He strode off with an aching gap in his chest where his heart used to be.

Chapter 16

As breakfast ended, gaily chattering groups drifted down the terrace steps to walk among the shrubbery. The crisp morning had turned into a clear day of sharp colors and bracing breezes, warmed by a bright sun shimmering in a cloudless sky. A rare day even for late May, one the Ashworths' guests seemed determined to take full advantage of before some of them left the estate later today. Sabrina was with her mother, seeing to the departure arrangements, ensuring luggage was brought down and carriages readied.

Holly should have felt buoyant. In fact, she *had*. Until her morning trek, she had fully believed that if Colin had Prince's Pride, he'd hidden the colt in the vale. The empty stall she'd found seemed to answer her prayers and clear Colin of the crime.

But then there had been Colin's plea, and that kiss. . . . As she caught up to her sisters strolling arm and arm down the garden lane, she glanced over at the topiary menagerie. Heat immediately tingled across her lips and cascaded down to her toes. But with the remembered pleasure of Colin's kiss came a sense of sadness she couldn't quite explain, like last night in the library. He seemed to be telling her something—good-bye, despite his protestation to the contrary.

Her imagination? Perhaps, because she knew she should not be kissing the man Victoria had sent her here to investigate. That must be it, not Colin's message to her, but her own admonishment to stay focused on her task.

Her sisters parted and then flanked her, and they all three linked arms as they continued strolling.

"Tell us what you found," Willow whispered. "I've been mad all morning to hear your news."

"I found nothing," she replied with a triumphant grin she was well aware didn't completely reach her eyes. "Colin—Lord Drayton—must be innocent."

If she had expected Ivy to happily concur, her sister surprised her. "How does not finding the colt in the vale exonerate Colin of all guilt?"

"Yes," Willow agreed. "I don't see how one necessarily follows the other."

"But . . ." Holly's shoulders slumped. Frowning, she regarded the path in front of her as they continued walking. "I was so certain that if he had the colt, he would have hidden it in the vale."

"He could have hidden it in any number of places," Ivy pointed out. "Do not misunderstand me. I am as eager as you to clear my husband's friend. But we would not be doing our duty to Victoria if we reached conclusions based on superficial evidence." Ivy halted their progress and turned to Holly. "Having served Victoria previously, I know whereof I speak."

Holly sighed, the action like wind abandoning sails to leave them sagging. "I know you do."

They proceeded, and Willow waved to Mrs. Fenhurst, who called a greeting from the Chinese footbridge that arced over the manmade brook. "I grow less convinced than ever that Prince's Pride is not at this moment occupying a stall in the Windsor mews," she said. "Victoria's perception might be easily explained. After all, a horse can be at the top of its form one day and falter the next."

"Very true." With her free hand Ivy adjusted the shawl draped around her arms. "Lady Sabrina's experience with Sport o' Kings proves a horse's performance can vary. The same animal might have appeared extraordinary to the queen when she first laid eyes on him, only to seem diminished once her initial excitement had waned."

Holly considered telling her sisters about the rock found in the paddock, but decided it bore little to do with Colin's possible guilt and could wait till later.

"Then what do we do?" Willow slipped her arm from Holly's and faced both sisters. "Return to Windsor and tell Victoria we don't believe there is another colt?"

"Not yet," Holly said firmly. "There is another alternative."

The idea had just occurred to her, perhaps *only* occurred because of the kiss, because of everything Colin had seemed to communicate to her through the touch of his lips. The memory of it gripped her with a certainty that he wanted—needed—to tell her . . . something. She plunged ahead. "We have been questioning the guests and sneaking about like thieves. Perhaps it's time to come clean with Col—er—Lord Drayton, and see what he has to say."

"Holly, you mustn't dream of any such thing!" Willow all but cried out. She clapped a hand to her mouth, darted a look about her, then spoke from behind her fingers. "You cannot betray Victoria's confidence."

But Ivy said calmly, "I think Holly is right. Never mind that I haven't for one moment believed Colin or any other member of the family could be guilty of an act as base as stealing a horse from the queen. The very notion! If anything, I thought perhaps the deed had been accomplished by an acquaintance from the racing world who knew of the colt and decided he must have it. But after all our questioning, not a single individual has given the slightest indication of ever hearing of such an extraordinary horse. The racing world forms a tight-knit community. Secrets of this caliber simply don't exist among turfites."

Holly agreed, but Willow tossed her hands in the air. "Before you run off to confess all, how do you explain the paddock you discovered in the vale? The colt might have been there, and been moved before you rode out there this morning."

"That paddock has stood for ages, perhaps built by a long-ago shepherd who saw the vale as a convenient place to seek shelter from storms." Holly shrugged. "Besides, no one but Lady Sabrina knew I'd be anywhere near the area today, so why would he have moved the colt?"

Yet a niggling memory belied that claim. Lady Sabrina had admitted that she had told her brother she and Holly would be riding that morning. . . .

"Perhaps Lady Sabrina moved the colt."

"Oh, Willow, don't be a goose. Sabrina Ashworth, a horse thief?" Ivy chuckled, and Willow bristled with indignation.

"Perhaps she and Lord Bryce conspired," Willow said. She scowled, and added, "Or she and Geoffrey. Or all three."

Ivy started to laugh outright, but Holly shushed her. "All the more reason to take their oldest brother into our confidence. We've accomplished little so far. It's time we took a risk. A leap of faith. Are you with me?"

Willow's worried look deepened. "If you cannot be dissuaded . . ."

"You have my support," Ivy said with more conviction.

"It's decided, then. On the pretext of purchasing a horse, I'll contrive to speak with Lord Drayton alone at his earliest convenience. Come, let's return to the terrace."

"What do you mean, gone?" Holly tried to conceal her dismay, but the news she had just received from Lady Sabrina delivered a startling blow. "Gone when? Where?"

"To Cambridge, apparently." Lady Sabrina walked at an unhurried, unconcerned pace through the terrace doors and into the drawing room. "If you'll excuse me, I believe it's time I changed out of my riding habit and into a more suitable frock."

"One moment, please . . ." Holly stumbled after her, nearly tripping over the train of her own riding skirts, the brim of her feathered hunt cap crushed in her fist as she hurried to keep up. At least a dozen people milled about the room. Holly lowered her voice. "Your brother left so suddenly."

Looking mildly annoyed, Sabrina stopped. "A letter arrived in the post for him. Something about an uproar involving university officials and an acquaintance of his, a dean. I believe your sister knows him. Benjamin Rivers?"

Ivy and Willow, standing amid a group in the curve of the pianoforte, looked sharply over at them as Sabrina spoke the name they all knew. Across the way, Lord Bryce, suddenly distracted from his own conversation, pinned a speculative gaze on Willow.

"Excuse me." At the masculine voice behind her, Holly moved out of the doorway. Young Lord Geoffrey stepped inside, and Holly wondered if he or Bryce were aware that their brother had left Masterfield Park. Colin's abrupt departure sent ripples of unease up and down her length.

"I'm well acquainted with Mr. Rivers," she said to Sabrina. "Did your brother say what sort of trouble?"

"Oh, university politics, from what I could make out. The matter seemed to require my brother's immediate intervention." Sabrina started walking again. They exited the drawing room and crossed the central hall to the staircase.

"Oh, dear . . ."

Sabrina lingered on the first step, her hand on the banister. "Is there a problem?"

"No . . . only that . . . I wished to make my purchase of a horse . . . and . . ."

Sabrina waved a dismissive hand. "You hardly need Colin for that. I'll arrange a meeting with our head trainer. The solicitors can smooth out the financial details." She resumed her ascent, saying over her shoulder, "I believe a letter came for your sister as well. It's behind you, on the salver."

Lady Sabrina left Holly gaping up at her from the bottom of the stairs. Now what?

Colin was gone. Abruptly and without a good-bye. Or *had* that kiss been his way of saying good-bye? But why the secrecy?

Crestfallen, she went to the round marquetry table beneath the massive hall chandelier at the center of the room. On the silver post tray, she found the envelope directed to the Marchioness of Harrow. Recognizing Simon de Burgh's familiar handwriting, she retraced her steps to the drawing room and handed the letter to Ivy.

Aware of the impropriety of lounging in the drawing room in her riding habit, she thought of bringing her sisters back out to the terrace where they would have more privacy. Ivy's flushed cheeks changed her mind, and she instead drew them to a settee that faced out over the gardens.

"Oh, that *is* good news." Ivy, her letter in hand, scanned the lines with a smile.

"What could possibly be good news at this point?" Holly asked without much interest.

"Simon writes that Errol Quincy arrived in London two mornings ago, and together they are going to continue the experiments on Victoria's stone." Ivy looked up, her smile widening. "Having the elderly gent on hand should prevent Simon from incinerating himself in my absence."

"But that's odd," Willow said. "Shouldn't Mr. Rivers have needed Mr. Quincy's help in whatever trouble is brewing at the university?"

With a shrug, Ivy continued perusing the missive. Her chin snapped upward. "Holly, you must read this."

She shoved the paper into Holly's hands. Willow peered over her shoulder. Aloud Holly read, "'Ben arrived several hours behind Errol, and I fear, darling, that under their influence I shall regress to the habits of my bachelor days. . . .'" She gasped.

Willow grasped the edge of the letter between her thumb and forefinger to steady it in Holly's suddenly trembling hands. "If Mr. Rivers is in London, then . . ."

"Then . . ." Ivy drew a sharp breath. "I cannot bring myself to say it, nor to imagine that it could be true. There must be some mistake. Perhaps Lady Sabrina misunderstood."

"She seemed awfully certain to me." Holly met Ivy's gaze and recognized the same reluctant conclusion. "Colin lied."

Willow released the letter, her hand falling to her lap. "What should we do?"

Holly stood up from the settee. "The only thing we can do."

Colin brought Cordelier to a halt and twisted round in his saddle. Raising a hand to shield his eyes from the steely glare of a late-afternoon sky that had turned overcast, he studied the road behind him. The dusty ribbon of byway curved out of sight around a bend, then reappeared a mile or so beyond the low swell of a hillside. Thatched roofs dotted the countryside, and curls of smoke drifting from chimneys indicated the ending of the workday and lighting of the evening fires. As he searched the distance he watched for any telltale movement, such as dust rising off the packed-dirt surface.

Beside him, the colt tugged its lead rope with a toss of its head, showing its impatience to be moving again.

"Easy, boy," Colin murmured soothingly. "You and I have the same goal in mind. To get you home, where you belong."

When Colin had started out from Masterfield Park, he had headed east in the event he was followed. Then he had doubled back, collected the colt from the hiding place where he'd moved it before dawn, and skirted the town of Ascot. He'd avoided the highway in favor of smaller, shadier country lanes until he'd traveled far enough and he felt it was safe to take the faster route. Here, he would appear as nothing more than a man transporting a young horse from one place to another, as many a fellow did during the spring, especially during the racing season.

Yet the fear of being followed, improbable though it was, never entirely left him, nor had the bristling of his nape. To his left, the roadside embankment gave way to forest that thrust the already pewter afternoon deeper into shadow. Beyond a low stone wall on the opposite side of the road, cows and sheep drifted like small craft in a gently undulating sea of green. Startled by a shrill caw, Colin followed the downward plummet of a speckled hawk, swiftly falling as if to collide with the ground. At the last minute it swooped low, then with a cry of triumph soared heavenward with some unfortunate creature dangling from its talons.

Closer to him, a cloud of dirt rolled along a field sown in neat rows of wheat, and he spotted a dray pulled by a stout little pony. His gaze darted back to the road, where in the far distance a swirling wisp rose like steam from a kettle. Instinct sent him to the side of the road. He dismounted, gathered both Cordelier's reins and the colt's lead rope in one hand, and pushed through the trees, seeking the cover offered by a dense, ancient wood.

As he went, he fumbled with the bag tied to his saddle. When he got it open he reached in and closed his fingers around his one bit of insurance, its weight solid against his palm. Then he waited, shielded by the luxuriant foliage and the cool, shady darkness.

The dray passed by at a lazy pace, its wheels creaking along the rutted road, the farmer humming a languid tune. More minutes passed. Cordelier stood patiently. Even the colt seemed resigned to the delay, and happily nibbled the moist spring leaves within reach.

Only Colin began to shuffle, grown weary of waiting for something that probably wouldn't come. He began to doubt the sensation that had raised his hackles. Since this business had begun, he'd read conspiracy in every sideways glance, deception in every young beauty that wandered lost in his home.

Obviously, he wasn't cut out for stealth. He missed his simple life at Cambridge, missed his laboratory and fellow scientists, his experiments, and the goal of one day accomplishing something extraordinary and proving that he was more, so much more, than Thaddeus Ashworth's heir.

Just as Colin was about to vacate his woodland hideaway, Cordelier's ears pricked forward. The stallion tensed, sniffing the wind. Without waiting for the colt to respond in kind, Colin covered his muzzle with his hands to forestall any whickers that might give away his location. Moments later, the clip-clopping of hooves echoed from down the road. Colin held his breath, knowing the approaching rider could be nothing more than a traveler like himself, yet thoroughly convinced otherwise. Ducking his head, he peered through the web of branches in front of him.

The lower half of a bay came into view, its flanks draped by a wide abundance of verdant green skirts. Taking care not to make a sound, Colin pushed an eye-level branch out of his way. The rest of a sleek horse took shape, and then the trim rider in her stylish habit. Fiery curls spilled from her hunting cap; its feather fluttered like a tiny flag.

He smiled grimly and placed his father's pistol back into his valise. Then Cordelier's snort alerted him to the presence of another horse coming along the road. Colin strained to see through the thickening shadows. He did a double take, and swore under his breath.

You can't just go off half-cocked. There may be danger. . . .

Willow's parting admonishment rang in Holly's ears, even three hours later. As she'd prepared to leave Masterfield Park, her sisters had argued against this plan of hers, protesting at her back all the way down to the stables. They had threatened to follow in their carriage, but Holly knew they wouldn't. Ivy wouldn't dare risk a jostling ride. And Willow wouldn't leave Ivy alone with the Ashworths.

Now, many miles down a lonely winding road bordered by vast fields and brooding forests, Holly wished they *were* with her. Already the trees cast long shadows across the road, and with growing misgivings she gauged the angle of the sun. In the fields, farmhands with their long, hooked staffs urged their herds of sheep and cattle homeward for the evening. She had not expected to be gone this long.

She had expected to catch up to Colin hours ago, but maybe she had been wrong about his direction. She had been so certain that if he hadn't gone to Cambridge as he'd claimed, then he must have headed west to the family's estate in Devonshire. She had found the records indicating that much of his work breeding horses took place at Briarview. Where better to bring the colt than that distant, isolated place?

But perhaps she had miscalculated. At this point, she might not make it back to Ascot before dark, and if she didn't turn back immediately, she'd have no choice but to spend the night at a roadside inn—one she hoped could offer her a clean room with a sturdy lock on the door.

"I say, Miss Sutherland?"

At the hail from behind her, she started and brought Maribelle to a halt, then with a flick of the reins turned the mare about. The face she saw snapped her eyes wide with disbelief. "Have you followed me all this way?"

Geoffrey Ashworth walked his horse up beside hers. "Yes," he said matter-of-factly.

Indignation unhinged her jaw. "Why? How could you have known . . . ? The drawing room—you overheard."

He hesitated for an instant, fingering his horse's mane. Then he glanced at her and once again uttered a single syllable. "Yes."

"Well . . . for your information, young man, I do not need a chaperone. I'll thank you to turn around this instant and go home."

"No."

"No? No?" Her temper surged, mingling with her chagrin. How on earth had this youth managed to trail her all this way without her knowing? She regarded the stubborn set of his youthful features. "Go!" she ordered with an outthrust finger.

"No."

Her frustration reaching a boil, she clamped her teeth, thought quickly, and drew a calming breath. "Lord Geoffrey, good friends of mine live in this area. I have decided to head there now, so I assure you I shall be quite all right on my own. I implore you to return home before your family begins to worry, if they aren't doing so already."

The boy faced straight ahead as if intent on some point in the far distance. "You are not going to visit friends, Miss Sutherland. You are following my brother."

"You had your ear to the door of our suite!"

"What I overheard in the drawing room worried me. So yes, I followed you upstairs and listened in."

"I've a good mind to tell your mother . . ."

He gave an unconcerned shrug. "Will you also tell her that you believe my brother has stolen something from the queen?"

"Good heavens . . ." She scrutinized him from head to foot and back again as understanding dawned. "It's like the other day on the racecourse, isn't it?"

He raised his eyebrows in puzzlement.

"When you raced beside your brother. You hardly flinched, for all you might have both been killed." She shook her head, smiling in spite of herself. "Everyone, and I do mean everyone, underestimates you, don't they?"

A twig snapped, and a voice from just inside the trees said, "I certainly have. I've underestimated both of you."

Chapter 17

"Lord Drayton!"

The exclamation came simultaneously with Geoffrey's calmer, "Brother."

"Good afternoon, you two," Colin said mildly. Having tied the colt securely to an oak some dozen yards behind him, Colin led Cordelier out onto the road. "Isn't this the oddest of coincidences?"

Holly was frowning down at him, obviously dumbfounded. With an amused smile, he angled his chin in her direction. "You're wondering why I should be hiding in the trees, Miss Sutherland. The answer is simple. I sensed I was being followed, and I was correct."

"Would one of you like to explain to me what the devil is going on?" Geoffrey demanded.

Despite the damned inconvenience of his brother's presence, Colin couldn't help feeling proud of the boy. Now, if he could only get rid of him before Geoff became any wiser about matters he was better off not knowing . . .

"Actually, whelp," he said with a laugh, "no. But I do thank you for delivering Miss Sutherland to me safely. I shudder to think of harm befalling her on the road."

He kept his tone light, but he wanted to hold her, shake her, assure himself that she was all right and at the same time make her swear never to behave with such recklessness again. Damn, but what was it about these Sutherland sisters that made them take such unfathomable risks? First Ivy pretended to be a man so she could attend university and assist Simon in his laboratory. Now this reckless, obstinate woman followed him.

They had played cat and mouse long enough.

He swung up onto Cordelier's back as if to continue on his journey. "The road is no place for a woman alone."

"I beg your pardon. I've as much right to travel the road as anyone else. And what do you mean, he delivered me?" Holly's horse lurched at the harshness of her tone. Colin recognized the animal from among the Ashworth personal stock: Maribelle's Fancy, a surefooted and dependable mare. Holly ran a reassuring hand down the animal's neck and said more sedately, "I came because . . . well . . . because I have an imperative question I must ask you."

"I can well imagine." He chuckled, then said to Geoff, "It's time you turned around. If you go now you'll make it back to Ascot just as it gets dark."

Geoffrey had the audacity to scowl. "What about Miss Sutherland?"

"She is under my protection now." He ignored her indignant huff. "She has questions for me and I shall answer them, but not here."

"Where, then?" Her chin came up; the question seethed with defiance and distrust.

"Devon," he told her.

"You're taking Miss Sutherland to Briarview?"

Colin nodded. "If she'll come. Otherwise she is free to return to Masterfield Park with you."

"It's hardly proper," Geoff protested.

"I assure you, it is," Colin replied. "We're traveling on horseback. Nothing improper about that. Along the way Miss Sutherland and I will secure separate rooms. You needn't fear for the lady's virtue, Geoff. You have my word on it."

Geoffrey looked unconvinced. The sun sank lower, nearly disappearing behind the tall trees; in another half hour it would be too late to send the boy home, and Colin would be stuck with him all the way to Briarview. He couldn't have that.

It was Holly who sent the boy on his way. "There is a favor I need you to do for me," she said. "If I am to ride on to Devonshire, I must assure my sisters that all is well, and that I shall see them in a few days." She glanced at Colin for confirmation. He nodded, and she went on. "You would be doing me the greatest kindness, Lord Geoffrey, and I should be forever grateful."

With a slight wheedling that reminded Colin of just how young his brother was, Geoffrey demanded, "And I am to learn nothing for my pains?"

Colin considered threatening the bounder with pain if he didn't hurry up and leave, but he dredged up a shred of patience. "If all goes well, I'll explain when we return. Until then, I believe Miss Sutherland would also be greatly beholden to you for watching over her sisters."

"That's very true," she said eagerly.

Geoffrey shook his head. "You don't need me for that. Bryce is already looking after Lady Harrow and Miss Willow."

"Need I remind you there is also Sabrina," Colin continued. "She is still angry and hurting, and I don't want her left alone."

Holly looked remorseful. "Yes, I'm sorry to have left her." She turned back to Geoffrey. "Please don't let your sister ride alone, or do anything alone, for that matter. She needs someone to keep her safe," she concluded in a whisper.

Geoff's scowl betrayed the silent argument raging inside him, yet he nodded finally and swung his horse about. As he set off at a brisk walk, Colin called out to him. Geoff stopped his mount and waited.

"You did a good thing today," Colin said quietly. "The honorable thing. I'm proud of you."

Geoff started to shrug. With a weight of disappointment, Colin witnessed his brother's obvious effort to keep his scowl in place. But just before Geoff turned and set his horse in motion, his mouth curved in a wide grin and his chest expanded. His own chest swelling, Colin watched the retreating figure until Geoff disappeared around a bend in the road. Once the hoofbeats faded, Colin dismounted again.

"What are you doing?" Holly looked nervously down at him, alarm sparking her eyes as he strode to her side and caught her around the waist.

"It's time you and I had a little chat."

She swatted at his hands. "Release me!"

"Down you go, my dear."

"Do not call me that. I am not *your* anything."

Panic lent her protest a hollow ring. He lifted her from the saddle, but when her feet touched the ground, he didn't release her. For the moment he had her exactly where he wanted her, where she could not run off. Soon enough there would be questions and each would demand their answers, but first . . .

He leaned his face over hers, his senses melting into heat, his body sinking into the fragrance of her skin, her hair, until their lips touched and he lost himself to the aching pleasure of having her in his arms again.

She stood stiffly for the span of time it took him to part her lips with his tongue. Then she pressed her body into his, wound her arms around his neck, and opened her mouth to admit him. Desire tightened his groin and opened his heart, and for several moments he indulged in the delight of crushing her to him as if she belonged in his arms, belonged to him. He drank her in, inhaled her, and swallowed her soft, sweet whimpers.

A whicker from within the trees prompted him to break the kiss, lift his head, and remember that, dear God, they were on a public throughway, and while their mounts partially shielded them from the view of anyone in the fields across the way, someone could come riding or walking along the road at any moment.

Even Geoffrey might find a reason to return.

She stared up at him, her lips parted and moist, her breath heaving in and out, matching his own rapid panting. "What now?" she asked.

Indeed. Now that the curtain was slowly being opened to reveal the truth behind the props and costumes and lies, how did they proceed?

"I have something I suppose I must show you," he said. "Because I've given up believing that you're simply going to go away."

A slight furrow gathered above her nose. "Do you wish me to go away?"

"No, damn it. But once I show you, you'll forfeit your right to leave. You'll have no choice but to continue on and see this play through."

"Play?"

"Oh, yes," he said softly. "We have both of us been playing parts, haven't we?"

"Yes." Her lashes swept downward to cast shadows over her cheeks.

He set his fingertips beneath her chin and raised it. "Shall we agree not to judge until we have learned all?"

The steadiness of her gaze as she raised it to his gave him all the answer he needed.

"Are you strong enough, or will the truth frighten you?"

"I won't be afraid," she said bravely. Her expression smoothed to one of quiet confidence, the serene look of a child at prayer. "After all, I have done no wrong and . . . I might even be able to help you."

Her sincerity pierced him through yet sent a smile to his lips, a smile of irony, and of regret. He released her chin and stepped back before he surrendered again to temptation. "Ah, but in this play the innocent are not always rewarded, and villainy often goes unpunished."

"Riddles." Her shoulders squared. "Why don't you show me whatever it is you've been hiding. Although I'll admit I'm fairly certain what it is."

The gleam of triumph in her eyes, and in her tone, was unmistakable. He only hoped the next few days wouldn't quash it completely. He stepped toward the trees and nodded. "Wait here."

Holly leaned for support against Maribelle's shoulder as Colin disappeared into the trees. Only halfheartedly did she wonder where he had gone or why. She was caught up in a dizzying unfolding of events where she no longer felt the urgency to press for the truth; she had only to wait and watch and learn. Maribelle turned her head to peer at her with one velvety brown eye, and Holly welcomed the warm wall of protection the horse's shoulder and curving neck formed around her.

But there were no walls to protect her from her feelings for Colin; no rationale to stop her lips tingling, her heart racing, her womb aching at the memory of his body against her, his lips pressed to hers. . . .

The snap of a twig brought her up sharp. Stepping away from Maribelle, she peered into the near blackness between the trees. She saw his golden hair first, bright against the shadows. His face was grim as he raised an arm to move the branches aside. At his shoulder, a star winked—or so it appeared. She craned forward and realized there was no disembodied star hovering among the trees, but rather the white marking on a horse's brow, the distinctive Ashworth star. At another crackling of underbrush, Colin's mount, Cordelier, pricked his ears forward, stamped a foot, and whickered.

An answering whinny came from within the woods as man and beast made their way through the foliage like players parting the curtains and walking on stage. Lead rope coiled about his hand, Colin walked the horse straight across the road, circled at the far side, and then walked the animal back. They stopped a few feet in front of Holly. Colin's gaze held her, but he said nothing. Cordelier gave a snort. Maribelle blew through her lips.

Holly glanced from Colin to the horse beside him, and everything around her seemed to fall quiet. Even her heartbeat, previously thudding in her ears, seemed to fade away.

"Oh . . . my . . ." And all at once, her heart thrust against her breast.

She could not have said what, pound for pound, inch for inch, made the animal presently tugging at its lead rope different from any other sleek, powerful, meticulously bred Thoroughbred. Essentially, it appeared the same as the colt she had seen in Victoria's mews, similar to Maribelle or Cordelier. And yet . . .

"It's him. . . . It's . . ." She stopped, startled by her own voice ringing loud in the silence. "The colt," she whispered.

A corner of Colin's mouth quirked.

She fought for breath, to control the panting she only now became aware of. "He truly does exist. The queen wasn't wrong."

Colin said nothing and made no move, but stood on the balls of his feet as if ready to spring away.

"All this time you had him." The truth should have astounded her, angered her. She had wished for his innocence—had believed, as early as that morning, that he *was* innocent. And yet somehow, this moment seemed as inevitable as . . . the warm press of their lips. "You took him," she said simply.

"And I hid him," he finished for her.

"In the vale."

"In the vale," he confirmed. "Until this morning, before dawn. Then I moved him to another location."

"Because of me."

"Because you are the most persistent woman I have ever encountered. More obstinate than even my sister."

Her thoughts raced. She and Colin had just made admissions that could not be taken back or ignored. The truth was out and must be reckoned with. He had taken—stolen—the colt from the queen. Colin Ashworth, Earl of Drayton and heir to the Duke of Masterfield, was no better than a common horse thief.

She had kissed a horse thief. More than once and, if given the chance, she would kiss him again. That, coupled with the fact that she was about to trust this man and follow him all the way to Devonshire without contacting the queen, made her nearly as guilty as he. Perhaps more so, for she had made a promise, taken a vow.

She was Her Majesty's Secret Servant, but, heaven help her, she was also about to become his lordship's secret accomplice.

"May I . . ." She swallowed and stepped forward. "May I touch him?"

Colin nodded, but it didn't escape her notice that he also tightened up on the lead rope until his fist hovered beside the colt's bridle. Holly stopped in front of them both, so close to Colin that his heady, masculine scent made her knees watery all over again. He gave another nod, this time one of encouragement, though he remained vigilantly close as if either Holly or the colt couldn't be trusted.

"I've never seen anything more beautiful. . . ." She held the flat of her palm under the colt's nose, her fingers spread open so he couldn't catch one between his teeth. He sniffed, then gave a tentative nuzzle. His head lowered, and Holly took this as a sign of permission. With one hand still at his warm whiskers, she raised the other and patted his neck, then ran it down the length of his nose.

A sense of reverence filled her like a stormy ocean breeze—bracing, charged, powerful. Astonished, she whisked both hands to her bosom. The colt lurched, but was just as quickly restrained by Colin's ready grip.

Holly held her ground. Her thoughts whirled like a dervish. She had found Prince's Pride—found him! She had doubted his existence, but here she stood, within arm's reach, her fingers still warm from his snuffling breath. Her mission should have been over, yet every instinct warned that in some vital way it was only just beginning.

She needed answers, and from somewhere in her heart sprang the conviction that acting without those answers could prove disastrous. Maybe it was because of the man silently watching her, gauging her reaction to the secret he had shared with her. With a fresh jolt she realized that Colin could have gone on pretending. He could have sent her back to Ascot with his brother, but he had chosen to trust her.

Just as he had kissed her. Impulse? Or something more, something deeper?

Reaching out a hand, she moved closer to the colt again, and felt swept up in a humbling sense of awe. "I don't understand." The animal lowered his head to allow her to scratch behind his ears. "What . . . what *is* he?"

"Special."

"One can see that, certainly." Her hand went still. "No, one can *feel* it. But why? How?"

"That is what you must come and see with your own eyes. If I explained, you would never believe me."

She darted a sharp gaze from the colt to Colin, but his handsome features caused her to look quickly away again. She needed to remain steady, to remember her duty to Victoria. "I wouldn't believe why you decided to play thief, and with the queen, no less?"

His gravity suddenly vanished. He had the audacity to grin, the curve of his mouth and the light in his eyes sending her pulse for a spin. "Am I any more of a thief than you, my dear?" With his free hand he gestured pointedly at Maribelle.

Heat crawled up her neck and into her cheeks. She *had,* after all, taken Maribelle's Fancy without asking. But with false bravado she set a hand on her hip. "That is altogether different. I only borrowed Maribelle, with every intention of returning her. Can you say the same?"

"Indeed not. But that isn't something to discuss here." His gaze had narrowed on her hips. Self-consciously, she dropped her hand to her side.

"What now?" she asked.

"Ah, yes, back to that essential question. There is a decent inn about a mile or two up the road. I suggest we head there before it grows dark."

"Yes," she said absently, once more spellbound by whatever enchantment the colt possessed. "I want to see him in motion."

Colin chuckled lightly. "You'll see him walk. You might even see him at a canter. But I promise you, you shan't see this horse move, not as he truly can move, until we've got him back home in Devonshire."

"I don't understand," she said, not for the first time. In fact, it was beginning to become a refrain.

He shook his head. "No. I'm afraid that, too, must wait for Devonshire."

The publican set two tankards on the table and retraced his steps to the bar. A small crowd filled the inn's tables and spilled onto the benches lining the side wall. Even so, the noise level remained subdued, and Colin had been relieved upon entering the place that it seemed to attract travelers rather than a rougher, local clientele. Even better, there were other women present.

He and Holly occupied a small table beneath a window that overlooked the stable yard. He would not have tarried here if he hadn't been able to monitor everyone that entered the stable, and every horse that went out.

Across from him, Holly raised her tankard but didn't drink. "How long have you known? That I was after the colt, I mean."

"I didn't know for certain until I saw you on the road. Before that, I kept telling myself my suspicions had spiraled out of control."

"And yet you moved the colt this morning."

He laughed softly as he lifted his own tankard. "There was something else that gave you away, actually, or at least heightened my reservations. Last night, you knew it was Ivy coming down the corridor to the library."

"Stupid of me, that slip." Spots of color brightened her cheeks, and for a moment she looked as she had after he'd kissed her on the road. It made him want to kiss her again. The temptation pulsed through him until heat suffused his own face, making him glad he hadn't requested a private room . . . and rather sorry, too.

He swallowed a deep draft of his ale. "And you? When did you know?"

"Victoria suspected all along and said you seemed the most obvious suspect. But until you walked the colt out onto the road earlier, I held on to the notion of your innocence."

"This must all come as a grave disappointment, then." He'd tried to sound lighthearted and unconcerned, but he hadn't quite managed it.

Her fingertip traced the grain of the wooden tabletop. "It does present a difficulty."

"You are free to turn around in the morning and return to Masterfield Park. I won't try to stop you."

She looked genuinely puzzled. "Why not? For all you know I'll go straight to the queen."

He didn't think she would. "My other alternative is to abduct you," he said. "Shall I add kidnapper to horse thief?"

Her brows knit, she leaned over the table toward him, her elbows propped on the trestle boards, her tankard suspended between her two hands. "*Why* would you do such a brazen thing as steal from the queen? How could you hope to get away with it?"

"There are times when *getting away with it* becomes a secondary consideration."

"Secondary to your future? To your family's future? What if you should be charged with treason?"

"Then I'll be stripped of my title and Bryce inherits."

"How can you be so indifferent?" She slammed the tankard down, splattering ale over the brim. She sank back against her chair and regarded him with a silent plea for a rational explanation.

He looked down into his ale, then back up at her. "Some things are more important than titles, and more important than one man's future."

"Such as what?" She held out the palm of her hand. "What can be more important? And don't tell me the answer is in Devonshire."

The innkeeper returned to place trenchers of steaming mutton stew in front of them. "Anything else, milord?"

"Have you checked on that room as I asked?"

"Aye. We've one left for the night."

"Good. Thank you."

The man tugged his forelock and sauntered away.

Holly simmered at Colin, her lips pinched, her nostrils flaring.

He pretended not to notice—he *needed* not to notice the sparks shooting at him from across the table, and the silent innuendo that gripped his loins and refused to let go. He picked up his fork and sampled a bite of his stew. "Not bad. Try some."

She went on staring, her gaze seething with questions while the notion of sharing a room with her, a bed with her, rendered his throat so dry it was all he could do to swallow chopped mutton and carrots.

"You never answered my question," she said, surprising him. He thought she'd have taken him to task for the single room he had secured for the night.

"You said not to tell you that the answer lies in Devonshire." He shrugged. "So I will say nothing."

She seized her fork as if intending to wield it like a weapon, but stabbed at her stew and not him. "I don't understand you. You stole something your father rightfully gifted to the queen, yet you refuse to offer any reasonable defense."

"My father did not—" He broke off as nearby patrons darted glances in his direction. His voice and his temper had both scampered out of his control, and that was something he didn't dare allow. There was too much yet to be accomplished, and too many people depending on him, for him to waver in his cool determination.

Besides, Holly Sutherland didn't deserve to bear the brunt of his anger, however much he sometimes needed to vent it. In a softer voice, he said, "My father did not rightfully gift the queen with anything. The colt was not his to give."

"He owns your family's estates outright, and everything on them, doesn't he?"

He reached for her hand, trapping it beneath his own. "He doesn't own the colt. No one does. Not even me."

Her skin burned like fire beneath his palm; her fingers trembled like trapped butterflies. He should have released her but he held on tighter, desperate for the slightest glimmer of understanding in her beautiful eyes, for even the most fractional lightening of the burden he'd carried since discovering the colt missing from the Devonshire herds.

But he saw only apprehension blazing in the brilliant green beneath her lashes, and he realized that he could offer explanation after explanation, and she still wouldn't understand. She couldn't, not until she walked the fields and saw the herd with her own eyes.

He eased the grip that had become tighter than he intended, and started to move his hand away. She stopped him, reaching out with her other hand and laying it on top of his. "Please promise me you're telling the truth. I want to understand, and I need to know you aren't lying. That this isn't all some bizarre trickery intended to cheat the queen and humiliate me."

All at once he saw her not as a reckless girl playing at spy work, or as an inconvenience to his already complicated venture, but as a woman with much to lose and wishing fervently to do the right thing. And he saw himself, during all these months of knowing her, and most especially in these recent days, fighting the infinite temptation she posed, struggling in vain, defeated from the first.

"I swear to you," he said, losing himself all over again in her vivid eyes and her sweet, springtime beauty, "if you can trust me a little while longer, you won't be disappointed. But you might be sorry."

"How could I be made sorry by the truth?"

"Because you'll become my accomplice. You won't intend to. Even now, you might be as strong in your resolve as ever to send the queen an accurate report and return the colt to her. But in the end, if you come with me and see all

I have to show you, you won't do that. You'll join me in treason."

Her entire body jolted in alarm, then stilled. "How can you be so certain of me?"

I couldn't love you this much if it were otherwise. Aloud he said, "The way you reacted to the colt tells me all I need to know about you." Unlinking their hands, he brought hers briefly to his lips. Then he released her and gestured at their trenchers. "Eat up, and then get some sleep. I'll be by early in the morning for you."

The alarm reclaimed her features. "You're leaving me here alone?"

"Of course I am. You didn't expect that we'd share the only bed left, did you?"

She blushed violent scarlet and darted a glance at their nearest neighbors. "I expected no such thing. I assumed you'd be a gentleman and sleep on the floor."

The urge to toss his head back and laugh nearly overwhelmed him. How long did she think he'd have lasted on the floor, with her occupying the bed right beside him, her lovely body heating the mattress, her voluptuous curves barely concealed beneath some wispy linen shift, her sweet and spicy scent beckoning to him all night long?

"You didn't think I'd leave the colt unattended all night in these stables, where any highwayman might ride off with him?"

"Oh . . . I hadn't thought of that. Where will you go?"

"There is a farm not far from here. I've lodged there before while transporting horses from one estate to another. The farmer is an honest man and I trust him. He'll be glad to accept my coin and have his boy watch the colt while I catch a few hours' rest."

She leaned forward, all eagerness. "I could come—"

"You are staying here. When I leave, everyone will see me leave, and they will see you retire upstairs alone. This way, should anyone recognize you tonight or any other night, they'll have no reason to cast stains on your reputation."

"A horse thief with honor." Her affectionate smile sent him to his feet before he changed his mind and dispensed with honor altogether. The thought stole the strength from his legs, and he gripped the back of his chair to steady himself.

"I'll see you early," he said, and exited the inn.

Chapter 18

True to his word, he came for her even before the sun peeked over the horizon. Speaking little beyond what was necessary as they broke their fast and prepared to leave the inn, Colin looked tired and tense and ragged, as ragged as Holly felt after hours of lying awake and thinking of nothing but him. Him and his strange colt and the circumstances that drew her farther from her duty to Victoria and, as he had said, into treason.

To take her mind off her misgivings, as they set off on the road, she asked him about the horse he so obviously valued above all the others—not the colt, but his own mount, Cordelier.

"You told me you considered him a 'young man's folly,' that he had presented a challenge to you. What did you mean?"

He remained silent for a long moment, so long she doubted he would answer her at all. Then he gathered a breath and raised his eyebrows. "My father wanted to sell him years ago. At the time, I didn't care who technically owned him. I'd carefully bred him, handpicked his sire and dame."

"Harvest Moon and Pilgrim's Delight," she interjected, remembering what he had told her during her tour of the stables.

"Just so. But my arguments meant nothing to my father and he insisted the horse be sold."

"Perhaps he didn't understand just how much Cordelier meant to you."

He smirked. "Oh, he understood. But you see, my family isn't like yours, Holly, or hadn't you noticed the difference?"

"I'd noticed," she said, gazing down at Maribelle's mane.

"So, as flatly as Father refused to let me keep Cordelier," he continued in a matter-of-fact tone, "I just as flatly bid him adieu, packed my bags, and returned to Cambridge. I swore I was through with the turf. Through with the whole damn business of racing."

"Did you mean it?"

"I most certainly did. Racing is a useless, self-serving endeavor that feeds no one, teaches nothing, and leads nowhere but to greed and pride. I decided my future lay entirely in the laboratory, where I might develop ways of improving agriculture and strengthening the crops and herds that *do* feed people." He laughed. "I even told my father I wanted neither the title nor the entail. To hell with them, I said. I wouldn't accept them."

Holly gasped and whisked a hand to her mouth. "What did he do?"

Colin's hand strayed to his jaw. "He hit me. A right hook to the chin."

"Good lord!"

"Split the skin. Can you see the scar?" Turning toward her, he raised his chin and pointed to the raised scar tissue. Then he shrugged. "After which I picked myself up off the floor tiles, strode up to my room, and packed my bags."

The ache in her heart prompted her to reach across the space separating them and press her hand to his shoulder. "I'm so sorry. Although something tells me you weren't quite so ready to forsake the rest of your family."

Turning, he bent his head and pressed a kiss to the backs of her fingers. "I honestly don't know what I would have done. About a month later, I received an invitation to return home, signed and sealed by Thaddeus himself. I let six weeks pass before I accepted, and when I arrived at Masterfield Park, I found Cordelier waiting right where I'd left him. Isn't that so, boy? You were happy to see me, weren't you? Or was it the sugar cubes in my pocket that made me such a welcome sight?"

"Why do you think your father changed his mind?"

"He had little choice. The truth was that he needed my knowledge, and more important, my instincts when it came to horses; he still does, because Father has none of his own."

Each day, they continued westward, riding hard until the evening shadows brought dangers to the road. Holly sensed that if Colin had been alone he would have pushed farther, perhaps reaching Devonshire in three days instead of four. For her sake he sought shelter. For her sake he delayed. But he spoke little, as if his lips were manacled by the brackets lying on either side of them, so that she didn't know if he begrudged her slowing him down or if he accepted the pace as a matter of course.

As proficient a rider as she was, and despite Maribelle's steady footing, Holly had never ridden so far in her life, and her body ached from the many hours in the saddle. Her shoulders and back, hips and thighs . . . all endured the punishment of each bumpy mile. It wasn't until halfway through the third day that her muscles suddenly relaxed and became limber, and she stopped estimating the remaining distance in terms of her discomfort.

Instead she measured the miles in terms of what she would discover in the end, and whether the close of their journey would mark the end of being close to Colin. She might no longer spend the days at his side, but she doubted that would stop her from spending the nights dreaming of him.

"How do you know her?" he asked that afternoon, just minutes after he'd informed her that they would soon stop for the night.

"Know who?"

"The queen, goose. Why are you spying for her?"

"Oh. I wondered when you would ask that question."

"And now I have."

She didn't marvel, really, that he had waited so long. Asking questions meant inviting questions, ones he obviously wasn't prepared to answer until they reached Briarview. That he could no longer contain his curiosity made her grin at him from across the space separating their mounts. "I have known Victoria nearly all my life, since before anyone guessed she would one day wear the crown. You see, my father was an officer under her father's command during the wars—"

She broke off, wondering about the truth of the story Uncle Edward had told her. In the past year, she and her sisters had discovered possible family ties to France, which could negate all they had once believed about themselves. With a shake of her head, she continued with the only truth she knew. "Victoria and her mother used to visit us at my uncle's estate, and on the day she told us she would one day be the queen of England, my sisters and I vowed we would always be her friends . . . secretly, if need be . . . always ready to serve her."

"My God . . ." He paled.

"I see I've shocked you. That does even the score somewhat."

He smiled grimly. "I'll see your horse thief and raise you one secret friend of the queen?"

"Something like that. Or three secret friends, so far. Remember when Ivy came to Cambridge dressed in trousers?"

His eyebrow rose in an arc of astonishment. "You mean she wasn't merely seeking a higher education?"

Holly flashed him a look of confirmation.

"It's damned dangerous, what Her Majesty asks of you."

"Are you saying I'm in danger now?" She tilted her chin in challenge.

He scowled. "No, but the queen doesn't know that. Ivy might have been killed last autumn."

"The queen doesn't know that either," Holly said firmly. "And she never will."

As they skirted the foothills of the Cotswolds, the countryside grew wilder and more rolling, the terrain rockier. "There is still plenty of light," she said, "and I'm not the least bit tired. We needn't stop if you'd rather press on. Colin, are you listening to me?"

He clearly wasn't. Ramrod straight in his saddle, he pricked his ears even as Cordelier did and held up a hand to silence her. He peered over his left shoulder, and then his right, and listened for another several moments, his brows knit in concentration.

A chill of foreboding swept Holly's shoulders, but she heard and saw nothing that shouldn't have been there in the miles and miles around them. Only birds and livestock and farmers with their plows. Only the half-stunted trees and clouds scudding overhead. She grew impatient, and then exasperated.

Finally, he dropped his hand to his thigh and relaxed. With a cluck he started the horses walking again.

The road before them dipped and entered the cool shade of a pine forest on either side, the branches reaching across to mesh like clasped fingers overheard. Holly welcomed the shadows. She loosened her collar and was tempted to drag her hunt cap off her head and free her hair to the cooling breeze. The nights and mornings might be temperate enough, but the days grew hot as the sun neared its zenith. Here beneath the trees she tipped her head back and let her eyes fall closed as Colin guided their direction and kept their pace.

A resounding crack broke the stillness. Holly's eyes sprang open as a tree limb split and came crashing down, spewing wood chips into the road. The horses jolted, their stride breaking. Maribelle's legs seemed to tangle as she pivoted, nearly tossing Holly from the saddle. Colin's voice echoed, sharp in her ears.

"Get down!"

Another blast rang out, and something whizzed past her face. Sulfur drifted in the air. The horses whinnied; the colt shrieked in fear. Maribelle reared up on her hind legs, then dropped down and kicked her back legs out behind her.

Holly tumbled headlong, her arms flailing, her legs caught in her twisting skirts. Sky and clouds and treetops spun in her vision. She was falling . . . falling . . . and then her hip struck the packed dirt road with a sickening oomph.

She had no time to blink away the pain. Colin's hands closed around her shoulders and hauled her to her feet. Within waves of panic an instant of clarity sent her hand lashing out. Her fingers closed around the reticule she'd hung from her saddle. She tugged the bag free just as Colin shoved her to the side of the road and dived with her into the trees.

"Quickly," he urged. "Go, go!"

On hands and knees they crawled through the underbrush, their clothes snagging, their faces whipped by weeds and trailing vines. Colin thrust Holly in front of him and half pushed her deeper into the vegetation. After they'd gone some yards the ground plunged to a narrow ravine. She would have slid down if Colin hadn't seized her about the waist.

Carefully he crawled up beside her and helped her to turn herself around. Then they lowered themselves down, lying on their stomachs on the sloping ground, their hands and chins resting on the edge, their faces turned toward the road. An unnatural stillness cloaked the forest around them.

Holly's heart pounded against her ribs. "Can you see anything?"

Colin shook his head. He rose a couple of inches and craned his neck. She could see his strained effort to control his breathing. The color had drained from his face; his lips were bloodless.

"The horses," she whispered needlessly. Surely he was as painfully aware as she that they had abandoned the horses on the road.

"Before I helped you up I gave Cordelier a good swat to set him running," he murmured back. "The others would have followed."

"What happened back there?"

He held up a hand again, first to silence her, then to indicate that she should stay put. She wanted to protest as he inched up the slope until he crouched on level ground. Wherever he intended on going, she didn't want to be left here alone. Then she remembered her reticule, which she'd dragged along the ground in her fist. Bringing the soiled satin pouch up in front of her, she opened the drawstring and reached inside.

Colin was on his feet now, and when he glanced over his shoulder at her, his eyes went wide. "Whoa. Where . . . ?"

He let the question go unfinished. She didn't meet his gaze, but stared straight ahead through the tangled underbrush, her hands wrapped around the cool grip of the handgun she'd brought.

Colin mouthed, "Stay." From his coat pocket he drew a weapon of his own, a double-barreled percussion pistol. If someone thought to continue assailing them, the scoundrel would find himself outnumbered and outsmarted. Unless . . .

There was more than one of them.

Holly swallowed and tried to stop her finger from trembling on the trigger.

Colin moved almost soundlessly through the trees. He had been right to leave her where she was, for she could never have maneuvered so quietly in her habit with its trailing train. The feather of her hat, bent and broken, sagged to tickle her cheek. She clawed the cap off her head and tossed it behind her into the ravine, then wished she hadn't when it hit the brush with a rustle that made her jump.

"I don't see anything, or anyone," Colin whispered when he returned. He crouched in front of her on level ground, the pistol hanging from his hand at his side. He switched the weapon to his left hand and reached to help her up.

He half dragged her to her knees beside him, and though she meant to be brave, meant to show him that she was made of firmer stuff than the average woman, the strength seeped from her spine and she slumped against him. Her head fell to his shoulder and she pressed her face into his collar. Her hand, the one not holding her pistol, grasped for purchase at his coat sleeve.

His arms swept around her. "I'm here. I've got you."

"Why would someone shoot at us?"

"We don't know for sure anyone did. I crept as close to the road as I dared, and didn't see or hear a soul. The shot could have been a hunter's misfire."

"So close to the road?"

"A poacher's, then. Or a drunken fool's. We simply don't know. We mustn't panic."

She heard the thud of his gun hitting the ground, and then his hands were on her, smoothing her hair, her back, rubbing up and down her arms. Setting a finger beneath her chin to lift her face, he peered down at her. Suddenly he pulled back and shed his coat. He draped the garment around her, then wrapped her in his arms again. "You aren't going to faint on me, are you?"

She shook her head against him, breathing in the reassuring starchiness of his shirt and cravat. "Of course not." Her words were slurred and unsteady, her protest a weak little thread. "At least, I'll try not to."

"Christ." He pressed his palm to her cheek, his fingers spread, the tips burrowing into her hair. He tilted her head back and then his lips were on hers, at first a gentle nuzzle that fast became insistent. He deepened the kiss until Holly's bones turned liquid and her mouth surrendered all he would take and render back with each stroke of his tongue.

His mouth slid to her cheek, and he held it there as he panted against her and gathered her closer still, her breasts melding to the contour and hollows of his chest. "Christ, I've never been so afraid. . . ."

His lips trailed downward, sliding over her chin and beneath, to her neck and the pulse in her throat. He latched on to it, suckled it, as if to draw strength, life, from its lashing beat. Perhaps only a few minutes passed; perhaps many. Holly knew only that she felt numb everywhere but where he touched her, where their bodies pressed. At some point she, too, had let her gun slip through her fingers and drop to the ground. It wasn't until Colin eased his lips away that she realized how vulnerable they were, in the middle of these lonely woods.

"We should seek shelter," she said. "And find the horses."

"Yes." His features grew taut, as if he struggled to recapture all the emotions that had escaped him in the last few moments. With a stoic expression he gained his feet and helped her to hers. "Quietly now."

She stifled a groan as a spasm radiated from her hip and shot down her thigh. She staggered slightly, and he reached for her. The stoicism slipped from his face again. "Dear God, Holly, were you hit?"

"No, no . . . I'm all right. When I fell, I struck the ground hard."

His shoulders sagged as the breath whooshed from his lungs. "I wish I'd sent you home with Geoffrey."

"Too late for that." She drew comfort from the birds gradually resuming their chatter after being silenced by the gunshots. Perhaps the danger had passed. Perhaps it merely *had* been a hunter's misfire. She managed a brave smile. "You're stuck with me."

"The only question now," he said, his voice dropping to a rumble that raised goose bumps at her nape, "is what I'm going to do with you."

His question had been one of practicality. What would he do with her; how would he continue the journey to Devonshire while ensuring Holly's safety? He had meant to sound pragmatic, not seductive, yet he saw from her shiver and the spots of color that bloomed on her cheeks that he had achieved the latter.

The truth was, with her he felt anything but pragmatic. With her he lost the control he'd honed in all the years of standing strong before his father and trying to hold his family together. With her, the honor he'd always adhered to— had *sworn* to adhere to because it was the one thing he could depend on to differentiate himself from his father— slid through his fingers like so much dust.

Damn it. They'd been shot at, had narrowly missed being hit. Holly might have *died* . . . and all he could think about was wrapping his body around hers and never letting her go. To protect her? Certainly. But how much more so to satisfy his constant craving for her sensual curves, the spicy challenge of her spirit . . .

By God, she filled him with admiration. Any other woman would have fainted dead away back on the road. But not Holly Sutherland. She'd even had the presence of mind to retrieve that deuced gun in her purse before he'd dragged her off into the protection of the trees. He might have guessed she'd have a weapon. He stooped now to retrieve both pistols, slipping his own into his coat pocket and handing hers back to her.

"Do you know how to use it? Can you shoot straight?"

Her chin came up. "Straight enough, especially at close range. I've practiced."

"I'll bet you have. Keep it at the ready. As we make our way through the trees, stay close behind me. But, Holly?"

"Yes?"

"Try not to shoot me in the back."

Her eyes shot daggers at him, and when he turned to lead the way it was with a small smile.

"Are you sure the horses will be this way?"

He nodded. "I saw their tracks on the road when I left you. Unless I'm greatly mistaken, they took off at a gallop in the direction they'd already been facing—west." At least he hoped to God that was the case.

They made their way just inside the tree line. Holly held her trailing hems over one arm and kept up admirably, though every few steps he heard a whisper of a groan. He glanced back at the determination etched on her face, but he didn't ask questions. He needed to convey her to safety, and as long as she continued to put one foot in front of the other they'd clear the area much quicker than if he carried her. Somehow he couldn't imagine her allowing that, no matter how bad the pain.

"Would the horses have dashed into the trees?" she

asked in a whisper after they'd walked for some minutes without coming upon their mounts.

He shook his head. "Not likely. Horses don't reason out the best course of action. They do the obvious, which for them means running in the open. They'll keep running until they forget their fear, and then they'll simply stop."

"I hope you're right."

They walked farther, their way hindered by underbrush, fallen branches, and rocky, uneven ground. A noise brought Colin up short, and Holly bumped into his back. He shushed her with a finger to his lips. The whicker he'd heard came again, and relief coursed through him.

"This way." In his impatience, he thrashed at the tangles blocking his path to the road, clawing at the foliage and ignoring the scratches to his hands. He broke through and stopped short, his heart plummeting to the soles of his feet. "No. Oh, God . . . no."

Holly stumbled out after him. When she reached him she braced herself with a hand on his shoulder. "What's wrong? Oh, Colin, the colt! Where is he?"

He didn't know . . . God help him . . . he didn't know. Colin staggered across the road to where Cordelier and Maribelle's Fancy stood tearing weeds from the grassy embankment. Cordelier lifted his head at Colin's approach and whickered in greeting. Bleakly, Colin grasped his bridle and leaned his forehead against the horse's neck. "Where is he, boy? Where's the colt? Please . . . don't let him be gone."

He didn't know how long he stood like that, hoping against hope that the animal would come trotting out of the woods as though nothing were wrong. Finally, Holly's scent drifted beneath his nose; she touched his arm tentatively. For her sake he raised his head and turned. Turned, but found no words. He could form no plan. The colt should have been here. Horses were herd animals, with instincts that told them to follow . . . always follow. There was no reason the colt wouldn't simply have galloped along with the other two . . . no reason . . . except for one.

"He's been taken."

"By whom?" she asked. "Who could have known about him?"

From within the eddies of panic, Colin noted Holly's pallor, the sheen of perspiration across her forehead that signified the effort she had expended tramping through the woods. Her lips were thinned and her features tight with pain, her breathing shallow and labored.

Even if he had been resolved to search every damned inch of forest and open countryside beyond—as if that would have done any good—the sight of Holly would have changed his mind. She might need a doctor. She might be hurt worse than she'd initially thought. Sometimes people appeared hardly injured at all, while inside they bled. . . .

Opposing obligations threatened to rend him in two, as if the tenants and villagers of Briarview had him by one arm while his feelings for this woman gripped his other. All along he'd been desperate to return the colt to Devonshire, yet that desperation paled beside his need to see her safe.

A strange calm came over him, that of a defeated man with nothing left to lose. With one hand still gripping Cordelier's bridle, he hooked his other arm around Holly's neck and drew her to him. It was a moment of weakness, just as when he'd kissed her in the woods. Her cheek touched his shoulder and he held her there for strength, for courage. He drew a fortifying breath that filled him with her very essence. Then he released her and drew himself up. The colt was gone. Holly might still be in danger. Those were the realities he must deal with now.

"Do you think you can ride?"

She blinked at having been released so abruptly, but recovered quickly enough and showed him her bravest face. "I can ride. But what about the colt? Surely we can't leave without him."

"It is he who has left without us." He shook his head, still disbelieving. "It's in God's hands now. It's all in God's hands."

She searched his face. "You make it sound like the world might end."

"No. Only a small part of it." He drew a breath laden with the scents of the forest, of leaves and timber and loam, fresh and rich. He took her face in his hands and sighed. "A small but beloved part of it."

He boosted her into her saddle and helped her arrange her skirts when her own attempts to do so made her wince. Then he swung up onto Cordelier's back. "There's a village some five or six miles from here, I believe. Can you make it that far?"

"Stop treating me as though I might break," she said sharply. Her features smoothed. "I'm sorry. That was uncalled for. I'm sore, but I'll ride as far as I must. All the way to Devonshire, if you wish."

He shook his head. "There's no longer any reason to rush."

They started down the road, Colin's senses on the alert. When they spoke, it was in subdued tones. Unwilling to take any chances, he rode with his pistol in his hand, resting on his thigh. His gaze darted back and forth, sometimes over his shoulder. He noticed Holly doing the same. The sun dipped beneath the horizon, blackening the silhouettes of the trees against the sky. Colin willed the village to be closer than he knew it to be.

He gestured at Holly with his chin. "Where's your weapon?"

"Where I can get it if I need it." She held up her drawstring purse, the cords wrapped around her wrist.

"I recognize that gun. The damned thing is more dangerous than you realize. It's only a prototype, not meant to be put to use. There's no telling how it might misfire. It could explode in your hand."

She flashed him an exasperated look. "Thank you ever so much for the reassurance. Are you always so optimistic?"

He smiled grimly. "It's not every day you have your life snatched out from under you."

"Your life?" She tilted her head, contemplating him in a manner that made him wish he could retract that last comment. "The colt represents more than a breeder's attempt to rear a champion racehorse," she said more accurately than she knew. "Or a scientist's endeavor to cultivate a species' best traits."

"Far, far more," he said softly. "But don't ask me more—"

"Until we reach Devonshire," she finished for him, and he nodded.

He raised a hand to point. "I see lights up ahead. We've reached the village." *Thank God.*

"I suppose you'll be spending the night with one of your network of willing farmers while I stay at the coaching inn?"

"We're not staying here tonight." He smiled at her surprise. "We're going to hire a carriage, tie our mounts on lead ropes behind it, and continue on to a safe place I know."

Questions creased her brow. It had been no slip of the tongue that he'd spoken of a safe place in the singular. They would not spend this night separately, as they had done on the previous nights. After the danger they'd faced today, he wouldn't risk leaving her alone.

But he knew well enough that spending the long, empty hours together would pose dangers of a different sort, and he didn't know how he'd protect her from those.

Chapter 19

After traveling nearly two hours in the carriage that Colin had hired for the remainder of the journey, Holly's joints protested at the slightest movement despite his obvious efforts to provide a smooth ride.

Under the intermittent light of a cloud-choked moon, they turned onto a narrow drive shrouded in tall pines revealed by the carriage lights swinging from the corners of the vehicle. When the trees fell away, the drive curved in front of a sprawling structure whose stone and stucco facade trimmed in slanting timbers suggested a cottage, but whose size suggested something more. Holly made out no formal gardens; few attempts had been made to torture nature into the geometric designs that surrounded most manor houses.

No lights brightened the windows behind their curtains. The front door appeared locked up tight, and not a sound disturbed the night but those of crickets and owls and the wind. Colin stopped the carriage and hopped down, quickly circling to Holly's side to help her down.

"Where are we? What is this place?"

"My father's hunting lodge, on the edge of Devon."

"Oh, then we must be close to your home."

"Another two or three hours, depending on the weather," he said. Then, as though reading her mind, he added, "I thought you could use a rest from traveling. The place is empty but for the couple who keeps the house and grounds. We'll be safe for the night, and can push on to Briarview in the morning."

Reaching onto the rear seat, he opened his valise and fished out a set of keys. Then he took Holly's hand and brought her up the few steps to the front door.

Inside, the air hung heavy with the pungent aromas of leather and books and tobacco, a thoroughly masculine essence that led Holly to guess that, besides the housekeeper, females were rarely if ever admitted here. Colin led her through a doorway off the foyer. Ghostly sheets draped the furniture. He dragged one off a settee.

"Sit," he commanded in a tone that brooked no debate. His large hands settled on her shoulders, spreading warmth through her. Her sudden shakiness had nothing to do with her earlier fall. She sank to the cushions as he gently urged her down. Then he bent to grasp her booted ankles. Turning her, he lifted her legs and propped them on the sofa cushion. Then he struck a match he retrieved from the mantel and lit a nearby lamp.

"Make yourself comfortable," he said unnecessarily, and retreated to the foyer. "I'm going below to let the Fulsomes know we're here. I'm sure Mrs. Fulsome can scavenge up something for us to eat."

"Tell her not to go to any trouble."

As she inspected her surroundings, she assumed this to be a drawing room, but the lamplight revealed strange, shadowed images looming just beyond its boundaries— exotic, startling shapes one would never have found in any civilized drawing room. The ticking of the mantel clock drew her attention first to a tapering snout, wide antlers, and the empty, glassy-eyed stare of a stag's head mounted above the fireplace. She flinched as other animals took shape, their glass eyes glinting at her in the darkness. A hare, a raccoon, a goose and—oh!—a wolf, posed as if stalking its prey.

Repulsed, Holly pressed deeper into the cushions. All these glorious creatures brought down, not to feed a family, but to the ignominious fate of being stuffed and mounted to satisfy a man's pride. Her gaze darted back to the stag's head, and images flashed in her mind. The duchess's bruised wrist ... Bryce's scarred hands ... Sabrina's bravado ... Geoffrey's timidity ...

Colin's rebellion, first against his father and now against his queen. Her heart wrenched painfully as the truth stared blatantly back at her from the buck's empty, spiritless stare.

She pressed to her feet, falling back when pain flared in her hip. She gripped the arm of the settee and, sucking in a fortifying breath, tried again. Ignoring the spasms, she made her way to the foyer and went to the front door. She grasped the latch, was about to throw the door wide when a voice behind her stopped her short.

"The horses are stabled and Mrs. Fulsome is warming a meat pie for us. Where do you think you're going?"

In a burst of defiance she whipped around. "I can't stay here. I won't."

"What are you talking about?" As though she were a cornered rabbit and he feared frightening her away, Colin approached her slowly. "The Fulsomes are trustworthy and there is no one here to recognize you. No one to go telling tales."

"I don't care about that. This place ... it's horrible. It's ..." She clamped her lips shut.

"It is my father's special lair," he said quietly, "but he's far away now. He can't bother us."

"Oh God, Colin," she whispered. "He's a very bad man, isn't he? He hurt you ... all of you."

He barely reacted, but the slight flaring of his nostrils and the clenching of his jaw told all. Until that moment she had hoped she was wrong, but she had guessed so horribly right, and now everything about this contrary family made sense. A pang gripped her heart as Colin momentarily bowed his head and shut his eyes. His stance remained determined and strong, and she saw how steadfastly he had shouldered the burden of holding his family together through the years, how bravely he had born the responsibility.

Surely even Simon de Burgh, his best friend, didn't know these most intimate and awful secrets about the Ashworths' lives. Surely if he had, Ivy would have known, too, but she had never given the slightest indication.

The thought of Colin's silent suffering sent Holly to him, her arms opening as she drew near. "I'm sorry. So sorry."

"No." He held up his hands as if to stop her, but then his arms went around her, seeking purchase, his forehead sinking to her shoulder and his face pressing to the curve of her neck. His lips, moist and parted, trembled against her skin.

"He doesn't give a damn," he said softly. "Not about his wife. Not about his children. He cares only for his cursed, malicious self." His hands sliding to her shoulders, he lifted his head, his eyes fierce, filled with the angry pain of an injured wolf. "How did you know? I know I told you he hit me, but fathers and sons often come to blows at some point in their lives."

"Everything I've seen and heard these past several days. And then—that." She thrust a finger toward Thaddeus Ashworth's macabre drawing room.

"Ah, yes." Colin's laughter echoed bleakly in the silent hallway. Releasing her, he turned half away to stare through the arched doorway. "That is essentially what he does to everyone and everything he touches. We are each of us his victim and his prize, to be stripped of spirit and hung on the wall for his friends to admire."

"Not you," she said emphatically. "Not Sabrina."

He shoved his fingers through his hair. "Me and Sabrina most of all. We're the special ones, you see—the heir and the only girl. Growing up, we constantly attracted his notice. He'd grow bored with Bryce and Geoff because they so rarely dared to oppose him, but Sabrina and I presented a challenge he couldn't resist, like that wolf in there. My father tracked that wolf for days before he put a bullet through its back, and straight into its heart."

He strode to the doorway and raised an arm to brace himself against the woodwork. "He's a great hunter, my father, an expert marksman. Invited by the past two kings every year to stalk with them in the royal forests. Of course, all that's changed now. The queen doesn't hold hunting parties, not like in the old days. And so Father found it necessary to court favor in an entirely new way."

Holly went to his side. "The colt. That's why he gave it to her, to curry her favor."

"He took something that didn't belong to him, something he could never understand if he tried for the whole of his ungodly life. And he simply gave it away, as if it were of no account, meant nothing."

"Couldn't you simply have gone to Victoria and—"

"And what?" His vehemence made her jump. "Tell her what? That this colt, most assuredly not a Thoroughbred despite its appearance, possesses qualities that no one, not even I, can come close to grasping? And because of that, she must give it back?"

Holly's shoulders sagged and she tucked her chin low. "No, I don't suppose she would have accepted that."

"And now it's gone." He released the doorframe and fisted both hands in his hair. "It's gone and I don't know how the bloody blazes to get it back. There'll be the devil to pay for it."

"I'm sorry," she whispered, her voice barely audible because even as she spoke, she dreaded admitting the truth. "It's my fault. If I hadn't followed you . . ."

"No." He reached for her and drew her close. "You're not to blame. You couldn't have known. I should have been brave enough to take you into my confidence back in Masterfield Park."

"Why didn't you? Have you always mistrusted me? I know you never cared for me, not as you cared for my sisters."

His sardonic chuckle vibrated into her. "Is that what you think?"

"It is what I *know*, the simple truth. You needn't spare my feelings."

His strong arms fell away from around her. Then his hands came up and seized her face. "The only thing I ever wished to spare you from was the reality of my ill-fated family, my fiend of a father. Do you think I'd ever let him near you, let him treat you as he's treated the rest of us? Good God, I'd die first. I'd see him dead first."

Her heart thundered inside her. Her throat and eyes throbbed with tears. "You were protecting me? All this time, when I believed you indifferent?"

He held her closer, his fingers burrowing through her hair and pulling it free of its pins. "As if any man could be indifferent to such a woman. A brave, bold woman who defies convention and meets life head-on, astride and with a pistol in her purse."

"I rode sidesaddle when I followed you," she reminded him around a sob.

"You did at that, and still you caught up to me, warrior that you are."

The world stood still as he bent his head, bringing the scent of his skin to swirl through her, his heat to warm her, the softness of his lips to melt over hers . . . melt and reshape and move, as molten rock moves over the earth, forming itself to the very landscape it conquers.

His arm hooked beneath her knees and all at once he swung her up off her feet. With her arms around his neck, their lips pressed and their tongues tangling, he carried her up the stairs.

Wrong. A mistake. Go back.

You have sworn . . .

His conscience railing at him, Colin cleared the top step with Holly secure in his arms. The first door he came to as he crossed the landing he soundly ignored, as he ignored the logic that shouted at him to return to the foyer below.

That first bedroom belonged to his father, and he would never take Holly in there. Colin had no permanent bedchamber in this house, but he strode to the guestroom he'd used in the past. The bed, curtained in heavy brocade and covered in supple satin, beckoned like a night-darkened glen dripping in foliage and draped in vines.

He moved past it and went instead to the window.

Letting Holly's feet slide to the floor, he kept one arm solidly around her waist while he flung the curtains wide. Cloud-dappled moonlight spilled into the room, gilding her milky skin and transforming her eyes to emerald-tinged stars. Those eyes . . .

Shimmered with emotion, and communicated the very gift he longed to see.

Downstairs, he had almost confessed all, almost told her he loved her and had from the very first. Now, seeing her glowing like a moon goddess with her lips parted and her heart in her eyes, he almost spoke those words.

Instead he expelled a long sigh that stirred the fallen tendrils beside her face. He swept his fingers through her hair again, filling his hands with an immeasurable treasure of rare crimson gold. "By God, you're beautiful."

A shadow dimmed her eyes, and he remembered that in their society, redheads were not accustomed to being considered beautiful. That she could think of herself as anything less than a goddess cast a pall over his own pleasure in having her in his arms. He couldn't bear it; he wouldn't have it.

Their time together would be too short for such misgivings.

"You are beautiful and I'll prove it to you," he said, as if she had demurred out loud.

He kissed her and swept his tongue into her mouth when her lips opened to him. Spurred by the unleashing of a passion too long held in check, he moved his hands over her, everywhere, seeking out her most feminine places, learning every curve and line of her through her clothing, while she panted into him and yielded her body against his. He filled his hands with the weight of her breasts, then claimed her hips and belly and buttocks. Trembling, all awareness of time and place lost to the rushing, aching heat that drove him, he bunched her trailing skirts in his fist and raised them.

She gave a desperate whimper, and he stilled his hands

while his heart shook his rib cage. The sound spilled through her lips again, but with it came a *yes*. She tightened her arms around him.

He swept her up again. This time he went to the bed and tossed her lengthwise into the pool of moonlight slanting across the coverlet. Crawling up over her, he braced his hands on either side of her face and dipped his lips to her smooth neck. Between kisses, he spoke her name.

"Holly?" It was a question, an appeal for permission, and it contained more vulnerability than he had dared express in many years.

"Yes," she repeated that single syllable, assuring him she knew as well as he why they were there, and what would follow.

Yes. Oh God, yes. His body responded with a surge of lust that strained his cock against his breeches. Whisking open the buttons of her riding jacket, he shoved its edges aside and dropped his face to her bodice, burying his nose and lips in sultry flesh. Tantalizing, spicy, her essence spiraled through him and made him tipsy with pleasure. He sat up and tore his coat from his arms. He ripped his neckcloth free. Without untying the laces, tugged his shirt over his head and tossed it away.

Raising her up to a sitting position, he went to work on the buttons down the back of her dress. Soon her bodice had joined the growing pile on the floor. She herself reached for the ties that held her skirts in place.

His conscience nudged, and he closed his hand over hers. "You should tell me to go to the devil."

The sudden swat to the side of his head not only startled him, but smarted, too. She grabbed his shoulders and pulled him to her, nose to nose. "If you wish to go to the devil," she said fiercely, angrily, "then go. Don't put it on me."

"I only meant . . ."

She shook her head. "No. You must do as you wish. Be here with me, now, because you wish to be. It is the only reason I am here." A fiery tendril slid into her face. She blew it back, and suddenly her vehemence faded and the vulnerability of a girl, a virtuous, untouched girl, peeped through. "I am here," she whispered, "doing as I have never done before because . . ."

"Why, dear heart? Why now?"

"Because of you," she said simply, the quiver in her voice resonating like the pluck of a harp. "And I will not take it back."

"Nor will I." No, were he granted one wish, it would be to change his life, his family, his father . . . his legacy. But to wish himself elsewhere but in that room and on that bed, gazing into the eyes of this one woman—*that* he would not have changed for all the priceless colts in the world.

For tonight, he would cease to be the Earl of Drayton, heir to the Duke of Masterfield. He'd merely be a man, with the world's most desirable goddess sprawled lushly beneath him, her body warm and welcoming, her eyes misty with desire and consent. The tenderness on her face made him feel good enough, blameless enough, for the first time in his life. Whatever else they would share, she had already bestowed a rare gift, the greatest possible gift.

"Nothing else exists tonight." His lips to her ear, his teeth nipped at the tender lobe. "We won't think of this as my father's house. We aren't in a house at all, but on a cloud just beneath heaven."

"And no one can hurt us or judge us or hinder us."

"That's right, dearest heart." He slid her loosened skirts down her long, slim legs. Crawling back up to her side, he kissed a trail from her chin down her throat to the swell of her breasts at the neckline of her chemise. "We're free."

Her hands ran through his hair. She locked her fingers behind his head and pressed him more fully to her bosom. "Free to rule ourselves."

"And our desires."

Her nipples, dark beneath the sheer muslin covering them, beckoned. Through the fabric he kissed each one, his lips demanding and taking more as she pressed higher, pushing her firm breasts into his mouth in the most innocently seductive way. His groin tightened, and the exquisite pain served as a reminder of the boundaries that must be set.

There were many ways to satisfy pleasure. Tonight he would be the teacher and she the student. Cut off from the entire world around them, the bed would be their secret classroom.

He lifted himself off her again. Sliding her chemise upward along those endlessly silky legs, he regarded her with a half smile, then considered her boots and stockings.

"Hmm. On . . . or off?" He ran a finger from the toe of her boot to the tasseled cuff that hugged her shapely calf. His finger wiggled inside an inch or two, causing her to squirm and stifle a laugh in her hands. "Ticklish?"

"No!" she said too quickly.

His smile widened. Removing his finger from her boot, he ran both palms up her stockinged legs to the tops of her knees. As he reached the toned swell of her thighs, he stopped. "Ah, what riding has done to this body." He squeezed her thighs gently, and she gave a squeal.

"Don't!"

"Too late, my dear. Your secret's out." Bending low, he kissed her belly through her chemise. "Holly Sutherland has a weakness, and I intend to work it to my full advantage. Now then, the boots and stockings . . . I do believe we'll keep them, for now."

Showing her the wickedness of his intentions with a rakish grin, he sat up, grasped her knees, bent them, and spread them gently. He settled his length over her, snug in the cradle of her thighs. He nuzzled her neck. "Tell me what you like."

"I don't know . . ." Her head tipped back. "Oh, I like *that*."

He had opened his mouth to suckle her skin, and now he put more effort into the endeavor until he had her squirming again, this time in earnest. He settled his palm over her breast, rubbing his thumb back and forth across the nipple. "What else?"

"Oh, *that*."

At her low moan, he stopped to raise her chemise higher and tunnel his hand beneath until nothing lay between his fingers and her body. Then he resumed his ministrations, making sure he didn't neglect either breast.

Through her purrs of pleasure, a question emerged. "What for you? What do you like?"

In reply, he grasped her hand where it lay clenched on the coverlet. He kissed it, then brought it to his chest, opening her palm flat against him and smoothing it across his pectoral muscles. She needed no more coaxing, but set about exploring eagerly, each warm touch raising heated shivers that shot straight to his groin. When her hand strayed lower, following the trail of his chest hair to where it became a narrow line down his belly, he nearly lost his fragile control.

His hand closed over her wrist, stopping her while he sucked air into his lungs and reestablished his strength of will. Ever bold, ever reckless, she tugged free and continued onward . . . downward.

"I don't know much," she murmured, "but I believe I can safely assume this . . ."

Her hand cupped him at the juncture of his breeches, her fingertips searching, testing, and then it was him writhing and moaning. No longer the teacher, nor even the student, he became a mindless supplicant in bliss, willing to do anything, say anything, to keep her hand precisely where it was.

Unless . . . it was to slide lower, against his bare skin.

He grasped her wrist again, and quickly eased off her.

Her brow puckered. "Did I do something wrong?"

"Oh, no, dear heart. You did it too, too right."

"In that case—"

He shook his head. "It is a matter of honor." At her crestfallen expression, he grinned. "Ladies first."

Perching between her still raised knees, he tossed the hem of her chemise high to expose her booted legs, her contoured thighs, her flat belly, and those luscious breasts, the nipples tipped and reddened and staring temptingly up at him.

With that, he parted her thighs wider and let his tongue guide his way between them.

Holly jolted at the first moist touch against her nether lips. Was that ... good heavens. His *tongue ... touching* her ... *there*. The shock of it radiated outward from that most intimate place to the very tips of her fingers and toes. Her head came off the mattress.

"I ... oh ... but ..."

He smoothly released one of her thighs, reached up to lightly grasp her chin, and pressed her head back down. Against her female regions, he uttered, "Shush," and "Relax," the vibrations of his lips sending more of those delicious currents through her.

Still, a scorching blush burned her cheeks at the thought of her position, his actions, the sight they must present. But then, oh, his tongue swirled and probed and speared, and her thoughts and qualms dissolved. She felt her body lifting, melting, heating, and she was consumed by a craving for more, ever more, only more of *this*—what Colin was doing to her—while nothing else mattered. Nothing.

Whimpers filled her ears, and she realized they were her own, rubbing her throat raw. Pleasure, hovering all around her, made her strain and arch, while Colin's mouth never left her, never stopped carrying her along a crest of pleasure she could not have imagined. As his lips suckled a place that seemed connected to her very core, her soul, she felt the sudden pressure of a finger pushing inside her, then a gentle withdrawal, and a reentering, this time wider, the width of two fingers.

She clutched at the coverlet, her entire being centered on the twist of fear and pleasure building inside her as Colin worked his fingers, spreading her wider. Suddenly a spasm gripped her, shook her. Another and another followed, until nothing else existed but the shuddering contractions of her womb, the booming of her heart, and her cries of ecstasy.

Before her body stilled, Colin was beside her, his lips

Allison Chase

pressed to her temple, his arm anchored tightly around her. His hand continued to cup her nether regions, pressing, gently massaging while her body quivered, shuddered again, and finally drifted back to earth. When she could finally open her eyes, it was to see him staring down at her, his own eyes filled with understanding and satisfaction and . . . a tender entreaty.

Her body still tingling, she laid her palm against his cheek. "It is the gentleman's turn now, if he'll be so kind as to advise me."

"It's all right if you don't wish . . ."

As she drew back with a warning expression, he fell silent, covered her hand with his own, and slid it down the length of his body. At his waistband, he released her and opened the buttons at one side of his trouser flap. It was enough to admit her, enough for him to fall free against her palm, to fill her hand with the solid, heated weight of his shaft.

She tried to stifle a gasp at the startling sensation, but he heard it and smiled so endearingly that she felt no embarrassment, only wonderment at this part of him, as substantial and unyielding as the rest of him. Her heart fluttered and swelled. But instead of speaking, she put every bit of what she felt into the rhythm of her hand, then both hands. She watched his face as his eyes fell closed, as a groan rumbled out of him. As the throes of passion claimed him, she couldn't look away from the chiseled beauty of his taut mouth, the tortured planes of his cheeks and brow, the hard press of his eyelids. Faster and harder she stroked him. His corded neck pulsed, his nostrils flared.

Then, just as she had done, he arched his back and thrust his fists into the mattress. His mouth fell open, and his groan became a roar. One hand lifted from the bed, found her thigh, and settled again between her legs. Her body responded with an echo of the pleasure he'd given her. With his shaft pulsing between her fingers, the power she held over him at that moment rushed through her like a stormy gale. She closed her eyes and let the potency of the act wash over and through her, and for a blessed instant she felt him to be part of her, joined in spirit: one mind, one intent, one great, billowing release.

Her small cry blended with his rumbles. Then he gathered her against his chest, held her and kissed her until their hearts ceased their mutual thumping.

As she lay nestled against him, her cheek resting in the hollow of his shoulder, she stared into the unfamiliar shadows and felt at home. She marveled at how high they had soared together, how heedlessly they had circled heaven and earth. And then she marveled all over again as she realized that through it all, she had remained a virgin.

Of sorts.

Chapter 20

Warm in the afterglow of their lovemaking, Colin lay against the pillows, one arm bent beneath his head. Holly lay quietly on top of him, though he could tell by her occasional movements that she wasn't asleep. His other arm draping her, he stroked her hair and absently twined a curl around his finger. "Did it frighten you, what we just did?"

She shook her head against him. "Not at all."

"Did you know about it?"

Her cheek moved softly against him as she nodded. "Generally speaking, yes," she said, and then added somewhat indignantly, "I grew up with servants, too, you know."

"What the devil does that mean?"

"It means that little girls press their ears to doors and hear conversations they shouldn't, as much as little boys do. Our scullion and laundress loved to trade stories. If Uncle Edward had ever found out, he'd have sacked them instantly."

"Ah." The notion of a much younger, saucer-eyed Holly pressing her ear to a door made him tighten his arm around her. "Tell me, what else do little girls do?"

"I don't know anymore about little girls, but . . ."

Her voice trailed off and her hands took over, accompanied by her lips, conveying exactly what it was about him that most fascinated her. Gently but boldly, she explored his shoulders, arms, and chest, touching, kissing, occasionally tasting until his muscles quivered, his skin burned, and his loins ached to take her—truly take her in the one way he had not.

In the back of his mind caution and logic spoke their piece. He didn't listen. Not tonight, not here, where he found himself blessedly free from his family, his father, society, and even missing colts. Tonight none of those burdens dangled from around his neck; he wouldn't allow it. He'd be what he wanted, *do* as he wanted. For tonight, he very much wished to continue testing the boundaries of pleasure with this extraordinary woman.

His groin tightening maddeningly, he rolled until she lay beneath him, and set about eliciting fresh moans and the occasional squeal, and replying in kind with groans and oaths murmured beneath his panting breath. Sometime in the early hours of the morning, they both fell into an exhausted, satiated sleep.

As he knew it would, the rising sun brought back all the harsh truths the night had concealed. As the first rays speared through the curtains he'd left gaping, he scrubbed a hand across his eyes, eased away from Holly, and struggled into his clothes. He chose another bedchamber at random and rumpled the covers to make the bed appear slept in. Last night he had temporarily donned clothes and gone belowstairs to collect the meal Mrs. Fulsome had prepared for them. He felt fairly certain neither the woman nor her husband had found any reason to climb all the way up to the second floor.

He went belowstairs again now and ordered breakfast brought up to Holly. Then he helped Mr. Fulsome hitch the hired horses to the carriage, with Cordelier and Maribelle tied behind. When the task was done, Colin lingered in the stable yard.

How on earth would he return to Briarview without the colt? How would he reassure a populace raised on superstition that the loss of the colt—a theft within a theft—would not destroy their lives? How would he convince them he would find the animal when he had no idea how or where to begin searching?

And how—God help him, *how*—would he set Holly free, as he must, without hurting her in the worst possible way? No, not the worst, for he had maintained at least that much control. They had indeed crossed a line last night, a splendid, glorious line, but he hadn't ruined her. Not in the truest sense. Holly Sutherland could go on to meet and marry a suitable gentleman, one who didn't have a horror of a father or a family mired in unhappiness; one who hadn't had to resort to horse thievery in a vain attempt to hold his world together.

Hands thrust in his coat pockets, he rearranged the lines of his face, clearing away the grimness before turning to head back into the house. A good thing, too, for as he glanced up he saw her peeking down at him from her bedchamber window. She raised one graceful hand, and when he thought she would wave, she instead smiled and touched her fingertips to her lips.

Yes, his lips still tingled from their kisses, from the sweet and tangy taste of her skin.

However wrong of him, last night had provided a badly needed respite, a rare taste of normalcy, and a brief but precious sampling of what other men took for granted. Ah, in truth it had been so much more than that. But he didn't dare dwell on what a night spent holding Holly Sutherland in his arms had meant to him.

He smiled up at her, then continued into the house. Why make these next, last hours together as bleak as they could possibly be? She'd done nothing wrong; it wasn't her fault he couldn't offer her what a gentlewoman had every right to expect . . . what she deserved. But once they reached Devonshire, he'd be leaving her almost immediately. After gathering a search party of trusted men, he intended riding out to find the colt.

If indeed the colt was anywhere to be found.

Holly met him at the top of the stairs, fully dressed. "I insist we ride today," she said in lieu of a proper greeting. "Have Mr. Fulsome arrange to have the carriage returned. We'll make better time on Cordelier and Maribelle."

He fought the urge to take her into his arms. Instead, he stood over her and mustered a stern, no-nonsense look. "You were hurt when you fell yesterday. We'll travel by carriage."

After a quick glance down the staircase, she tipped her chin and flashed him an irrepressible grin. "In case you hadn't noticed, my injuries didn't prevent me from achieving some highly acrobatic feats last night."

Against his better sense, his arms spanned her waist. "I don't wish to take any chances."

"Then leave me here while you search for the colt. You can't afford to lose so much time. Already he could be miles away."

He had considered that very strategy, but he'd deemed this house with its two elderly custodians as not nearly safe enough. The colt's disappearance shed doubts that those shots yesterday had resulted from a badly aimed hunting rifle. But whether highwayman or poacher, if the villain showed up here, the Fulsomes could provide little protection. At least Briarview boasted a house full of servants, including a footman or two versed in the firing of weapons.

She was right, though. They could travel much faster on horseback. He held her cheeks between his palms. "Are you certain you're not hurting?"

"Watch me." She eased out of his hold and performed a nimble pirouette. "If anything, I'll stiffen up if I'm confined to a bumpy carriage seat all day. In fact, Simon's research in muscular regeneration suggests that motion, rather than rest—"

"I give up." With a laugh, Colin held up a hand. "I can't possibly out-argue you, not if you're going to quote Simon de Burgh at me. We'll untie the horses from the carriage and be off. But you're to say something at the first uncomfortable twinge. Promise me."

She walked back into his arms. "I promise."

"Why does that do so little to reassure me?" He scowled as he gave in to temptation and kissed her. In many ways he was grateful for her insistence on traveling by horseback, for now there would be no close proximity on an enclosed carriage seat to tempt him further.

As she predicted, they made good time and entered the village of Briarview by midmorning. On a ridge two miles to the north, Briarview Manor, the Ashworths' ancestral home, glared down like an exacting patriarch at the small collection of farms, cottages, and tiny, rickety shops as if to admonish such underlings to know their place and heed their betters.

Colin felt no joy at this homecoming. On the contrary, his misgivings mounted as, on both sides of the road, the effects of the "Exmoor curse" became more and more apparent.

The fields that had flooded weeks ago had not been replanted, and the surrounding moors threatened to encroach on the cultivated land. The barn roof that had fallen in had not been replaced. Worse, he saw sure signs that all but the most basic labors had ceased. Farming and herding beyond what the inhabitants required for their own survival, as well as local business and trade, seemed to have come to a screeching halt because these people, most of whom could trace their families to this wild, craggy land for centuries back, believed their efforts were cursed.

An unnerving quiet permeated the air. No clangs of the hammer rang out from the smithy. No pungent tanning fumes clashed with savory aromas from the Dancing Mare Tavern. The only scents Colin could make out were those of rotting crops and general decay, oddly mingled with fresh wisps of the heather clinging to the surrounding hills.

The first nudges of true fear crept up his spine. Was he too late to reverse a self-fulfilling prophesy?

"What's wrong with this place?" Holly asked in a whisper.

He had opened his mouth to reply when he noticed the faces peering at them from either side of the road, gaunt silhouettes gathered in the windows of cottages and shops. As they passed the greengrocer, the shop door opened. The proprietor, a bull-faced man named Harper, stood in the doorway and gazed out without any trace of the deference Colin had been used to receiving from these villagers. Another door opened, and then several. In every case, men, women, and children spilled onto front stoops and stared, their fears and worries evident in the shadows beneath their eyes.

"What is this?" Holly whispered again. "What does this mean?"

"The colt," he whispered back. "They are the reason it must be returned."

"What can a colt have to do with—"

A shout pierced the air. "Where is it? Where's the Exmoor? By God, what have ya done with 'im?"

"The Exmoor?" Holly twisted round in her saddle to view the stout farmer wearing rough woolens and threadbare corduroy. "What is he talking about?"

A chorus of disgruntled voices joined in the jeering; a forest of fists waved in the air. When something—perhaps a packed ball of dirt, perhaps a small rock—sailed across the road and thudded to the ground close enough to make Maribelle stumble, Colin tapped his heels to Cordelier's sides.

Both horses broke into a canter, a pace Colin didn't break until they reached the gates of the manor. There they were forced to stop and wait for the gates to be opened, and Colin tossed many a cautious glance over his shoulder to see if they'd been followed. An indignant frown creased Holly's brow, and she looked as though she were practically choking on the questions she longed to ask. Colin guessed that only the gatekeeper's presence checked her tongue.

"Thank you, Oliver," Colin said to the man as they turned onto the drive.

"Milord." Oliver Long, a burly man somewhere in his fifties whose father and grandfather had also occupied positions on the estate, dragged his cap off his head. But he didn't smile or offer the enthusiastic greeting Colin had come to expect from him over the years. He didn't ask after Colin's health, or inquire after the rest of the family. He didn't relate the latest news, as he'd always done after one of Colin's absences. Except for an initial glance, Oliver kept his eyes averted, his thoughts shielded by the sooty sweep of his lashes.

They moved past him, past the stone gatehouse and upward along the open expanse of drive. Before them, the home's austere facade looked out over fields and moors, and down at the village behind them, its stone and thatch structures reduced by the distance to a collection of insignificant dots.

Holly brought Maribelle to a halt. A few yards ahead of her, Colin also stopped and wheeled Cordelier around. "What?" he asked, but by the look on her face, he already knew what she would say.

He was not surprised, then, when her chin came up and her delicate eyebrows arched. "I'm not budging another inch until you explain what the blazes is going on here."

"No more putting it off." Holly injected into her tone an obstinacy she hoped would intimidate the truth from him. But she nearly laughed at the thought of anyone ever intimidating Colin Ashworth. The very way he sat his horse, tall and proud, his strong profile etched against the stark noonday sky, declared him a nobleman very much in command of his world and his fate.

Oh, but not completely so, she remembered. What happened in the village had momentarily shaken his authority; she had seen the crumbling of his confidence, however briefly, in the dimming of his blue eyes, usually so bright and sharp. In that moment she had sensed that the loss of the colt had stripped him of whatever plan he had devised, and that presently he steered his course one small step at a time.

She moved Maribelle up alongside Cordelier and reached to place her hand on Colin's wrist. "You need help, and I am here."

Heightened color suffused his face. His fingers tensed, but his hand didn't move to clasp hers. "Do you know what an Exmoor pony is?"

"I've read about them." She glanced up at the granite

facade of the house, catching the flick of a curtain up on the first floor. She couldn't see in, but she felt certain a gaze met hers. Then the curtain fell back in place. A servant? Puzzled, she returned her attention to Colin's question. "An ancient breed, England's purest native pony. Surely the colt isn't—"

"The colt *is*. Partly, at least. We have a herd of Exmoors on our land here, and for years I've been crossing ponies with Thoroughbreds."

"But why?"

"The Exmoor is one of the hardiest breeds on earth, resistant to many of the diseases that strike other horses. The Thoroughbred, despite its speed and power, is far more fragile in comparison. Have you any idea how many are injured in the races and must be put down each year?" When she shook her head, he didn't elaborate. "So I'd thought . . ." He broke off, thumb and forefinger pinching the bridge of his nose.

"You thought to create a super breed. But the Jockey Club would never allow it. All racehorses must be descendants of those three original Arabians. I forget their names."

"Darley, Godolphin, and Byerley Turk. And the colt *is* a direct descendant of Byerley Turk. Thoroughbreds themselves were created by crossbreeding those stallions with native Galloway mares. My experiments were meant to show the value of introducing new, hardier stock into the existing breed, but in infinitesimal amounts. The colt, you see, was the result of several generations of crossbreeding, with the Exmoor element having been added early on and not again. For all intents and purposes, he is a Thoroughbred, with a residual strain of Exmoor in his blood, but not at all evident in his physical traits."

Holly paid close attention to every word, trying to understand. "This is all very scientific. But I've a notion that those villagers couldn't give a fig about your experimentations."

"They don't. The problem is that nothing can be kept secret here, not when it comes to the Exmoors or anything else that takes place on these moors. The local populace knew full well what I was doing, and I had their approval, up to a point."

She narrowed her eyes at him as a suspicion dawned. "When did you lose their support?"

"At the exact moment my father removed the colt from Briarview. They don't know why he did it, and they don't know where the colt was taken. They only know it is gone."

She twisted in her saddle to peer down the hillside to the village, from here as picturesque as any rustic Devonshire hamlet. But what she had witnessed close up had left her more than unsettled. An inexplicable foreboding had taken root in her very bones. "I understand the villagers might be protective of the ponies, but, Colin, they threw things at us. They shook their fists. That is no way to treat their future duke and patron. It's downright unpardonable."

"Their bile is fueled by more than mere protectiveness." He might have gone on to explain, but at that moment the front door of the house burst open.

"Colin? Is that you, my boy?"

Holly shaded her eyes with her hand. Through the open door, liveried footmen and black-and-white-clad maids poured out and down the steps, hastily arranging themselves in a line facing the drive with men on one side, women to the other. In their wake a woman in an elegant, high-necked gown of black silk descended from the top step, her gray hair pulled back from a lined face and tucked beneath a lacy matron's cap.

Despite its wrinkles, the woman's face held an ageless beauty that to Holly spoke of resilience, even of defiance, as if she'd laughed at the passing years and dared them to rob her of her finest qualities. In that face, that expression, Holly recognized Sabrina's bold spirit and Colin's stubborn determination.

The woman started down toward them, balancing on each step with the help of an ebony cane. Her features tightened with the effort, but her smile remained fixed. Halfway down, a man—a butler Holly guessed by his formal suit and rigid bearing—scurried down after her and offered his arm.

"Your Grace, I beg you, please do wait for me before attempting stairs."

"Oh, yes, yes, Hockley . . . Thank you."

Holly needed no introductions to guess the woman's identity. "Your grandmother, I presume."

Colin nodded. "Maria Ashworth, the Dowager Duchess of Masterfield."

"You didn't tell me anyone would be here." A sudden misgiving lodged in Holly's stomach. "What will she think of us, arriving together this way? I knew you should have left me at the hunting lodge."

To her confusion, he let out the first true, wholly unburdened note of laughter she'd heard from him since . . . perhaps ever. "It's perfectly all right. Grandmama is the one member of my family to whom I do not shudder to introduce you."

"But she is the Ashworth matriarch. She is sure to disapprove."

"Come." His eyes twinkled like a mischievous boy's, throwing Holly into further bewilderment. Surely this couldn't be the same man with whom she had ridden all the way from Masterfield Park, the Colin Ashworth of the solemn looks and bleak pronouncements. "The old girl is sure to surprise you," he said irreverently. Then he sobered. "When I was a boy, sometimes I'd pretend she was my mother. She was the only person able to tell my father to go to the devil and get away with it."

"Colin Ashworth," the dowager duchess cried out with a force that belied her physical limitations. She thumped her cane on the ground in front of her foot. "You come here to me this instant."

Holly chewed her bottom lip as the horses trotted the remaining distance up the drive. Cordelier had barely come to rest before Colin leaped from the saddle and rushed into his grandmother's outstretched arms. Just before he did, the woman thrust her cane into the butler's waiting hands.

She held her grandson for far longer than most dowager duchesses would have deemed dignified. She even patted his back and rocked him like a child as her delighted laughter rang out. This woman did indeed surprise Holly with an outpouring of affection she would not have believed possible from any of these Ashworths.

"Do you have him?" the woman pulled back and asked.

Colin's hands wrapped around her thin, black-clad forearms. "He's still at large, I'm afraid."

The last thing Holly expected was the grin that split the duchess's aged countenance. "Well, I've every confidence that eventually you'll bring him home."

A few words from Colin produced curtsies and bows from the servants. Then footmen and maids scampered back up the stairs and into the house. Colin took the duchess's hand and placed it in the crook of his arm.

"Grandmama, there is someone I'd like you to meet."

"Oh, indeed, dear. I've been wondering about the exceedingly pretty lady sitting atop the mare. Is that Maribelle, by the way?"

"It is, Grandmama. You haven't lost your eye for horseflesh, have you?"

Leaning heavily on his arm, the duchess moved stiffly at his side. When they came to Maribelle he released her and reached up to help Holly down. Once her feet were firmly on the ground, Colin removed his hands from her waist and reclaimed his grandmother's hand. "Grandmama, this is Miss Holly Sutherland. You remember my good friend Simon de Burgh. Miss Sutherland is Simon's sister-in-law."

"A great pleasure to meet you, my dear."

Holly curtsied and managed a polite answer that she herself couldn't hear over the roaring in her ears. How on earth would Colin explain their having traveled all this way together? Would he lie and claim she was staying somewhere in the area with her sisters, perhaps in a neighboring village? Surely he wouldn't—

"Miss Sutherland has been kind enough to offer her help in recovering the colt," he said. "And we had him, Grandmama, for a brief time. I'm afraid he's been taken by highway thieves."

What? No honor-preserving pretense? No white lie to spare the elderly woman from an unseemly shock?

"My goodness, but that *is* dreadful." Despite the duchess's pronouncement, she didn't look nearly as distressed as one would suppose. On the contrary, she leaned slightly forward and surveyed Holly with what appeared to be an amused and speculative gleam. She might as well have been ogling Holly through a quizzing glass, her scrutiny burned so deeply. "You are very lovely, my dear."

Holly tried to smooth away a puzzled frown. "Thank you, Your Grace."

"Tell me, have you any lofty connections?"

"Lofty?" Holly blinked. What could the duchess mean? Could she somehow know of the Sutherlands' friendship with the queen? Uncertain how to respond, she looked to Colin for help.

"Miss Sutherland is an orphan, Grandmama," he said gently, "raised by an uncle who, too, has passed away."

The duchess's silver eyebrows rose in sympathy. "Oh, I am most sorry to hear it." Slipping an arm through Colin's again, she linked her other with one of Holly's. "I suppose one shouldn't stand outside on the drive all day, should one? Ah, here is the groom to take your horses. Let us go inside and take tea, and you may regale me with your adventures. Between the three of us, we'll devise a way to find the colt. By the by, Colin dear, have you explained to Miss Sutherland about the Exmoor curse?"

Chapter 21

"Good night, Colin. Miss Sutherland. I shall see you dears in the morning."

Colin watched his grandmother as she made her way out of the drawing room, her cane thudding against the rug. Her voice drifted from the hallway as she greeted her lady's maid, come to help her to her room and to bed.

He made use of the interval to take a fortifying sip of his brandy as Holly rose from the settee with an angry rustle of her skirts. Well, Sabrina's skirts; Grandmother's maid, Anne, had found a gown that fit Holly well enough after some adjustments. The flowered muslin swished around her ankles as she took a stride toward him. "Was it your intention all along to make a fool of me? To make a fool of the queen?"

Outside, a light rain pattered against the windows. Colin stared down into his brandy, cupped between his palms. "Of course not," he said calmly. "Don't you think I'd have prevented all of this if I could have? My father took the colt and gave it to the queen without my knowledge."

"Perhaps. But then to concoct such an absurd story. An ancient family curse, cast by a Celtic priestess who'd been jilted by her lover? What manner of simpleton do you take me for?"

"She was a princess and hereditary mistress of the ponies, and when her lover spurned her for another, he left behind a butchered Exmoor pony to dissuade her of any notion that he'd ever be back. My grandmother—"

"Is silly and misguided if she believes the spirit of this priestess . . ."

"Briannon, and don't speak ill of Grandmama."

"I'm sorry, but if Her Grace believes this Briannon lives on through the ponies, waiting to visit her fury on all who dare to harm or separate any animal from the herd . . ." Scowling, she left off and tossed her hands in the air. "What am I to think but that the dowager duchess, however gracious, has taken leave of her senses, while her grandson makes convenient use of her delusions?"

She raised a valid point, but that didn't prevent Colin's indignation from surging. He set his brandy on the table beside his wing chair and stood. As he started toward Holly, her eyes widened and she backed a step away so quickly that he doubted she realized she'd done it.

"I will not tolerate anyone speaking of my grandmother in such terms."

Her gaze, boldly adhering to his up till now, abruptly dropped. Her bosom rose sharply and she nodded. "Again, I'm sorry."

The frock had rendered a profound change in her bearing. Her riding attire had lent her an air of authority, even strength—aided, of course, by the presence of the revolver in her purse. But the gown brought out her most feminine traits, setting off the flame of her hair, the green of her eyes, the flawless white of her shoulders, arms and . . . he swallowed . . . the swell of her breasts. The broadcloth habit had concealed all that Sabrina's evening gown, with its shoulder-hugging décolleté and tiny, delicate sleeves, revealed in ways that were sure to keep him ruminating long into the night.

The dress also reminded him of how young she was. She looked so vulnerable, peeking at him from beneath her lashes, he nearly retreated to his wing chair. He didn't wish to frighten or intimidate her; he merely wished to make her understand. He felt it as a pressure in his chest, this urge to gain her approval and wipe the distrust from her features.

"As for me making convenient use of anything," he said, "can you conceive of anything convenient about stealing a horse from the queen? Was riding all this way, only to lose the colt, convenient? Did those jeers from the villagers strike you as being at all convenient?"

He savored the gradual lowering of those glorious breasts as she released a breath. "No, I suppose not. But surely, as a scientist, you should be able to explain to your grandmother and the villagers how the world works. That the forces of nature are not propelled by ancient Celtic curses."

He laughed softly. "This is Devon, a land of legends and superstition. The beliefs held by the villagers go back count-less centuries. Do you think they'll easily relinquish those beliefs to scientific treaties founded on mere decades of re-search? And as for Grandmother . . ."

He shoved a hand through his hair. Holly watched him intently, a little crease above her nose, her pretty lips uncon-sciously pursed and kissably plump. How could he explain to her that his grandmother had taken refuge in the old beliefs as a way to escape the realities of her life? Colin's father hadn't arrived in this world eager to torment, hu-miliate, and occasionally bruise those who fell under his authority. No, Father had learned such behaviors from his own father, and he from his father before him. And so it had gone in the Ashworth family, for many generations.

In Devonshire's archaic mythology Grandmama had found a certain comforting order, a stability based on ma-triarchal traditions, until a sudden apoplexy had freed her from her tyrant of a husband.

"Grandmother hasn't always been happy," he said softly. "Her life hasn't always been easy." He paused as compre-hension etched pain across Holly's countenance. "Believing in mystical powers, including that of the Exmoor ponies, has provided her with a sense of her own power." He shook his head. "Does that make sense?"

Holly came closer, clouding his thoughts with the heat of her skin. Her small hand closed over his sleeve. "Yes, oddly it does. You aren't like them, you know. Your father, your grandfather. Not at all."

His reply was to pull her into his arms and bury his face in her hair.

When he released her, her eyes narrowed until her lashes framed shards of green. "You don't believe it, do you? About the ponies?"

"That they are cursed? No. My scientist's brain wouldn't allow it. But logic and science offer an explanation that may sound just as fantastical." At her quizzical look, he warmed to his explanation, which he had never shared with another living soul. "I believe that just as matter cannot be destroyed, only converted, so too may hereditary traits become dormant, but never die out. The Exmoors and the colt project a magical quality because of traits that are thousands of years old, and which no other breeds share."

"That is why Victoria insisted her colt was so extraordinary," she said excitedly, "and how she recognized the replacement colt for what it was."

Colin nodded. "And why you sensed the colt's remarkable nature as well."

She remained quiet for a moment, frowning pensively. "But even if the ponies *were* magical and the curse existed, Prince's Pride carries only a small fraction of Exmoor blood."

"Prince's Pride?"

Her smile held a trace of irony. "Victoria's name for him. He is—was—to be given as a gift to Prince Frederick of Prussia, to forge stronger relations with the future king. And to help Victoria regain her ministers' confidence and her people's regard. Her first two years as queen have been . . . shaky at times."

"Christ." Colin raised a hand to his eyes. "This gets worse and worse." He dropped his arm to his side and met her gaze. "But as for the colt's Exmoor blood, it doesn't matter how little runs through his veins. A single drop is enough to render him part of the herd and cloaked within the terms of the curse. I knew this when I created the crossbreeds, but I never intended for any of them to leave Briarview. Not for many more generations. They were meant only for my private scientific pursuits."

Or so he had told his younger, more cavalier self nearly a decade ago when he'd first conceived the idea of crossbreeding an Exmoor stallion with a Thoroughbred mare. Then, he'd dismissed the curse as so much balderdash. He still did . . . except that whether it was real or not, the damage it inflicted still took its toll.

"'I charge the lords of this land with the safekeeping of the ponies, forever and always, or you and yours shall know my wrath.'"

"What?" Holly tilted her head in puzzlement.

"Those were supposedly Briannon's last words," he explained, "before she took her own life and scattered her soul among the herd."

"Such a tragic story. Briannon . . ." Holly repeated the name silently, her lips moving. "Is that where Briarview's name came from—the beginning of her name?"

He nodded. "Her legacy is everywhere."

"Legacies can be altered."

"Perhaps." He shook his head. "Without the colt I have very little chance of altering the downwardly spiraling fortunes of this place. But it's getting late. You must be exhausted from our ride today, not to mention the very odd greeting you received upon arriving."

Her eyes filled with uncertainty.

"Grandmother ordered the rose bedchamber opened for you," he said to make it clear where she would be spending the night.

"Colin . . . we haven't talk about . . ." She compressed her lips, then released them. Red and moist, they parted gently.

Again, he shook his head. "No, Holly. What we did—"

"A mistake?" When he didn't immediately answer, her head went down.

With two fingertips he raised her chin. "Under any other

circumstances, no, it would not have been a mistake. But surely you see that my life is not one I can share with an outsider."

The color drained from her face, and he realized his mistake.

"What I mean is . . ." His fingers grazed her jawline, her cheek, then smoothed back a wisp of hair. It was on the tip of his tongue to say that she deserved better, but if he'd learned anything about this woman in past days, it was that she could be as stubborn as the most spirited filly. If he were to deter her from the feelings that even now made him ache, he must deny them himself.

"We are from very different worlds. I have obligations, not the least of which is to calm the villagers' fears and restore order to Briarview. I haven't time for . . ." He stroked her cheek again—one last time—and turned partly away to stare at the reflections of the room in the night-blackened windows. He died a small death inside as he concluded, "For dalliances."

He saw her scowl reflected in the windowpanes. "You're a terrible liar, Colin Ashworth, and I'm suddenly suspecting you're something of a coward."

It was all he could do not to spin around and react to that statement.

"Far be it for me to interfere with your self-inflicted martyrdom," she said tightly. "Good night."

Good. She could rely on that stalwart pride of hers until he could safely return her to her sisters. Her words continued to mock him. *Was* he a martyr? Perhaps, in a way. He was an Ashworth male, latest in a long line of arrogant sots who had put their own needs and desires before those of the people in their care. He wouldn't be like them. He would *not*. Nor would he allow Holly Sutherland's spirit to wither away among this family, as his mother's spirit had, leaving her a shell of the woman she might have been.

Tomorrow, he would ride out and find the herd. He owed them his attention, and he must ensure that they continued to run free and thrive. Then he would gather his most trustworthy servants from the estate, and perhaps a few from the village who still held him in some esteem, and begin his search for the colt.

Turning about, he remembered that he hadn't wished Holly good night. And that left him feeling as empty as the room in which he stood.

Holly strode past the stables and continued down the path to the high stone wall that enclosed the farthest borders of Briarview's formal gardens. Using the key the dowager duchess had lent her, she let herself out of the arched gates and emerged onto the estate's forested riding lanes. The duchess had wanted to send a maid along with her on her walk, but Holly had assured her she wouldn't go far, that she only wished a brief glimpse of the moors she had heard about but never seen for herself. Here in the country formalities such as chaperones shouldn't matter so much anyway ... and she had particular reasons for wanting to go alone.

Following the duchess's directions, she trekked along a main riding path for about another quarter mile due east. There she came upon a cart track, little more than a depression in the encroaching weeds, twisting ivy, and wispy fern, that veered from the Ashworth's cultivated property and entered the open wilderness of the moor, a landscape as natural and wild as the tiered gardens behind her were planned and formal.

She knew she would be safe as long as she kept the rooftops of the manor house within view. The warnings she had received minutes ago from Mr. Hockley, the Ashworths' butler, had proved correct, however. After last night's driving rains, the soggy terrain made for unsteady walking. She employed her closed umbrella, which the duchess had insisted she take with her, as a staff to help her along. The butler had also cautioned her to stay clear of the nearby stream, sure to be overflowing its banks this morning.

Some fifty yards away, that very stream boiled furiously high, tossing up plumes of foam where it dashed around boulders. The impatient current, winding its way between Holly and the greater expanse of the moor, matched her present mood, and she chewed her bottom lip as she regarded the stone footbridge arcing across the water. It appeared solid enough. She angled a glance over her shoulder. Surely neither Mr. Hockley nor the duchess need ever be the wiser.

Once across, she proceeded at a brisk pace from the farther bank, using the exertion to vent her frustrations. She had awakened this morning alone, naturally. Certainly she had not expected Colin to come to her room with his grandmother sleeping beneath the same roof, but the change in him last night had left her unsettled. Disappointed.

Crestfallen.

And very worried about him. No matter his excuses for pulling away, she'd never again believe he didn't care for her. Her doubts had been forever silenced by their night together at his father's hunting lodge, where they'd shared so much more than lust. This sudden cooling of Colin's ardor, she suspected, had little to do with their differing worlds, and everything to do with his fears for his future, his punishment at the hands of an angry queen.

Didn't he realize those consequences didn't matter to her? That she would wait for him however long, no matter the circumstances?

She suspected he did, and he had decided to act in what he believed to be her best interests. Blasted, stubborn man.

She continued on despite a quick scattering of raindrops. As she topped a low rise, a sweeping vista spread out before her, a lush, rolling landscape blanketed in bright yellow gorse and crowned by granite crags gleaming wetly under the cloudy sky. The view stretched on for miles until it dissipated on a misty horizon; it seemed the world had been laid out before her.

Mr. Hockley had informed her that Colin had risen at dawn and taken Cordelier out for a ride, and she searched for him now amid the rugged hills, sudden ravines, and the distant, gold-carpeted landscape. She worried about him, fretted that his burdens might drive him to take dangerous risks. As crows and jays cawed in disharmony above her head, she poked the tip of her umbrella into the sodden ground and tramped over the next hill. If she could only reassure him . . .

Thunder rumbled across the moors. Holly came to a stop and searched the sky. Should she turn around? Only occasional drops continued to fall and no lightning pierced the clouds. Odd . . .

A glance over her shoulder brought a shock. She hadn't thought she'd walked far, but the house had disappeared from view. The thunder rumbled again, or rather, continued to rumble, building from those first, faint tremors to a din that shook the ground beneath her feet.

Even in the worst of storms, thunder didn't roll on and on without pause. The longer she listened, the more she realized the drumming came from the earth itself. Mystified, she hoisted her skirts and scrambled up the side of the nearest granite-crested mound for a better view.

She gasped at the sight before her. About half a mile away, a herd of sturdy, bay-coated ponies, their darker manes and tails streaming behind them, coursed over the landscape as if with the will of a single being. Exhilarated, she pressed a hand to her mouth, so entranced that she didn't at first notice the flash of gold amid the dark-coated ponies. Then she recognized the significance of that flash, and her pulse hammered all the more. Colin was galloping amid the herd, not on one of the ponies but on powerful, sleek Cordelier, who stood several hands taller than the rest.

She detected other differences among the trampling herd, horses that stood taller, whose flanks rippled with the musculature of Thoroughbreds, though they streamed over the terrain with the same nimble grace as the ponies. With their bay coats and the distinctive Ashworth star flashing white above their eyes, these, she realized, were the other crossbreed horses—siblings and cousins to the missing Prince's Pride.

Her breath quickened as she realized that Colin wasn't

herding the animals, but rather riding with them, swept along in the tumult of their flight. He wore only breeches, boots, and a shirt whose fine linen caught the wind and arched like a sail away from his back. He seemed transformed, no longer the duke's heir burdened by the misfortunes of his family, but as free and fearless as the Celtic warriors who once inhabited this land. Suddenly a powerful arm, bared from the elbow down, shot into the air, the hand fisted in a gesture of jubilation. His shouted whoop echoed across the moor.

The spirit of his madcap ride infected Holly until she, too, might have been galloping wildly across the countryside without a thought to the risks posed by the unpredictable ground. She should have been alarmed at the very real possibility of Cordelier stumbling, of Colin falling and breaking his neck, but somehow she trusted, as he apparently trusted, in the ponies' collective instinct. The prospect left her giddy and laughing, with a wordless exclamation dancing on her tongue.

The umbrella dropped and forgotten, she lifted her skirts and sprang forward, breaking into a run. Raindrops splattered her cheeks and forehead and clung to her lashes. Sodden grass and gorse streaked beneath her feet. Puddles splashed her legs. A gust of wind pushed her bonnet backward until it slid off and hung by its silken strings down her back. She laughed louder and shut her eyes.

When she opened them again, she started. The herd had surged closer to her, and the earth beneath her shook, rattling her very bones. Colin and the Exmoors were heading straight for her, his expression fierce, indomitable, his eyes riveted on hers. She wanted to back away, to turn and run, but her feet wouldn't move. It was as if his forceful determination had changed her to stone, leaving her no choice but to await her fate at his hands.

Her fear suddenly dissolved and she no longer wished to run. Standing straight and tall, her chin lifted, she longed for the ponies to engulf her like a rushing tide. She yearned for the instant Colin would reach her side, his powerful body leaning low, one strong arm sweeping down to lift her off her feet. She wasn't afraid of being trampled or of falling. She had no doubt that within seconds, she would be cradled in the saddle before him. He would carry her off and, oh, she would let him . . . she would happily be this wild warrior's captive.

But as she stood waiting, her eyes and heart wide-open, the herd veered and streamed eastward, taking Colin and Cordelier with them. They pounded over a hill, and disappeared down the other side.

Soon the only sounds were those of the wind and the rain hitting the ground. Holly stared into the emptiness where the horses had been, her body tingling, throbbing, as if the echo of the Exmoors' riotous gallop lived inside her still. As if Colin had somehow swept her up and had his way with her, tantalizing every inch of her body before setting her down again.

A sense of foolishness swept through her. Nothing about the last several seconds had been real outside of her imagination. All had been a figment of her lusty desires, her unquenchable fascination with Colin Ashworth. Mortified, and all too thankful the man couldn't read her thoughts, she covered her face in her hands. Despite the chilly breeze and the cool rain, her skin felt hot. Her fingers shook. Her legs barely supported her as she turned about and searched the sodden grass for the duchess's umbrella. At last she found it.

She began walking, hoping she had pointed herself in the right direction. When, after several minutes, the peaked roofs and stone chimneys of the house failed to rise up into view, a smidgeon of panic blossomed inside her. She hurried her steps, and felt a burst of relief when the sound of voices reached her ears.

She heard the rushing waters of the stream, but still no sign of the house or the entrance to the riding lanes. With no other choice, she followed the voices. A ragtag band of village men came into view, about seven or eight of them gathered beneath an alder tree. Their voices were raised, some of their fists as well.

"I don't care who them Ashworths think they are," growled a man with heavy, bullish features. Holly remembered him from yesterday. Had he been the one who threw the first rock as she and Colin passed through the village? "The colt don't belong to them. It belongs to the herd, and 'tis us 'n' ours that'll suffer."

A tall, lanky man with a tattered scarf wrapped round his neck ran his fingers through his wet hair, making it spike. "I damn near died when he rode in yesterday without the colt."

"Lord Drayton never had no business fooling with those ponies," another asserted.

"Didn't matter, so long as those crossbreeds of his stayed here where they belonged."

"He swore he'd bring the colt back," a youth said in whiny tones. "I remember it. He stood on the village green and swore."

"Yeah, and he'll pay for this," the bulldog said. "Them Ashworths'll be made to pay. Today, if we have anything to say about it. 'Tis time we pounded on their door."

Oh, dear. Holly began backing away, retracing her steps even at the risk of becoming lost on the moor again. She'd rather take her chance among the granite crags than with this hostile band. If she could just retreat over that last hill without their seeing her. . . .

"You there!"

Incensed faces blurred in Holly's vision as she whirled and ran. Behind her, footsteps hammered the ground while cries of "She rode at his side yesterday" and "Get her!" nipped at her heels. For one daft moment she considered wielding the duchess's umbrella in their faces. Idiot. There were too many of them; they'd surround her in seconds and ply the makeshift weapon from her hands. Fervently wishing she had thought to bring the revolver instead, she ran as hard and as fast as her legs would take her—legs toned and strengthened by her many years of riding. The scoundrels kept up their pursuit, but Holly maintained a distance between them.

Behind her, a voice barked out a demand that the village men leave off. She couldn't make out the words, only the commanding tone of a man accustomed to being obeyed. She slowed her steps slightly to cast a glance over her shoulder. Her pursuers had been brought to heel, but not by Colin or Mr. Hockley or anyone else she recognized. As the ragged men tossed malice-filled stares at her, another, clad in the calf-length greatcoat of a gentleman, positioned himself between them, his arms outstretched as if to act as a shield to protect her.

His intervention should have brought reassurance, yet it didn't, especially not when, after a final word to the villagers, he turned and strode toward her. The gunshots on the road, the missing colt, and even the incident at the Ashworths' ball all urged her to run faster. Dropping the duchess's umbrella once again, she gripped her skirts, raised them high, and pumped her legs as fast as they'd go.

Beyond a doubt, she had taken a wrong direction. As she raced around the rheumatic twist of a dead rowan, the stream, foaming furiously, wound its way across her path and brought her to an uncertain halt. Some dozen yards to her left, a very different footbridge from the one she'd first crossed spanned the flooded banks. This one, made of wood, appeared much older and narrower. She sprinted to it only to discover the planking to be faded and splintered, even broken in places. The structure hardly looked trustworthy.

Another glance behind her revealed no sign of either the villagers or the man in the greatcoat. Had they given up their pursuit, or slipped into hiding to await her next move? She scanned the horizon ahead of her and to her great relief detected the corner of a chimney scraping the sky. The rain began to fall harder, obscuring her vision.

Grabbing hold of the rail, she gingerly placed a foot on the first plank. The bridge trembled slightly but otherwise seemed solid enough. The way across couldn't be more than a dozen yards, a stone's throw. If she went quickly and remained light on her feet . . .

Halfway across, the bridge sagged beneath her weight. The stream lapped at her feet, shocking her toes with frigid water and making her afraid to move in either direction. Logic demanded she continue forward, but her next step produced a resounding crack.

The slat splintered in half and one foot fell out from under her, plunging calf deep into the racing water. She gripped the rail with both hands and for several seconds clung to hope. Then the bridge shuddered and broke apart. Holly felt herself falling, splashing into the frothing, frigid water, engulfed in her own terror and the relentless current.

Chapter 22

Deep into the valley a mile and a half from Briarview, Colin shortened Cordelier's reins to slow the stallion's pace. The Exmoors coursed around him and pounded past, their ranks narrowing as they surged between the rocky granite tors that ringed the valley's eastern rim. Cordelier came to a restive halt, snorting and pawing the ground while the last of the herd disappeared at a gallop.

As the trembling of the ground stilled and the air quieted, the euphoric thudding of his heart eased and the rush of blood through his veins calmed. They were his responsibility, those ponies, and his duty to protect them brought him joy he never spoke of, not to another living soul. However much his father believed he owned the herd that roamed his land, Colin knew the ponies belonged to no man. They belonged to the earth, to tradition and legend. They were free, and only by the dictates of their collective will did they tolerate an outside presence among them.

As they tolerated Colin and Cordelier. As a boy he'd discovered that all he needed to do was ride out across the moors, and the ponies would gallop with him, accepting him as one of the herd. He didn't understand it, but the realization had dawned that he belonged to them far more than they could ever belong to him. True, they needed his protection from those who would separate or abuse them—men like his father—or those who would destroy their native habitat, but he needed them just as much, for it was only with them that he felt truly alive.

He laughed out loud at the notion, a bitter sound bitten off by a rainy gust. Ironic that it took a herd of wild ponies to remind him that he was a free man with passions and dreams of his own, and not merely Thaddeus Ashworth's heir. Here, on the upper reaches of the Devonshire moors, with the ground coursing beneath him and the sky stretching above, the pounding of hooves drowned out the cynicism and self-doubt his father had planted inside him at an early age.

At least, all that had been true as recently as two days ago. Now, however . . .

The conviction had filled him that with Holly at his side, he had the power to break free of whatever curses, real or imagined, held him and his family. With her in his life, he might finally know happiness.

Sucking a draft of soggy air deep into his lungs, he swung Cordelier about and headed for home. Bringing Holly into his world would more likely change her life for the worse. It was not a chance he'd willingly take.

He neared Briarview's forested acreage, preparing to jump Cordelier over the stream that looped around it. He leaned low over the stallion's dark mane just as a tangle of rotten, broken boards rushed by on the water. Screams pierced the wind. Colin lurched upright in the saddle, prompting Cordelier to bounce to a stop. Colin pricked his ears, and another desperate cry sent Cordelier rearing up on hind legs, his front hooves thrashing.

Colin's blood ran cold. *The old footbridge.* With a tap of his heels he and Cordelier set off at a gallop.

In less than a minute he came upon a half-submerged flurry of dark skirts and white petticoats; a pair of hands groped frantically at the air. Holly's desperate face appeared briefly in the foaming waters. The current closed over her, flipped her around, and thrust her back up. All Colin could see of her now were glistening, streaming ribbons of red hair. His heart rocketed into his throat. *Oh, God . . . oh, God.*

"Holly!" he shouted, "I'm coming!"

He turned Cordelier again and urged him to a full-out gallop along the bank of the stream. As he went, Colin slid free of the stirrups and slung a leg over the stallion's neck so that both his feet dangled toward the water. Holding his breath, he waited until he rode up even with Holly, and then passed her by several long paces. In a few more yards the watercourse would narrow slightly—enough, he prayed, for what he intended.

A tightening of the reins slowed Cordelier to a canter. Colin mentally counted to three, then propelled himself from the saddle, hitting the bank with a force that clacked his teeth together. Using the momentum, he slid down into the water. Submerged chest deep, he fought past the chill and battled the current to reach the middle of the stream.

His arms outstretched and his feet braced as solidly as possible against the rocky streambed, he waited as swirling fabric, streaming hair, and Holly's white, terrified face rushed closer. She hit him with an impact that knocked the breath from his lungs. His feet threatened to slip, his legs to swing out from under him. He closed his arms around her and she went limp against him, her own arms hanging slack, her legs tangling with his. The water clawed at her saturated skirts, almost prying her loose from his arms.

Clutching her tighter, he called on all the strength he possessed to hug her to his chest. He sidestepped toward the far bank, where the overhanging branches of a willow tree skimmed the current. Limbs stiff with cold and muscles aching from the exertion, he fought his way closer to the tree and chanced lifting one arm from around her. Reaching out, he gripped a branch and hauled himself and Holly out of the water and onto the muddy bank.

Her eyes closed, her body wilting against the ground, she showed no signs of consciousness. On his knees beside her, he swept the sodden snarls of hair from her cheeks and cupped her face in his hands. "Holly. Oh, God . . . please . . ."

He rubbed her cheeks, hands, and arms in a desperate attempt to force the blood to flow. Hunching over her, he slipped an arm beneath her shoulders and lifted her against him, pressing his lips to her forehead, to her mouth. Then he remembered something vital. As her sister had once done for Simon after an experiment had nearly killed him, he opened her mouth and breathed into her, forcing air in and out of her lungs. All the while he prayed and raged and promised God anything . . . anything. . . .

A sputtering cough sent dizzying relief all through him. Her eyelids fluttered, and a racking cough shook her frame. Over and over she coughed, cringing from the force, her shoulders wrenching.

Twisting away from him, she doubled over, her face hanging low over the ground as she gagged and purged the stream water from her lungs. Helpless to provide relief, Colin thrust an arm across the front of her shoulders to support her while with his other hand he gathered her hair and held it back from her face. Each convulsion echoed through him until the tension flowed from her body.

"What . . . happened?" Her head hanging, her voice came as a tremulous flutter. Wiping shaky fingers across her lips, she gazed feebly up at him. Her image blurred before his eyes, obscured by tears he couldn't prevent. He felt her cold palm against his cheek. "You saved me."

Then her hand fell away and she collapsed against him in a dead faint.

Holly's lungs ached. Her head throbbed, and the voices that reached her ears sounded muffled and waterlogged. What were they saying? She wanted to ask, but her tongue adhered thick and heavy to the roof of her mouth. Her throat rasped for a drink . . . yet somehow the very idea sent a bolt of terror through her, as if at the mere parting of her lips, water would gush in and drown her.

Panic nipping at her consciousness, she tried to open her eyes. They felt weighted . . . as heavy as lead. . . . The world tipped, and she slid once more into blackness.

"You've been here for hours," a woman's voice murmured, but how many minutes or hours later, Holly didn't know. "Stretch your legs. I'll stay with her."

Through a swarm of images, Holly swam back toward consciousness. The voice, a feminine whisper close to her ear, peeled back the layers of panic that had engulfed her for an unknown length of time. Though not entirely familiar, she had the strongest sense she had heard the voice before, that it signified safety, acceptance. She struggled to remember where . . . when she had heard it. . . .

"I can't leave her until I know she's well, Grandmother."

That voice she knew. *Colin.* Her heart turned over, setting off a cascade of memories. She was in Devonshire, at his family's estate of Briarview. She went out on the moor, saw him riding. . . .

The din of the ponies' hooves echoed inside her, a near physical beat thrumming through her limbs, her ribs. She had seen Colin racing among the ancient breed, his fierce resolve interwoven with their feral instincts to form a single purpose, an audacious challenge to the power of the moor.

Then the angry faces of the villagers swamped all thoughts of him. They had chased her, forcing her to run . . . run to the swollen banks of the stream. Her only refuge had been the footbridge, old and rickety. The creaking of the boards reverberated in her mind, then the splintering, the snapping . . . and she was falling, falling. . . .

Her eyes flew open and she sprang upright, only to have her momentum checked by a solid wall in front of her. No, not quite solid. A pair of arms closed around her and her cheek met a ripple of muscle covered by the smooth sheen of a silken waistcoat.

Her breath clawed at her dry throat; she coughed and coughed, unable to quell the urge until a pair of aged hands held a cup to her lips. "Little sips," the woman's voice crooned. "There, there. Not too much at once. That's right. There's a good girl."

Cool water trickled sweetly into her mouth, vanquishing

the torturous urge to cough. Still half-dazed, she relaxed her cheek against Colin's shoulder.

"Easy now, Holly. It's all right. *You're* all right." Colin's voice sifted gently through her hair. Though a thousand questions prodded, she leaned against him, grateful. . . .

To be alive. Good heavens. She would have been dead—drowned—if not for him.

She lifted her chin, her gaze meeting the reassuring stubble that lined his angular jaw. "Thank you . . ." Her voice sputtered and died in her throat.

"Shhh." He rubbed her back gently.

"Here, try some of this, dear." The soft, wrinkled hands reappeared in her vision, this time holding a snifter filled with liquid fire. The strong aroma of brandy stung her nose, but she took a small sip.

The liquor immediately spread its restorative heat through her veins. Little by little she assessed her condition. Someone—the duchess's lady's maid, Holly presumed—had stripped away her sodden clothing and replaced it with a warm flannel chemise. Her hair, though dry now, streamed in tangles down her back.

A hand stroked lightly down those tangles. Holly half turned to discover the dowager duchess perched on the other side of the bed from Colin, the snifter balanced on her thigh. Her clear blue eyes, so like Colin's, twinkled with myriad sentiments: relief, gladness, affection . . . and something . . . a secret to which only the woman was privy, but which Holly suspected amused her no end.

"Well, now," Maria Ashworth said, "didn't I say the lass would soon be right as rain? She's got pluck. I saw it the first time I laid eyes on her." The creases across her brow deepened. "Though perhaps rain is not the proper reference in this instance. One would not suppose our Miss Sutherland would wish to think of rain or water for quite some time to come."

"Grandmother . . ." Colin said in an admonishing tone.

A laugh bubbled to Holly's lips. Hilarity rose up inside her, unstoppable, the laughter pouring out until her belly shook and her eyes teared and her throat ran dry again. The duchess's softer laughter blended with hers. From the corner of her eyes, Holly saw Colin looking on uncertainly until a smile tugged at his lips. His deep bellows rang out, until anyone passing by the doorway would have thought surely three lunatics had escaped their asylum.

When she could laugh no more for the stitch in her side, Holly pressed a hand to her belly and gasped for air. "I haven't the slightest notion how any of this could be funny." She met the duchess's eye and found herself chuckling again.

The woman reached out a hand to Holly's cheek. "Better to laugh than to cry, yes?"

Holly couldn't argue with that. "How long did I sleep?" she asked.

Colin glanced at the little pendulum clock ticking on the dresser. "About three hours."

His grandmother leaned to whisper in her ear, "He never left your side. Not once."

"Grandmama . . ."

"He was terribly worried," the older woman went on, "but all is well now. You seem little the worse for wear."

"All is not well, Grandmama. Far from it."

Colin's return to gravity reminded Holly of the many troubles still facing them. The colt was missing. They'd been shot at. And now an incensed band of villagers wanted retribution for misfortunes they blamed on Colin's family. Her eyes went wide. He still didn't know about that.

"What happened," she said, "there was a reason . . ."

"I should have warned you about that bridge." Colin's eyes darkened with an emotion approaching anger, though whether at her or himself she couldn't say.

She shook her head. "Mr. Hockley warned me about the stream. I knew better than to cross onto the moor."

"Then why on earth would you do such a dangerous thing in weather such as this?" His expression turned so severe she drew back against the pillows. "Why would you cross that broken old bridge?"

"That's what I'm trying to tell you, if you'd only calm yourself and listen."

"She is right, Colin. You should calm yourself."

His eyebrows knotting, he glanced from Holly to his grandmother and back again. "I am perfectly calm." The white lines of tension on either side of his nose belied that claim, a fact not missed by the duchess, who winked at Holly. Colin reached for her hand. "Tell me what happened."

He absently stroked his fingertips across her palm, and for a moment she could focus on nothing else. Another memory flashed, that of his lips pressed to hers, not tenderly in a kiss but desperately, distractedly. She remembered a shrieking pain in her lungs, an inability to draw even the smallest breath . . . sinking closer and closer to death.

He had breathed life back into her. There on the bank of the stream, he had brought her back to the world. *Dragged* her back when she might almost willingly have succumbed to the waters . . . he had claimed her, as a warrior claims what is his. . . .

Tears of gratitude and sheer awe burned the backs of her eyes, and her throat tightened around a powerful ache. She swallowed and returned the pressure of his hand. "I'd been out walking on the moor and . . . I saw you out there . . . riding with the ponies. I'd strayed too far and lost sight of the house. As I tried to make my way back I came upon a group of villagers. They were ragged . . . and angry. They talked of pounding on your door and demanding answers about the colt. When they saw me, they remembered me from yesterday when we passed through the village. They began to chase me—"

She broke off as a ghost of panic chilled her and left her shaking. Colin rubbed her hands between his own. His grandmother patted her shoulder.

"Damn them." His features hardened. "They won't get away with this. How did you manage to outrun them?"

"I didn't. Someone else . . . appeared. A gentleman, judging by his clothing."

Colin's grip on her hands tightened. "What do you mean, he appeared?"

"I don't know. I didn't see where he came from and I'd never seen him before. At least I don't think I have. He ordered the villagers to abandon their pursuit."

"This man, did he speak to you?" The duchess frowned. "Did he identify himself?"

She shook her head. "I hardly lingered long enough to give him the chance. Something about him . . ."

"Yes?" Colin placed his fingertips beneath her chin, and steady courage flowed into her.

"He frightened me," she said evenly, calmly. "Those shots on the road the other day—"

"Shots?" The duchess turned an alarmed expression on her grandson. "Colin, you didn't mention this."

"Not now, Grandmother. What else, Holly?"

"You remember the night of the ball."

"The man who accosted you in the corridor."

"Good gracious!"

Holly clasped the woman's hand. "It's quite all right, Your Grace. Nothing untoward happened then, either. But now I'm wondering . . ." She turned back to Colin, meeting his gaze with her own deadly serious one. "Could this stranger be the same, and is there a connection between these incidents?"

Colin rode Cordelier at a sedate walk to the end of the driveway. He might just as easily have walked the short distance from the house, but he desired the air of authority that sitting atop his stallion would lend him.

Given the situation, he needed every advantage he could muster.

A group of representatives from the village, some twelve or so strong, milled outside the gates. They had gathered nearly an hour ago, but he'd put off the confrontation long enough to assure himself Holly had suffered no lasting injuries from her accident.

Before he'd gone halfway down the drive, their petulant

voices reached him. He eyed each man sharply, wondering if any of them had been part of the gang that had chased Holly. If he discovered any of them had been . . .

He forced himself to remain calm, at least to put up the appearance of composure. That the delegation of village men waited peaceably at the base of the drive, rather than storming past to threaten those within the house, was something to be grateful for. But he didn't know how much longer his good fortune would continue.

Or whether one of them might brandish a weapon and take aim. Would they stop to consider that the person most worthy of their enmity was at this moment on his way to some sunny island halfway across the world?

Damn you, and damn you again, Father.

The morning's drizzle had abated, but the leaden skies and moist breezes promised more rain to come. Colin prayed for inclement weather to chase the villagers back to their homes and keep them there. For now, however, he'd enjoy no such luck. He collected his thoughts as Cordelier brought him inevitably to the end of the drive.

"Where is it?" Ed Harper, the greengrocer, flourished a formidable-looking fist. He'd been among the first yesterday to throw up his clenched hand and shout. Regarding his bulldog face and massive shoulders, Colin narrowed his eyes. Holly had described just such a man among the rapscallions this morning.

He tightened his own fist around the reins. "The colt will be returned to Briarview," he said, raising his voice against a gust of wind. "You have my word on it."

"That's no answer." Harper strode forward, and Cordelier lurched.

"I've had another lamb die, two days ago." A sallow-skinned man hovered slightly behind Harper and spoke with considerably less force. Colin recognized him as Jon Darby, a tenant farmer. The man held his cap between his hands and met Colin's gaze only briefly before ducking his head in a show of customary if reluctant deference. "That makes three this month."

Colin raised his chin. "I'll come out and see to your sheep. Most likely there's some blight in your feed that's affecting the ewes' milk."

"And where'd the blight come from? I wonder." Harper shoved his hands in his pockets, hunched his shoulders, and dug in his heels.

"From the curse," murmured another among them. Ken Fanning, who ran the smithy, glanced around at the others for encouragement. "My boy was nearly blinded last week when the coal door of the forge burst open with a spray o' embers."

At those words, sparks showered behind Colin's eyes and a scream burst from his memories. There had been another forge once, but what happened there had not been an accident. Bryce had eluded his Latin tutor yet again and was happily assisting Masterfield Park's smithy when their father had found him. Bryce had always preferred physical pursuits to academic, but that day Thaddeus had decided to teach his son a lesson. To deter him from ever shirking his schoolroom duties again, he'd gripped the seven-year-old child's hands, twisted them around, and held them over the heat of the smithy's fire until the skin had begun to scorch . . . until Bryce would bear scars for the rest of his life and his hands would be so weakened that he'd never be able to handle a high-spirited Thoroughbred again.

Shutting his eyes, Colin forced the memory away and focused on the matter confronting him now. "An accident," he said to Ken Fanning. "Had anyone checked the latch?" He raised his gaze to encompass all of them. "Such things happen in every village across England."

"Not like this," Harper shouted. Mutters of agreement circulated through the group. "Damn you Ashworths . . ."

"That will be enough, Edward."

The firm but unperturbed admonishment came from beneath the wide, round hat of northern Devonshire's traveling preacher, who until that moment had hovered to the rear of the group. Now the man pressed forward, parting the others by placing his hands on their shoulders. Colin had never been so relieved to set eyes on him; if anyone could penetrate the wall of superstition built up in these people's minds, Daniel Fairmont could, a man of Colin's age who possessed an astuteness that made him seem much older.

"Mr. Fairmont, surely you agree with me that—"

The preacher did something neither he, nor any of these villagers, had ever done before. He interrupted the firstborn son of his benefactor. "Lord Drayton, however much you and I might agree is a moot point. The day the colt was led off Ashworth land, reason went with it."

"Is it lack of reason that brought disease upon our live-stock, floods, and blights to our fields?"

This came from Fanning the smithy, reminding Colin that no matter a man's profession, in this part of England all families farmed their plots of land and raised their small herds, supplementing other income with homegrown food-stuffs and textiles. Some years, a decent yield was all that stood between such people and starvation.

"Our livelihoods are at risk while you Ashworths take your ease and grow fat." Harper again. And he had a point, and for exactly that reason Colin couldn't afford to show even the slightest sign of weakness.

His grandmother lived in that house at the top of the drive, his beloved Grandmama who had once stood up to her husband and her own son on a regular basis, but whose strength was all on the inside now. She could never defend herself against a band of hammer- and pitchfork-wielding vagabonds. Should the villagers' patience wear out . . . dear God, what would happen to Grandmama?

"Well, my lord?" Harper's biting tone dripped sarcasm into what should have been a term of respect. With no vis-ible show of effort, the man's biceps flexed, straining the sleeves of his soiled woolen shirt. "Just what are you going to do?"

"I'm glad Colin's gone out to visit with the villagers." The dowager duchess turned away from the scene outside the window. Her cane thudding on the rug, she moved stiffly back to the bed and carefully lowered herself to perch at the edge beside Holly. Holly reached out a hand to help steady her, and the duchess grasped it warmly. "You and I may become better acquainted."

"You're very kind, Your Grace." Holly couldn't keep the surprise from her voice. Considering the circumstances of her visit, she'd had every reason to expect glaring disapproval from this woman. But to be welcomed, pampered ... She remembered how the other duchess, Colin's mother, had doted like a mother hen on Ivy after she fainted. The Ashworths were not nearly as devoid of kindheartedness as they might appear at first glance. The women, at least, showed uncommon generosity. Even Sabrina was not without her gentler side. As for the men ...

They were nothing if not perplexing, especially one Ashworth man in particular. She knew Colin had feelings for her, yet she knew just as surely that he saw no way for them to ever be together. He had given up without fighting, just as the villagers had given up their livelihoods because they believed they were cursed. Didn't he see that his view was as self-defeating as theirs?

She tried to shake those thoughts away, only to discover it was the very topic the duchess wished to discuss.

"Colin explained to you about Lady Briannon," the woman said, "who presided over the Exmoor ponies centuries ago?"

"He mentioned it, Your Grace. He said the villagers believe the loss of the colt has led to their misfortunes." She drew on a lifetime of common sense and added, "Anyone can see these misfortunes are the sort that can happen anywhere, to anyone."

"You believe that, do you?"

"Of course I do. Surely, Your Grace doesn't think ..."

"I believe there are forces in this world that cannot be explained as my grandson would like, with logic and formulas and what he calls intrinsic evidence." The woman leaned close to brush a hair from Holly's cheek with the back of her fingers. "His problem is that he doesn't stop to look at the full picture."

"Full picture, Your Grace?"

"Men are so shortsighted." Maria Ashworth smiled, revealing the curves of high cheekbones. "So limited in their scope of understanding. They want their answers here and now, tied in neat little bundles. Women, on the other hand, are much more patient. We must be. We experience the long hours of childbirth, spend years raising our children, make sacrifices in the here and now and put our hopes in the future. We have a special power all our own, which a man can never understand."

"I'm not sure *I* understand." Holly drew herself up straighter against the pillows and looked into eyes that held the brightness of youth and optimism, despite the duchess's advanced years.

"A woman can see the connectedness of life in all its many aspects. She might not receive what she wants when she wants it, but if the rewards of her labors are reaped by her children and her grandchildren, then she has not toiled in vain."

Holly took this in. "Are you speaking of Briannon?"

"I am. Her lover betrayed her in the worst possible way, but she has been patient."

"You believe she is finally taking her vengeance?"

The duchess tilted her head and laughed softly. "No, dear child. Goodness, no. What Briannon seeks is not retribution, but resolution. Through the centuries, her spirit has reached out for peace—for herself, for her ponies, and for those who are touched by her legacy. And that means all of us who walk the land she once walked."

The duchess fell silent, the knowing gleam in her eye mystifying Holly as much as her words had. Yet she found herself trusting that gleam, and heard words spilling from her own mouth. "Your Grace, yesterday on the moor, I saw Colin riding among the ponies, and I felt something . . . extraordinary. And most peculiar."

"Do tell, my dear."

Holly searched the old woman's face, seeing not a proud noblewoman in the once-lovely features, but someone kinder and wiser. Someone who might understand. "The ponies' raised a thunder across the moor, a sound that took control of my heart, my pulse, my breathing. Even my thoughts. I could think of nothing else but the herd, and I felt as if I were among them, surging wildly over the land, but at the same time safely. I . . ."

"Go on."

"I felt an unaccountable trust, as if the rain-soaked ground posed no threat whatsoever. And then there was Colin. Oh, when I saw him, I . . ." Holly swallowed and gained control of her breathing. "I don't know quite how to say this to you."

Maria Ashworth grasped Holly's chin between her fingers with surprising force. "Tell me. Leave nothing out."

"Well, I . . . I'd have gone anywhere with him, let him sweep me up . . . and I'd have done anything. . . ."

"You'd have trusted him."

"Yes, completely. It sounds mad. A woman in my position, entertaining such notions . . ."

"Not mad, my dear. Understandable. It was *her*."

"Briannon?"

"Her spirit . . . guiding the ponies, and guiding you. This is an ancient land. Briannon's land. You felt what she wished you to feel. As you watched the herd, her spirit entered you and revealed the truth to you in its baldest form."

"What truth, Your Grace?"

A slow smile spread across Maria Ashworth's face. "Do you truly need me to tell you?"

No. What she'd felt on the moor was no different than what she felt every time Colin took her in his arms; every time he kissed her, touched her. She loved him, and she didn't need an ancient Celtic princess to tell her that.

"There is more." The woman gestured for Holly to come closer, as if she wished to whisper a secret in her ear. The duchess pressed a palm to her cheek. "There is a part of the curse the men of this family have long since dismissed. Until now it is only passed down through the women, from wife to wife."

The curse again. Holly subdued a groan of frustration. "Yes, Your Grace?"

"Briannon's curse can be broken forever if the lord of this land, which in our modern times means the duke, were to take a bride of royal blood."

Even before Holly fully realized the meaning—and consequences—of those words, her heart began to sink, and sank deeper still as the duchess went on.

"It must be a love match, pure and simple. Nothing less will do. And that is why the Ashworth men dismissed it long ago. For centuries, you see, they scrambled to take royal brides, but to no avail. That is because they married for advantage, not love, and without love the curse cannot be broken."

Holly thought of Lady Penelope Wingate, the young woman with the corkscrew curls and an overabundance of jewelry who had simpered at Colin the night of the Ashworths' ball. "Then . . . when Colin marries. . . ."

"If he loves and marries a woman of royal blood, a princess, the Exmoor curse will no longer hold its power over us."

"And the colt won't have to be returned to the estate." Holly's voice came small and flat.

The duchess shrugged. "The colt should be returned because it is the right thing do to. Because it belongs here, with others of its kind, and because my son had no business removing it from the moors."

"Why did you tell me this, Your Grace?" Holly asked in a whisper as she sank back against the pillows.

But the woman only regarded her with eyes that were so like her grandson's.

Holly realized that in relating her experiences on the moor, she had openly admitted her feelings for Colin. Maria Ashworth obviously disapproved, and she sought to discourage what she perceived to be an affection that would come to naught. To her mind, Colin must marry a woman of royal blood—a woman like Penelope Wingate—not a common miss like Holly.

Well. The duchess needn't have bothered. However Holly might feel, Colin had apparently made up his mind. His heart lay imprisoned within a wall of self-sacrifice, thick and secure. Each time Holly discovered even the slightest gap, he hurried to seal it tight.

Chapter 23

Well, my lord? Just what are you going to do?
The greengrocer's question shivered palpably in the rain-chilled air and sent ripples of tension through the unhappy group. If Colin could only make them understand that ancient curses didn't exist, and superstition couldn't hurt them . . . but how to break through centuries of narrow thinking?

Besides, there were times when he half believed the curse himself. Holly's accident today could easily be seen as the curse at work. Of course, a series of factors had contributed to her falling into the stream, but these people would argue that the curse had caused every one of his so-called factors to fall neatly, lethally into place.

If he were to deal with them at all, he realized, it must be in terms they could understand and believe. And he must be utterly honest, because men like Ed Harper and even the quiet Jon Darby could spot a liar like a hawk spots a mouse dashing across a field. They'd be on him just as quickly, with equal fierceness.

"I'll bring the colt home, but I'll need more time." He held up his hand at their grumbles. "A month at most."

Harper visibly bristled. "A week!"

Colin shook his head. "It could take longer than that. I had the colt—upon my word, I had it—but it was stolen along the road between Ascot and here."

"Ascot?" The information sifted through the group. The preacher held up his arms to quiet them and turned back to Colin.

"Why Ascot?" the man asked. "The horse is a mixed breed, useless for the racetrack."

Colin hesitated. He had enough trouble without mentioning the queen's part in all of this. Finally, he settled on an abbreviated version of the truth. "My father had a notion to test the colt's strength against its Thoroughbred counterparts. He didn't understand the damage he might inflict—"

"Your father's an arrogant sot." Harper's voice boomed, interrupting him for a second time.

Yes. But Colin would accomplish little by publicly agreeing with that assessment. Instead, he assumed his own most arrogant expression and prompted Cordelier forward until he forced the villagers to part ranks. "Since my father is not here to defend his actions, you've no choice but to deal with me. Here are my terms: this village and our tenant farmers have, and always will have, the support of the Ashworth family. Take account of your recent losses. Any that have occurred through negligence on our part will be immediately recompensed, and that includes roofs that should have been repaired at winter's end, riverbanks that should have been reinforced, and fields that should have been properly drained."

Indeed. The estate records offered indisputable evidence that his father had let his responsibilities toward these people lapse in the most shameful way. While he had demanded payment of the rents the very day they were due, he as often as not reneged on the age-old obligations of landlord to tenant. They had every right to be angry, even to lash out, but as acting head of the family and acting lord of Briarview, Colin had no choice but to deny them that right, for the result would be chaos.

"Return to your farms and your shops," he told them in the tone of a commander, "and resume the work you've abandoned in recent weeks."

"And the colt?"

His nostrils flaring, Colin turned a cold glare on Ed Harper and hoped his next words would not prove a bald-faced lie. "The colt will be returned, and soon. That is all I can tell you for now. Be the men you were born to be and stop making matters worse," he added in a softer voice that he knew would strike at their very hearts.

He wasn't wrong. At the inference that they were behaving as less than proud Devonshire men, they traded sheepish looks. Their heads down, shoulders hunched against the damp breezes, they began to disperse. Colin watched them go, relief pooling in his gut.

"You've perhaps borrowed yourself a bit of time, my lord."

He jumped, the sudden movement sending a shiver through Cordelier's flanks. In watching the others and willing them to keep their feet moving away from Briarview, he hadn't noticed that the preacher had lingered.

Turning his hat slowly in his hands as if it were a ship's wheel, the man leveled a shrewd look up at him. "But if you don't make good on your pledge, sir, they'll be back."

Colin gazed out at the village rooftops huddled at the foot of Briarview's sloping approach. The faint curls of smoke rising from the chimneys reminded him of all that could be lost. Bleakness filled his spirit. "I know."

The preacher set his wide hat back on his head. "In the meantime, I'll see what I can do to keep them calm."

Colin turned Cordelier around and started back up the drive. Tomorrow at first light he would leave here and begin his search for the colt. He would also begin distancing himself from Holly. If he'd had any doubts about involving her in his family's troubles, today's incidents confirmed his qualms. His world held neither safety nor security for her.

Upon happening to glance up, he saw her peering out at him from her bedroom window, and flimsy denials of that last assertion began eroding his resolve. Despite the haven he had made for himself in his work and his circle of friends, he found the prospect of resuming his life without her too grim to contemplate. Without Holly to share them with, his future successes would mean next to nothing.

She raised a hand to wave, then let her fingertips stray to the base of her throat. He could all but feel the beat of the pulse there, taste it on his lips. The first stirring of lust tugged at his core. With a sweep of her lashes she broke the connection of their gazes, but the blaze of her scrutiny had seared a path straight from his heart to his loins.

Christ. What was she doing out of bed? Did she never exercise the slightest caution? Must she always test her limits, as she continually tested his?

His limits proved short enough as he found himself trotting Cordelier back to the stables and cursing the slowness of even that speed. The image of her fresh features and voluptuous curves sent ideals of duty tumbling away like so much water beneath a broken bridge, leaving him with a rising passion that would not be contained. When the groom ran out to take Cordelier, Colin leaped from the saddle.

He found her waiting for him in the open doorway of her bedchamber. The near run that had brought him across the grounds and up the curving staircase had left him slightly breathless, but the rise and fall of her bosom declared her to be no less so. The borrowed nightgown still swathed her shapely body, the soft fabric hinting at so much more than it concealed, the ruffled collar framing her pale face and fever-bright eyes.

Seeming impossibly large, those eyes held him, mirroring the emotions roiling inside him. Even as his own passion fired anew at the sight of her, so too did some inner yearning infuse her cheeks with heightened color.

He strode to her from the landing. "Where is my grandmother?"

"Resting in her room."

"How long ago did she retire?"

"Not long, perhaps a quarter hour." A small frown etched her forehead. "She winked at me and told me the day's excitement had wearied her, and that she'd see us at tea. Why do you suppose she winked?"

"I couldn't say." Nor did he, at that moment, care. His lust flared like dry kindling as he considered various possibilities for filling the time.

With single-minded determination, he closed the distance between them, forcing Holly to back up into the room. He followed her inside, shut the door, and for added security turned the key in the lock.

The startled look on her face doused him like a bucket of cold water. He went still, arms at his sides. "Now is when you should probably slap me and scream."

She hesitated for an instant. Then her expression changed to one of certainty, a look that transformed her from innocent girl to a woman who knew what she wanted. "Now is when you should take me in your arms."

He went to her and swung her off her feet. "I don't wish to hurt you. The accident earlier . . ."

"I am as right as rain." Her arms slid easily around his neck. "I've had it on the authority of a very wise duchess."

Perhaps, but he certainly didn't want to think about his grandmother now, or about curses or missing colts or the rabble that was eager to storm Briarview's gates. Shoving those thoughts away, he dipped his face to the curve of her neck and immersed himself in the fragrance that was uniquely hers. Holding her firm against him, he carried her to the bed, laid her down, and leaned to cover her with his torso. His lips pressed to hers, he let his nightmares melt away into the warm flush of her skin and heady dream of loving her.

Yes, merely a dream, but one he needed to believe in if only for a few more hours. He needed to pretend that something in this world possessed the power to vanquish ancient curses.

And if anyone held that power, it must be the brave and bold Holly Sutherland.

For the second time that afternoon, tears pricked at Holly's eyes. She lay on her side, nested in a deep depression in the down mattress, her back framed by Colin's length, his

strong arm draped around her waist. His body warmed her
even through the layers of clothing they wore: her chemise,
his shirt and trousers. His steady, even breath gently stirred
the curls at her nape. The beat of his heart thudded reassur-
ingly against her spine.

She felt utterly at peace . . . and utterly floundering in
turmoil.

Her breasts ached with the irrepressible yearning to
feel his palms on them once more. Her body at once
thrummed with pleasure and echoed with a hollow note.
Despite his lifting her chemise and exploring all of her—or
nearly all—once again her deepest feminine core had not
been breached. And while she knew she should rejoice in
that, she couldn't dismiss a profound and crushing disappointment.

Nor could she help wishing that Colin Ashworth were
not such a gentleman.

Not that gallantry had prevented him from taking his
pleasure. With his hand wrapped around hers, he had shown
her where and how to touch him, hold him, move him, until
rapture had forced his head back against the pillows, his
neck strained and corded, while he gave himself up to her
control.

She had relished every moment of it. Closing her eyes,
she had glimpsed him again as she had seen him on the
moor, riding free among the ponies like a Celtic warrior of
old. In a rush of shared, exhilarating passion, she had whispered to him that it would be all right if he were to . . .

But in the darkening of his gaze she'd had her denial. A
gentleman's denial, for he was unwilling to ruin her for the
sake of an afternoon's pleasure. Then, laughing, he'd rolled
her across the bed and done unspeakable, delicious, wicked
things to her.

But things that had left her maidenhood intact and commitment unnecessary.

Tangled up with her conflicting emotions lurked a sense
of betrayal. . . . She had betrayed Victoria's trust, and now
the dowager duchess's as well. Obviously the woman had

meant to warn her away from Colin, and earlier, alone in this guest chamber, Holly had formed the resolve to do just that. When she had waved to him outside the window, she had meant it only as a friendly gesture—

No. Even now, she lied—lied to herself as she would be forced to lie to Maria Ashworth, in manner if not in actual words. In a short time she must sit before the kindly woman and pretend she felt nothing—nothing at all but polite regard for her grandson, while in truth she continued to ache for the moorland warrior who had raided her heart and stolen her soul.

But he had not marauded her body, at least not in the way that mattered most. She supposed that however Colin felt about her, on some instinctive level, he believed she was not the woman for him. He could not trust in her strength, her loyalty, her resolve to stand by him. So while he had left her sated, he'd also left her craving more . . . more than she would be allowed to know.

As the sun slanted across the open country beyond the estate, he stirred and gathered her in his arms. Coming fully awake, he kissed her, but a change had come over him. His lips no longer communicated the passion of their stolen hours together. Their touch was brief, almost chaste—the kiss of a man bidding good-bye to a woman he happened to esteem.

He rolled away quickly and gained his feet. They exchanged few words, mostly about what time he would expect her at supper. After refastening his trousers, tucking in his shirt, and pulling on the rest of his clothing—boots, waistcoat, cravat, and coat—he opened the door a crack to ensure no one would see him leave. Then like a reiver in the night, he slipped away, unaware that he took with him the whole of her being.

Some half hour later, a soft tap sounded at her door. After a beat the duchess's maid entered with a sumptuous silk gown draped over one arm. "Her Grace sent me to ask if you felt well enough to attend supper, miss."

With a fortifying breath, Holly prepared to face the evening.

*   *   *

"I wish you'd let me come with you." Holly followed Colin across the stable yard to where Cordelier stood saddled and ready to leave Briarview. The sun had not yet pushed above the horizon, and long gray shadows draped the gardens and plunged the forested riding lanes beyond them into dense, inky midnight. She caught up to Colin as he leaned down to check Cordelier's girth. "Maybe I could help," she said to the broad sweep of his shoulders.

"No." He straightened and reached up with both arms to test the straps holding his bag to the back of the saddle. "I've no idea where my search might take me. It would be too dangerous having you along."

Her hands fisted around the corners of the cashmere shawl she'd borrowed from his grandmother. "I wouldn't slow you down. You know that . . ."

"I said no." He pivoted suddenly, his face so close to hers that she pulled back with a start. "Did our journey here teach you nothing?"

"You were shot at, too. Or . . . perhaps neither of us was shot at. You yourself said it was probably a hunter's misfire."

"And you think I'll let you run that risk again?" His features pulled tight; his mouth thinned.

She shrank back again, but lifted her chin in a burst of defiance. "You needn't look so severe . . . nor be so stubborn."

His scowl deepening, he reached for her and pulled her close. His face dipped, bringing his cheek against hers, his lips brushing her hair. "I don't know what will happen in the days to come. Ah, Holly, how will I ever find the colt? It could be anywhere by now."

"If you'd let me help you . . ."

He was shaking his head before she completed the thought. He lifted his face, his gaze filled with pain. "If I am to fail, I'll fail alone. But I'll rest easier knowing you'll be here with my grandmother. At the first sign of unrest from the villagers, the slightest indication that they might be turning their anger toward Briarview again, you're to make certain the house is locked up tight and no one—and I do mean no one—is to venture outside."

The very notion chilled her. "Do you think it will come to that?"

She expected him to shake his head and profess the warning to merely be a precaution. He surprised her by nodding. "If I don't lead the colt through that village within a fortnight, then yes, it very well might. Sooner, should any further misfortune befall the local families. Now bid me good-bye."

He set his knuckles beneath her chin and swept his lips across hers. The kiss sent tingling heat showering through her, ever more so when his tongue prodded the seam of her mouth. She opened to him, drinking in the taste of him and accepting the bittersweet reality that where honor and obligation took him, she could not follow. His lips melted hotly, wetly, over hers, only to break away when a voice called his name.

"Colin!"

The duchess. His head snapped up. Holly looked up at the garden path, searching for the source of the voice. Perched in an open sedan chair carried by two broad-chested footmen, the elderly woman craned her neck to see past the shrubbery into the stable yard. A youth dressed in boots and breeches walked beside her chair. Behind her, a lantern swung from its post at the rear corner of the chaise, making the shadows dance.

"Colin, are you still here?"

At this indication that Maria Ashworth hadn't yet seen them, Holly sighed with relief. Colin strode across the stable yard to the half wall at the base of the gardens. Holly hurried along behind him, tucking behind her ear the strands of hair that had fallen loose during their kiss.

Colin reached for his grandmother's small, veined hand when the sedan chair stopped beside him. "I thought we'd said our good-byes, Grandmother."

"Indeed we did, but this lad arrived only moments ago."

She thrust an envelope into his hands. "He has a message from Sabrina and he says it is urgent."

"More theatrics from my sister?"

The footmen stared straight ahead, pretending deafness. Holly laid her hand on Colin's forearm. "You often underestimate your sister," she said quietly. "Let's hear what she has to say."

Colin shifted his gaze to the boy, whom he recognized as one of the head groom's lads-in-training. "What is it, Joshua?"

"My lord, it's the horses. Nearly all of them. A ravaging illness has swept through the stables, one even Mr. Peterson, our veterinarian, cannot identify. If someone doesn't find a cure soon, they'll begin dying. . . ."

As Colin heard those words, his skin darkened. His fingers began to shake. "Wyatt!" he shouted across the stable yard. A moment later a young groom came running out of the building. "Unsaddle Cordelier and put him away. I'll need the carriage readied, and a team hired from the village. Send Douglas. Immediately!"

"Aye, milord!"

The duchess's eyes flashed with horror. "Yes, go . . . go at once!"

Chapter 24

Colin strode back to the stables, unsure how he could keep his panic at bay during the long ride back to Masterfield Park. Joshua's description of the symptoms almost suggested that the horses had been poisoned.

Then he heard Holly scrambling across the cobbles to catch up with him. "It could be nothing more than a severe case of colic. Surely your Mr. Peterson is increasing their water and walking them, perhaps administering a dose of mineral oil. . . ."

Colin whirled, his fears translating to anger. "Colic that strikes an entire stable of horses? This is more than a common bellyache. At the very least it signifies tainted feed. A blight, or perhaps a parasite. If so, it won't be cured by a walk and a bit of oil."

Frowning at his tone, Holly retreated a step. But neither her chin nor her direct gaze wavered. "I'm coming with you."

Her declaration sent relief through him, as if simply having her at his side would cure the horses and fix everything. He wanted her with him, wanted to reach his arms around her and anchor his world with her earnest faith and her forthright courage. But that was a false perception. She could not help him; he could only drag her down with him into the mire.

"No," he said bluntly. "I want you here, with Grandmother. As we agreed."

"I only agreed because you were going off to search for the colt. Now that you're returning to Masterfield Park there is no reason I shouldn't accompany you and return to my sisters. Ivy may need me and besides . . . perhaps I can help with the horses."

More false hopes. They triggered his temper. "Are you a veterinarian?"

The determination in her expression dimmed. "No, but—"

"Then you cannot help."

She shot a glance over her shoulder at the approaching sedan chair. His grandmother waved a hand as she urged the footmen to hurry their steps into the stable yard. Before she reached earshot, Holly whispered, "Have you forgotten the queen? It's time I reported back to Her Majesty. She has a right to know her colt may never be recovered."

"And do you intend on telling her the truth?"

An eternity seemed to pass before she answered. She owed him nothing and God knew he had no right to make demands. Yet as the moment stretched he felt himself dying, withering inside.

"No," she finally said, and he drew air into his lungs as though he were being born, as if it were his very first breath. Relief eased the tension from his shoulders, the knots from his gut.

"Thank you." Across the way, the footmen had passed through the garden gate and into the stable yard. "What *will* you tell Her Majesty?" he asked quickly. "I don't wish you to lie for my sake. If it comes down to it—"

"I will, though," she whispered. "I'll lie for you, but not *only* for you. I'll protect the colt. Should you ever find him, you must return him to the moor. I understand that now."

"Ah, God . . ." A sharp ache wrapped itself around his chest.

"And I *am* coming with you."

How could he tell her no when he wanted her with him so badly? Yet how would he withstand the ride all the way to Masterfield Park with her sitting within arm's reach?

He'd already compromised her. How could he be such a blackguard as to continue to do so, when he knew he couldn't offer more? He shook his head, trying to stand firm. "This won't be a leisurely three- or four-days' ride. The pace will be brutal, for I intend to travel nonstop, except when I must change teams."

"That doesn't matter—"

"What is this?" When his grandmother reached them, she signaled the footmen to bring the sedan chair to a halt, but not to set her down. As a result, she hovered imperially at Colin's eye level. "Did I hear correctly that you wish Miss Sutherland to remain here while you return to Masterfield Park?"

"I thought it would be best, for her comfort and your safety, Grandmother. The villagers—"

"I'll be the judge of what's best for my safety, young man. For your information, the villagers do not frighten me in the least. Bluster, that's what they are. Angry, true enough, and with cause. But they belong to Briarview as much as we do, and they will not make good on their threats. Miss Sutherland is to return to Masterfield Park with you." With a dismissive sniff, she crossed her arms over her bosom.

"I'd still feel better if—"

"Colin." Holly's hand came down on his forearm. "If Her Grace wishes me gone, we must not argue."

"Oh, my dear, don't misunderstand," his grandmother said. She reached out to grasp Holly's hand. "It isn't that I wish you to go. Quite the contrary, I should like nothing more than for you and me to become better acquainted. However, you *must* go. Your place is no longer here. Not just now, at any rate," she added.

"I don't understand, Your Grace."

"In time you will." She smiled brightly. "Now, then, the two of you had best make yourselves ready to go. Douglas will be back with the team before you know it."

Colin didn't know whether to laugh or tear at his hair in frustration. "Grandmother, the Ashworth family and all our prospects lie in shambles. How can you be so optimistic?"

She had no answer for him, only an enigmatic smile whose meaning eluded him. No matter. Within the hour he and Holly were barreling along the eastbound highway, Colin having entrusted the driving of the carriage and four to the capable hands of Douglas, Briarview's longtime coachman. Joshua would remain in Devonshire for a much-needed rest after his harried journey there, and then make his way home at his leisure.

Colin put his efforts into remaining on his end of the velvet bench seat, his spine pressed to the cushioned squabs and his hands fisted on his knees. How easy it would have been—too easy—to pull Holly into his arms and allow his hands to roam beneath the hems of the riding habit she had resumed wearing.

How easy to indulge their desires within the shadows of the carriage's interior. Like the tree that falls in the forest with no one to hear . . . would Holly be ruined if there was no one to see? No one to tell tales?

How easy to form the answer he would like to be true. But that wouldn't make it true.

He clenched his hands tighter. Bad enough they would arrive in Masterfield Park together like this—like the pair of lovers they almost were. He glanced over at her, his gaze tracing her profile. She sat with her hands clasped lightly in her lap, her body swaying with the motion of the coach. She seemed far less perturbed than in those final moments at Briarview, as if she'd reached a conclusion that gave her comfort. It made him wonder . . .

"What did Grandmother mean when she said your place was no longer at Briarview?"

He'd expected her to be startled by his sudden question, cutting like a knife through the silence. But as if she'd been pondering the very same matter, she only compressed her lips and peered at him through the ever-moving shadows. "I'm not sure. I thought at first she was angry with me, and wanted me gone." She smiled wistfully. "Apparently your grandmother is confident that everything will come out well, and somehow my returning to Masterfield Park plays a part in that plan."

"Do you believe she's right?"

She shrugged. "At this point I neither believe nor disbelieve. Events will unfold as they will. Your grandmother told me a story yesterday, and I believe it meant we must be patient and not resist what fate has planned for us."

"Must we be passive?"

"No, we must believe that all things are possible."

"Even curses?"

She took a deep breath and let it out slowly. "Perhaps that most of all. For what is a curse but the results of our own failure to have faith?"

He angled a gaze out the window at the passing fields dotted with sheep, cattle, and the occasional worker. "Faith is something I lost a long time ago."

"Your grandmother hasn't lost hers."

"Grandmother is an idealist." A pang struck his chest, a sharp pain that was half remorse and half anger that his grandmother and mother had had so little to depend on in their lives, enduring husbands who had scorned their every attempt to usher happiness into the Ashworth family. For their pains they'd received ridicule and disregard, intermingled with bouts of drunken violence. Perhaps this was the truth of the family curse, not a spurned Celtic princess but a legacy of abuse handed down from one despicable individual to another.

He had escaped such a heritage only by *literally* escaping—into academia and his science, where the steadiness of logic overruled emotion and irrationality. His life at Cambridge had saved him.

But saved him for what? In the end, he was still Thaddeus Ashworth's son.

Crossing one leg over the other knee, he hunkered down lower on the seat and leaned his head back. "Faith is something Grandmother clung to by necessity, when she had nothing else."

"On the contrary." Holly paused, and he raised his face to regard her. A shrewdness that mirrored Grandmama's spread across her features. "The dowager duchess may resort to mythology to explain the world around her. She may even believe in that mythology to a point. But I assure you, your grandmother is a realist. And she possesses something you lack." She chuckled softly. "And which I lack, too."

"And what is that?"

"Patience."

"Ah, true. Then what of faith, Miss Sutherland? What, if anything, do you believe in?"

"I have faith in God. And in my sisters." She was quiet for a moment, then added, "And in Victoria."

His hand reached across the seat before his mind even formed the intent to touch her. He caressed her cheek, a slight graze of his fingertips. "What about me? Does Holly Sutherland have faith in me?"

She hesitated in answering, and just as in Briarview's stable yard, he died a dozen small deaths while he waited, wishing he hadn't asked—wishing he hadn't *needed* to ask. Yet everything he'd always believed himself to be as a man hung in the balance, dependent, somehow—irrationally—on her answer.

Ha. Science hadn't really saved him at all.

But when it came, her whispered *yes* renewed him as nothing else could. He slid to her, and then she was in his arms, their mouths pressed, their breath mingled. His lust prodded, sprang to life, even as his heart opened on a torrent of emotion that enveloped him and sent unexpected words sliding from his lips into the sultry interior of Holly's mouth.

"If things had been different, had I not been an Ashworth, I'd have asked for your hand months ago."

She went utterly still in his arms.

He drew back, then pressed his forehead to hers and shut his eyes. "You deserve to know that. Since our first ride together at Harrowood, I knew you were the perfect woman for me, that I could never want another as much as I wanted you—"

"You took pains to hide it," she whispered hoarsely, her lips brushing his.

"Yes, I did, because I feared bringing you into my family, letting my father anywhere near you. . . . But I thought about you constantly. Then, just weeks ago, I thought I'd finally gathered the courage to face whatever the future brought—as long as I had you at my side. I was determined to speak to you, not to ask for your hand just then, but to reveal something of my feelings. I'm sure you've forgotten that morning in Simon and Ivy's morning room—"

Her hands tightened around his forearms. "Box hedges."

Surprised, he pulled away to peer at her. "By God, yes. It was that morning."

Tears glimmered in her eyes. "But why did you never get past asking about those blasted hedges?"

He felt as though a dagger was slowly piercing his chest. "You were so beautiful that morning. So lovely and fresh and candid. It made me think of my family again. Good God, Holly, how could I bring you into such a family?"

"I'm stronger than you know."

"Perhaps, but I found myself unwilling to take the chance, to risk losing the person you are by exposing you to things that would change you." He sat up straighter, moving his hands to her shoulders and creating space between them. "I did right. What if I had spoken of my feelings, my intentions?" She started to answer, but he pressed his fingers over her lips. "No, Holly. Look at me now. I am a horse thief and a traitor, with a curse over my head. It doesn't matter if curses are real or not. The result is the same. I cannot offer you the life you deserve."

She blinked her tears away, and swiped angrily at the one that still spilled down her cheek. "You're a fool, then, Colin Ashworth. I would have stood by you." She pulled away from him and angled her gaze out the window. "I'd have stood by you through everything."

Yes, and that would have hurt most of all. Not the consequences of stealing from the queen, not the repercussions at Briarview should the colt never be returned, but knowing she suffered for his sake.

"Why did you even bother telling me?" she asked in a flat voice.

"Because surely my feelings must have become obvious to you these past several days. I thought it only right you knew the truth."

She turned back to him, her countenance sharp, her eyes accusing. "You believe that to be the truth? That you were protecting me?"

He nodded.

"As I said, you are a fool. You weren't protecting me. You were *underestimating* me, as you do with everyone else in your life." His mouth opened but she cut him off. "You were right about one thing—you don't have faith, not in anyone. You believe you must face adversity alone because no one else is strong enough to stand with you. Because in your eyes no one else can be trusted not to wither away and die. You'd rather wither and die alone than risk putting your faith in anyone. In me."

"You don't understand . . ."

Holly stopped listening to him. He could go on and on about wanting to spare her from the unpleasantness of his family, but he would never dissuade her of what she knew to be the truth. He didn't believe in her, didn't believe the love that had been growing steadily between them was stronger than any difficulties life could throw at them. For better or worse. She believed in that. She was strong enough to live by such a vow.

Perhaps if she had been a woman like Penelope Wingate, she could see the sense in his actions. If she were a woman who wanted little more than the status and wealth of being a future duchess, then yes, of course such a marriage would be unsatisfactory. But she didn't care a whit for the *things* he could give her. She wanted only him. Colin Ashworth the man. And while his hardheaded, noble desire to step between danger and those in his care was part of that man, and part of what she loved about him, his stubborn refusal to accept help made her want to slap sense into him.

What angered her most was his refusal to allow her a choice. He had simply decided what was best for her, and brooked no debate. As though she were a child. Even now, as he moved away to occupy the far end of the carriage seat, his troubled expression held a certain self-assurance, because no matter who suffered, he apparently felt justified in his decision.

She crossed her arms in front of her and tried to settle in for the remainder of the ride. He had promised a grueling pace, and he hadn't lied. She had long since lost track of the hours, even of how many times they stopped, each respite proving all too short before she'd had to fold her aching limbs back onto the carriage seat and endure endless miles of incessant jostling.

His confession had denied her any comfort she might have derived from traveling together toward a shared fate, a common goal. Instead, she understood now that they were traveling to an end, and that once they arrived in Masterfield Park she would no longer have any claim on him, or hold any significant place in his life.

She dozed, then awakened to find him staring across the seat at her. For a moment her heart gave a lift as she thought perhaps her reproving words had forced him to reconsider.

"Where does my mother believe you to have gone?" he asked.

The question caught her off guard, and filled her with disappointment. "I . . . er . . . down to London. Why?"

"I think we should separate at the next coaching inn. I'll arrange transportation to take you the remaining distance to Masterfield Park."

"What on earth for?"

"You know how quickly the rumors will fly if we're seen returning together." His words struck her like rapid gunfire, equally as jarring. "There is no reason to sacrifice your reputation."

The irony of that statement, considering the unnecessary sacrifices he seemed willing to make, pushed mirthless laughter from her lips.

His nostrils flared as if she had offended him, rather than the other way around. "I won't be responsible for destroying your future," he said.

You already have, irreparably. "You are not responsible for me, and you don't owe me anything," she said evenly, proud that she could prevent the mutinous tears from putting a tremor in her voice. For it had suddenly occurred to her that along with not believing in her sufficiently, perhaps he simply didn't *love* her sufficiently. Perhaps that had been the trouble all along. Oh, he admired her, esteemed her, perhaps found her an intriguing contrast to the elegant young women who typically crossed his path. But when it came to actually marrying her . . .

"Very well, then, we'll continue on together." He slid the window open. "Can we go any faster?" he called out to the driver.

"We'll be changing teams at the next coaching inn, my lord," the man shouted back. "I daren't go any faster till then."

She shivered at the cool air streaming in the open window, then wished she hadn't when she once again felt his scrutiny. She very nearly admitted she was cold so he would hold her, or at the very least remove his coat and drape it around her shoulders. If she couldn't have his arms around her, couldn't have *him*, his sleeves, warm with his musky scent, seemed the next best thing. "I'm all right," she said to his unspoken question. "Just stiff."

Without a word he slid closer, and in a haze of exhaustion she watched his arm come up and his hand reach for her. As it closed around her shoulder and pulled her toward him, anger and longing fought inside her.

"Don't," she protested weakly.

"Let me." He tugged the ribbons beneath her chin and tossed her bonnet onto the seat at his other side. She felt his lips on her hair. "I am an ass," he whispered.

"Yes, you are."

Her head tipped, angling to the heat of his mouth until their lips met, easily, inevitably; a perfect fit. The taste of him filled her, and imbued her with the sense of how life could be. . . .

The pain became almost too much to bear until he lifted his mouth. "You may have been right about me," he said.

"I know I am right."

"But not entirely. Perhaps I should have had more faith in you sooner, but I didn't know you then as I do now. I couldn't even have fathomed just how much there was to learn about you. But what I could not believe was that there could be a happy ending in all of this. That I could return the colt to Briarview and simply walk away from the crime I'd committed. That my father would no longer have a hold over me."

"Or that I would stand by your side through it all. You wouldn't believe that, either."

His embrace tightened. He held her close, his face in her hair, his heart beating against her breast. But when he pulled away again, he was shaking his head. "I won't allow you to sink with me. But—" He broke off, and the look that came over him held her spellbound. "If by some miracle I find a way to extricate myself . . . I haven't the least idea how . . . but if I do . . ."

"Yes?"

"Then I shall be speaking to one of your brothers-in-law."

For an instant they held each other as joy enveloped them, flowing like golden light around them. But as he dipped his head to kiss her, she saw it in his eyes—that glimmer of doubt that belied his hopefulness. He didn't believe their happy ending would come. He wanted it, treasured the possibility, but in the end, he still didn't believe strongly enough.

Still, she let him hold her, kiss her, allowed their pretense to continue. Desire flamed to life, fueled by the memory of all the things they had shared, the kisses, the caresses, the secrets rendered by their bodies when touched just so.

"Colin . . ." She whispered his name like the desperate entreaty it was.

His own whispered reply tore from his throat. "I only mean to hold you."

"I know."

"Damn it, it's not enough. It'll never be enough."

"No, never."

The world tumbled, and then the carriage seat pressed her back and the biting muscles of Colin's chest and abdomen and thighs pressed her front. Pressed her painfully, deliciously.

His hands dived beneath her hems and raised them. Without permission or prelude he thumbed his trouser buttons open. Her own impatience beyond enduring, her soft cries filled the carriage as his hips pinned her and the impossibly hot length of his shaft rubbed between her thighs. She instinctively parted for him, her arms encircling his waist, her own hips coming off the seat to meet him.

She braced for pain—it should hurt, she'd been told—but she felt only the gently demanding nudge at her nether lips.

He came to her barrier and stopped. Above her, Colin lay completely rigid as if he feared making the slightest motion, while he pulsed within her contracted muscles, their joined spasms hinting at something greater, a shared communion of pleasure, a completion.

But just as she seized upon the notion and tried to rock her hips to bury him deeper, he began to recede. She gripped his arms, fingernails biting through his sleeves. "No."

"I must." He paused as if agonizing over the decision he'd made. "While the future is still so uncertain, what else can I do?"

Have me, ravish me, love me . . .

"Live for now," she said, "because we don't know what we'll find when this carriage stops and its doors open."

He shook his head, and without another word he retreated from her. Before she could fully mourn the loss of him and of what her body craved so intensely, he leaned between parted her knees, and she felt the warm brush of his hair against her thighs.

She gasped as his tongue entered her. Yet a protest rose up, and she tugged at his shoulders until he slid off the seat and knelt on the floorboards beside her, his torso within easy reach. His mouth never left her, not even when her hand followed the trail of fine hairs from his navel downward, and her fingers closed around his shaft. As she stroked up and down, his lips moved all the more fiercely against her and his tongue lashed deeper, all in a mounting rhythm goaded by the rocking carriage.

Then she turned her face into the velvet squabs to muffle the sounds of her ecstasy, while his shudders traveled like silent thunder all through her.

Chapter 25

M asterfield Park lay dark and silent when Douglas turned the carriage up the drive sometime between midnight and dawn. Colin didn't have him stop at the house, but ordered him to circle to the stables. With sleepy eyes, Holly nodded her agreement. They would see to the horses before seeking their own comfort.

A haggard-looking Mr. Peterson met them in the cobbled forecourt as Colin handed Holly down from the carriage. "It's not like anything I've ever seen before, my lord. One or two horses at a time, yes, but not an entire stable full."

"Tell me exactly what the symptoms have been, starting with the earliest ones."

"First we noticed a slightly unsteady gait on some of the horses, and a tightening of their flanks, as though they were holding their bellies. The intestinal symptoms began soon after, and I've noticed dilated pupils on some."

"What about the guest horses?" Colin asked.

"All moved elsewhere, at the first sign of illness. But your family's personal mounts are fit as fiddles—so far. It's the racehorses and hunters that are affected."

"And you've tried all the traditional cures for colic?" Holly asked.

Peterson's gaze traveled up and down her cloaked form, and Colin experienced a moment's remorse in having exposed her to speculation. The expression of concern never slipped from the veterinarian's features, however. If he found anything unusual about the two of them having traveled through the night together, he didn't show it.

"That we have, miss." The man gestured to the archway that separated the two wings of the stables. "The grooms have been alternating the sick animals, walking them all night long. I've ordered extra water and they've had nothing to eat but the purest hay."

"Has anyone inspected the grain?"

"Yes, my lord. It appears sound, but . . ."

Peterson trailed off. He and Colin both knew that a blight might not be apparent to the naked eye. "I want samples brought to my office."

"Lady Harrow ordered samples sent to London, sir, to her husband."

"Good." Colin pinched the bridge of his nose and attempted to blink the fatigue from his eyes. "Still, I'd like to run my own analysis. Bring me clearly labeled samples of the hay and the water. I need to know exactly where each sample comes from."

"The water comes from our own wells, my lord."

"Even so. Wells have been known to become poisoned."

Holly shot him a sharp look but said nothing.

"My lord, the horses are all fed from the same sources. If there was a contagion of some kind, they'd all have fallen ill."

Colin thought a moment, and then a notion struck him. "Are you sure all the horses are consuming the same feed? Didn't some of our guests bring their own feed formulas for the horses they boarded here for the races? Could some of it have been left behind and gotten mixed in with our own?"

"My word, sir, it's possible."

"Get me those samples." Colin filled his lungs with misty, predawn air and gazed up at the house. "Where is my sister?"

"Retired, I believe, sir, though she was here helping direct the grooms until long after midnight. I caught her yawning and insisted she get some rest. Your brothers helped as well. We needed as many hands as possible to keep the horses moving."

Colin nodded, glad to hear the family was getting much-needed rest. Exhaustion dragged at his bones, but not merely due to the present crisis. He'd spent his lifetime holding his family together, mediating, consoling, encouraging, protecting . . . only to be faced now with circumstances that stretched beyond his control. What would happen should events continue careening down their present course? What future would there be for the Ashworth family? Financially, they would remain unscathed, for the bulk of their fortune came from other sources. But these horses provided so much more than money, rewards such as pride and a sense of accomplishment.

He extended his arm to Holly. He found himself needing the support of her stubborn spirit, her frankness; heaven help him, even her rebukes bolstered him, forced him to admit the truth and take action, rather than brood and accept defeat.

He needed that now. Needed to believe, as she did, that they could fight their way to happiness. As if sensing his need, she slid her hand into the crook of his arm and walked with him across the forecourt to the heavy door that led directly into the office he kept here in the stables. Before they went inside, he turned back to Peterson. "Would you send one of the grooms up to the house to ask that tea be brought down, please?"

"The kitchen sent down some fresh buns and oatcakes not a quarter hour ago. I'll have some brought in to you."

Inside, a groom appeared and lit the brazier. Some minutes later Peterson himself brought in a tray of refreshments. Holly had removed the cloak she'd borrowed from the dowager duchess and stood warming her hands in front of the hissing coal heater. Colin dragged the only other chair besides his own closer to the desk.

"Come and sit. Have something to eat."

"We've been sitting for hours and hours." She sent a rueful glance over her shoulder, but then turned and approached the desk. "But something hot and filling sounds heavenly." She unstacked two cups and placed them on their saucers. She poured tea into both, spooned in some sugar, and added trickles of milk. Then she selected a treacle bun from the platter Peterson had brought.

Colin perched on the corner of the desk and drained half his tea, not caring that the hot liquid burned his tongue. The brew was black and strong, precisely what he needed to start his mind working. All he required now were the samples.

He held out a hand. "Come here, please."

She popped a remaining morsel of bun into her mouth and set her teacup down. When she came to stand in the V of his knees, he drained the last of his tea, set it aside, and encircled her waist with his arms. "I'm sorry for the way I behaved on the way here."

"For which behavior?" Her eyebrow rose in a show of censure, while the twitch of her lips hinted at humor. "The dismissal or the ravishment?"

Her forthrightness drew a laugh from him in spite of everything. "Both, I suppose. Holly . . ." He ran his gaze over her—her lovely figure with its athletic curves, her straight, brave posture, her beautiful face with its endearing blend of fortitude and innocence. He reached up to caress her cheek. "The time isn't right for us."

Her eyebrow arched higher. "Do you think there will ever be a perfect time?"

"Perhaps, someday . . ."

She pressed her fingertips to his mouth. "First we have horses to diagnose and cure."

As if on cue, a knock at the door separated them. She returned to the heat of the brazier; he opened the door and admitted three young grooms, their arms filled with sacks, scripted notes pinned to each. A fourth groom carrying a bucket half filled with water followed them into the room.

"Your samples, my lord," one of them said.

Colin helped the lads arrange the parcels on the long table against the far wall of the office. They exited single file and shut the door behind them. Colin opened a cabinet and reached inside.

Behind him, Holly exclaimed, "Oh, is that what I think it is?"

He drew out the wood and brass contraption, which appeared much like a short telescope mounted on a wooden stand, and set it on the table. "It's a microscope."

She heaved an appreciative sigh and joined him at the table. "It's beautiful. Even Simon doesn't have one as grand as this."

"It's my own design."

She bestowed upon him perhaps the proudest smile anyone had ever afforded him . . . the sort of approval a young boy longs to see on his father's face, but which, of course, he never had.

"May I?" she said with a note of awe. With a forefinger she reached out, nearly but not quite touching one of the brass brackets. He gestured his permission, and she leaned over to place an eye over the viewing lens. She wiggled the small round mirror set in the base. "I don't see anything."

"That's because you need more light, and something to examine." He'd already moved across the room to the shelves where he stored the small lanterns he had designed specifically for this purpose. With polished steel reflectors that directed the light exactly where he needed it, he could illuminate the tiniest particle brightly enough to be explored through the telescope's lens. Returning to the table, he lit the lanterns and reached for the first of the samples. "I'll need your help," he said.

"Of course. Anything."

He nodded toward his desk. "You'll find a notation tablet and pencils. Bring them here. You're going to record my findings."

"Yes, sir," came her enthusiastic reply, followed by a delighted little laugh. "This is how Ivy must have felt the first time she assisted Simon in his laboratory." Her gaze met his and her face immediately fell. "Colin, I'm sorry. This is no time for merriment."

He smiled sadly. "No. But I do understand. I was once a young science student." After selecting a scoop from an assortment hung on the wall just above the table, he opened the first of the sample bags, poured a small amount of grain into a mortar, and ground it into a powder. From a drawer he took two glass specimen plates, sandwiched a pinch of powder between them, and set them into the base of the microscope. "Now then, let's see if we can't determine what the devil is going on here."

Nearly two hours later Colin removed the last specimen from the microscope and set it onto the tabletop with a force that made Holly flinch. She peered around his shoulder to see if the plates had shattered beneath his hand, but seeing neither bits of glass nor blood, she gave a little sigh of relief.

And of frustration. They'd gone through every sample of grain and hay as well as numerous droplets of the water and discovered nothing unusual. Holly had taken copious notes, copying down nearly every word Colin had spoken, even what he had absently murmured under his breath.

He propped his elbows on the table and let his head fall into his hands. "It's useless. I see no sign of any sort of blight."

The flatness of his tone worried her. He was once more losing hope, and with it his confidence in his abilities as both a scientist and a horse breeder. Her hand hovered over his sagging shoulder; uncertain how best to offer comfort, she settled her palm against the curve of his neck. "Perhaps we missed something."

His eyes were glazed and red-rimmed from anxiety, lack of sleep, and the intensive concentration of the past two hours. "Maybe the answer is under my nose. I've been looking for a foreign element. Perhaps it's the feed itself. Pass me another sampling."

"Pressed onto a new slide?"

"No. Just bring me a scoopful."

When she did, he brought the lantern closer, poured the

feed onto the table in front of him and leaned down to examine it closely. He sat like that for some minutes, running his fingertips through the grains, separating them, piling them together, rolling them apart. Then he picked up a leafy granule between his thumb and forefinger and peered at it with one eye.

"There is something about the color of some of this grain ... it's too green. . . ." His head snapped up. "I need the library. Let's go up to the house."

He gathered up the strewn piles of her notes and grabbed the feed bag. Without looking back to see if she followed, he was out the door.

She half ran to keep up across the cobbled forecourt and through the gardens. Glimmers of dawn reflected on the house's black windows, except at the lowest level where the kitchen staff were awake and preparing the day's meals. Whiffs of baking bread and savory meats floated on the breeze, making Holly's stomach rumble despite the breakfast they'd shared. Colin appeared oblivious as he took the terrace steps two at a time. At the main door that led into the rear corridor, a bleary-eyed footman admitted them. Colin murmured a preoccupied thank-you and kept going, practically bounding down the hallway to the library.

Holly couldn't step across that threshold without remembering what had occurred the last time she'd entered that room. Their first embraces, their first kiss. The first time she'd heard her Christian name fall gently from his lips.

Colin strode to the desk, found a box of lucifers and began lighting the lamps. A mellow glow settled over the settee where he'd first held her, where her passion had first awakened. She compressed her lips and angled her gaze away. "What can I do to help?"

He seemed not to hear her as he surveyed the bookshelves. Then he said, "Look for books on plants and horticulture."

They each began snatching books off the shelves. When a small pile had grown on the desk, he sat and began flipping through the first volume. Holly lifted one. "What are we looking for?"

"Something I couldn't identify through my microscope, nor with my naked eye, but which I'm almost positive doesn't belong in horse feed."

"Such as?"

"Poisonous plants that could have gotten mixed up in the feed."

"Good lord."

Painstakingly they read through countless plant descriptions and compared the tiny, mysteriously green particles he'd isolated with the sketches and engravings contained in the books.

"I hadn't realized how many species of plant life are poisonous." She pointed to a sketch of a trumpet-shaped blossom. "A flower as lovely as the lily, for example."

"I don't think it's a flower we're looking for," he mumbled, "but something heartier, with tougher leaves and stems." He snapped a book shut, making her jump. Pressing the heels of his hands to his eyes, he leaned his elbows on the desktop.

"We will find it," she said.

"Not if I'm mistaken." He lifted his head and balled his hands into fists. "This may be beyond my capabilities."

The statement chilled her. If a man educated at one of Europe's most prestigious universities, who associated regularly with some of the finest minds in the scientific world, could not find the answer, then. . . .

"You mustn't lose hope."

He shook his head slowly. "Terrible things happen in this world. Why should the Ashworths be immune?"

She had no answer for him.

"Because you see, this is about more than saving horses. They are magnificent beings, yes, and surely worth our most prodigious efforts. But it's also about the well-being of my family. These horses, the stud—it is who we are. What we are about. It may sound melodramatic, but can you understand?"

"I can, yes."

He reached for another book, pulled it to him and, like a man reconciled to a dismal fate, began thumbing through the pages. Her gaze settled on the bag of grain he had set on a corner of the desk. She slid a lamp closer, thrust her hand into the bag, and then examined the contents of her palm. She did this several times, each time digging deeper. Colin went on reading. Finally, she noticed an inch-long particle of plant matter in her palm, a frond that, if ground up smaller, would not have caught their attention among the granules. "Colin, this looks like a bit of fern mixed in with the grains. Is that correct in horse feed?"

He pushed the book away. "No, that is not correct. Let me see."

He held out his hand, and she tipped the feed from her palm into his. Then she slid the lamp close to his elbow. He studied the specimen, his frown deepening. Without looking up, he said, "Open that book." He gestured with his chin. "The one on indigenous ground cover."

The slight tremor in his voice filled her with urgency. She fumbled the book and it thwacked to the floor. Once she had retrieved it, he said, "Find the entry for bracken."

"Bracken? But doesn't that grow—"

"Everywhere. And it's poisonous to horses. A nibble or two won't hurt them, but if they ingest large amounts over time . . ." He sat up straighter.

She opened the book, flipped through and found the entry. She began reading out loud, describing the traits and habitat, but Colin stopped her. "Do they list the symptoms of livestock poisoning?"

She used her finger to skim down the page. "Unsteadiness, skittishness, stomach pain, blockage of the intestines . . . dilated pupils." She stopped short, compressed her lips, and met his gaze. "This is it, isn't it?"

He lurched out of his seat to read the entry over her shoulder. Then he grabbed her, spun her around and kissed her breathless.

He pulled his lips away, his own stretched in an elated

grin. "Wait here. I want to get a message down to Mr. Peterson."

He sprinted from the room, returning within minutes, his step buoyant, his relief palpable. She had begun replacing the books on the shelves. He crossed the room, took the stack from her arms, dropped them onto the nearest tabletop, and took her in his arms. He danced her in circles to a silent waltz.

"Now that we know what it is, they'll live." He sounded youthful, filled with a childlike wonderment. He brought them to a halt. "Thank you. Thank you!"

"You're welcome. But I think I only noticed the frond because . . ."

"Because you hadn't given up hope, as I had," he finished for her. When she nodded, he kissed her brow, then straightened, looking sheepish. "You'll laugh at me, but I had actually begun to believe Briannon was at work here. Some scientist, eh?"

Chapter 26

H olly reached her arms around his neck. "The last thing
   I imagine Briannon would ever do is harm innocent
horses."

"You say that like you believe in her."

"I think I do believe in her spirit, and what she stands
for. Your grandmother told me that Briannon doesn't seek
retribution, but *resolution*. Curse or no, we have free will,
the choice to do what is right, no matter what."

A slight smile tugged at his mouth. "Was I right to steal
the colt, then?"

"Oh, Colin." An ache pinching her throat, she pressed
her face to his shirtfront. He gently stroked her hair, kissed
the top of her head.

"I'm sorry. I didn't mean to make you sad. I meant it as
a joke. Because you see, suddenly I'm not quite as appre-
hensive of the future as I was." He cupped her damp cheeks
in his palms and lifted her face. "I can't quite explain it, but
you've made me . . . I don't know . . . *believe*. And no one
has ever been able to do that for me before."

As his words dissipated he took her mouth—took it as
though she belonged to him, as if she always would, and the
tears that ran down her cheeks became joyful. She held on
to him and kissed him back, until his mouth slid away from
hers and he lifted her into his arms.

The room blurred as he brought her to the settee and laid

her across the cushions. Briefly he left her to lock the library doors. When he returned, the look on his face frightened her even as it thrilled her, and she made a swift decision.

She melted into the cushions as he pressed his lips to hers in a conflagration of possessiveness that left her heart pounding. He left her briefly again, opened a cabinet, and retrieved a dark blanket that proved lusciously soft when he tucked it beneath her.

If she expected the next moments to be a heated rush of mindless passion, she was only partly right. Oh, her body heated by impossible degrees, and her thoughts dissolved to mindless pleasure as Colin slowly stripped away her clothing. Ah, but there was no rush. No haphazard tangle of limbs. No frenzy of kissing and groping.

But then, she had momentarily forgotten the scientist in him, the careful observer who formed a meticulous plan for everything he did. Just as they'd examined and catalogued the samples, Colin took stock of all of her. From the kisses he planted on the arches of her feet, the undersides of her knees, the inner sides of her thighs ... to the contours his fingertips traced with torturous caresses, he moved with purpose, precision.

And slowly but relentlessly he drove her to a mindless, frenzied brink, until she fisted her fingers in his hair and clenched her teeth to stifle her cries.

At some point, she didn't know when, he'd shed his coat, his waistcoat, and cravat. With both hands she reached up and worked the laces of his shirt free, and with mounting passion spurring her, she tugged the garment over his head. Ah, she loved his chest, hard and rippled, the muscles deeply carved by the hand of some masterful god ... or goddess. The thought curved her lips to a smile, one that put a temporary halt to his ministrations.

"What?"

She wanted to tell him how happy he made her. How eagerly she would spend the rest of her life at his side, for better or worse. But she feared the words would remind him of all they still faced and would drive him away. She didn't want him to think, didn't want his sense of duty to rise up or awaken his instincts to protect her.

She pulled his head back down, and as their mouths joined she slipped her hand between their bodies and plucked his breeches flap open. Using her other hand as well, she tugged his breeches lower to expose the chiseled lines of his hips.

His shaft rose against her belly, but just as quickly slid lower to prod between her thighs. "Holly . . ." His tongue swept her lips, speared between them, then slowly retreated. "I am who I am. I can offer nothing. . . ."

"I'm not asking for anything," she whispered. "Only you. Only now."

"What I feel for you . . . I believe . . ."

The tip of his shaft nudged at her nether lips. He rocked his hips and slid inside her. As in the carriage, he reached the barrier and stopped. "I believe if I searched forever I'll never find another woman like you." He gave a thrust that threatened to shatter the barrier, that sent a jolt of pain . . . yet not *quite* pain . . . shuddering through her.

She pushed against him, and the barrier gave way, breaking apart with searing suddenness. She clung to him, tears leaking from the corners of her eyes and rolling to her ears. Tearfully she smiled up at him, knowing he spoke the truth—that she could search the world over and never find another man like him, a man who made her feel whole and alive and beautiful.

"I believe," he repeated in a whisper as, like an undulating ocean tide, he began to move inside her, the sweet mingling of pain and pleasure filling her heart and clogging her throat and sending more tears spilling from her eyes.

Tighter she wrapped her arms and legs around him, tipping her pelvis to take him deeper, so that each thrust filled her completely, and each retreat brought the full length of him gliding like heated satin at her opening. Her muscles tightened around him, took possession of him. The intensity rose, stretched, carrying her higher. Her body tensed and arched. The world disappeared and there was only sensation and need, desperate, urgent, until the tautness inside her broke in a blinding burst that racked her from her core outward. A thousand tiny bolts of lightning sparked through her, and she muffled her cries against his shoulder as he plunged, deeply, a final time.

His seed pumped into her, filling her, draining him, and leaving them spent and breathless in each other's arms. And as he settled his solid, perspiring weight over her, he completed the sentence he'd begun.

"I believe in you. I believe what I feel for you is love."

He should not have spoken the words. He should not have done many things these past several days, but most of all, he should not have envisioned what his life would be like if he were free to take Holly as his wife.

If he had entertained any doubts previously, the last hours of working together had proved how perfect a wife she would have made for him. Like Simon and Ivy, who shared a laboratory and together devised new and startling ways of conducting electricity. Who knew what he and Holly could have achieved together, what methods of strengthening equine breeds, or ensuring that England's yearly harvests would feed her people?

Yet as the minutes passed, joy moved farther and farther away, until dejection hung over him, pressing down on his shoulders, becoming heavier with each tick of the clock. For now he knew, wholly, what he must give up.

He stroked his fingertips over the bare curve of her shoulder. Had she fallen asleep? Dear God, how he hated to wake her. How he hated having to wake himself from this perfect dream.

He shifted until he lay beside her. "Holly?"

Her lashes fluttered. She smiled up at him.

"Did I hurt you?"

"Yes. It was wonderful."

"Are you . . . going to be all right?" He didn't mean only that moment. He meant for the rest of her life. "We should not have . . ."

"I don't regret it. I won't."

"But if—"

Her eyes came fully open, and she pushed up onto her elbows. "I will live with any consequences. My sisters would never abandon me, no matter my disgrace. If nothing else, I do have that assurance."

The words cut him deeply, for they attested to the kind of love that was lacking in his own family. They also attested to all he would not be able to give her.

"I understand that nothing has changed." She smiled sadly.

"And you don't hate me?"

"Never."

That stabbed deepest, caused him the most pain. This was his curse, perhaps Briannon's doing after all: to know love, to want it, to have it not just within reach but between his very hands, yet be forced to push it away. To have to walk away, while knowing he would not be the only one suffering for his mistakes.

If that wasn't a curse, what was?

He forced his shoulders not to sag, his chin not to fall. "At least be angry with me. I can bear your resentment. Right now I don't think I could bear the tenderness of your heart."

Her expression changed, hardened, the flare of her tempter glinting in the lamplight. "Why not? Because you insist on breaking my heart? Mine and yours together? In the carriage I called you a fool. You never seem to stop proving it. You want anger? You may have it. Not because of what we've just done, but because of what you refuse to do. You refuse to have courage. And you lied to me."

That last charge came as an affront even as it inflamed his sense of guilt. "I never lied. I never promised you more than I could give."

"Moments ago you said you believed in me. But you don't. In all likelihood you never will."

She sat up and turned her back on him then, and began gathering up her clothes in tight-lipped silence. Funny, though, how the simple act of dressing required a truce of sorts. He needed help securing his cuffs; she needed his assistance in rehooking her corset. By the time he laced the bodice of her riding habit and draped the little jacket around her shoulders, they were trading civil words again.

"What will you do now?" she asked as she tried, with limited success, to twist her hair into a tidy knot. No matter her efforts, tendrils fell about her flushed cheeks. She looked warm and sleepy and sated, as fresh as a country milkmaid who'd just tumbled with the stable boy in a pile of hay.

God, he wished his life could be so simple.

He yanked the blanket from the settee and folded it into a small bundle to bring to the laundress. He'd noticed the light streaks of blood on Holly's thighs and wondered if she had, too. Each stain seemed both a pledge made and a promise broken. And evidence of the lie she had accused him of uttering.

"I'm returning to the stables," he said, picking up his neckcloth from a side table and shoving it into his coat pocket. Outside, the sky was turning gray; the dew clinging to the library windows ran in silver drops down the panes. "I sent orders to clear out all the remaining feed. I need to see that it's properly done. Then I need to initiate an investigation into how this happened."

"I'll come with you."

He shook his head. "Get some rest." When she started to protest that he might need her help again, he held up his hand. "And see to your sisters."

That convinced her, for she nodded. He walked her to the library door. He turned the key, was about to open it and bid her good morning, when instinct seized him and he pressed his mouth to hers. She did more than simply accept the kiss. After the minutest of hesitations, she parted her lips, closed her eyes, and arched her neck. A purring whimper slid into his mouth, and suddenly, unexpectedly, his hopes soared. This woman cared for him, wanted him. Loved him. Surely they were meant to be together. Surely, together, they could find a way to set their future to rights.

Their lips still meshed, he turned the knob and opened the door. A gasp flew at them from across the threshold.

Colin broke the kiss, and like startled rabbits he and Holly stared back at the shocked faces filling the doorway. Sabrina, the duchess and her brother, and, good God, both of Holly's sisters. Then an outraged cry drew Colin's attention to a figure standing behind the others, to blond curls and a haughtily pointed chin. His stomach dropped.

Lady Penelope Wingate. He had forgotten that she and her parents were staying on at Masterfield Park. His family could be persuaded to discretion, but Penelope and her parents? He darted a sideways glance at Holly. She was blushing furiously and seeming not to have drawn a breath since before he'd kissed her.

He wanted to demand of Penelope, demand of them all, what the bloody hell they were doing up so early. And why, of the many doors in this house, they'd chosen to congregate outside this one. They were all of them dressed for riding, except Penelope, who wore a gown far too elaborate to be called a country morning dress. A partial answer arrived—and made matters worse—in the form of parlor maids Tildy and Emily, who at that moment turned into the corridor carrying trays laden with breakfast victuals. Their murmured conversation suddenly went silent, and they came to abrupt halts and surveyed the scene with wide, uncertain eyes.

For several unbearable seconds no one spoke a word. Then Penelope huffed, pivoted, and stomped noisily away. Ivy compressed her lips. Colin's mother exchanged a scandalized look with her brother, Colin's uncle Horatio, Lord Shelby.

It was Sabrina who blithely broke the silence. "Well. What a surprise. We didn't know you two had returned."

As if matters weren't bad enough, their audience grew by yet another member as Geoffrey sauntered down the corridor. "I say, Tildy, is breakfast ready?"

Denials and excuses slid through Colin's brain. But there was no denying the obvious. The aftermath of their love-making hung about them as sweet and languid as the dew on the morning landscape. The blanket tucked in the crook of his arm didn't help.

"I'm glad you're both safely back," Willow said with an attempt at a smile, though the corners of her mouth never quite achieved an upward tilt. "We . . . er . . . missed you."

The silence stretched to breaking. Colin could feel Holly's mortification emanating in waves from her skin, flushed now to an alarming scarlet—a hue reflected in her sisters' faces. His mother's as well. Yet when he hazarded another sideways glance, he saw that Holly held her chin high and her shoulders level. She gestured behind her to the library desk.

"We have been testing samples of feed and water and researching our findings against known causes of acute colic. We believe we found the answer."

His chest swelled with pride at the unwavering note in her voice. And after all, she hadn't lied, and what she'd left out was no one's business.

It seemed to work a charm on everyone, for the tension broke and excited questions tumbled forth. Uncle Horatio turned to Tildy and Emily and bade them take the breakfast trays to the drawing room, telling them everyone would be along soon.

"Bracken!" Sabrina exclaimed. "How did you ever discover that?"

"It was Holly," he said proudly. "She found a small but identifiable particle among the feed."

"But how?" Uncle Horatio asked. "Accidents like that don't simply happen. Someone, somewhere, was negligent."

Colin nodded. "I hope to find out who that person was." He didn't add that he also intended to ascertain whether the act was accidental or intentional, but the look his uncle flashed him said their thoughts were not far apart.

"I appreciate everything you all did in my absence," he said to the group. "Sabrina, I know you headed up the efforts to keep the horses moving, well watered, and fed with only fresh hay. If not for that, we may have seen many deaths."

"You're welcome," she said quietly, without the hauteur he might have expected. "At times it felt rather like pushing a boulder up a slippery slope."

"We also sent samples to Simon," Ivy said. "He and the rest of the Galileo Club can utilize the Royal Society's best facilities. Perhaps they'll help you find where the bracken originated."

Colin nodded his thanks. Then he couldn't help being curious. "Has Lady Penelope been helping?"

Sabrina shrugged. "She has a horse of her own here, remember. She's been overseeing his care, though he shows no sign of the illness."

Probably ordering the grooms about at the expense of the other animals, Colin couldn't help thinking, perhaps unfairly. But Penelope had never impressed him with acts of generosity or kindness. He wondered what tales she might be telling even at that moment about what she had seen when the library door opened.

Clearly he would have to marry Holly now.

The duchess's speculative gaze shifted back and forth between Holly and Colin, and Holly could all but see the wheels turning in the woman's mind. The family reputation, the scandal, her husband's reaction when he learned of the incident, as he most assuredly would. What words must her mind be forming to describe the woman who had just, for all appearances, trapped her son into a commitment?

"You have no choice but to marry," Ivy said once they were alone in their rooms a short time later. "Even if Her Grace and Lord Shelby were willing to turn a blind eye, Lady Penelope certainly will not. I'd be astonished if all of Ascot didn't know of this by luncheon. And from there, well . . ."

Willow raised her eyebrows and nodded. "Lady Penelope appeared rather furious."

"She had good reason to be." Holly inwardly groaned as she remembered the look on the duchess's face as the library door had opened. "They all have good reason to be livid."

"Colin will be better off," Willow said with a decisive sniff. "And if you ask me, the duchess agrees. And I don't believe Her Grace looks at all unfavorably upon you."

Holly grimaced at her sister's naive assertion. "How can she not? I essentially stripped her eldest son of his most important choices in life."

Ivy sat on the bed beside her and put an arm across her shoulders. "Who could be a better choice for Colin than you? The circumstances are perhaps a smidgeon less than ideal, but I think the result is splendid."

"Neither of you understands." Holly shook her head. "I cannot marry Colin. It would be wrong. He . . ." Dismay squeezed her heart.

Willow made a face of incredulity. "No else believes it to be wrong. Except Lady Penelope and her parents, of course."

"Indeed. I can think of no one more ill suited for Colin than Lady Penelope," Ivy declared with a shudder.

Holly shot each of them a pensive look, and made a decision. "There is something you don't understand." She gestured for Willow to sit beside Ivy. Then Holly herself stood and faced them. "Colin doesn't wish to marry me."

"I can't believe that."

"It's true, Ivy. You may think you know him, but you don't, not as well as I have come to know him these past few days. It isn't that he might not like to marry me. He expressed quite the opposite desire. But he believes that not marrying me is the best way to protect me. You see, he *did* steal the colt."

"No!" This came from both sisters at once.

"His reasons were noble enough," Holly was quick to add, "but he refuses to link his fate to mine."

"Oh, but that's silly . . ." Willow started to say, when Ivy interrupted her.

"You did bring the colt back, did you not?"

Holly clutched her hands at her waist. "The colt has been stolen . . . again. This time, neither Colin nor I know who took him or where he might be."

"You *lost* the colt?" Willow whispered around her splayed fingers. "Good heavens, what *will* Victoria say? What will she *do*?"

In a burst of frustration Holly began pacing. "That is precisely why Colin is convinced we cannot marry. Although . . . I don't believe that is quite true." She stopped pacing. "It seems he simply can't believe that any love can be strong enough to prevail over the adversity we face. He doesn't believe I, or anyone, can possibly love him enough to stand by him if matters become dire."

"Oh, but that is fearing the worst." Ivy rose from the bed and pressed a hand to Holly's cheek. "We must hope that the colt will eventually be found. Colin is a man of vast resources. Surely he will—"

"Perhaps the colt will be found," Holly said solemnly, "but he will not be returned to Victoria."

"But of course he will . . ."

Holly shook her head. "There is more that you need to understand."

She spent the next few minutes explaining the curse and Briannon's legacy, beginning with her tragic heartbreak and ending with the loss of the colt and the tribulations that had recently befallen the tenants of Briarview.

"So you see, the colt must return to the Exmoor herd in Devonshire," she concluded.

"You talk as though you believe in this curse." Ivy exchanged an incredulous look with Willow. "And Colin, too. How can he, a man of science, and you, my own sister, put stock in such nonsense?"

"Indeed," Willow eagerly agreed, "to make the leap in logic from extraordinary animals to an ancient Celtic curse is, well . . ."

"Neither of you was there," Holly insisted. "You didn't witness how the local folk reacted to the colt's absence. It doesn't matter if curses exist or not. They *believe*, and so the results are the same."

"Can't they be reasoned with?"

Holly released a breath. "No, Ivy, they cannot be." Her eyes widened at a sudden realization. "If Colin and I are forced to marry, the Devonshire folk will be more horrified than they are now. Good heavens, it could lead to a greater disaster there than Colin envisioned."

She explained to them what the dowager duchess had told her, that the curse would be broken if the next duke were to take a wife of royal blood. "So you see, in light of the colt being lost, Lady Penelope, with her royal connections, would make a far better wife for Colin."

"I beg to differ," Ivy murmured with a sour look. "Oh, this is all simply too irrational. Neither you nor Colin can be thinking clearly."

"After what occurred this morning, can you blame them?" Willow asked softly.

Holly regarded each of her sisters in turn. Their inability to understand what was at stake felt like a betrayal and made her feel more alone than ever before. She had told Colin she didn't regret their lovemaking, yet now she realized the consequences of that act, not to herself, but to him, and to the people of Devonshire, even to the Exmoor ponies. She realized suddenly what he had been attempting to protect when he stole the colt from Victoria's mews: a way of life, long-reaching traditions, a belief system. It didn't matter whether those beliefs were founded in logical thinking. It only mattered that people believed with their hearts and souls.

What Colin had been trying to protect were the very things he never knew growing up as Thaddeus Ashworth's son, but which he longed for so deeply.

He wanted to *believe*, as the Devonshire people did, in *something*. Briefly today, he *had* believed—he had believed in *her*; he had said as much. And what had she done? Accused him of not believing strongly enough. Good heavens, what had she expected, an overnight miracle? Considering

his upbringing, that he had believed at all, even momentarily, was miracle enough.

During the next three days, events spiraled even more out
of her control as the duchess set about planning a wedding.
Her Grace recruited Ivy's and Willow's assistance, and even
Sabrina made her opinions available now that the sick
horses had begun to recover, a welcome development that
lifted the mood at Masterfield Park for the better. Each day
that the horses were no longer fed the tainted feed, their
condition improved.

Holly saw little of Colin in those three days, and never
alone. The duchess and Lord Shelby made certain of that,
the former always surrounding Holly with a bustle of activity, and the latter offering his assistance with the horses and
thus remaining always at Colin's side. Lady Penelope and
her parents had vacated Masterfield Park in a huff, glower-
ing their recriminations at Holly as they paraded past her
on their way out the door. Most of the other guests had left
as well, those with Thoroughbreds making alternate arrangements to board their animals for the upcoming races.

The engagement was to be announced at a ball given by
the duchess following the opening of the Royal Meeting in
less than a week. And then there would be no righting
things . . . unless Holly eventually freed Colin with an an-
nulment. Could she muster the strength to pursue such a
course? Sabrina had spoken of slippery slopes. Holly felt
like a snowball careening down an icy slope of her own.

That third afternoon, while her sisters and the few remaining guests were resting or walking in the garden, Holly
wandered the house alone, strolling into the various rooms
until finally the drawing room appeared to offer an empty
but cozy haven.

She didn't notice the flickering lamp on the card table in
the far corner, or the two women bent over their work, until
it was too late. She might have backed quietly out of the
room had Sabrina not spoken.

"Good afternoon, Holly. Do come in."

The young woman sat with a basket at her elbow and an array of fabric swatches spread out on the tabletop before her. One of the parlor maids who had brought breakfast to the library on that ill-fated morning two days ago sat beside her, her starched linen cap and apron glowing starkly against the room's gilded furnishings and rich upholsteries.

Sabrina tapped the back of the chair on her other side. "Come sit with me, for this concerns you." She turned to the maid. "That will be all for now. Thank you, Tildy."

The girl bobbed a curtsy to Holly as she walked briskly past her. Was it Holly's imagination, or did the corner of the maid's mouth quirk with the slightest bit of derision?

Holly slid out the chair and sat and peered down at the swatches. "This concerns me?"

"Mother is shopping in Windsor today. She asked me to sort through the colors and fabrics for next week's ball." Sabrina cast a significant look up at her. "Which will now double as your engagement celebration."

Holly's stomach clenched. "How may I help?"

Sabrina held up three satin swatches. "These are the blue, gold, and burgundy of the Masterfield crest. Mother plans to incorporate the colors into the ballroom decorations in the form of draperies, bunting, and table linens. The flower arrangements as well. The orders must be placed immediately, mind you, or they'll never be ready in time. Is there a Sutherland crest whose colors we might include?"

Holly chuckled. "The Sutherlands don't have a crest."

Sabrina caught and held her gaze. "You do realize you have no choice in this. You and Colin must marry." From outside came the faint echo of voices. "I, on the other hand, had a choice, thank goodness."

"What do you mean?"

"Hadn't you noticed the absence of one guest in particular?" She sat back and let the swatches in her hand drop to the tabletop. "Mr. Bentley."

In all that had happened, Holly had forgotten about Colin's fellow Jockey Club member. She frowned. "You mean to say he didn't stay to help with the horses?"

Sabrina shrugged a shoulder. "He might have, but I sent him packing before the trouble began."

"Did you?" Holly couldn't keep her astonishment from showing. "What offense had he committed?"

"He asked me to marry him," she replied with a moue of distaste.

"Well, I cannot say I'm surprised. What did you tell him?"

"No, of course. And then he became angry. He had the impertinence to call me a tease. Can you imagine?" Sabrina's narrow chin tilted defiantly. "He even threatened to speak to Father when he returns. That is when I showed him the door."

An unsettling suspicion sent goose bumps up Holly's spine. "You say this all happened before the horses began showing signs of illness?" At Sabrina's nod, Holly continued. "Do you know where he went? Did he leave the area?"

"No, with the races coming I don't suppose he did. . . . What are you driving at?" She drew back against her chair, shaking her head. "Surely you aren't suggesting that Mr. Bentley is responsible . . ."

"Is it possible?" The image of a sharp pebble flashed in her memory, bringing her back to the day Sabrina lost control of Sport o' Kings. Mr. Bentley had disapproved of Sabrina's riding that day.

"But he is a devoted turfite. And a Jockey Club official." Sabrina scowled down at the swatches, but the compression of her lips revealed her uncertainty.

"Sabrina, I am not accusing Mr. Bentley. I am only suggesting a possibility that should be explored." Holly stood. "Whatever you select for the ball will be splendid, I am sure. If you'll excuse me, I must speak to your brother."

Chapter 27

Colin handed the horse he'd been walking in the paddock off to a groom and scrubbed a hand across his eyes. They felt bloodshot and swollen, chafed by the morning glare. No matter. In these past two days the sick animals had rallied, marginally perhaps, but enough to raise his hopes. He hadn't wished to alarm his family, but he hadn't been at all certain they had discovered the bracken poisoning in time.

The truth was, they could still lose horses. But not, as he had once feared, all of them. What frustrated him was not knowing the cause, how a lethal substance had ended up in sacks of horse feed, and how those particular sacks had found their way to Masterfield Park. If he were to prevent another such incident, he needed answers to those questions.

He was glad, then, that he had left Cordelier in Devonshire. Maribelle, too. As he picked his way from the paddock to the stable yard, he couldn't help smiling at how in a very short time the mare had become Holly's own. He intended making the transfer official by offering Maribelle as a gift.

A wedding gift? Dread settled over him. Maribelle would provide paltry comfort when the authorities clapped Holly's new husband in irons and led him to Newgate.

Had his thoughts conjured her? She suddenly stood framed in the archway between the stables. Her hair was loosely drawn up at the crown of her head, ringlets tossing in the breeze. His pulse quickened at the sight of her. Waving, he broke into a sprint that he hoped looked casual and not the overeager act it was.

"Good afternoon," was all he could think to say when he reached her. She flashed an uncertain smile, but the careworn shadows beneath her eyes raised his concern. "What is it?"

"Did you know Stuart Bentley intended asking Sabrina to marry him?"

Her bluntness took him aback. "No. Has he asked her?"

"He has, and she turned him down. He became angry."

Colin glanced out at the paddocks. "So that's why he left before we returned. I'd wondered."

"He left because Sabrina insisted he do so." Holly pressed a hand to his wrist. "Colin, all this took place *before* the horses became ill."

"And you think Bentley . . ."

"The rock in the paddock," she said with emphasis.

"We never found any proof that he threw the rock, or that anyone did. The stable lads might simply have missed it with their rakes."

"But when you consider all three incidents—the rock, the spurned proposal, the ailment . . ." She gasped. "Why, perhaps he followed us on the road to Devonshire, and it was his bullet that nearly struck us. Colin, perhaps Stuart Bentley has the colt."

His hands went to her shoulders. "Don't you think you're heaping a bit too much suspicion onto Stuart Bentley's narrow shoulders?"

That seemed to rob her of fervor. "Please, even if you don't wish to take me seriously, at least look into it."

Despite the grooms' and even Mr. Peterson's nearby presence, he drew her to him and wrapped his arms around her. "I take you seriously. Don't ever believe otherwise."

"I'm sorry. Forgive me for saying that." She raised her chin against his shirtfront, and he lowered his mouth to hers.

"My lord! A message!"

He and Holly broke apart as a footman approached. He held out a folded missive. Colin's first thought was that other horses in the area had become afflicted with the bracken poisoning. He broke the unfamiliar seal and read: *If you wish your precious colt returned, meet me at . . .*

The note gave detailed directions to a small manor located to the northeast, about halfway between Ascot and Windsor. In stunned disbelief, Colin glanced up from the page. "The colt . . . Is it possible?"

Holly had been attempting to read over his shoulder. "What about the colt? Colin, you've grown as white as the paddock fence!"

His mind worked frantically. Was this some sort of bizarre game? A trap?

Was Stuart Bentley involved? *Come alone* the note insisted.

"The hell I will," he said decisively.

"Will what?" Holly gripped the arm that held the note.

He shoved the letter into his coat pocket. "I'll be meeting with the author of this note, but I'm not about to go alone, or unarmed for that matter."

Her face filled with alarm. "I'm coming with you."

His expression turned thunderous. "The hell you are."

"I should have insisted on going with him." Her fingers laced tightly, Holly stood at the bay window that overlooked the drive and the sweeping front lawns of Masterfield Park. She and her sisters occupied the formal receiving salon, a room seldom used by the family but desirable today because of the view it offered of the far-off road. She stared hard into the distance, as if she could make Colin reappear by the force of her will.

"Even if he had been amenable to your accompanying him," Ivy said from the settee behind her, "I'd certainly have stepped in your way."

"You'll accomplish nothing by fretting," Willow reminded her, not for the first time. "Come take your tea.

Colin will be safe with his valet, Kirkston, at his side, and they'll both be home before you know it."

Holly knew her sisters were right, but she couldn't force herself to turn away from the window. Would Colin return with the colt? At least then the people of Devonshire would rest easy and continue with their lives, though she and Colin would have to face the queen's wrath.

Whirls of dust arose from the road. Her hopes surging, Holly craned her neck, only to be disappointed a moment later when an unfamiliar phaeton turned onto the drive.

"Holly, did you just groan?"

Willow's query turned her away from the window. She lifted the teacup Ivy had poured for her some five minutes ago and sipped the cooling liquid. As she did, she heard the front door opening. Voices drifted in from the main hall.

"I am sorry to say His Grace is away from home, sir."

"Good gracious, is he indeed?" a man's voice said with surprise. "I had written to tell the duke of my coming, but my letter must have gone astray. How unfortunate. I am told by a mutual acquaintance, Lord Kinnard of the Jockey Club, that the Ashworth stud is the finest in all of England. Dear me, what to do now?"

A short silence ensued, whereupon the voice took up again with, "Might I speak with the duke's eldest son?"

"Lord Drayton is in residence, sir, but presently not at home. Perhaps Lord Bryce might be of assistance?"

"Ah, yes, Lord Kinnard mentioned Lord Bryce. Would you tell him Mr. Anthony Verrell wishes to see him about a certain of the family's Thoroughbreds."

"If you'll kindly wait in here, sir, I'll see if his lordship is receiving."

"Thank you, my dear man."

The door of the receiving parlor opened and the footman stopped short, nearly causing the visitor to stumble into his back. The young man in the Ashworth livery blushed furiously, his startled gaze lighting on Holly and each of her sisters.

"I beg pardon, ladies. I . . . I didn't know anyone was in here. This room isn't typically occupied. . . ."

Ivy smiled up at him. "Quite all right. Perhaps Mr. . . . er . . ."

The visitor stepped around the footman and doffed his beaver hat. "Verrell. Anthony Verrell, at your service, madam."

Willow lifted the teapot. "We were just having tea, Mr. Verrell, if you would care to join us."

As the gentleman expressed his delight at the idea, the footman strode off to summon Bryce Ashworth and procure a fourth cup and saucer. After initial introductions, Holly sat quietly while Ivy and Willow made polite conversation with their guest. She found him to be a distinguished-looking gentleman of about fifty, tall and slender, impeccably dressed, his hair thick if slightly graying. She thought it oddly ironic that he should come now of all times to inquire about purchasing a racehorse, but perhaps news of the illness hadn't spread as far as London, or wherever he had come from.

Judging by the questions he asked, he seemed to know very little about horses, but Holly found she didn't have the energy to enlighten him. That would be Bryce's job, or Colin's when he returned home. She was nonplussed, therefore, when not only Bryce but also Sabrina entered the room, made Mr. Verrell's acquaintance, and bade Holly accompany them as they took the man on a tour of the stables.

"I'll come, too, if I may." Willow stood up from the settee and smoothed her skirts. She glanced back at Ivy. "Unless, of course, you need me here."

Ivy waved a hand at her. "You've been shut up in this house with me quite long enough. Go and enjoy."

Holly eyed her youngest sister. Exactly when had Willow stopped hiding from Bryce Ashworth and begun volunteering to be in his company? Had Holly been so absorbed in her own concerns since returning to Masterfield Park that she'd missed a significant development?

She herself preferred to remain behind with Ivy so she could wait for Colin *and* discover what had transpired between Willow and Bryce in her absence. As the small group gathered to escort Mr. Verrell to the stables, she gestured Sabrina aside. "Surely you don't need me to come along."

"On the contrary," Sabrina whispered back from behind her hand. "You've worked closely with Colin these past several days. Should our guest ask questions about the ailment, who better to answer them? Who better to offer assurance that the cause has been found and the worst over?"

"But . . ."

Sabrina's features sharpened. "Do not think I am worrying about making a sale to this gentleman. You know how I view financial matters." Holly didn't particularly, but she remained silent as Sabrina continued. "I couldn't give a fig whether he makes his purchase from us or from any of a host of other studs. As things now stand, we will have to withdraw most or all of our entrants from the Royal Meeting. It cannot be helped when the horses have suffered so. But there will be other races, and it is of the utmost importance that people perceive the Ashworth stud as settling back to normal. Otherwise, can you imagine the havoc to be wreaked in the betting boxes this racing season?"

Holly knew she was right. Fortunes were made and lost at the races. Inaccurate information could easily cause a panic and skew the betting in artificial, damaging directions.

But *had* the Ashworth Thoroughbreds been irreparably weakened? With that question in mind, Holly followed the others through the gardens and to the stables. As they proceeded, she kept an eye on her sister, but Willow showed no interest in Bryce other than the polite deference a guest owed her host.

As they moved from stall to stall, Bryce or Sabrina explained the particular attributes of the animals, along with their sires and dames. Meanwhile, Holly closely examined each horse: the color of the eyes, the rhythm of the breathing, the sheen of the coat. Whenever asked, she offered her opinions on their condition and soon held Mr. Verrell's attention more than did either Ashworth. But it wasn't until Mr. Verrell commented on her obvious devotion to the Ashworth stud that she gave an inner start.

The gentleman was right. Somewhere during the past several days, she had begun to think of the stud in very personal terms, and these horses as being as much a part of her as her own family. And that led to a further revelation that, in her heart, she had already taken on the role of Colin Ashworth's wife.

"If I may ask, where do you come by your expertise, Miss Sutherland?"

She hadn't noticed Mr. Verrell's accent before then, but now she heard something in his pronunciations that suggested English was not his first language; that hinted at a Continental upbringing. "Merely a lifelong interest in horses," she replied.

"Ah, it must be more than that. The average rider boasts far less knowledge than you, miss."

She smiled. "I suppose I was lucky in that the uncle who raised me was kind enough to indulge a young girl's fixation. I was always happiest either in the saddle or trailing our grooms as they went about their business. I cannot think but they must have considered me quite the nuisance."

"I am pleased you were not shooed from those stables. Your uncle raised you, you say . . . ?"

He strolled with her down the stable's center aisle, the conversation turning to the pros and cons of purchasing either a filly or a colt for investment purposes. Again Holly answered his questions as best she could, advising him to wait for Colin's return before making any decisions. Once she glanced back over her shoulder to see her sister walking with Sabrina and Bryce, but it was with the latter that Willow quietly spoke. A vivid blush suffused Willow's cheeks, and in response to something Bryce murmured, her laughter echoed through the stables. Then Mr. Verrell once more claimed Holly's attention.

*   *   *

Colin stopped his mount just outside a pair of open gates that looked in jeopardy of falling off their hinges. At the other end of a drive choked with brambles and weeds, a stand of neglected elms and twisted hawthorn half concealed a smallish manor of whitewashed brick. Darkened, dirty windows, a number of them cracked, stared blankly back. Colin neither saw nor heard signs of habitation.

"It appears deserted, sir." Beside him, his valet, Kirkston, lifted his face in a houndlike gesture as if scenting the breeze.

"It most certainly does." Caution put Colin's senses on the alert. "The message said to bypass the house and go round to the stables."

He clucked his gelding forward. Kirkston followed, a telltale click letting Colin know the older man held his pistol at the ready. Colin's own weapon weighted his coat pocket.

To the rear of the house, overgrown shrubbery signified what had once been a garden. A long stone building with a broken slate roof squatted off to one side, its narrow windows shuttered with splintering, weather-warped panels.

"The stables," Kirkston said unnecessarily.

Stopping in the concealing shadow of the terrace steps, Colin dismounted and fished his double-barreled percussion pistol from his pocket. "Watch over the horses," he said.

His valet was off his own mount in an instant. "I'm very sorry, sir, but that's one order I feel compelled to disobey. I'd prefer to watch over you."

Colin regarded the man's squared jaw, tight mouth, and most of all his obstinate gaze, and thought better of arguing. Leaving the horses to graze, he led the way past the ground floor of the house, passing dusty kitchen windows and storage cellar doors. Like the house itself, the stables were small, more befitting a prosperous country farm than an estate. Heaps of dead leaves and what might have been kitchen scraps lay moldering against the back wall of the structure. Using the unkempt foliage for cover, they crept close, taking only shallow breaths to avoid the stench. Moving to one corner, Colin flattened himself against the granite stones and attempted to peer through the closest window.

He opened the shutter slightly and had just put his eye to the gap when a *thunk* from inside sent him back around to the rear. He came to Kirkston's side, and the valet put a firm hand at his elbow.

"Did you see anything, sir?" he asked in an undertone.

Colin shook his head, then eased forward again. To his mild annoyance, Kirkston grasped the hem at the back of his coat as if ready to pull him away at the slightest hint of danger. This time Colin heard no sound, and now that he thought of it, the original *thunk* might have been nothing more than a falling tree limb.

A snort reached his ears, followed by a soft whicker. He nearly set off at a run to the front of the stable. Kirkston, however, still held his coat.

"Prudence, sir," he advised in a whisper.

Colin nodded, and the other man released him. Together they crept along the wall. As they went they heard more sounds of a horse inside, as well as a human occupant. The possibility of that person being Stuart Bentley raised spots of fury before Colin's eyes, until the man inside spoke again.

"There, there, my good boy . . ."

Not Bentley. Colin couldn't make out the rest, and it took him a moment to realize the man spoke in French. Then his brain began to loosely translate.

"We must return you to your rightful owner," the man murmured, and received a whicker in reply.

Colin and Kirkston reached the stable yard and each straddled the low stone wall. A lone horse stood tied to a railing across the way, stretching its neck to munch the grass that had pushed between the stones. They moved soundlessly to the double doors. One stood open a few feet, admitting a triangle of light across the filthy, hay-strewn cobbles inside.

Swiftly Kirkston darted across the doorway so that they now flanked the opening. His vantage point giving him the better view, the valet leaned over to survey the scene inside. With his gun at the ready, Kirkston held up one finger to signal that he had spied a single man. He questioned Colin with a glance. Colin tightened his grip on his pistol and nodded.

Kirkston kicked the door wider. As it slammed against the inner wall, they strode inside, taking aim with their pistols at a tall, lean man who was about to feed the missing Exmoor colt a carrot.

"Put your hands above your head where I can see them," Colin ordered.

The bright carrot floated upward in the dimness.

Colin raised the revolver higher. "Now turn slowly toward me, and make no sudden movements."

The middle-aged face that met his gaze was that of a complete stranger. Somehow, Colin had expected to find someone at least partially known to him, a member of the racing world who coveted his success, perhaps even one of his recent guests. Colin took a moment to survey the colt, or what he could see of him above the stall gate. He noted the proud angle of the head, the forward, alert set of the ears, and the sharp gleam of the eyes.

With a tentative surge of relief, he returned his attention to the man. "Who are you?"

The Frenchman took a step forward. Kirkston held his pistol higher. "His lordship didn't bid you come any closer."

True, but something in the man's stance prompted Colin to relax a fraction. Unless this Frenchman was the most practiced of assassins, Colin didn't deem it likely that he would suddenly procure a weapon and start shooting. His lined features held a mild expression, as if holding his arms above his head were part of an amusing game.

"My name is Henri de Vere." The accent intensified as he pronounced his name. "And I am pleased to make your acquaintance, Lord Drayton."

Colin narrowed his eyes. "How do you know me?"

The man smiled. "I know much when it comes to my

Sutherland cousins." The assertion sparked a jolt that ran through Colin from head to toe. De Vere's eyes once more registered amusement. "*Oui, monsieur*, the woman you know as Holly Sutherland is my cousin, and I have spent the past year shadowing her, shadowing all four of them."

Colin exchanged a quick glance with Kirkston; then he approached de Vere. "You can put your arms down. But start talking. How can you be connected to the Sutherlands?"

Chuckling, de Vere fed the carrot to the colt. "They are not the Sutherlands. Their name is Valentin." He fell silent but turned back to study Colin closely, waiting for his reaction.

"Valentin . . . I've heard that name before. Wasn't there a Roland de Valentin during the wars who—"

"Opposed Napoleon and worked with English spies to rout him." The Frenchman nodded. "And for his pains, his own relatives plotted his death, and the deaths of his family."

"Holly . . ."

"Hélène. That is her true name. But yes, she and her sisters were all meant to die in a fire that razed their manor in Artois to the ground. Their friends learned of the plot, but too late. They arrived in time to save only the children. The man they knew as their uncle Edward bore no blood relation to them. Only an undying loyalty to their father."

"Then he was a British spy as well."

De Vere nodded, and Colin's pulse hammered as his mind worked through this information. "There is more to this story than the machinations of the war," he said. "Otherwise, why murder innocent children?"

De Vere nodded wearily, his shoulders sagging. "That is a story that must now come out. But not here. The details are for the Valentin sisters alone."

The colt snorted and pawed the cobbles, reminding Colin of his presence. His pistol pointing downward, he gave it a wave in the animal's direction. "Why did you take the colt?"

"That was not me, *monsieur*. That was my brother, Antoine. His way of obtaining your attention, one can only suppose. I am here because I traced my brother to this property."

"And which one of you shot at Holly and me on the road to Devon?"

He fully expected de Vere to implicate his brother, but the man surprised him. "That, regrettably, was me, but I certainly did not aim at either of you. If I hadn't frightened the two of you off the road, Antoine would have taken more than the colt. He would have murdered you and taken Hélène . . . Holly. You see, until a year ago when he encountered the eldest sister in Bath—"

"Laurel, now Lady Barensforth."

"Yes. Until he saw her, he believed the sisters were dead. But Laurette resembles their mother, Simone, so greatly, there could be no mistaking the relation between them."

"The night of the ball . . ." Colin murmured. When de Vere looked puzzled, Colin explained. "We held a ball at Masterfield Park last week, and a man accosted Holly in what appeared to be a fit of drunkenness. Could your brother have gained access to the house?"

"Easily, one would imagine. You had many guests that night, no?"

"What did he want from her?"

"That is for the sisters' ears."

Colin decided to let that go . . . for now. He narrowed his eyes. "You said you traced your brother here. What were you planning to do when you found him?"

De Vere's smile chilled his blood. "For too long my brother has been a blight on this earth. I intend to protect the girls he wronged so grievously." He jerked his chin toward the floor near the stall gate, and Colin saw what he hadn't noticed previously, and what de Vere could have used against him if he'd wished: a small pistol he had apparently set down when he'd decided to feed the colt.

Unexpected revulsion pitched in Colin's gut. There wasn't anything he wouldn't do to protect Holly; if he had to, he knew he could kill to keep her safe. But his own brother? He thought of Bryce, of Geoffrey, and the notion of taking either of their lives raised bile in his throat. But then, he couldn't conceive of either of his brothers ever doing anything as heinous as what de Vere described.

"You wanted my help," Colin guessed. "Is that why you summoned me here? To help you kill your brother?"

For the first time, de Vere's aplomb slipped. He frowned in puzzlement. "I did not summon you. I came expecting to find Antoine. Only Antoine."

"You didn't send me a message earlier?"

De Vere shook his head.

"Oh, God," Colin whispered. "Then I've made a fatal mistake."

Chapter 28

"Your sister seems to have abandoned us, Miss Sutherland. Where do you suppose she has gone?"

Holly and Mr. Verrell strolled between the paddocks toward the racetrack. Sabrina was busy overseeing the saddling of several horses, for it had been decided that she and the head trainer would display the animals before their guest.

Holly glanced over her shoulder to the stable yard. Where was Willow, indeed? Not to mention Bryce.

"Are you and your sisters close, Miss Sutherland?"

As he spoke, Holly frowned slightly in concentration as she tried to place his accent. French, or perhaps Flemish? She could surmise only that he'd originated or spent much time on the Continent. "Yes, we're very close," she replied. "I suppose it shows, doesn't it?"

"It is most charming." He paused, then asked, "Your other sister, she is not well?"

"Oh, no, she's—" Holly faced forward again, suddenly struck by Mr. Verrell's interest in Ivy and Willow. She had very nearly mentioned Ivy's pregnancy, a detail far too intimate to be disclosed to a complete stranger, and a male stranger at that. Yet something about his manner as she had answered his queries about the horses had set her at ease, perhaps too much so, and only now did she sense that his amiability strayed beyond the proper boundary. And then she realized something else: although he had asked many questions about the horses, he hadn't seemed to take much note of the answers.

"Mr. Verrell, may I ask you an impertinent question?"

His eyes twinkled kindly. "You may, my dear."

They reached the wide elm that grew beside the racetrack. She glanced out across the course, the lush lawn at its center tinged gold by the late-afternoon sun. "Did you truly come here to purchase a racehorse, sir?"

He took a long moment in answering, his lips pursed as he regarded her. "No," he finally said. Her stomach knotted even before he added, "I came here hoping to meet you, my dear."

Her heart pounding, she took a lengthy stride backward. "Who are you?"

In the instant or two before he replied, she became aware of the clamor of a pair of blue jays squabbling overhead. She noticed it now because as she waited for Mr. Verrell to identify—*truly* identify—himself, everything inside her went still and silent with an impending dread she could not name.

"My name is not Verrell," he said. She felt no surprise, only a vague apprehension at having ventured so far from the others with a man who had suddenly transformed into a complete stranger yet again. "It is de Vere," he continued. "Antoine de Vere. And I am here to help you."

The name echoed in her ears and propelled her back another step, until her shoulders struck a solid form. In dismay she realized she'd retreated up against the tree trunk, which held her trapped. "I know that name. Except . . . it wasn't Antoine. It was Henri."

Henri de Vere, a man with an enigmatic past who might have attacked Laurel in Bath last year, but who had disappeared immediately afterward, taking his secrets with him.

"Henri is my brother," he said gently. "And he is an exceedingly bad man."

"My sister Laurel . . . ?" Holly broke off, uncertainty clogging her throat with fear.

"If you speak of your eldest sister, then yes," he said in that soothing way of his. "Henri might have killed her a year ago had the Earl of Barensforth not interrupted their struggle."

Holly tried to move away from him, only to have the bark of the tree bite into her back through her clothing. "But why? Who are we that anyone would wish us harm? And you . . . what do you want with me?"

His smile both reassured her and left her unsettled. He stood too close, close enough to touch her should he raise his arm but a few inches. "Your name," he said, "is Hélène de Valentin. You and your sisters, Laurette, Yvonne, and Wilhemine, are the direct heirs of a vast fortune. A French fortune seized by the crown at the close of the wars, and only now about to be restored into the hands of its rightful owners."

"I don't understand. We are English. Until my sisters married we were poor. We are orphans. We are nobody."

His soft chuckle triggered an onslaught of memories . . . of having heard that very laughter before, in her very distant past. "You are indeed somebody, the last of a very great French family. You were orphaned because your manor was burned to the ground."

"Yes, I—I have vague memories of running through the flames. Of my uncle lifting me into his coach . . ."

"He was not your uncle. He was your father's friend, his comrade against Napoleon's forces. He and I and the father of the young queen, and many more besides, worked secretly to bring the tyrant down. But before Napoleon fell, he learned of our network, and he sent a man who knew your father well, who knew your manor as he knew his own home, and who had much to gain in destroying your family."

The world began to spin before Holly's eyes. She shut them, only to feel the ground tip beneath her feet. At the pressure of a hand at her elbow, her eyes flew open, and with a gasp she pressed tighter against the tree. Far off—an impossible distance away—she saw the tiny figures of Sabrina and the head trainer leading the horses into the upper paddock. Sabrina would wonder where Holly and *Mr. Verrell* had gone. Would she see them here, or would the shade of the elm hide them from view?

Antoine de Vere released her, his hand dropping to his side. "Forgive me, my dear. I didn't wish to startle you, but you seemed unsteady."

"I'm all right." Her fingers clenching, she drew a shaky breath. "This man sent to destroy my family . . . what did he have to gain by it?"

"My family, the de Veres, are cousins of the Valentins, and for over a century the two sides have fought over the rights of inheritance to a great fortune, rights left ambiguous by the terms of the original will. Many times the battle has turned bloody, with cousin murdering cousin and the fortune changing hands like the ball in a tennis match. At the beginning of this century, your family stood triumphant. But then the wars started, and with it came chaos. My brother, Henri, decided to use that chaos to his advantage."

"By murdering my parents . . . trying to murder my sisters and me? No, this cannot be true . . . Uncle Edward . . ."

"Saved your lives." De Vere gave a deferential nod. "And now *I* am here to save you once again."

She narrowed her eyes at him. "Why are you turning up only now? Why not when we were children? Or even a year ago, when our lives were suddenly endangered again? Why have you kept this secret?"

"I have kept watch," he said. "But I feared if you and your sisters knew of your legacy, your inheritance, there could be more bloodshed. I thought as long as you were cared for and safe, there was no reason to devastate you with such a truth. Why raise such sorrowful ghosts when you could simply go on being the Sutherland sisters?" He heaved a regretful sigh. "Forgive me, my dear, if I judged incorrectly."

Fear closed around her as she thought of her sisters, of Laurel, whose child would soon enter the world; of Ivy, still months away from giving birth but so vulnerable; and of Willow, the youngest, who had yet to fully experience life and love. In truth, Holly didn't know if she *could* forgive this man, this bearer of grievous tidings and a specter of her violent past. Perhaps it wasn't his fault and she was being unfair, but how to pardon him for ripping away her very identity?

Her identity. Even now she couldn't absorb it . . . her entire life, her memories . . . all lies?

No. She was still who she'd been moments ago. Only now, there was more to her story . . . and suddenly so much of that story made sense. Her isolated upbringing, Uncle Edward's reluctance to ever leave the safety of Thorn Grove, their very few friends . . . other than Victoria, whose father had been involved in the subterfuge against Napoleon, along with . . .

Along with Holly's own father. Her father and her mother, nameless, faceless voids in her life . . . until now.

"What were their names?" she asked hoarsely. She swallowed, surprised at the pain of doing so. "My parents. Who were they?"

"Your father was Roland de Valentin. Your mother's name was Simone."

"Simone." The name struck a memory. "The man who attacked my sister—"

"My brother," he interrupted.

Holly nodded. "He spoke that name to her."

"Because she resembles your mother so strikingly. For an instant, he believed your sister to be her."

Tears, raw and burning, sprang to her eyes. "D-do I look like either of them?"

He smiled sadly. "You take after your father's mother, who had hair the color of fire."

Holly's hand went to her hair, her fingers absently tracing a curl that strayed from beneath her bonnet. There were so many questions she longed to ask, about her family, her kin, her home . . . yet one concern clamored with even greater urgency.

"These things that have been happening to me . . . last week, during a ball here, a man accosted me in a corridor.

And then only days ago on the road to Devonshire, Lord Drayton and I were shot at . . ."

To each reference, he nodded. "My brother."

"But wait . . . on the moor . . . was it he who protected me from the angry villagers?" She studied the man before her. "I didn't see him close up, but it couldn't have been you that day, though you do resemble the man I saw. Why would your brother protect me if he wishes me ill?"

If she'd had any suspicions that it might have been this man on the moor that morning, the surprise that flashed in his eyes dispelled them. "Obviously he had plans for you, my dear, ones he dared not implement in front of witnesses."

She shuddered. "And the colt—what has he to do with all of this?"

"Henri has been watching you closely. He knows the colt is important to you, that he can use it to manipulate you. Your sisters have remained secluded, always under the protection of family or friends. Only you have strayed from that haven in recent days. Henri guessed that with the colt he could lure you farther from safety."

Holly's hand flew to her throat as her pounding heart sent the blood pulsing through her veins. "Oh, God . . ."

"Mademoiselle, what is it? Why have you grown so pale?"

"Colin . . . the earl . . . he's gone after the colt . . ."

"Where?"

Her thoughts lashed in confusion. "I don't know. He received a message earlier telling him that if he wanted the colt he must go . . . oh, he wouldn't tell me where. He didn't wish for me to follow." She looked wildly around her, taking in the paddocks, the racecourse, the open heath beyond.

"I have an idea where he might have gone," de Vere said.

"Then take me there, immediately."

"It could be dangerous."

"I don't care. We must help him. Perhaps we should bring footmen with us."

De Vere hesitated, then shook his head. "There may not

be time for that. If indeed Lord Drayton has gone for the colt, he may be in grave danger. We must go at once."

Instead of retreating the way they had come, Monsieur de Vere led her along a path that bypassed the stables and gardens, passing through a wooded garden that skirted the manor's west wing. As they stepped from the shade of tall oak, pine, and walnut trees into the bright sunlight of the front lawns, Holly saw three riders racing up the drive.

"The earl has returned," she exclaimed. She started to run, but de Vere caught her by the wrist and held her back. She scowled down at the offending hand. "What are you doing? Release me, sir." She waved her other hand over her head. "Colin!"

"Have a care, my dear," Antoine said sharply. He peered toward the riders. "Who accompanies him? *Mon Dieu*, I believe it is my brother."

Holly struggled against his grip. "Then surely there is no danger, or they would not have ridden back together. Surely this has all been a vast misunderstanding."

"No, my dear, there has been no misunderstanding."

Still maintaining his hold on her, de Vere tucked his free hand into his coat pocket. To Holly's horror, when it reappeared, it held an ebony-handled pistol.

"You don't dare fire upon us, Antoine," Henri de Vere shouted across the way to his brother. "There are three of us, and only one of you. You cannot beat such odds."

Kirkston and Henri flanked Colin as the three of them strode across the lawn, their weapons at the ready. At the sight of Antoine restraining Holly, Colin's heart lodged in his throat.

Suddenly, almost comically—if Colin could have found even a particle of humor in the situation—a window on the ground floor opened and Geoffrey popped his head out. "About time you returned. We've a visitor, and he—"

"Stay inside," Colin ordered tersely and kept walking, the other two men keeping apace.

Near the trees, Antoine continued to train his gun on

them. To all appearances he might have been protecting Holly. Confused, Colin experienced a crippling doubt about the man striding beside him.

"You don't dare fire upon *me*, Henri," Antoine called back. "Your odds of hitting Hélène are too great. Or would you murder our young cousin in cold blood, before witnesses?"

"I wish to kill no one, Antoine," Henri yelled. "Not even you. Put your weapon down."

"And you drop yours as well," Colin ordered the man. From the corner of his eye he saw Henri flick him a glance. The barrel of his pistol dropped toward the ground, but to Colin's continued frustration the weapon remained in his hand.

"I wish you would all put your blasted guns down." Holly attempted to wrest free of Antoine's hold. "Nothing can be accomplished this way."

Antoine, not as graying or as sharp-featured as his brother, held her fast. Colin and the men with him continued their approach until Antoine gestured with a flick of his weapon. "That is close enough. Lord Drayton, my brother has tricked you. You would do well to take him into your custody."

Colin heard the words, but his attention was riveted on Holly, on her expression, her every movement. If he could only get her away from there, he wouldn't care who fired or who was hit—not even himself.

She had stopped struggling against Antoine and the fear had left her gaze. She seemed to be communicating a message to him, and it took him all of a split second to understand it.

I love you. I trust you.

The message held no reservations, not the slightest hesitation. She believed in his ability to save her; she believed in him. And in the faithful shimmer of her eyes, he found his courage, his confidence that he *would* save her, that somehow, together, they would save each other.

He pulled his gaze away from her. The two de Veres

were arguing, leveling charges at each other that seemed to encompass several decades of bitterness. Colin caught references to the wars, to aristocrats sent to the guillotine and innocent people chased off their lands or massacred in their beds ... he heard accusations of arson, and of the cold-blooded murder of family members. ...

"You cannot win, Antoine." His voice unnaturally calm, Henri took several steps across the grass, stopping only when Antoine raised his pistol and took what appeared to be lethal aim. Henri held out his arms, his own weapon pointing benignly toward the shrubbery off to his left. "The secret is out. What is more, the sisters are not the anonymous orphans you believed them to be. They never were. The man they called their uncle Edward saw to that when he deliberately established ties between them and England's young queen. Surely you realize you cannot kill them and expect their inheritance to be handed over to you. It is time to listen to reason. ..."

Still talking, Henri started forward again. Antoine tensed in response, his grip on his gun tightening. Undeterred, Henri extended a hand. "Perhaps we might find a way to share the inheritance with our cousins and end the violence—"

A blast drowned out the rest of his words. Henri crumpled to his knees. Across the way, as smoke wafted from Antoine's gun, the recoil sent him staggering backward. His grip on Holly loosened and she pulled free, then stumbled and fell, landing on her bottom and sliding on the leaves at the base of an oak. With several feet now between Holly and Antoine, Colin took aim and squeezed the pistol's trigger. The shot rang out, the explosion deafening, dizzying. Colin kept his stance, cocking the second barrel to fire again when Antoine lurched an unsteady step toward him. Another blast was fired, one so violent that it launched both Colin and Kirkston to the ground. Colin wasted no time in scrambling to his feet. When he looked toward the trees, Antoine had vanished.

Chapter 29

Holly landed hard on her hip, her back striking the tree trunk behind her and knocking her half senseless. The last thing she saw before the impact was Colin being thrust to the ground, and the boy . . . Geoffrey, running into harm's way.

Run, run somewhere safe she tried to call out to both of them. Whatever was happening, whoever these Frenchmen were, it had nothing to do with the Ashworths. This was *her* past, *her* ghosts, rising up to commit violence.

But she was on the ground, her senses in a sickening whirl, her voice caught in a throat inundated with the rancid stench of gunpowder . . . and something else. Something metallic and moist and frightening. Upon forcing her eyes open, the first sight to greet her was the splatter of blood—on the grass, on the roots of the oak, on her skirts. Whose blood? She looked wildly about her. *Dear God, whose?*

Footsteps thudded toward her, and then a pair of arms closed around her and a torso nearly crushed her. She felt herself being rocked and smothered as frantic, frenzied hands traveled over her. A voice rumbled in her ears, the same words repeated over and over again.

"Are you hurt? Are you shot? Oh, God, Holly, dear God . . ."

Even as she tried to form words of reassurance, she

could not prevent her own hands from desperately searching Colin's body, spurred by both hope and dread. They were talking, whispering, shouting all at once, until she realized they were asking the same questions and speaking the same answers.

She found his dear, handsome face and framed it in her hands. "I am all right. I wasn't hit," she said slowly and carefully, repeating it until she saw the panic leave his features. Only then did she release him and slide her palms over his shoulders and down his chest, searching for holes, moisture. . . . "And you, my love?"

His hands tightened around her upper arms. "Not hit."

Relief came in a consuming wave, but a brief one. "That man . . . he's vanished."

"He had to have been shot. Badly." His gaze dropped to the ground. "So much blood. God help me, for a moment I thought it was yours." His eyes reddened, misted unabashedly.

A commotion from the house drew their attention to the team of footmen spilling around the corner. Some half dozen of them came to a halt, taking in the scene. Two went to where Colin's valet crouched over the fallen man. After helping Holly to her feet, Colin beckoned to the remaining four.

"There is an intruder on the premises. We believe he's been wounded, so he can't have gotten far, but he is armed, so proceed with caution. Summon all the menservants and raise a search."

They raced off, and Colin, his arm secure around Holly's waist, started toward the man lying on the ground. She stopped him, one hand clinging to his coat front. "How do we know which man is telling the truth? Perhaps they were both lying."

"I don't think so." He covered her hand with his own. "Henri refused to fire his weapon. He didn't dare risk hitting you." His eyes glistened with tears again. "Just as I couldn't take that chance until Antoine had released you and you stumbled out of the way. Even then . . . it took more courage than I knew I had to aim straight and fire that shot. But I had no choice, or I'd risk allowing Antoine to seize you again. Or worse."

His last word ended on a strangled note. Holly pressed her lips to his cheek and tasted salty moisture. She wrapped her arms around him. "I heard two shots. Who fired the second? Your valet?"

"No. I did."

She turned toward the house and gasped. "*Geoffrey*?"

The youngest Ashworth strode toward them, a rifle clutched in his hands. "I shot the bastard, and I shan't apologize for it. Someone's got to look out for you, Miss Sutherland."

Colin grasped Holly's hand—tightly, as if he feared she would vanish into thin air—and together they met his brother partway across the grass. Colin's eyebrows hovered like storm clouds above his eyes. "Damn it, Geoff, I told you to stay inside."

"Yes, but you didn't tell me not to listen in. And having heard what I did, I acted in the only logical way possible. I ran to my room and pulled this"—he held the rifle up higher in front of him—"out from beneath my bed. You can't blame a fellow for taking decisive action."

Colin snatched the weapon away. "Where did you get this? Father—"

"Keeps his firearms under lock and key." Geoffrey angled his face. "That never stopped you. Besides . . ." The boy's eyes narrowed and his features hardened in a way Holly had never seen on him before, but that reminded her very much of his eldest brother when he was angered. When Geoffrey spoke again, the words sizzled bitterly on his tongue. "Father isn't here, is he?"

"No. Indeed he is not." Colin stared down at the rifle, his knuckles whitening around the dark, polished wood. He lifted his gaze to regard his brother, and without another word passed the weapon back to him. Geoffrey's mouth quirked, and Colin nodded, and for some odd reason tears stung Holly's eyes and a lump pushed against her throat.

"My lord! I have sent for a physician. This man is badly wounded."

Kirkston's cry sent Holly, Colin, and Geoffrey running across the lawn. The valet and remaining footmen moved aside, and Colin and Holly knelt down on either side of the Frenchman.

"Hélène . . . Holly?" Henri de Vere attempted to sit up, but Colin placed a hand on his uninjured shoulder. Holly gasped at the crimson stain spreading all too quickly across the other side of his coat. His head turned toward her, his eyes searching. He stretched out a hand. "Hélène . . ."

"He means you," he said.

She nodded. "His brother explained it to me." She shuddered involuntarily. "Or at least he told me a fantastical story about—"

"It is . . . all true." A bubble of blood formed at the corner of the Frenchman's mouth. "Except in his version . . . I am no doubt . . . the villain."

Colin gently pressed his shoulder again. "Don't try to speak. Not now."

"But I must . . . explain. . . . There is . . . more."

Holly's eagerness must have shown on her face, for Colin met her gaze and gave a nearly imperceptible shake of his head.

"Later," she said to Henri, "after the physician has seen you."

The two footmen had retreated to the house. Now they reappeared, carrying between them a door that had been taken off its hinges. One also had a blanket slung over his shoulder. When they reached Henri, they placed the door on the ground beside him, covered it with the blanket, and eased the man onto the surface. As steady as they could, they struggled back to their feet and carried de Vere inside.

A carriage came rumbling up the drive.

Holly shaded her eyes with her hand. "The physician is here already?"

Colin shook his head. "My mother. She's back from Windsor."

"Good gracious. However will we explain all of this to her?"

Colin wrapped an arm around her and drew her close. "Prudently."

They walked around to the front steps, where Ivy met them. "What is going on?" she demanded. "I was napping and awakened to the most dreadful clamor. And now I see this gentleman being carried into the house. Why, is it Mr. Verrell?"

For the first time since they'd fallen into each other's arms on the ground near the trees, Holly left Colin's side. She climbed the three or four steps until she stood level with her sister, and threw her arms around her.

Ivy let go a startled laugh. "What is all this?"

Holly looked deeply into her sister's eyes. "Yvonne."

"Who?"

"Come into the house, Ivy. I have much to explain to you. Where is Willow?"

"I thought she was with you."

"I'm right here."

Willow and Lord Bryce stood at the base of the steps. Holly went down to her youngest sister and caught Willow's hands in both of her own. "There is something I must tell you. Something both you and Ivy must hear."

"What is everyone doing gathered around the steps?" With the help of both a footman and her lady's maid, Colin's mother stepped down from her carriage. "And why do you all look so grim?"

Colin touched Holly's shoulder. "You speak with your sisters. I'll explain to my mother. And take care of de Vere."

She smiled sadly up at him. "Thank you."

"No, thank *you*." He grasped her chin, and warmth traveled her length even before he brushed his lips across hers.

He strode away, going to greet his mother and escort her into the house. Holly watched his retreating back, sensing a profound change in him. Oh, so much had changed since her arrival, since that day outside the Ascot Racecourse when he had nearly struck her down with his curricle. She had believed him to be indifferent to her, to disapprove of everything about her. But it had never been her he disapproved of; it had been himself. He had judged himself in terms of his heritage and the mistakes of those that came before him. That such an extraordinary man could think so little of himself brought tears to her eyes.

She impatiently blinked them away. Their future still lay in uncertainty. Their trials were far from ended, and she knew that in the coming days she would have to be stronger than ever before. All she knew was that, no matter what happened, she would stand by him. Even if it meant angering Victoria and sharing his fate.

"Holly?"

Ivy's quiet summons jarred her from her thoughts. Steeling herself for the immediate task at hand, she pulled her gaze from the man she loved, linked an arm through each of her sisters', and went with them into the house.

They were the most difficult words Holly had ever had to utter. The tale, defined by greed and brutality and murder, left Ivy and Willow pale and speechless. Willow wept silently. Ivy pressed a hand to her belly.

They had retreated to the privacy of the ground floor receiving parlor where they had met Antoine de Vere. The silence, as her sisters took in all she had told them, stretched on until it resounded in Holly's ears.

Then Ivy tilted her head, her brow wrinkling. "Uncle Edward's garden."

"I'm sorry?" Holly could understand her sister's turning to Thorn Grove, the estate where they had grown up isolated but protected, but why the garden in particular?

"Can't you picture it?" Ivy closed her eyes for a moment. "The towering laurel tree. The ivy clinging to the back of the house, the old dovecote and the stables. The holly growing in tangles around—"

"The giant willow," Willow finished for her. Her mouth dropped open, then snapped shut. "He brought us to his home and found names for us in what he saw outside his windows." She swallowed audibly and wiped her palms across her cheeks. "Then I am . . . Wilhemine? Wilhemine de Valentin?"

"Yes." Holly, who had stood as she wove her tale for them, walked behind her younger sister's chair and pressed a hand to her shoulder.

"Yvonne." Ivy seemed to test the fit of the name on her tongue. She shook her head. "It is as though we are speaking of strangers, not ourselves."

Holly agreed. "I am perfectly content with who we are. *Were*. I mean . . ."

"The Sutherland sisters," Ivy finished for her. "No matter our past, we *are* the Sutherland sisters, with all that entails. This changes nothing, except . . ." Her eyes filled with tears. In a whisper she said, "Now at least we know what happened to our parents."

Holly went to sit beside Ivy on the settee and put an arm around her. She held out her hand to Willow, who immediately jumped up from her chair and hurried to them. Taking Holly's hand, she sank to her knees on the rug and rested her cheek on Ivy's knee.

"I don't care about the fortune. I don't want it," she declared, sounding much like a recalcitrant child refusing the offer of a treat. "That money is tainted. It killed our mother and father and I . . . I never knew them. I have no memory of them." She lifted her tearstained face. "Do either of you remember anything at all about them?"

Her heart clenching, Holly started to shake her head, but Ivy whispered, "I remember a scent . . . like lilacs . . . Whenever I smell lilacs I feel . . . I don't know . . . soothed. Calm. Almost . . . happy." She reached down and stroked Willow's hair. "I think perhaps Mother wore that scent. I like to believe it."

Something not quite a memory, more of a sensation, pushed its way through Holly's thoughts like a ship breaking free of an ice flow. "Rumbling. I remember a rumbling against my cheek, and . . . and reaching up and tangling my fingers in the curly softness of a beard. Uncle Edward never wore a long beard . . . so it must have been Father's." She bent down and put her arms around Willow. "Think, dearest . . . perhaps there is something . . . even the smallest thing."

Willow's face filled with eager hope. Her brow furrowed and she closed her eyes. But the upsweep of her lashes revealed only a deep and unshakable sorrow. "There is nothing. I was too young. Oh, it isn't fair." She bowed her head, and Holly thought she heard words slip out beneath her breath, ones that sounded very much like, *Damn those men for doing this to us*.

Ivy was the first to gather her composure. "I agree with Willow. I don't care a whit about this fortune. Of course, we'll have to confer with Laurel, but I say we either give it all away or allow it to remain in abeyance indefinitely."

Holly related the details Antoine de Vere had revealed to her, that after Napoleon's defeat, the newly restored French monarchy had seized the family's holdings, or what remained of them. In those chaotic years following the wars, it had been unclear which branch of the family, the de Veres or the de Valentins, had betrayed their king and so many of their peers, and equally unclear which cousin had preyed upon which. Indeed, many had believed the fire that killed Roland and Simone de Valentin had been an accident, and that their four daughters had perished with them.

"Yes, give it all away." Willow lifted her blotchy face higher. "I've no wish to be suddenly French."

Madly, that assertion sent laughter bubbling up in Holly's throat. She tried to stifle it, for there was nothing humorous here, nothing at all, but not even biting her lips kept the chuckles from spilling out. Certain her sisters must be appalled, she tried to apologize but could barely form the words. Suddenly Ivy was laughing as well, her shoulders shaking. Willow frowned with a mixture of puzzlement and hurt, but after a moment her lips parted and she, too, fell to uncontrollable guffaws. Holly laughed until her cheeks ached and her belly cramped. Scarcely able to sit up, she half collapsed against Ivy's side, while Ivy, in turn, wilted helplessly back against the cushions and Willow, red-faced and nearly shrieking, huddled against their knees.

Their laughter gradually subsided with tears and sniffles and more silence, until a sobering, but not unhappy thought made Holly smile. "Well . . . it would seem we are still indeed the Sutherland sisters, aren't we?"

Colin wasn't certain his mother fully understood what he had spent the last quarter hour trying to explain to her. Sabrina, who had come running from the paddocks at the first sound of shots, sat dumbfounded beside the elder woman as Colin's story unfolded. Geoffrey added his version of events as witnessed from the music room window, leaving out, however, his part in wounding Antoine de Vere.

In the end, their mother nodded her head with something of a dazed look. "So, then, Miss Sutherland and her sisters are not misses at all, but ladies in the aristocratic sense of the word?"

"One would make that assumption, Mother. Their father was le Comte de Valentin, or was so before the end of the wars. The title has been in abeyance ever since."

"Ah, well, no matter." His mother gave a little shrug. "Miss Sutherland will be the Countess of Drayton as soon as the two of you are wed."

Unease mingled with the joy he should have felt. For several precious moments out on the lawns, he had wholeheartedly believed that with Holly at his side, there wasn't anything in life he couldn't do, couldn't face.

But now that the immediate danger had passed, it was remorse and not relief that filled him. If he married Holly and the queen sent him to prison, Holly's life would be ruined. If he didn't marry her, Lady Penelope and her family would waste no time in sullying Holly's reputation, and thus ruin her prospects. Either way, he had wronged her grievously, given into temptation and failed to protect the one person he loved most dearly.

It was time to see exactly what the future held. Leaving

Geoff to answer his mother's questions as best he could, Colin excused himself from the library. He intended first to check on Monsieur de Vere. Then he must return to the abandoned manor. In his haste to save Holly from Antoine, he had left the colt—around which so many fates hinged— alone in the dilapidated stable.

Chapter 30

Colin left Masterfield Park without informing Holly, but she was with her sisters, the three of them struggling to come to terms with the startling truth of their origins. The revelation had so shocked Holly that she hadn't even remembered to ask him whether he had found the colt. He couldn't blame her. Even now he could hardly fathom this new identity of hers, and he wondered how Simon de Burgh would react to the news that his wife was not the obscure miss he believed he had married, but a member of the French aristocracy.

Colin quickly realized it wouldn't make the slightest difference to Simon, because it didn't make the slightest difference to him. Holly was still Holly: sensual and surprising and courageous. She could be a queen or a washerwoman for all he cared; he'd still be intrigued by her, at times awed by her. He'd still wildly crave the spicy warmth of her skin and the taste of her lips. Still love her to distraction.

At the pair of rickety gates he'd entered earlier, he and the others turned down the dilapidated drive. Halfway to the house he brought Kirkston and the footmen to a halt. "Weapons out," he told them. "Eyes and ears sharp. We don't know what we'll find."

Not that he believed Antoine would have returned here, even if he could have, but it paid to be prudent. Judging by the amount of blood the man had left splattered on the ground near Holly, Colin doubted Antoine had gotten very far in his flight, perhaps no farther than the heath beyond Masterfield Park's pastureland.

Had he survived? And if not, would his brother join him in death? Henri had lost a good deal of blood, and the physician feared the bullet might have nicked a lung. If that was the case, Henri de Vere had only hours to live.

"I believe the young devil just gave a snort," Kirkston said, interrupting Colin's bleak musings. They had ridden through the derelict gardens and dismounted just outside the low wall encircling the stable yard. "The colt must smell us coming."

With great relief they found the animal safely in the stall where they had left him earlier. They made short work of their errand and turned toward home, the colt's lead rope wrapped securely around Colin's hand.

The next morning, Colin stood beside Holly in the stables as she reached up and stroked the animal's neck. In her other hand she held a halved apple. She raised it and the colt snatched the fruit from her palm.

"I believe I would recognize this horse if I were blind-folded," she said.

"Perhaps more readily." Colin smiled, remembering how yesterday, when he'd first brought the colt home, Holly had insisted on examining him from every angle to make certain he was the same horse the queen had named Prince's Pride. "He looks much like the rest of the Ashworth stock. What is inside him makes him unique."

"The enchantment."

He chuckled softly. "Have you become a believer in Celtic magic?"

"No." She turned her face to him, her expression causing his chest to tighten. "I am a believer in the magic you have created through your science. Through your brilliance as a horse breeder."

"I don't think . . ." His throat constricting, he closed the small space between them and pressed his forehead to hers.

"I don't think any compliment has ever made me more proud."

Her arms encircled his neck and she pulled him lower still for a kiss—one quickly interrupted by the colt's impatient nudging. They broke apart, and Holly fed the animal the other half of the apple. "The bracken . . . do you think it was Antoine who poisoned the horses?"

Colin scrubbed a hand across his eyes. "I wish I knew. All I can say is I won't rest until I have the answer. The investigation shall continue."

"If it *was* Antoine, I shall certainly feel guilty about having accused Mr. Bentley."

"He need never know."

"That's true. Isn't it, boy?" she cooed to the colt. She laughed softly as the animal lowered his head and snuffled as if searching out further fruit. Then she sighed. "We do need to bring him back to Devonshire as soon as possible."

Colin started to question the claim that *they together* must bring the colt anywhere when he realized that if he went to Devonshire, he would most assuredly bring Holly with him. And everywhere else he happened to go. He'd almost lost her yesterday; he wasn't about to let her out of his sight, at least not until the queen's decree forced their separation.

"There is no need to bring that colt anywhere," a voice said from down the aisle. They turned to peer through the dusty shafts of light streaming through the narrow windows. "At least not with any immediacy."

Colin squinted into the intermittent shadows and brightness. "Grandmama?"

With her butler, Hockley, trailing behind her, Grandmother walked—not hobbled but walked at a pace that had Hockley almost running to keep up—down the aisle. When she reached Colin and Holly her smile tilted like that of a young debutante. "It is I."

"But . . . how? When? I don't . . ." Realizing he was stammering, Colin closed his mouth and simply marveled at the sight before him. Grandmother still clutched her cane, but she'd used it haphazardly, as if out of habit more than from any true need. With a delighted grin he kissed her cheeks. "I don't understand. How can this be? You haven't visited Masterfield Park in . . ."

"At least five years," she finished for him. Then her gaze shifted to Holly and her eyebrows angled to an amused slant. "How are you, my dear?"

"I am well. Thank you, Your Grace. And you . . ." What began as a question quickly transformed to a statement that echoed Colin's own sentiments. "You look positively splendid."

"Thank you, dear. I feel splendid. More splendid than in . . . goodness . . . I don't know how many years." She placed a gloved hand on Colin's cheek. "Since those first few years after your grandfather passed away."

Colin nodded his understanding. Before he could comment, however, she moved past him and stood before the colt. "So, here is what all the trouble has been about."

"He can go home now, Your Grace, where he belongs." Holly absently stroked a hand down the colt's nose.

"Yes, he should go home. But it is no longer of the utmost urgency." Grandmother's exuberant expression melted years, even decades from her age. "Everything has changed. Two days ago Jon Darby's sow birthed a healthy pair of piglets. The sun has come out, and the seed crop we had believed to have been washed away when the river flooded is beginning to sprout. Apparently, everyone has taken these occurrences as a sign, for the farmers and shopkeepers resumed the tasks that had gone ignored these many weeks. And me . . . well!" She held her arms out, the cane dangling in the air. She then turned a narrow-eyed gaze on Holly. "One wonders . . ."

Holly backed up half a step. "Your Grace?"

Grandmother thrust her cane into Hockley's hands. Then she gripped Holly's shoulders and drew her closer. "Hmm. Yes, there is a difference about you, too, my dear." She glanced over at her butler. "Hockley, would you mind?"

The man gave a nod and, with Grandmother's cane in hand, he retreated down the aisle.

Holly's gaze darted to Colin, and then returned sheepishly to Grandmother. "I don't understand."

"Oh, I think you do." Grandmother released her. Gripping Colin in similar fashion, she studied him as if he were a specimen under a microscope. "When I arrived Sabrina informed me of an impending wedding. Ah, yes. It is clear to me now."

Her capriciousness was beginning to exasperate him. "Good grief, *what* is clear, Grandmama?"

"The two of you. You've ..." Her eyebrows arced in amusement.

"Grandmother." Colin injected a good dose of warning into the word, but she went on smiling shrewdly while Holly blushed furious shades of red.

Finally, Grandmother threw back her head and laughed. "Do you children not see? Your union has lifted the curse." She clapped her hands together. "Briannon has her resolution and we are free."

"Oh, Your Grace, that cannot be so. You *know* it cannot." Holly gently clasped his grandmother's hand. Colin feared she would attempt to dissuade Grandmother of her romantic, magical notions by denying the existence of the curse, but Holly only said, "Whatever your grandson and I have done, we are not married ... not yet ... and therefore—"

"My dear," Grandmother interrupted, "do you not realize that in Briannon's time, marriage was a simple matter of handfasting and ..." She lowered her voice, though her whisper rang with delight. "Consummation, though not necessarily in that order. In Briannon's eyes, in her heart, you are married *enough*."

"Grandmother's right," Colin murmured quickly. Curses or no, he agreed that in his heart of hearts, he was already married to Holly Sutherland and nothing could change that.

But Holly wasn't finished trying to reason with his

grandmother. "Your Grace, you're forgetting one essential part of Briannon's legacy. Perhaps the most important part—"

Colin cleared his throat loudly, and Holly broke off with a bewildered scowl.

"There is no arguing with my grandmother once she has made up her mind," he said.

Holly hesitated; then her scowl faded and she nodded.

Later that afternoon, Holly stood alone in the doorway of the guest chamber where Henri de Vere had been brought. The physician still could not say with any certainty what the man's fate would be, though his having held on this long was cause for optimism.

Willow and Ivy asked after the health of their distant cousin often, but other than an initial visit, neither had showed any inclination to venture to this wing of the house. To them, the man represented danger and changes neither of them welcomed. These forebodings loomed over Holly as well, but after being caught smack in the middle of the two brothers, tricked by one and rescued by the other, she alone understood that her future hinged on finding a balance between the past and present, between danger and change, between what she wished for and what simply was.

How Henri de Vere, still unconscious, could possibly provide the answers she sought, she didn't know. She only knew she was drawn to him and helpless to resist that almost magnetic pull. While Colin continued to care for the horses down at the stud, she slipped away from her sisters whenever they appeared not to need her, to see if Henri had awakened. To will him to recover.

Because if he died, how many secrets about the Sutherland sisters would go untold?

Usually she stood only in the doorway, but this time she couldn't resist tiptoeing to the bedside. Dr. Fanning, who'd come all the way from Windsor, had slipped out moments ago to stretch his legs. Holly and Henri were alone.

She leaned over the prone man, noting his linenlike pallor, the blue shadows beneath his eyes. Even bluer veins stood out like frozen rivers on his temples, and his lips stretched thin and bloodless across his face. Could a person hover so close to death and still recover? She said a little prayer, not only for Henri but for everyone—her sisters and the Ashworths, and the faraway folk of Devonshire. She even included the horses, with thanks that the illness had passed. Everyone here went about in a state of relief, almost happiness, though they curbed the latter emotion out of respect for their injured guest.

Sabrina, however, could scarcely subdue her elation. Lately she was all smiles, and told anyone who would listen how her horsemanship skills had returned to their former level. With the dowager duchess's help, Colin's mother contentedly planned the upcoming ball, and the wedding to follow. And just this morning Holly had caught Colin whistling to himself—whistling! As if he hadn't a care in the world.

If only that were true. . . .

"Hélène?"

With a gasp Holly drew her gaze away from the window. But when she stared down at Henri, his eyes were closed and he appeared as unconscious as ever. She leaned lower. "Mr. de Vere . . . monsieur . . . did you say something?"

Though his eyes stayed closed, his lips twitched, and "Hélène" slipped out on a shallow breath.

"Yes, I am here. Right here beside you."

"Must . . . have . . . care."

The last word ended on a raw wheezing, and Holly felt guilty for having encouraged him to speak at all. That guilt only intensified when a rusty bubble broke at the corner of his mouth.

She laid a hand on his upper arm through the blankets. "Please don't speak. Not just now. The doctor will return any moment, and he will make you comfortable." As if to prove her point, sunlight glinted on the vial of laudanum left on the bedside table.

"Must . . ." He struggled against the coverlets, perhaps to sit up, perhaps to speak.

Holly laid a gentle finger across his lips and spoke in his ear. "I promise I will have a care, if you promise to lie still."

He gave a nod, or perhaps his neck merely spasmed, for in the next instant he coughed. Suddenly his eyes blinked open and he stared lucidly up at her. "Danger . . . not past."

His intensity frightened her, and she pulled back with a start. "What danger? Your brother, or something else, something more?" She leaned close again, but she saw that he had fallen into a faint. Moments later, Dr. Fanning returned and took her place at the bedside.

Outside in the corridor, raised voices from the ground floor sent Holly hurrying to the stairs. In the hall below, all the Ashworths and Holly's sisters milled about in turmoil. Questions flew haphazardly; some were answered, others went unheard.

"Oh, how beastly!"

"He was a beastly man! He deserved what he got."

"Whatever brought him here, to us?"

"And what of his brother?"

Colin met Holly at the bottom of the staircase. "He's been found," he told her. "He's being laid out in a storeroom belowstairs."

She didn't need him to elaborate. "Alive, or . . . ?"

Colin shook his head, then gathered her to his chest while around them the pandemonium continued. "The wound was to his gut. There was no way he could have survived, even with medical attention. He bled out during the night."

"Where . . ." Her pounding heart made it impossible for her to form full sentences. But she discovered that she didn't need to, for Colin anticipated her thoughts perfectly.

"Quite close to the vale, where I'd hidden the colt."

A dismaying thought brought her head up off his shoulder. "Geoffrey . . . oh, I hope it wasn't his bullet. . . ."

"It wasn't. Dr. Fanning has already pronounced the

wound indicative of a smaller ball than the rifle could have held. It was my shot that killed Antoine."

Her arms were around his waist, and now she tightened them, squeezed with all her strength. He clung just as tightly. Tears sprang to her eyes and flowed freely, soaking his coat front, while her sobs echoed into him and shook his frame. "It's all right," she whispered between her weeping. "You had no choice. You did it for me."

"I'd do it again," he whispered back.

From behind her, a hand came down lightly on her shoulder. "Everything will be all right now, Holly-berry. We're safe again. We can go on with our lives."

She eased away from Colin, loath to let him go. Turning, she beheld Willow's teary-eyed smile. Her hand went to her sister's cheek, even as dread plummeted to the pit of her stomach. They were not safe. Even before Henri had spoken to her, she had known, deep down, that their lives would never be the same again, and that the danger would not pass even if Antoine left this world.

They had to discover the truth—all of it.

For now, she smiled for Willow's sake, and for Ivy's, too. She encouraged them to take tea with the Ashworth women, but no, she would not join them, not now, for there was something she must do. After assuring them she was perfectly fine, and watching them stroll into the drawing room with the duchess, the dowager, and Sabrina, Holly pulled Colin aside before he could slip away to the stables again.

"This isn't over."

"No, I didn't think it was," he agreed simply.

"For good or ill, we must stay with Henri in the event he speaks again. He knows more than he admitted, and I believe he is regretting that now."

Colin nodded. They had just started up the stairs when a footman called to him.

The freckled youth, his sandy-brown hair slicked neatly away from his face, held out a sealed missive. "My lord, the morning post arrived a little before . . . before the unfortunate gentleman was brought in. I'm dreadfully sorry, sir. In all the commotion I nearly forgot."

Colin reached for the letter and tucked it into his coat pocket. "That's all right, Michael. Thank you."

The youth bobbed his head and went about his business.

They sat at Henri's bedside for nearly three hours. The man never moved, much less spoke. Yet Dr. Fanning seemed encouraged. He hadn't expected the Frenchman to last this long.

Colin scrubbed the fatigue from his eyes, reaching with his other hand to massage Holly's shoulder. From her chair, she leaned a little in to him, then straightened.

"Why don't you get some rest," he suggested, not for the first time.

She stubbornly shook her head. "He could awaken at any moment."

Or never. But he didn't say it aloud. Instead he took her hand and raised it to his lips, holding it there even when the doctor reentered the room to check on the patient. Without much interest, Colin watched Fanning, a middle-aged man with graying muttonchops, a balding head, and a large nose that reminded Colin of misshapen dough, lift each of Henri's eyelids. The man had repeated the examination several times, had listened to de Vere's breathing and heart, had checked his pulse. Always he clucked his tongue, raised his eyebrows, and shook his head.

This time the doctor flinched as, without warning, Henri's hand came up and gripped his wrist. The man let out a whimper as his patient's fist tightened. Holly surged to her feet, and Colin beside her.

"Hélène . . ."

"I'm here."

Henri released the doctor and with a weak gesture beckoned her closer. Colin moved with her to the bedside, believing that whatever the man might utter would affect him equally as much, for better or worse, and would define his future as much as hers.

Henri struggled to push the words out. "Hélène . . . there is more . . . more than a fortune . . . at stake." He had been straining to lift his head. Now, his scant strength waning, his head fell back against the pillow. His eyes closed, and Colin could feel Holly's disappointment though she said nothing.

Henri's lips moved again. "The de Valentins . . . the Bourbons . . . one family. Danger. Succession. You and your sisters . . . your sons. Danger."

Holly darted an alarmed glance at Colin, then bent over de Vere. "What are you saying? That the de Veres and the de Valentins are—"

"Not . . . the de Veres. Il-illegitimate. The de Valentins only . . . in line. Claim, even now."

"Claim . . . Claim what?"

Colin slipped an arm around her shoulders and pulled her closer in an effort to calm her. If what de Vere was saying held any truth . . . dear God. His heart heaved against his ribs. When Henri didn't answer, Colin said as gently as he could, "The French throne."

Holly wrenched away from him, half turning and backing into the bedside table. The impact sent a cup and a vial onto their sides; they rolled off the table and onto the rug. She faced him like some frightened, infuriated young fox, her eyes glittering dangerously, her nostrils flared, her chin outthrust in defiance. "That isn't possible. It's . . . it's . . . madness."

"My love." He held his arms benignly out on either side of him. He moved closer to her, but when she stiffened as if ready to run, he halted. "It is what I believe he is trying to tell you."

She began shaking her head. Her mouth opened, but no words came out. From the bed, Henri sputtered through his half-parted lips and opened his eyes. His hand came up, fingers groping at the air.

"Hélène—"

"Do not call me that." Holly made no move to go to him. "I am Holly. Holly Sutherland."

Henri compressed his lips, and tried again. "You are . . .

who you are. There are those in France t-today . . . unhappy to have the king . . . restored. Want re-republic. Should Louis-Phillippe lose control of his crown . . . violence . . . like before. And you . . . your sisters . . . your heirs . . . perceived as threats. Next time . . . *all* claimants . . . dispatched . . . leaving no one . . . no one to claim the throne."

The words reverberated through Colin and rendered him weak-kneed, immobile. But seeing Holly's legs about to give way beneath her, he reached her in a bound. His arms went around her and she sagged against him, a whimper of despair groaning like a winter wind from inside her.

Holly opened her eyes, only to shut them again against a blinding light. She turned away from it and tried opening her eyes again.

This time the rich tones of a burgundy and gold canopy met her gaze. She blinked and looked about her, taking in the unfamiliar surroundings of a bedchamber furnished in heavy, dark mahogany and deeply burnished cherry wood. The bright light had come from the window a few feet from the bed on which she lay, the sunshine spearing through a gap in the curtains someone had hastily drawn. Where was she? With a sense of alarm she braced her hands against the mattress and pushed upward. . . .

Into Colin's waiting arms.

His lips brushed her eyelids, the bridge of her nose, her cheeks, and finally her lips. Against them he whispered, "You fainted, but it's all right. You're in my room but no one knows we're here. They're all still drinking tea in the drawing room."

She clung to his shoulders, her lips nestling against the warmth of his. "I fainted? How long . . . ?"

"Not long."

"And Henri?"

She felt his lips curve. "Dr. Fanning is feeling encouraged."

She pulled back a little. "Oh, I *am* glad. I was unkind to him. . . ."

"He understands."

Her guilt persisted. "However distressing the tidings he brought us, and however much he erred in not confiding in my sisters and me sooner, I do believe he meant to protect us."

"I believe that, too."

"And if everything he says is true, then he is something exceedingly rare to us. A blood relative." Holly couldn't yet determine exactly what that would mean to her and her sisters' lives, but it warmed her to think that from now on, there would be a new—or rather an old—family member in their midst.

Even so, a faint repugnance seeped through her. "I've never fainted before in my life. The Sutherland sisters are *not* swooners."

Colin laughed, pressing his mouth to her cheek and holding it there. "Perhaps not, but in this instance it's no wonder. You're exhausted."

Her fingers tightened around his shoulders. "What Henri said . . . do you believe it can be true?"

"Do I believe you and your sisters are descended from royalty?" He lifted his head and smiled, a grin that held boyish mischief on the surface, yet revealed something raw and vulnerable and endearingly humble beneath. "Do I believe a colt and a madcap herd of ponies hold mystical powers? Or that a Celtic princess once cast a spell over my family? Or that because I happened to fall in love with a stubborn, reckless goddess of a woman that spell has been broken, the princess appeased, my grandmother cured of her ills, and the people of Devonshire satisfied?"

She made a fist and pummeled it into his shoulder. "Stop toying with me. I asked you in all earnestness."

He bewildered her by releasing her, sliding off the bed, and holding out a hand to her. "Are you feeling quite restored?"

"Yes, much better. But—"

"Then come with me."

He refused to explain as he practically towed her through the house, down a set of back stairs, and through the service corridors to avoid being seen by their families. Her curiosity got the better of her when they came upon Maribelle—newly returned from Briarview in Grandmother's wake—saddled and waiting on the wide garden path. Digging in her heels, Holly demanded to know where they were going, but Colin refused to elaborate. He said only that there was something she must see. He boosted her into the saddle and swung up behind her.

It wasn't until they'd cleared the stables and the paddocks that Holly understood what he wished to show her. Within the racecourse, two bay horses with black points galloped and reared and kicked their hind legs as if with an inexpressible joy, their distinctive Ashworth stars flashing silvery in the sunlight. As Holly watched, the pair ran the length of the closer straight, then veered and parted, racing away from each other. From opposite corners they each let out piercing whinnies and kicked at the turf, arching their sleek backs and tossing their formidable heads in the air. At some agreed-upon signal the larger of the two animals galloped back to the youngster's side, and they began a neck-and-neck race round the track.

"Cordelier and Prince's Pride," Holly whispered. Her heart clogged her throat and her eyes swam with tears she could not blink away, that stung painfully each time the wind buffeted her face.

Colin nodded. "I sent word down to Mr. Peterson to have Cordelier and the colt brought out to run together."

"Good gracious ... they're ... glorious. So beautiful. So free." Her tears trickled over, and a sob, mixed with irrepressible laughter, bounced on the breeze.

"And magical, no?" His arms tightened around her, his fingers splaying possessively over her abdomen. His mouth moved against her hair. "Up in my bedroom you asked what I believed."

"Yes." The word slid from her lips as a breathless gasp. With the exultation of the two Ashworth stallions before her and Colin's heat at her back, she felt wrapped in magic, in the certainty that anything was possible.

Colin abruptly dismounted. Standing at Maribelle's side, he reached up for Holly. She slid into his arms expecting him to set her down. Instead he cradled her and began whirling her round and round. Maribelle trotted away, going to the fence rail and calling out to her equine mates. Holly, meanwhile, encircled Colin's neck and pressed her cheek to his shoulder, while the racecourse and horses, the pastures and paddocks, and the bright sky blurred around her.

"I believe in all of it," Colin said so loudly that he might have been heard from as far away as the stables. She instinctively shushed him, but that only made him throw back his head and laugh. Meanwhile, he continued dancing in dizzying circles, mindful not to trip over rocks and tree roots.

"I believe," he said even more loudly, as if addressing the sky itself, "that there are phenomena in this world that science cannot explain. That there are forces even greater than those that can be studied in a laboratory."

He suddenly stopped, though the world kept whirling madly around Holly. Feeling slightly ill, she might have succumbed to dizziness if not for the strength of his arms holding her secure and the wall of his chest steady against her. "I believe in love, Holly. I believe in the power of it. And most of all . . ." he murmured, but trailed off again.

With his lips he nuzzled her face upward, putting her mouth right where he apparently wanted it—entirely at his mercy. He seized her lips with his own and kissed them until they magically opened; then his tongue swept inside, sweeping *her* up in a giddy swirl of sensation. He kissed her again and again, deeply, wholly, until their surroundings went spinning away, leaving only tingling heat, safety and strength, and the love bursting from her heart.

He released her legs, but before her feet touched the ground he whirled her once about, then held her, still suspended, against him. "I believe in you, Holly Sutherland. I believe you and I are meant to be together, curses and naysayers and even the queen be damned."

Her gasp was muffled by another kiss. Then he loosened his hold just enough to let her slide along his body until her half boots touched the grass. As they did, Holly's arms slid lower, too, and the sound of crumpling paper came from Colin's coat pocket.

"What's this?"

"Ah, yes, I'd forgotten. Just a letter that arrived today." With a shrug he pulled it from his pocket and glanced down at the sender's direction. His brows knotting, he slipped a finger beneath the seal. "It's from a Captain Percival Smithers. . . ." His head snapped up and his arm dropped to his side, slapping the page against his thigh. The blood drained from his face, leaving him as white as the clouds drifting overhead.

His pallor raised an alarm inside Holly. "More dreadful news?"

His lips moved, but for a moment no sound came out. Then he drew a ragged breath. "There was a storm. My father . . . his ship went down."

He swayed slightly and Holly drew him beneath the shade of the elm tree. He leaned against the trunk, and she grasped his free hand between both of hers and searched his pallid features. "Is he . . . ?"

Colin nodded. "Captain Smithers writes that his ship came across the remnants of the *Sea Goddess* a mere few hundred leagues off the European coast. He says there could have been no survivors." The letter drifted from his fingers and fluttered to the ground. "He died only days after he left England. By Christ, do you realize what this means?"

"Yes. It means that you are the Duke of Masterfield." She framed his face with her hands, her palms fitted snugly against his cheeks, her fingertips burrowing into his golden hair. "It means that since before the colt went missing, you have been the head of the Ashworth family."

The beginnings of a smile tilted the corners of his mouth. It was neither humor nor amusement that gleamed in his eyes, but a look of awe and of love. "And you, my darling, have been and always shall be my princess."

Chapter 31

Holly smoothed a hand over her carefully arranged curls—again—and gave her bodice a tug to ensure all sat smooth and straight. She'd checked her appearance in the mirror this morning at least a score of times, and now as she trailed the liveried footman down the seemingly endless corridor, she craned her neck for last-minute glimpses in each pane of glass she passed.

"Do stop fidgeting." Colin's warm hand briefly cupped her shoulder. "You look perfect."

She tossed him a grateful smile, at the same time realizing that how she looked wouldn't make the slightest difference. Perfect or no, within minutes her fate—their fate—would be sealed. She didn't understand how Colin could remain so calm.

At last the footman, a tall, handsome young man with a head of dark, wavy hair, brought them to a halt where the corridor ended abruptly before a formidable set of paneled, carved mahogany doors that stood twice as tall as a man. Two guards dressed in regal red and black stood at attention, one in front of each door, their legs braced wide, their right hands poised on the hilts of their gleaming swords. Their gazes remained fixed on some distant spot over Holly's and Colin's shoulders.

"Here is where I must leave you," the footman said.

"Thank you, Roger, for everything."

With an encouraging smile, he nodded. She had begun this journey with Roger Linwood on that night that now seemed ages ago, when he'd come for her in London at the queen's behest. She wondered how much, if anything, he knew about her failed mission. Touching her fingertips to his sleeve, she held them there a moment and said, "I wish you all the best."

"Good luck, miss," he said affably. He tipped his head to Colin. "My lord."

He retreated down the hall, and Holly returned her attention to the pair of royal guards. Perhaps they'd refuse to open the doors, she thought with a twinge of hope, and she and Colin could go home. All too quickly, however, one of the doors opened. As she took a step forward, Colin's hand came down on her shoulder.

"No matter what happens," he said, "I am yours."

"And I yours." She flashed him a shaky smile, a reflection of the unsteady courage she tried desperately to prevent from crumbling. "At least horse thieves are no longer hanged."

"Perhaps Her Majesty will allow us to share a cell in Newgate."

"I would happily reside there, or anywhere, with you."

Then they were inside, Colin bending at the waist and she sinking into a deep curtsy after catching the briefest glimpse of deep blue silk trimmed in ivory lace. She hadn't dared to lift her gaze as high as Victoria's face.

The lie Holly had rehearsed for nearly twenty-four hours, ever since the royal summons had arrived at Masterfield Park, ran through her mind. Would she be able to speak the falsehoods, to break the sacred vow she and her sisters had made that sunny day in Uncle Edward's rose garden, so many years ago?

The colt would return to Devonshire, not because of any curse but because it was the right thing to do, because he was meant to run free with the herd, with his own kind, under the watchful protection, perhaps, of Briannon's spirit. For Holly that meant facing her queen, her friend, and breaking faith. Her conscience gave a painful twist. . . .

Behind her, those intimidating doors closed with a soft thud that jangled her nerves. Somewhere in front of her, a familiar voice spoke quiet words, followed by briskly receding footsteps and another closing door. Holly wondered what was happening but didn't look up or so much as blink. Then. . . .

"Holly, dearest, surely you know there is no need for such formality. We are quite alone now. I've even sent Lehzen away." At that, a pair of soft, slightly plump hands appeared in her vision, reaching for her own. Holly clasped them and let herself be raised from her curtsy.

Lifting her face the few necessary inches, she met her queen's gaze. "Your Majesty, I beg you to understand . . ."

Victoria smiled broadly. "I just told you. No need for formality. And if anyone must beg, it is I, Holly dear. I must beg your pardon for my foolishness." Victoria's gaze, filled with an odd mingling of amusement and chagrin that only a queen could achieve, shifted to Holly's right. "I must beg your pardon as well, Lord Drayton."

Holly exchanged a startled glance with Colin. "I don't understand."

"The colt, of course. Oh, Holly, such a wild-goose chase I sent you on. And you, Lord Drayton . . . dear me, such things I suspected of you. Wrongly, of course. Oh, so very wrongly. That is why I summoned you here as well, sir. I don't know how much our dear Miss Sutherland has explained to you, but I thought it only right that I make my little confession with hopes that you will both forgive me."

Astonishment and confusion and a tiny seed of hope pulled Holly's brows tight. "I . . . I'm afraid I don't . . ."

"Prince Frederick returned early. Yesterday morning, in fact. He went straight to the mews to take possession of the colt. My head groom—you remember William—sent a message to warn me, so naturally I hurried down to the mews to explain to the prince about the colt's disappearance and to apologize most humbly. And do you know what happened?" Still grasping Holly's hands, Victoria tossed her head and laughed. "I never got the words out. Frederick saw nothing amiss at all. He was so pleased with the colt, so grateful, that suddenly I realized how foolish I'd been. Goodness, to send you to find 'the real colt' when all along he was right there in my stables."

Victoria released one of Holly's hands to dab a mirthful tear from her eye. "Truly, I can't imagine what got into me. You must have thought me mad, yet off you went in good faith to do my bidding, like the true and steadfast friend you are. Thank you. Thank you, dear soul. And I *am* sorry."

Again, Holly shot a glance at Colin, who only gave an infinitesimal shrug. She turned back to Victoria. "Then . . . you're saying all is well?"

"Of course that is what I am saying. And to make it up to you, I'd like you and your sisters to ride with me in the royal procession to open the Ascot meeting. And you as well, Lord Drayton. All of you shall ride in a coach of honor right behind my own. And then you may watch the races from the royal box." The young queen looked suddenly stricken. "Oh, but that is hardly reward enough for the trouble I've caused you."

Holly waved a hand in the air. "No reward is necessary. Your satisfaction is quite enough, and I'm simply elated to see that everything has worked out." This time she flashed Colin a grin she couldn't contain. "Truly."

"That won't do." Victoria was shaking her head. "I must reward you somehow."

Colin offered Her Majesty a smart bow. "Ma'am, if I may make a suggestion."

"Yes, Lord Drayton?"

He took Holly's hand and cupped it in both of his own. "Your Majesty, I shall be bold and ask your permission for this lady's hand in marriage."

"Really?" Victoria beamed at each of them in turn, her approval plain to see.

"Yes, ma'am. And as soon as possible. We were even thinking, with your consent of course, of obtaining a special license and eloping. We simply don't wish to wait a day longer than necessary."

"Good heavens." Victoria's eyes narrowed and her lips puckered speculatively, causing Holly to squirm slightly as she considered what her friend must be thinking. In fact, did the royal gaze just drop to her belly? Did Victoria suspect they'd been intimate . . . in essence, suspect the truth?

Holly couldn't have denied it, nor could she with certainty know yet if Colin's child had taken root inside her. Impatience might have played a role in prompting his request, but prudence certainly advised that they marry as soon as possible.

Except, there was still one small matter remaining. . . .

"I believe I understand," Victoria said. "If only I could marry quietly, when and as I wished . . ." She gave a decisive nod. "Yes, if this is what you both wish, then consider it my gift to you. Holly?"

Oh dear. It wasn't that Holly felt the slightest hesitation in wishing to be Colin's wife, but securing Victoria's permission to marry prompted yet another lie, or, at least, an omission of the facts. Immediately after reading the news about his father's fate, Colin had carefully resealed the letter and tucked it away. He would not, he declared, spoil the Ascot races, the coming ball, or his mother's announcement of their engagement. Most of all, he refused to wait through an entire year of mourning before becoming her husband. Not until they had said "I do" would the letter suddenly *turn up*.

"My father has caused enough upheaval in our lives," he'd told her. "This time—perhaps for the *first* time in his life—Thaddeus Ashworth is going to be obliging and cooperative, albeit from his watery grave. We'll give him his respectful due, to be sure, but not until you and I are happily and irrevocably wed. No one, my darling, ever need be the wiser."

Holly slipped her hand from Colin's now and in a surge of affection and gratitude threw her arms around her childhood friend. "Thank you, dearest. Yes, *yes*, this is what I want. The *only* thing I want. Except . . ."

She drew back to gaze into those large, solemn eyes that had changed so little over the years, that might as well still have been those of the eleven-year-old princess to whom Holly and her sisters had once sworn their lifelong allegiance. Through a veil of tears Holly said, "I wish for you to be as happy as I am. I wish for you to have the love of a good man, the finest of men, and for you to know he loves you for yourself, as you are, and that he'll sustain you and never falter from your side."

Victoria's eyes filled as well, their magnified depths mirroring Holly's own brimming emotions. "Goodness," she whispered through quivering lips. "Is that the kind of love you two have found? Can you be *that* happy? It sounds too, too good to be true. It sounds like magic."

Holly gave a little sniffle and cast a loving glance at the man grinning beside her, not with his lips so much as with his clear, beautiful, honest blue eyes. "It *is* magic, Victoria. But I've learned that magic is real if you only allow yourself to believe."

Epilogue

"Yes, good night, Mrs. Eddelson. Don't worry. I'll lock up presently. Bid Mr. Eddelson a pleasant evening for me." Perched on the high stool behind the counter of the Knightsbridge Readers' Emporium, Willow propped an elbow before her and let her chin sink into her palm.

She should be happy. After all, she had much to be grateful for. Two weeks ago Laurel had been delivered of a healthy baby boy. She and Aidan had named him Edward Roland, for the "uncle" who had raised them and the father they had never known, who had died protecting them.

A few days later, Holly and Colin had slipped away to Scotland, to Gretna Green. The Duchess of Masterfield would still hold a post-wedding ball, but the next time Willow saw Holly and Colin, they would be man and wife. Meanwhile, Ivy had gotten over her daily dyspepsia; she now seemed to enjoy her state of impending motherhood with her former zeal for life, not to mention her zeal for science. She had taken to recording every facet of her pregnancy in a little ledger book and planned to publish a treatise for expectant mothers.

That left Willow back here in the Emporium for want of anything better to do when she wasn't helping Laurel with little Edward. Oh, he was an adorable child and she dearly loved being his auntie, but she couldn't help admitting, privately, that the sweet tot helped to remind her of all that was missing from her life.

She sighed and experienced a stab of regret, one of many that, for the past month, sneaked up on her without warning to slice at her heart. She had made a horrible, dreadful mistake back at Masterfield Park, and there was no fixing it. The evening after Willow and her sisters learned the truth of their parentage, Bryce had tried to speak to her. To ask her a question. The look in his eyes . . . the fierce emotions she had seen there . . . had frightened her. Her world had just been upended, and she had wanted only time and a bit of peace to come to terms with such drastic changes. She had meant to tell him as much, but the words had come out all wrong, had been harsh and impatient, a rebuff.

His demeanor toward her had changed after that. No longer had he sought her out, or sat by her in the drawing room before supper, or coaxed her to go with him to the stables. And when it had come time for her to leave Masterfield Park, he had bidden her a terse good-bye with a blink of his dark, troubled eyes, a quick wave of his scarred hand. . . .

Her heart aching and heavy, she slid off the stool and dragged her feet to the street door, ready with the key to lock up for the night. She had just jiggled it into the lock when the *clip-clop* of horses and the rumble of carriage wheels came to a halt directly out front. Seconds later a knock reverberated through the tiny bookshop.

Willow gasped. Could it be Victoria? Was it suddenly *her* turn to be Her Majesty's Secret Servant? For an instant the weight lifted from her chest. She sidestepped to the window and thumbed the curtain aside to peek out. Her hopes plummeted to the very soles of her feet, for the carriage that stood at the curb bore no resemblance to the brougham that had stopped here three times before. No, this was a curricle, open and sporty, not at all the discreet vehicle Victoria would have used.

Just someone looking for a book, she supposed with a sigh. Another knock sounded, and she opened the door. A tall figure ducked in the doorway.

"Willow . . . er . . . that is . . . Miss Sutherland, I am pleased to find you in."

Her mouth dropped open. Had she summoned him here with her fanciful thoughts and painful regrets? Was he even here, or had her yearnings conjured those dark blue eyes and broad shoulders, and those hands . . . the hands that had once unsettled her, but which she had come to realize were the outward manifestation of the secret pain he'd lived with most of his life. Holly had explained Thaddeus Ashworth's cruelty toward his second son, how he'd held a little boy's hands over an open fire to teach him . . . what? That children should not be curious? Should not be mischievous? The thought of it brought tears to burn the backs of Willow's eyes.

As if his heart ached as much as hers, he held one of those dear hands to his coat front. "Miss Sutherland, may I step inside?"

She blinked the moisture from her eyes. "Oh, yes. Do forgive me. I'm just so . . . so surprised to see you here. I had not heard that you were in London."

"I arrived this afternoon." His footsteps thumped solidly on the floorboards, and his formidable presence filled the little shop. Willow suddenly found herself laboring for breath, as if Bryce Ashworth had sucked the oxygen from the room.

"Are you here on business?" she asked, pushing the words out hoarsely.

He shook his head, for a moment saying nothing, merely regarding her with an expression that seemed so unfamiliar on his typically serious features. It was an expression she couldn't decipher. Was he amused? Had he learned a secret about her? Had he come merely to gape?

"Do you perhaps seek a particular book?" She gestured to the shelves surrounding them.

Again he shook his head, that enigmatic expression deepening, his eyes piercing the evening shadows. Finally, his chest swelled and his shoulders lifted. When they dropped back into their hard, straight line, he said, "I came to see you, Miss Sutherland. And to bring you something you left behind at Masterfield Park."

"Left behind?" Wondering what it could be, she closed her eyes a moment to think back.

"I was going to ask you to do that."

Her eyes popped back open. "Do what?"

"Close your eyes. Please do so again."

"Why?"

"Please, Miss Sutherland."

"Oh. Very well." It was all she could do not to peek, especially when she heard him step closer, felt the heat of his skin against her cheek, heard the soft wisp of clothing being drawn aside. Good heavens! She found herself panting for breath, yearning, needing . . .

"Put out your hands."

"Pardon?"

"Your hands, Miss Sutherland. Or, if I may, Willow," he added with a soft rumble, as if her name were some reverent, fragile thing to be spoken in hushed murmurs. She did as he asked, holding her hands out, palms up. Her fingers trembled. Her heart pattered.

"There," he whispered, and something warm and furry squirmed in her hold.

"Oh, my!" Willow opened her eyes to behold a golden-striped kitten curled in a wispy ball between her hands, its sweet little face tilted up at her. One eye blinked, and a tiny pink tongue shot out for a taste of Willow's fingertip. "Oh . . . oh, how delightful!"

She raised her gaze to Bryce's eager expression. "Now that they are old enough to leave their mama, I took the liberty of selecting this one for you." He smiled a little self-consciously. "You see, she reminded me of you, all golden and sweet and ladylike, but with a spark of spirit I doubt many people recognize."

Willow's throat tightened. "You are so very correct," she whispered. "Most people don't see it."

"I do. I have from the first." He leaned closer, bringing his masculine heat to scramble her senses. He reached out a scarred finger to stroke the kitten's tiny head. "Do you like her?"

"Oh . . ." She brought the kitten to her lips and kissed the top of its silky head exactly where Bryce had touched it. Then she nudged its nose with her own. "I positively love her. Kittens are my favorite things. How did you know?"

"One has only to look at you, Willow, to see the obvious."

"I cannot thank you enough." Not for the kitten, and not for his ability to see what other people missed. How tired she had grown of always being the most proper sister, the patient sister. The sister who always smiled, rarely complained, and never, ever experienced adventures of her own. Nestling the kitten between her belly and the crook of her arm, she reached out the other hand to him. "Thank you, my lord. Thank you so very much."

"Bryce. I insist." He took her hand in his own, gently at first, and then with a tug drew her to him. With their bodies touching and their hearts practically pounding in unison, he held her chin in place and kissed her soundly, as she had never been kissed before, as she had dreamed of being kissed—by him and only him—these many weeks.

When he lifted his lips from hers, her elation was such that she couldn't help grinning up at him, nor could he seem to stop himself from grinning back. Their sudden laughter startled the kitten, who dug her sharp little claws into Willow's sleeve.

"Ouch!" Still laughing, she removed her free hand from Bryce's steady shoulder and hugged his darling gift to her bosom. "Bryce, will you stay for tea and help me name her?"

"I did so hope you'd ask."

And just like that, Willow's own adventure began.

ALLISON CHASE

Most Eagerly Yours

Her Majesty's Secret Servants

*First in a spectacular new series
of historical romance*

Raised on their uncle's country estate, the four
orphaned Sutherland sisters formed a close friendship
with the young Princess Victoria. Shortly before her
coronation as queen, Victoria asks the sisters to serve
her in matters requiring the utmost discretion.

They are to become her secret servants. The first to
serve is Laurel—who poses as a widow to uncover a
traitor, and discovers instead an irresistible rogue
conducting his own undercover investigation.

**Available wherever books are sold or at
penguin.com**

ALLISON CHASE

Outrageously Yours

Her Majesty's Secret Servants

A precious gem gifted to Queen Victoria by her secret beau has been stolen, and Her Majesty believes it has been delivered into the hands of the Marquess of Harrow. Ivy Sutherland's task is to assume the role of science student, "Ned Ivers," win the Marquess's trust, and recover the stone. But when Simon de Burgh, Marquess of Harrow—and a lonely widower—discovers "Ned" is actually a woman, he is unable to resist his growing desire for her.

"A masterful storyteller."

—*New York Times* bestselling author Catherine Anderson

Available wherever books are sold or at
penguin.com